For Kelly
who hears every word

1

I know a stage-door Johnny when I see one, and I know a tough guy. This was no Johnny. I had my reasons not to look at the facade of the Duke of York's and perhaps that's how I came to notice him down the alleyway on the south side of the theater. The midsummer's late sunlight was almost gone and the play-going crowd was hubbubbing at the front doors, and here was this lurker in the shadows, around the corner, on the way to where only the company of actors was supposed to go. He'd crammed a bouncer's body into a three-piece serge and his trilby hat was pulled down and tipped forward.

I gave off pretty much the same impression, I realized, but I wouldn't want to see somebody like me down this alley either. He was turned sideways and looking in my direction, probably thinking similar thoughts.

There was nothing to do about it. Sniffing around on the sly for my government while still trying to more or less sniff the same way for my newspaper had made me excessively suspicious of my fellow man. I would have been a busy guy indeed if I'd tried to deal with every mug who put me on edge.

The trilby and I stared at each other for a long moment, and then he broke the gaze and slid away down the alley, fading into the shadows. I shrugged him off and figured it was time to go to my seat. Which meant I had to face the wired sign thrusting out over the Duke of York's portico. In my coat pocket was a ticket for the front row of the stalls, so I had to deal with this.

I turned.

The theater event of the decade, for a limited run only, was ringed in electric lights: ISABEL COBB IS HAMLET.

My fifty-six-year-old mother.

When this ticket showed up on a bellhop tray at my hotel without a note, it took me by surprise. As close as I'd been to the theater all my life, I'd been unaware that the theatrical event of the decade was about to happen in London, much less that it involved my mother. I hadn't heard from or about her for fifteen months. A couple of years ago she retired from the legitimate theater, refusing to carry on in a profession that no longer let her pretend she was a twenty-year-old beauty. She was still pretty much a beauty. But she wasn't Juliet anymore. Or even Kate in *Shrew*, which an audience in Memphis finally, infamously, made clear enough to her, summer before last.

There would be no older-woman roles for her, by god. She would rather leave it all behind. But here was a clever way around that problem. She was playing the most famous man in the history of the stage. A young man, even.

Under the portico now, I found myself on the edge of a gaggle of shirtwaisted women, talking low among themselves, a few with a bit of purple, green, and white ribbon pinned near the heart. Suffragettes, their focus shifted by the war. Instead of marching and chaining themselves to railings, they were starting to drive trams and buses and work in factories. Some of these women near me even gave off a whiff of sulfur from a munitions plant, their hands and faces beginning to turn faintly yellow from the chemicals.

As we pressed together through the doors and into the foyer, my mother's name floated ardently out of these voices. Their new exemplar. She was to be a man. To be and not to be, of course. But tonight a man.

I sat on the right end of the first row, very near to her as she came downstage, alone and soliloquizing, wishing that her too too sullied flesh would melt, thaw, and resolve itself into dew. I was trying hard to relinquish myself to the illusion of the stage, trying to forget who, in life, this was before me.

To my surprise, this was not difficult. Isabel Cobb was indeed a man. She was a small and slim Prince Hamlet, her hair cut shoulder length and died dark blond and worn loose and wavy, as a young man of the time might, being hatless in distracted grief, and though my mind knew how tightly my mother was wrapped inside her black doublet and though I recognized her voice, which was always low and a little husky even as a woman, and though I recognized those vast, dark eyes as the maternal origin of my own, she convinced me.

And I wondered: did she convince herself? Perhaps. I heard no tang of irony in her voice as she, being a man, a son, railed against a mother's hasty sexuality. And though this Hamlet before me was believably his own man, he and his qualms reminded me of my mother. Not that I shared the prince's vehemence. But as he rolled the word "frailty" in his mouth like an overripe grape and then named it "woman," stirring the suffragettes in the crowd to a titter, I stopped seeing the play. I lifted my eyes from Hamlet's indictment of his mother and looked up, far up into the fly galleries—uniquely visible to the residents of the front row—and to the catwalk there, its pin rail wrapped with thick hemp ropes. The catwalk was empty and my mind lifted much farther than the flies: I stood outside a room at the Gilsey House in New York. Though it could have been a room in any of a hundred hotels or boarding-houses around the corner from a hundred theaters in a hundred cities on the headliner circuit, where one of the great stars of the American stage and her son lived while she worked. The star was my mother, and she was my father too, my Gertrude and King Hamlet both, though my actual father was no king, was not even a ghost, was an unknown to me, to this very day. But what son needed a father with a mother who could convincingly become anyone?

This flash of memory, me standing in the hushed and carpeted hallway of New York's Gilsey House, could have been any from a multitude of memories of my childhood or adolescence in any of those other hotels, but in the front row of the Duke of York's it was the Gilsey and I'd just turned thirteen and my cheek was still damp from her kiss and she expected me, as always, to understand that she was about to shut the door in my face and send me away—it had been thus for as long as I could remember—I was much younger than this when I'd first been cooingly sent away from her door—and at the Gilsey House her leading man had pitched in, had given me a wink and a nod and a *Good lad*, and her play—what was it? a Clyde Fitch, perhaps—had run a tryout month in Boston where I'd been bid a similar affectionate adieu in the hallway outside a room in the Hotel Touraine with a different leading man, and I liked this Boston guy okay, and I thought he and I would have this understanding for as long as the play ran, which everyone hoped would be at least a year in New York. But the producer canned him before the play left Beantown, and this guy at the Gilsey was a new wink and a new nod. My mother always seemed to have a hasty hankering for her leading men. And I always seemed to be seeing them off together at a hotel door and then turning and walking away. Having quickly learned not to linger, not to listen.

All this ran quickly and hotly and stupidly in me from the front row of the Duke of York's, so it took me a moment to realize what I was looking at. The guy from the alley was on the catwalk. Once I focused on him, I could picture the last few moments. He'd eased out slow to a place at the rail. And now he squared around to look down to the stage where Hamlet was finishing his soliloquy, bidding his heart to break, and this guy had a real intense interest in this Hamlet, who was my mother.

I had a real intense interest in *him*. I concentrated on his face as he watched Hamlet greet Ophelia with feigned madness. I wanted to read his eyes, but they were a little too far away, and I wasn't looking straight into them. But the stillness of him, the casual privilege of his pose, made them seem hard, as insolently hard as his stare from the alleyway. Shakespeare and Isabel Cobb faded into a buzz in my head as I focused on this man and on my instinct that he was up to no good.

And then he turned his attention to me, casually, as if he'd known I was there all long.

We had a second extended face-off.

I was right about his eyes. They seemed dead, these eyes. As dead as a bullet casing.

He returned his gaze to my mother.

I was tempted to slip from my seat—right that moment, with Hamlet tormenting the girl he loved—and go through the stage access door into the wings and find my way up to the flies.

And then do what?

Cool off now, I told myself. For weeks I'd been sitting in a London hotel room preparing for the next assignment. Necessarily so. But I'd been idle for too long. This guy reminded me what my body had been trained for and primed for. Which, however, certainly *hadn't* been to cause a public ruckus over some lug because I didn't like his looks or his sneaking around.

I lowered my face. I concentrated on Hamlet advising his girl to be off to a nunnery and then making a flourish of an exit. A few moments later, with Ophelia still boohooing about her boyfriend's madness, I looked up once more into the flies.

He was gone.

I let it go.

At the first intermission, after Hamlet vowed to catch the conscience of the king, I went out of the theater and down to the side alley and smoked a cigarette there, watching the shadows, waiting for a tough guy in a trilby. Nothing doing.

Back in the theater, through to the next curtain, I kept a frequent but fleeting eye on the flies. No sign of him, and now Hamlet was swearing that his thoughts be bloody or be nothing worth. At the beginning of the act I'd have embraced that recommendation. As the curtain came down for the second intermission, I'd finally been able to drift in the other direction. So I went out and smoked another Fatima and kept my back to the suffragette chatter nearby on the sidewalk and thought about how my mother was indeed Hamlet, as it said rimmed in electric light above my head, and she was a good one, neatly balancing the classic introspective inaction with the strength to kill.

Inside the theater once more, she held my undivided attention through to the prince's last words—*the rest is silence*—and in the script there is but a single word of stage direction: *Dies.* For most actors who have taken on Hamlet, the rest is *not* silence. The rattling or sighing or moaning or gasping are considered by the usual tribe of actors to be the sweet dessert to a long night of emoting. I feared for my mother now, in spite of the surprising subtlety of her performance so far, feared for her excesses. And she surprised me once more by dying with simply an exquisite lifting of the face to the spotlight and a closing of the eyes and, thereby, an ineffably rendered release of spirit.

I admired her performance, but I did not like to witness this, in much the same way as I did not like her closing a hotel room door upon me. I felt she had left me forever. And with her death upon my mind—for it was hers as well as Hamlet's that I was thrumming to—I lifted my own face once more, to the flies.

And there he was. He was watching once again at the railing, and as my mother played at death he leaned toward her and his jacket gaped briefly and showed a holstered pistol on his left side. I wished ardently that I was carrying my own.

From the early days of my reporting career I got close to a fair number of criminals. Tough guys, all of them. Tempered-steel tough. But I'd heard a number of them talk about their mothers, think about their mothers, and inevitably these tough guys turned into simpering idiots of a variety of sorts, from weak to reckless.

So it was that even as I wished I had my own pistol with me I was grateful I didn't. I felt trigger-itchy at that moment and it was possible my hand would have drawn my Mauser and would have pushed the safety button and would have waited for the slightest movement of this lug's right hand toward his pistol, with the wrong kind of look on his face, and I would have shot him. Maybe not aiming to kill. Maybe just to disable that right arm.

Without this option, however, I clearly understood that shooting him would have been the wrong thing to do. At least till his pistol was out and coming to bear on her. And then I would have simply killed him.

2

As it was, he didn't do anything but watch for the last few moments of the play. Then the curtain fell, and when it rose and the calls began, he was gone for good.

The audience clapped loudly and the rest of the cast came and bowed and lined up on the sides and they joined the applause as my mother appeared. She bounded downstage center and the women in shirtwaists and suffragette ribbons all stood up and cried, "Bravo! Bravo!" and my mother bowed deeply to them as a man and then she straightened and flounced her hair and she curtsied as a woman. The suffragettes cried, "Brava! Brava!"

All the while, the rest of the viewers were applauding loudly, some of them rising to their feet as well. As did I. My mother did not look my way.

A boy brought roses from the wings.

I'd seen bigger ovations for my mother, but the few actresses who'd done Hamlet before had been pilloried in the press and heckled from the cheap seats. I hadn't read her reviews, but I heard not a single rude sound from this audience, and that seemed a triumph to me.

I lingered to let the crowd murmur its way out of the auditorium after Mother had finally stopped taking bows and the house lights had come on. Then I crossed before the front row. But instead of going left, up the aisle to the exit doors, I went to the right, up the steps and through the stage access door and into the wings with its smells of greasepaint and sweat and dust burning on the electric stage lights. The actors had all vanished, and squaring around before me was a lanky man in shirt sleeves and bow tie. The stage manager, I assumed.

I was ready to explain myself to him, why I felt privileged to go through an unauthorized door and head straight to the dressing rooms, but he immediately said, "Mr. Cobb."

"Yes," I said.

"Would you like to see your mother?"

"I would."

"This way." He turned on his heel to lead me toward a door at the back wall.

I stepped up quickly to walk beside him.

"There was a man with a gun up on your fly floor," I said. "Are you surprised?"

He stopped. He turned to me.

"A gun?" he said.

"Inside his coat."

"Yes," he said. "I'm surprised."

"Do you know who he might have been?" I asked.

The stage manager hesitated at this. He was thinking in ways that I could not clearly interpret. Then he said, "Not if he was in my flies."

"And if he hadn't gotten that far?"

"Your mother has fans."

This was no fan.

He turned and moved on. "Please follow me," he said.

Something was odd here, but I didn't push the point.

As we passed through the doorway at the back of the stage wings, I said, "How did you know me?"

"Your mother has a picture of you in her dressing room."

This didn't surprise me.

I followed him along a short passageway and we cut back at the next turning and entered an enclosed staircase.

Her dressing room was on the second floor. The door was ajar and emitting female laughter.

The stage manager knocked and the laughter faded.

"Prithee show thyself," my mother called out, using the lowest Hamlet register of her voice.

More female laughter.

The stage manager leaned his head past the edge of the door to look in. "Your son," he said.

I did not hear her reply, if she made one. Perhaps she gestured. The stage manager pulled back at once and opened the door and I stepped in.

She sat with her back to her makeup mirror, still in her costume of trunk hose and doublet, the doublet unbuttoned, however, showing a finely embroidered lace blouse beneath, straight from a Mayfair shop no doubt, her own private joke throughout the night's portrayal of Hamlet, a secret assertion of her modern womanhood. She was flanked by four suffragettes, two on each side, their uniform dark skirts and white shirtwaists making them look like a ladies string quartet about to go off to play in a palm court at a local hotel.

I stopped a single pace into the room, my hat in my hand. My mother rose. Quite formally, even solemnly. Then she took a step forward and opened her arms. "My darling Kit," she said.

I came to her and we hugged and she smelled of greasepaint and mothball camphor and she felt all bones and sinew inside her man's clothes.

"Isn't he handsome, my dears?" she said.

The women simply made little muttering sounds in response, ready for the vote but not for boldly voicing the sort of sentiments my mother was challenging them to have.

I focused on her suffragettes, as my mother resisted my incipient withdrawal from her arms, assessing them as she would have them assess me.

They were varying degrees of young—Mother had brought only the more impressionable acolytes into her closest circle—but three of them did not hold my eye even for a moment. One, though, had a strong-jawed, wide-mouthed sort of farm girl prettiness, the kind of girl you'd enjoy trying, briefly, to pry away from her horse.

Mother was letting go of me now, pushing me back to arm's length but keeping her hands on my shoulders. "Where have you been for the past year?"

Where *she* had been was a more interesting question, but I politely did not ask it in front of the young women for whom she was still performing.

"Ah yes," she said, as if just remembering. "I read your stories lately. What a fine writer you are. I taught him to write by making him read a thousand books in countless star dressing rooms on three continents." The "him" was the only indication she'd suddenly started to talk directly to the other women, as her eyes kept fixed tightly on mine, shining that light of hers on me, making me a willing part of her present performance.

She said, elaborating on her perusal of my stories, "But Constantinople of all places," she said. "All those poor people suffering under the Ottomans. A terrible business. Why would you ever go out there? I thought you were the great chronicler of bullets and cannon shells and men in battle dress, my darling."

I did not have a chance to reply.

"And your ordeal on the high seas," she said, the light changing in her eyes, giving off more heat and less illumination. "Did you get my telegram?"

"No."

"Well, I didn't know where to send it."

Then you already knew I didn't get it. But I didn't say this.

"He was on the *Lusitania*," she said.

The suffragettes clucked softly in sympathy.

"Closer to three thousand," I said.

Her eyes narrowed. "Utter non sequitur, my darling," she said.

"The number of books you had me read. I figured it out not long ago."

She brightened.

"In an idle moment," I said. And then, to the others: "She and an ever changing cast of theater people she enlisted taught me everything I knew, before I knew to teach myself." As she had done, I did not look directly at the suffragettes, letting the pronoun suggest I was addressing them.

Mother let go of my shoulders.

She introduced me to the young women, and I smiled at them and shook their hands, their grips still limply disenfranchised, but I did not endeavor to remember any of the names. Even, though it went against my natural inclinations, the name of the pretty one. Immediately after the introductions, my mother ushered them all out of the dressing room, everyone fluttering ardent good-byes and comradely good wishes every step of the way.

Mother closed the door and leaned back against it. "Was I splendid tonight?" she asked.

The question was not rhetorical, though I knew she knew the answer. "You were," I said.

"Yes I was," she said.

"Does all of London realize it?" I asked.

"Much of London."

Some of the critics surely sneered at any woman playing the role. But she seemed content, so I did not ask.

"Poor Bernhardt," she said.

Sarah Bernhardt played Hamlet in London in '99 to vicious reviews. Mother was inviting the comparison. "You did better?" I asked.

"Yes," she said. "But I was referring to her leg. They cut it off only a few weeks ago and she gave it to a university."

From Isabel Cobb's Hamlet in London to Sarah Bernhardt's losing a leg, service to my government had put me behind in my reading.

"Gangrene," my mother said.

"So you're doing better than the Divine Sarah in legs as well," I said.

Mother lifted her face to the ceiling in a loud bark of a laugh. But when her face came back down, she grabbed a chaw of my cheek between her thumb and forefinger and gave it a squeeze and shake to match the laugh. "I feel bad for her," she said.

I have a pretty high threshold of pain, but like those Chicago thugs going soft about their mothers, I felt the same at thirty-one years old about Isabel Cobb's uninhibited mother-cheek-pinch as I did at ten: it hurt like hell.

She finally let go, and she sat down in the chair where she'd been presiding over her suffragettes. I sat in the chair at the idle makeup station next to her. Edged into the frame of her mirror was my formal portrait in a cabinet card, a thing she'd insisted I do for her six years ago upon hearing that the *Post-Express* was sending me off to Nicaragua on my first war assignment.

She caught me looking at it.

"I carry you with me everywhere," she said.

I turned to her.

In spite of her being made up as a man—a melancholy man, no less—and being an age that tormented her always for what she no longer was, my mother was still beautiful, her face, in impact, all dark eyes and wide mouth, both restlessly shaping and reshaping in attentiveness to whoever was before her.

It had long pleased me to be able to make her eyes and mouth abruptly freeze. Like now. "Can you think why a tough guy with a gun would be stalking you?" I said.

But I had her for only the briefest of moments. Then, with a tilt of the head, her eyes veiled themselves like a cat showing its trust, and her mouth made a dismissive moue. "Not at all," she said.

She sounded sincere. But she was arguably the greatest living actress of the American stage. She could sound however she liked. What I needed to figure out: had the oddness of the question itself been enough to make her pause for that brief moment or had it revealed she was now lying?

I had good reason to suspect the latter.

Last year she got involved in some undercover detective work in New Orleans while she was trying to make an escape from the theater.

"Are you still in bed with Pinkerton?" I said.

"What do you take me for?" she said. "Old man Pinkerton's been dead for thirty years."

She winked.

"Okay, Mother," I said. "I usually let you get away with ending a serious conversational topic with an ambiguous theatrical gesture. Not this time. Does the wink mean you're not sleeping with a dead man but if he were alive it would be a different matter, or does it mean you're not sleeping with a dead man but you may still be working for his detective agency?"

This stopped her face once again.

She squared around to me, leaned forward, straightened her back, and pressed her hands onto her knees. A manly gesture. A man with more backbone than Hamlet. But I recognized it from a lifetime with this woman as a no-nonsense Isabel Cobb gesture. She said, "Listen to me, my darling. Consider my ego. Did you think I would be happy to play that role for long? Going after two-bit hoodlums for a corporation of private dicks?"

I kept my own face still. I wasn't going to let her get away with the ambiguity of a rhetorical question.

She knew. She smiled a that's-my-boy smile. "It was beneath me," she said. "I am not now nor will I ever again work for the Pinkertons or any other detective agency."

She held my eyes steadily with hers.

Okay.

"Okay," I said.

She didn't move.

"That leaves the man with the pistol in his coat," I said. "He was in the flies above you."

She didn't flinch. Her face was placid, but she said, "That's unsettling."

How to read my mother? That had been a daily challenge for much of my life. It probably made me the hell of a good newspaper reporter that I was. Right now I believed what she was saying about the detective work; her reasoning acknowledged who she was behind the mask. This quiet in her also felt real. I supposed. But she was perfectly capable of playing, from her actor's book of tricks, *Placid and Calm.* Playing the untrue thing was her life. If the calm were true, wouldn't she be squeezing every flinch and flutter from a fictitious endangerment?

She said, "Maybe the theater put on some security. A woman playing a man provokes a lot of people on both sides."

"Your stage manager said he didn't know who he was."

She nodded faintly. Then she shrugged. "We do only a matinee tomorrow and the run ends Thursday night."

There wasn't much left to say about this. It worried me. But this was my mother I was dealing with.

I let her change the subject. "Do you tour on from here?" I asked.

"Yes."

A few moments of silence clock-ticked away as we looked at each other, as if casually.

"As Hamlet?"

"Yes," she said. "And you? Will you be waiting in London for the German bullets and cannon shells to arrive?"

Another beat of silence and then she smiled. And she winked. She was reminding me that we'd long ago tacitly agreed not to question how we led our lives.

"I'll be touring on," I said.

3

I asked nothing more of her. Nor she of me. By the very early hours
of the next morning, however, as I lay sleepless in bed in my rooms at
the Tavistock Hotel across from Covent Garden Market, I'd become
less and less convinced by her performance. Not her Hamlet. That
remained swell. In temperament she'd always been something of a
man—a tough guy, in fact—trapped in a leading lady body. Indeed,
last night she'd played the catching of the murderous uncle at his
prayers so fiercely and had so clearly kept that edge in all her character's later delays that she'd utterly transformed Hamlet's Wilsonian
vacillation into the overriding desire to kill his uncle only when it was
most likely to send him, unrepentant, to Hell. That was Mama. She
knew how to draw on her toughness, play it as if that were all there
was. Which was why it took me till three in the morning to begin
to doubt her nonchalance about the man in the flies with the gun.
Something more was going on.

But it wasn't my affair. I was still a war correspondent. There was
that. But I was also working for my country's secret service now.
Primarily now. She wasn't the reason I was awake. I'd always figured
she could take care of herself. And I was my tough-guy mother's son.
Which wasn't to say certain things in my new profession didn't get
to me. It meant I played the essentials of my character convincingly
and I did what I needed to do.

I just might not sleep for long stretches in the night.

I fidgeted mightily around on the bed. I paced about the room, smoking Fatimas. A room I'd occupied for going on ten weeks now. My own issues were about the thirteen months prior to that.

But I was tough guy enough to keep any extended replays of those scenes out of my head. From the battlefields I'd covered I'd learned the attitude I had to hold on to: the man you watched die yesterday doesn't exist today; he fell to yesterday's bullets and you've got today's bullets to deal with. Nevertheless, sometimes it got me to brooding. Only it was in indirect ways.

Like noticing a little girl, maybe nine years old or so, from a working family, passing in James Street with a sad face.

Or a newspaper headline about a film actress—a star—formerly thought rescued but now assumed lost on the *Lusitania*.

Or the arcaded portico along the front of the Tavistock, which felt, in spite of obvious differences, very much like the *portales* of a certain hotel in Vera Cruz.

And making all this worse was the Corona portable on my desk, which I'd paced past a hundred times already tonight and kept my eyes from seeing. This time, however, I stopped. The electric bulb above the desk, wired into the gas-jet fixtures of this sixty-year-old hotel, pissed its yellow light onto a blank sheet of paper in the roller. One more story to write under a phony name.

No. I couldn't think of it as phony. That was the point.

I was Joseph W. Hunter speaking through my Corona now. Joseph William Hunter. Formerly Josef Wilhelm Jäger, which I was keeping quiet about. From Chicago he was publishing widely in the German-language newspapers and the German-American English-language newspapers in the U.S.A. He was a damn good writer, sentence to sentence at least, though he clearly had an agenda. He was a justifier and apologist for the home country.

No. Not *he*. *I*. I was this guy Hunter. Becoming him, at least. I was still in love with *mein Vaterland* and anxious that my fellow Americans understood why. I was writing about the war as if America was smart to remain out of the fray. As if we were getting the wrong dope about Germany and its goals and its intentions. We had far more in common with the Germans than we did with the Brits.

It turned my stomach but it had to be done. It was quite likely, given recent events, that Christopher Cobb was known to the German Foreign Office as a dangerous man. Journalism was what I knew best as a cover identity and Germany was still courting sympathetic American journalists. Joe Hunter would be useful.

He was in the works even before my mix-up with the Huns this past spring. I'd been creating him ever since I came out of my secret service training in February speaking damn good German, the language training aided by a lifetime of intense and varied private education in the back stages and dressing rooms of the thousand theaters of my childhood and by my mother's gene for mimicry.

I'd lit the electric light with the reasonable intent of making good use of my sleeplessness. I had a story to cook up about a movement among Chicago school administrators who advocated more classes in German in anticipation of a new order in Europe. But I reconsidered. I was Cobb alone tonight. Only Cobb. I reached up and turned the key and extinguished the light.

I moved to the window and opened the heavy blackout drape. It was the newest thing in the room. Since January London faced the nightly possibility of a Zeppelin attack. Since May the attacks had come to the city center and were increasing in number and bomb load. The Brits still hadn't figured out how to defend themselves. The airships could climb faster and higher than the Sopwiths and Blériots of the Royal Flying Corps, and the best the anti-aircraft ground defenses had were Hotchkiss six-pounders whose range was less than half the Zepps' attack altitude. The city was defenseless.

My rooms were at the back of the hotel on the upper floor, the fourth. I looked along the parapets and chimneys of the rooftops stretching north on James Street, all of it barely visible, blacked out, as was the whole city in the overcast night.

And as I watched, the darkness to the west cracked open from ground to clouds with a white searchlight and then with another, the two beams stiffly scanning the ceiling of clouds. I took in a quick breath. These Zeppelins were as vast as ocean liners, piston droning a mile overhead, slowing down almost to a float to aim their bombs, giving off a strange kind of elegance in their dangerousness. They were unlike anything you knew, no matter how much tough stuff you'd seen. They could set off a quick reflex of fear you didn't quite know how to suppress.

I watched the two restless pillars of light searching, searching, and then one abruptly vanished and, moments later, the other. The darkness resumed unmitigated. It had been a false alarm.

In this part of the city the dark was not silent. Though I was high up and facing away to the north, I could hear the muffled bustling at the Covent Garden Market across from the front of the hotel. The market carts and wagons were rumbling in and unloading cabbages and cauliflowers, turnips and tomatoes, broad beans and brussels sprouts to await the greengrocers of London before dawn.

I closed the drape.

I'd been here too long.

I knew too much about this neighborhood.

I was too much like a Londoner, waiting for bombs from the night sky with nothing to do in response but keep the lights off and duck.

I went to the armoire and opened the doors and I felt my way into the bottom of my Gladstone bag. I put my hand to the Luger there, which I'd acquired on a difficult night in Istanbul. I drew it out.

I faced into the darkness of the room and held the pistol as if to fire, holding the grip with the crotch of my thumb pressed into the curve beneath the hammer, the trigger snug in the tip-joint of my forefinger, my hand part of the Luger now, an exact prolongation of its axis. Calming.

And unsettling. I'd been calmed through the other wars by typewriter keys. What had I come to? But this reservation was of the mind. My body, my beating heart were calmed by holding this pistol.

I let the thought go.

I put the Luger back into the bag and I moved to the bed and lay down and slept.

And a knock at the door awoke me. I did not know what time it was. I didn't even know if the sun had risen, the blackout lingering in the be-draped room.

I rose. I moved to the door. There was no peephole in this aging hotel. I turned my ear to the place where a peephole should be.

"Yes?" I said.

"Mr. Cobb?"

I recognized the voice. A bellhop as old as the Tavistock.

I slid the chain lock off its metal groove and opened the door.

"Good morning, Mr. Cobb."

"Good morning, George," I said.

George lifted a long, paper-wrapped parcel with the hook of a clothes hanger protruding from the top. "From a gentleman," he said.

With the door closed and with the blackout drape opened to reveal the light of an advanced morning and with the parcel laid flat on the bed, I tore away the paper and found a tuxedo.

The note pinned to the paper gave an address in Knightsbridge and the present date and a time. No name.

I took in a quick breath, aware how similar the reflex seemed to the anticipation of the Zepps a few hours ago. But with a different feeling altogether. The last time that I'd been sent off on a serious assignment, it began with a tuxedo. My waiting, I figured, was over.

4

That night, after the late-coming summer dark, gussied up and still fiddling with my white bow tie in the back of one of the ubiquitous French-made London taxis, I thought about a guy named James Metcalf, my contact from the embassy in May who dispatched me a tux and took me to dinner at the Carlton Hotel to give me a train ticket to Turkey and a license to kill. I expected him to be waiting for me in Knightsbridge.

The taxi drove to the end of Basil Street, just south of Hyde Park, where Basil Mansions stretched a full block long, a continuous row of posh, red-brick, Queen Anne revival mansion flats with half-octagonal, Portland-stone bay windows. The mansions flatironed at the angled intersection of Pavilion Road, and the northernmost door I'd been brought to led into a massive wedge of a very fancy multistoried flat, four floors from basement on up, joined by a circular staircase.

A manservant in tails answered the door and he bowed to me and he said, with lugubrious upper-class overprecision, "Good evening, sir. May I announce you?" Which was just his way of saying, *Who the hell are you?*

I gave him my name. The Cobb one.

"Of course, Mr. Cobb," he said. He had the acceptable list in his head.

"This way, sir," he said, and he led me across the marble foyer and up one circular flight to the second floor, the central feature of which was a large, oak-paneled drawing room. The furniture was all done in the heavy, dark Jacobean style. Oak wainscot chairs mostly hugged the walls; overstuffed, out-of-period wingbacks and a matching couch sat before a walk-in fireplace; and a couple of major, fat-legged trestle tables lined up in the center of the room, one with a side of beef and a guy in chef's whites, the other with drinks and a bartender. But among all this was plenty of stand-around room.

There were a dozen of us, or a few more. All men, all done up in evening wear, arranged in little broods of two or three just out of earshot of each other. I smelled government.

The butler stopped and so did I, just behind his right shoulder. "Lord Buffington will be here momentarily, sir," he said.

Indeed, from near the beef, a large, fleshy man who seemed no less large and fleshy for his perfectly bespoke evening clothes, a man who once might well have been the primary bully among Charterhouse upperclassmen, broke away from his group and moved toward me.

"Mister Christopher Cobb, your lordship," the manservant said, stepping out of the way.

"Cobb," the man said, presenting a large hand and a firm grip that I was lucky to get good enough hold on to return effectively. "I'm Gabriel Buffington."

"Lord Buffington."

He'd given me his casual name, but he nodded to acknowledge that I'd done the right thing in returning his title to him.

And now a man emerged from behind Gabe Buffington. A man I recognized. But it wasn't James Metcalf. It was my other James, the guy who came to Chicago and persuaded my publisher to let him hire me away for the government while remaining ostensibly at work for the *Post-Express*. James Polk Trask. Woodrow Wilson's right-hand secret service man.

Trask appeared around Buffington like a half-back running the ball behind Gabe the Grappler's block.

I sidestepped to take him on. "Trask," I said.

"Cobb," he said.

We shook hands.

"Lord Buffington is our host," Trask said at once, turning his face around to look at the Brit.

Buffington nodded two little smiles, one for each of us.

"Thanks," I said.

Buffington said, "The windows are secured, the food and the drink are plentiful, we have a splendid space belowground. Let the wretched Huns do their worst." Having made this declaration, the lord nodded once more, firmly, for both of us, and he moved off.

Trask watched Buffington. "He's one of the good ones." He turned those blackout-dark, empty-seeming eyes back to me. He waited, as if it was obvious that I was supposed to say something. Since he'd come to recruit me, I'd seen those eyes in other people in his business. *Our* business. I figured he expected me to acquire the knack of putting on these show-nothing eyes, just as I'd acquired the knack for planting an enemy in the ground. A couple of moments of silence had already passed between us since he'd declared Buffington a good one.

I said, "As in 'one of the *few* good ones' or 'stay close to the good ones because the bad ones are very bad.'"

Trask smiled. Very faintly. "Both," he said. "You want a drink?"

"Sure."

"I've taught the Brits to make a Gin Rickey, at least here in Buffington's joint."

It was the only drink invented by a Washington lobbyist. "That may be a violation of our neutrality," I said.

"Too bad," Trask said, and he led me to the drink table and another of Buffington's servants in tails. This one, however, was armed with cocktail shaker, ice shaver, lemon squeezer, long-handled spoons and toddy sticks, a jigger, and a couple of fine, small knives. He used one of the latter to cut us a lime, the halves of which ended up in our two glasses of Beefeater.

Trask took us off to a corner of the room and we sat on a couple of high-backed, carved walnut chairs facing, at right angles, into the room. We were able to watch for anyone approaching, no doubt Trask's intent. We would speak low.

"What's this get-together all about?" I asked.

Trask gave a tiny snort through a whistley sinus. I looked toward him at this commonplace noise he'd made. It didn't go with his eyes. It didn't go with him, this peep of human frailty.

He said, "This is a high-class version of a thing you're starting to find all over London. A blackout club."

"The Zepps," I said.

He nodded. "All you need is a basement and some nervous friends."

"Are these guys nervous?"

"From the air attacks, a few. But mostly from their long neglect of homeland defense and the task of correcting that. They'd all gotten complacent about their island fortress. Their vaunted navy can't do anything about airships. Churchill warned them before he got canned. He foresaw a major air war. I suspect he'll turn out to be correct. Unfortunately, Winnie didn't know crumpets about sea war and land war."

Trask was referring to Gallipoli. Churchill had authored the disaster in the Dardanelles, which wasn't over yet. "I got pretty close to all that," I said.

"Right," Trask said. "Which reminds me. Good work in Istanbul."

I grunted.

Yesterday's bullets.

"That compliment wasn't as incidental as it sounded," Trask said, as if he were a sensitive guy, not wanting to offend. His eyes hadn't moved from me, hadn't flickered through any of this. Not even when he added, "Not incidental at all."

I practiced on my own dead stare.

Trask said, "Sorry to reward you by hitching you to a post in London for so long."

I didn't even grunt at this.

Trask knew how to justify it. He said, "Your Mr. Hunter has been getting some nice response in various places."

"Good for him."

"Now we're trying to do our British friends—the good ones—a special favor."

This declaration was the kind of rhetorical setup Trask liked to execute before taking a sip or a drag of whatever was in his hand. A Rickey in Washington when he sent me off on the *Lusitania*, a Fatima when he asked to enlist me in his covert tribe. And yes, a Rickey again now. I sipped too, waiting.

"They've got a traitor inside somewhere," he said.

"Inside the government?"

"They think so, given what they suspect is getting through to Berlin."

"Will I be involved with this?"

Trask shrugged. He looked off into the room. "We have someone on it at the moment. Looking into a suspect."

He said no more.

I took a pretty good hit on the gin and lime. Old Joe Rickey and his Washington bartender friend had a real inspiration, simple though it was.

"We're still feeling our way along," Trask finally added. "It might be a good time to introduce Mr. Hunter."

"Here?"

"I have a slightly different crowd in mind." He leaned toward me, lowered his voice even further. "Do you know how many of the most powerful men in this country have German blood in their veins? It goes back two hundred years. George I, King of Great Britain and Ireland, previously Georg Ludwig, Duke of Brunswick-Lüneburg, the only eligible heir of the dead Queen Anne. He didn't even speak English. This was Queen Victoria's great-great-grandfather, mind you, progenitor of four British kings before her. And who did Victoria up and marry? Another Hun, Albert, of Saxe-Coburg and Gotha, who thus named the present royal house. For Christ's sake, the Kaiser himself is Victoria's grandson. There's been a powerful lot of German-blooded begatting over those two hundred years, which has now produced, beneath the Brits' virulently anti-German surface, a small but strategic shit pot of conflicting interests at a very high level."

"Your suspect is one of the begotten?" I said.

Trask nodded. He glanced into the room and back to me. He bent near. "A baronet by the discreetly adjusted surname of Stockman. Given-named after Victoria's German prince. Sir Albert Stockman. He's the great-nephew of Christian Friedrich Stockmar, a German-born physician who became the personal doctor for Prince Leopold of . . . where else? . . . Saxe-Coburg and Gotha. Great-Uncle Chris was sent by Leopold to a marriageable Victoria to vouch for his own nephew Albert. Stockmar vouched well, and after the marriage he stayed on as the young couple's personal adviser. So Victoria took good care of this guy's extended family, including the baronetcy of our Sir Al."

"Why don't the Brits just grab him and interrogate him?"

"It's all suspicion at this point," he said. "And the operative phrase was 'very high level.' Sir Albert was beloved-by-blood by the Great Queen herself, which counts in this country. And though a baronetcy doesn't quite rank the House of Lords, he got himself elected as a member of Parliament. Which, if he's dirty, tells you something about his guile."

From outside, very near, a whistle sounded, shriller, simpler than the bobbies' whistles. An air raid constable. This the Brits were well prepared for. Guys in uniforms with whistles. The conversations instantly stopped in the drawing room. All the faces turned in the direction of the sound—the southern wall and the street beyond.

I looked at Trask. He looked at me. "Here come their cousins in a balloon," I said.

Trask snorted.

I snorted.

But we both rose and moved with all the other white ties and dinner jackets into the circular staircase, going along in a quite orderly fashion, quite calmly, even as the sound of the Hotchkiss six-pounders began to pop pathetically in the distance.

We descended to the ground floor and then we circled on down, into the basement, and we emerged into a large, open space. At one end sat wine in barrels and more wine in bottles in racks, and on half a dozen of the barrels, candles burned in silver candelabra. Against the far wall were more racks, of a different sort, layered with Buffington's guns. In the center of the open space a billiard table was disappearing even now under a white cloth cast over its surface by still another liveried man.

Beyond the vanishing billiard green were three, round dining tables already draped in white and each set with half a dozen dinner places and lit, as well, by candles. Beyond them was an opening to a corridor in deep shadow, leading into the recesses of the basement floor. On one side of the doorway was a piano with a lit stand-up lamp. On the other side was a wall of books, two-shilling editions, books for a man to actually read. For that purpose he had a couple of over-stuffed Morris chairs with another stand-up lamp between them, this one dark. The basement—at least on this side of that corridor—was Buffington's guy's retreat.

We all now vaguely drifted in the direction of the set tables until Buffington's voice boomed from behind us. "Gentlemen, the food and the drink will soon follow, and there will be more of both. But first a word."

We stopped drifting. We began to turn toward our host.

He was drawn up to full height, hands behind him, framed against the final swoop of the staircase. He watched us turning to him. He approved. He waited. He encouraged us as we gathered our attention to him by addressing us once more. "Gentlemen." Firmly he said it, though the tone of his voice had mellowed up as well, become comradely, almost affectionate.

When at last he had the full and silent attention of every man before him, he said, one more time, "Gentlemen." This time he rolled the word out as if he were asking us to consider its full meaning. Which no doubt he was, for he went on, "They come now, showing their true and savage selves. They come in the night, sneaking in, dangling beneath gas bags to throw bombs on our homes and schools, on our women and our children. And a few months ago they unleashed poison gas upon our troops at Ypres, violating what civilized men from time immemorial have understood to be fields of honor. This is no longer a war of nation against nation. It is a war of civilization against a new barbarism. We fight to preserve the entire world from a second dark age."

As if, offstage, the sound effects man heard his cue, a bomb thumped distantly and shuddered faintly beneath our feet.

Buffington paused only for a single beat as if to let his point sink in. Before me and to the side I could see most of the men in the room, and I knew I could assume the same of the others: not one of us had flinched. And here in this London home, the bomb's fading vibration in our feet and legs and chest supported Buffington's point.

He said, "Gentlemen, if we fail, this dark age will be longer than the last. Those previous five centuries will seem the winking of an eye compared to this. And the new dark age will be infinitely more terrible. Mankind's vaunted advances of manufacturing and technology can be used for good, but they can just as readily and effectively be used for evil."

One more drub of a bomb, much closer, rattled our knees and stirred the silverware on the tables.

Buffington boomed in response, "Consider *that* the call to roast beef and Yorkshire pudding."

We all certainly were happy to take that attitude, but no one moved. Not even Buffington. We waited for the next one. This moment and the next. The Germans were still working on aerial warfare. So far the raids were widely spaced and had come with one or two airships following a single, ongoing path across the city and flying away. This bomb was very near and from the direction of the earlier, distant blasts; the next would either be farther away along the flight path or it would be right on top of us.

We waited.

"Shall we sit?" Buffington's voice had diminished a little. This was a question now, not a defiant suggestion.

And there was a stroke of sound. More distant. Barely felt in Buffington's cellar.

"Bloody hell," someone said nearby, very low, to himself.

We heard no more until we were sitting with four others at the far table. Trask and I were beside each other and I could look, if I wished, between two steel-gray, slick-maned Brits across from me and down the darkened corridor leading to the rest of the basement floor. We heard one more bomb before the food, like a distant stroke of thunder, someone else's storm.

And then we ate. Our companions introduced themselves but did not declare their work, nor did they ask ours, which made me suspect they were Foreign Office types, secret service no doubt, at least some of them. Their talk was casual but it was bluntly critical about Britain's progress so far in the war. About the disastrous four-week gap between the sea attack and the land attack in Gallipoli, about the severe shortage of artillery shells, about the hasty training of a million new troops, about the U-boat threat and the Zeppelin threat and the sudden vulnerability of sacred British soil after centuries of comfortable insularity.

Trask and I said little.

When the four began to lean toward each other and debate the need to dissolve the government and form a new one, I leaned too, toward Trask, and said, low, "Are all these guys in your line of work?"

Trask nodded. "In varying degrees."

The four men stopped talking abruptly.

I thought at first that they'd overheard us, trained as they perhaps were. But their faces had turned not to us but to a point higher up and beyond Trask's far shoulder.

I looked, and Buffington had arrived and he put his hand on the shoulder of a stout man with a crooked cravat sitting next to Trask. The man needed no word. He nodded and rose and moved off and Buffington sat down.

He said to the other three, "Sorry, gentlemen. Continue."

And they did, with one of them saying Kitchener—who was the secretary of state for war and who all three agreed was responsible for the shortage of artillery shells—had to resign no matter what they did with Asquith.

Buffington drew Trask toward him. I leaned along as well and neither of them made the slightest gesture to suggest I was not invited.

Buffington said, "Stockman's throwing a weekend house party."

"Your man?" Trask said.

Buffington said, "In the vicinity."

Trask nodded. And then he made the tiniest intentional movement of his head, so tiny that I instantly doubted my perception, figured I was an example of how you can overtrain a secret service agent. The movement, I thought, was this very slight turn in my direction—since I'd drawn near, behind Trask's right shoulder—as if it was a subtle gesture to Buffington, reminding him of my presence. "Is she ready?" he said.

What did all that have to do with me?

I sat back in my chair.

My eyes moved across the table and between the two steel-gray heads, who had sat back as well, now that they'd agreed to throw out Asquith and Kitchener and all the rest of them.

I looked into the darkness of the corridor.

And the darkness moved.

That was the first impression, lasting only a brief moment. The darkness shifted, swelled, and then points of light began to clarify into a face, hands, and a piano started playing the instrumental introduction to a song—and I recognized it, the intro to "Keep the Home Fires Burning"—and the face emerging from the shadows of the corridor, heading this way, became clear, and now I recognized it as well, even as I had a sense of movement to my left, Buffington no doubt standing up to address us all. He said, "Gentlemen, in the interests of preserving civilization as we wait out this latest barbarous attack, I give you the great Isabel Cobb."

My mother emerged fully into the room, dressed in black, and she stopped, framed in the doorway, as the men at our table wrenched around, turned their chairs, applauded, and cried out "Hear! Hear!"

The introduction was over and Mother shot the piano player a brief glance as he fumbled a bit with the transition to the verse. I glanced with her, and it was the stout man Buffington had replaced at the table. This was a select and secretive group; Isabel Cobb's accompanist was drawn from one of our own number. He wasn't terrible at this, however, and he found his way into the verse and Mother looked back to us and began to sing.

I heard her voice, but for a few moments, as far as I knew, she could have been singing a soliloquy from *Hamlet*, as I grappled with my surprise at her presence here. And then she was inserting that phony ache into her voice that she was so good at. Phony mostly to my ear, of course; fans loved it. But, indeed, she drew even me in with it now as she sang:

"Let no tears add to their hardships
As the soldiers pass along,
And although your heart is breaking,
Make it sing this cheery song."

The secret service pianist did all right with the transition to the chorus and Mama floated on in, more achy than ever. "Keep the home fires burning, while your hearts are yearning," she sang and she began to work the room, gliding along the tables, singing to each stiff upper lip individually—"Though your lads are far away, they dream of home"—and bringing a tear to each eye and a stirring to each stirrable part—"There's a silver lining, through the dark clouds shining"—and she gave me a little less eye contact than the others and a pat on the shoulder as she slid by. "Turn the dark cloud inside out, till the boys come home."

I watched her as she moved on to Trask.

He lifted his face to her, and a son knows certain things for reasons he can't put his finger on easily. Or the reasons seem minute and in-substantial. But Trask's eyes and my mother's held on each other for one pulse beat, one intake of breath, and I knew there was something between them. This particular son knowing certain things about this particular mother made me think in my usual, weary little way: *lovers.*

Then he nodded, once, very faintly, with those blank eyes of his, and I felt my intuition shift. She was not sleeping with him. She was working for him. *Is she ready?* he'd said. Ready for Sir Albert Stockman's weekend party.

She moved along, singing, "Overseas there came a pleading, help a nation in distress," and Buffington extended his hand and she took it and she sang to him and I had the same first, fleeting hunch about him. She was working for Trask, but she was sleeping with Buffington. And then I felt like the punk kid I once was, standing outside a closed door in a theatrical boarding-house trying to will his mother to live her life in some other way. What way, I couldn't imagine, just some other way.

But in fact I was thirty-one years old and she was fifty-six and we had long ago disentangled ourselves from our shared life. And rightly so. We wrote letters. An occasional telegram. But all of that was strictly private. As public as I had subsequently become and as she had always been, it was not really known—outside of a few of my journalist pals and the close-knit tribe of American theater people—that we were mother and son.

She let go of her host's hand and I let go of the hunch and she moved off to the next table to urge everyone to keep the home fires burning while their hearts were yearning.

I thought of her lying to me in her dressing room. No. She hadn't lied. It was no doubt true that she was not now working nor would she ever work again for a detective agency. But she didn't say anything at all about working for the U.S. secret service. She'd convinced me about the Pinkertons by invoking her ego. Her ego would be thoroughly satisfied playing the role of spy for her country. Just the thing for a great actress who was furious with the theater for not overlooking her advancing age. As a spy she could still be a glamorous leading lady. And her performance had a special edge: her life could depend on it being convincing.

I turned around in my chair, shut out her voice, poked at a roasted potato.

My mother segued from the home fires into an upbeat "Pack Up Your Troubles in Your Old Kit Bag," and then she finished with an even more achy "There's a Long, Long Trail."

The music stopped, the gentlemen cheered, she left, and a rhubarb crumble arrived. In the midst of all this, Buffington rose and followed her up the circular stairway and Trask turned to me as the ramekins landed before us.

"Your mother is working for us," he said.

"I surmised," I said.

And though I felt the irony, given my recent bout of musty hunches, I asked the obvious question. "Is she going after Sir Albert?"

"Yes," Trask said.

And then he added, "So are you."

5

The next night Isabel Cobb ended her run in London as Hamlet, Prince of Denmark. She'd swept out of her basement cabaret on the night of the most recent Zeppelin attack on London and it wasn't until Friday morning that I saw her again, when she stepped into a first-class compartment at Victoria Station for the train to Broadstairs in Kent and she sat down across from the American journalist and German apologist Joseph W. Hunter.

Trask had booked the compartment so that she and I would be alone. But she entered playing a stranger, nodding at me and then ignoring me as she settled in, arranging her handbag next to her just so, its corners squared to the edge of the upholstered bench seat. I watched this with a vaguely squirmy sense of recognition. I always did that very thing with the pages of a story as they came out of my typewriter.

She finished with her bag and then smoothed her overskirt, though it hardly needed smoothing. It was a stage gesture. She looked quite summery in a blueberry bolero jacket and straw boater with a matching ribbon and pleated bow.

She turned her face to me now, even as I was thinking how she looked pretty good, and she tightened her forehead as if I were a young man on the mash.

I refused to play along. "We have the compartment to ourselves, Mother," I said, in a tone of *We both know this, so what are all the theatrics for?*

She flared her hands in front of her. "Can't we have a little fun, my darling? Improvisation? How long has it been since we rode a train together? We used to have so much fun."

I shrugged and looked out of the window beside me. A conductor strode past blowing his all-aboard whistle.

"You were always a clever boy," she said. "A talented boy."

We rode enough trains together between theater towns to circle the earth and circle it again. For as long as I could think back, we would play roles together to pass the time. Over the years, I was everyone from a beggar boy running away from an orphanage to a dry goods commercial traveler who was Isabel Cobb's biggest fan and overwhelmed to meet her. She once had hopes I'd follow her into the theater.

The train was moving now, and I turned back to Mother. She was watching out the window. Her face was blank. I knew the look. I'd seen it often, in stage wings just before she would make her first entrance. This blankness was all she would show of the actor's inevitable terror of reinventing herself before a thousand strangers watching from the dark.

This time her audience would be smaller and she would walk among them and things were at stake far beyond entertaining a theater crowd.

I knew to let her be. The outward blankness would last until her entrance cue, and then she would come suddenly alive as if she'd flipped an electric light switch. I glanced at her only briefly and stealthily, but her preparatory state went on and on, through our run across the Thames and through Clapham and Herne Hill, with their old estates turning into middle-class commuter houses, and through our plunge into the dark of the long tunnel beneath the Crystal Palace. Here, the electric lights in the compartment flickered us into total darkness. We clattered through the blackness for a long moment, and when the lights flared back on again, I looked frankly at her and she had closed her eyes.

I believed her fear.

I wanted to reach out and take her hand.

But I knew better.

What would she take as her entrance cue on this day?

The lights blinked off once more and then almost instantly back on and her eyes were open, as if they had been all along and what I'd seen was wrong.

But she was still preparing.

Only when we were above ground and finished with London and into the county of Kent and we were rushing through vast hops gardens, the plants beginning to bloom into gold, ready for the seasonal pickers to come down from the slums of London, only then did she turn her face back to me.

"The curtain goes up," she said.

I nodded.

"What the hell are you doing?" I said.

"What do you mean?"

"This role of yours."

"And you, my son? I was quite surprised to learn about your own specialized acting career."

"You already knew about me the other night."

"Of course." She leaned forward and patted me on the knee. "Aren't we having fun?"

There was nothing to say to that. Of course she was.

I decided to watch the hops for a while.

Trask had briefed me before we parted at Buffington's. I'd been invited to stay the weekend at Stockman House, his family estate high on the chalk cliffs between Broadstairs and Ramsgate. I was following Isabel Cobb, doing a feature story on her for the de facto syndicate of German-leaning American newspapers that were making my reputation. The news hook was the next stop on her tour of *Hamlet*. Berlin. A detail she deliberately withheld from our discussion of her tour in her dressing room. I was to stay alert to—even, at my discretion, seek out—evidence that Sir Albert was indeed actively aiding the German cause. My mother was doing the same.

"This will be an interesting test of your new identity," Trask had said.

I wasn't worried. There had been almost no images of me in the press over these half dozen years of my war correspondent notoriety. I'd insisted on that. My printed words were my public face. There was, however, another issue. I'd said to Trask, "She and I have kept it quiet for more than a decade, but the Germans surely know she's my mother."

He'd simply nodded. We were drinking brandy in the two Morris chairs after everyone else had cleared out of Buffington's basement bunker.

"This is very risky for her," I said.

Trask did a lift of the left shoulder and a tilt of the head in the same direction, both equally minute. A characteristic shrug I'd seen more than once. It usually was meant to stop a line of inquiry. But this time he also said, "She understands the risk. She's made it very clear how disaffected she is with you. I understand she can be very convincing."

I let that sink in. I tried to believe it. I said, "But why recruit *her*? Why take on that extra burden?"

"She was already undercover."

"I know about that."

"So I gather." He smiled, slow and sly. Her Pinkerton work.

"You're not saying she came to you," I said.

He shrugged again. This time it did stop the inquiry. But he added, "It could actually make her more interesting to them."

At that, I should have had a thought about something I'd seen in her dressing room, but I got distracted by her being "interesting" to the Germans.

Trask even followed up on my distraction, though he figured he was simply giving me a more direct answer to my question of *why her*. He said, "She happened to be the best possible person for our Sir Albert. He is her ardent fan."

The hops seemed to have vanished. The field passing was full of cows.

I turned back to Mother.

"There *is* something to say to that." This came out of my mouth before I realized I was alluding to a thought of a few moments ago that I'd not given voice to: what was there to say to her "Aren't we having fun."

"Have I missed something?" she said.

"We can't take this as fun," I said. "Of course you knew about me and Trask when I saw you in your dressing room. You knew long before that."

"So?"

"So what the hell were you doing making a show of my being your son? The stage manager knew me on sight. My photo was stuck in your mirror. You did your underappreciated-and-deeply-concerned-but-proudly-loving-mama act with the suffragettes."

"I *am* underappreciated and deeply concerned," she said.

"Trask surely told you these people are dangerous."

"I am proudly loving too," she said.

"Your fate . . ."

"Always that," she said.

"Your fate with the Huns," I said, firmly, "depends on their belief that we are estranged, you and I."

"I know that," she said.

"Then how could you publicly play the opposite?"

"It wasn't public. This man would never in an eon talk with suffragettes or stage managers. And when he came backstage I hid your photo."

I flipped my hands in the air in exasperation.

"So Mr. Hunter," she said, suddenly lighting up in her stage-star way, immediately turning me into this guy. As if that was all it would take to put my concerns to rest. "You and I share some strong sympathies that are, I'm afraid, quickly becoming unpopular in our country."

She engaged my gaze and she was looking at me with veiled but lively eyes and she was smiling a very small, crooked smile. This pose was filed under *Faintly Superior Solicitousness*. She was inviting me to get into character with her now. Like old times on a train on the way to a performance.

"Wrongheadedly so," I said. "This is not the first time our country has had trouble choosing its friends."

For a very brief moment her smile flashed wide: Isabel smiling at her son Kit playing along with her. Then she plunged back into her playlet. "You are so right, Mr. Hunter. So right indeed. But this weekend you will have a chance to write about the greatest actress of the American stage celebrating her triumph as Hamlet in London and then traveling on to play the tragically fated prince in Berlin. I will, by my art, build a bridge between these two warring nations. I take no sides. I love the English but I also embrace our German brethren."

"And do you embrace our host this weekend?" I asked.

There was a stopping in her and then a fluttering out of her part, just a little, in her hands. I tried not to show any pleasure at getting her to briefly lose her performance composure. My sense of our old *game* of this indeed made me feel a sort of pleasure. But for me to have flustered her with that cheap innuendo meant there was some bit of truth in it. And there was no pleasure in that at all.

She recovered quickly. "Mr. Hunter, I never took you for a yellow journalist."

I played at backing off. "I mean, of course, in the same way you would embrace the good people of *Das Deutsche Reich*."

"Well, do forgive me, Mr. Hunter, for misunderstanding you. I am sadly accustomed to young men taking an inappropriate interest in my private life, which is none of their business."

I turned my face to the windows. The cows had given way to apple orchards, the small, green earlies already beginning to appear.

"We need to talk in our actual selves," I said.

"And what are those, exactly?" she said.

I looked at her.

Our eyes connected but didn't hold. She turned her face to the long, even rows of apple trees whisking by. "All right," she said.

"Your man Albert . . ."

"He is not my man," she said.

"Your target Albert."

"Yes?"

"What can you tell me about him?"

"I've said things about America privately to him that make your little pseudonymous odes to the Fatherland sound wishy-washy."

"Wouldn't that make him suspicious?"

"I'm exaggerating." She said this instantly, shrugging.

"Let's talk straight," I said.

"What I said *felt* that extreme," she said. "It's easier for you to write this drivel than it is for me to say it face to face. But I've made myself look as potentially good for the German cause as your J. W. Hunter. And I worked up to it. I know how to play that role with a man. Oh, sir, I've got this little secret that some people would think unsavory but I feel I can trust you."

"Sounds effective." I said this with an edge I didn't want. She didn't either. It was her own fault for putting it in those terms.

We looked at each other and silently called a truce.

She said, "I think he believes me. And he was receptive. You could feel him expanding, glowing. But this was just loose, still rather indirect talk. His receptiveness is nothing like proof."

"There's one thing I worry about," I said.

"What's that, dear?"

"He'll see a resemblance in us."

"I don't think so," she said.

"The eyes," I said.

"No," she said.

"We have the same eyes."

"Nonsense," she said. "You have your father's eyes."

In those rare occasions she'd let herself refer to him, however vaguely—*always* vaguely—she meant it to stop the present conversation. She had never identified my father except that his name was Cobb and he was dead and I'd received from him some good traits and some bad traits. Unspecified. To her credit, she had never once, no matter how angry or frustrated she became with me, never once had she invoked my dead Cobb of a father as being responsible for my behavior. And perhaps a dozen times over the years she'd said that the one thing I got from my father were my looks, which she heartily approved of. Just *my looks*. The eye thing—that they, specifically, were his—this was new. And unwelcome.

I found my next breath hard to take. Impossible to take. And I could hear the clatter of my heart in my ears. Perhaps I had my father's heart as well. Perhaps he'd died of a heart attack. Perhaps I wouldn't have to worry about Sir Albert Stockman looking into my face and seeing my mother and smiling and nodding and later telling his men to kill us both in our sleep. Maybe this clatter was my last.

"You'll be just fine, Mr. Hunter," my mother said, quite low. Not a stage whisper. Not stagey at all. She meant to sincerely encourage me. Encourage us.

I nodded and turned my eyes to the window and saw nothing and then I turned back to her.

"What did Trask say he expected of you?" I asked.

"Whatever I can give him," my mother said. "But at worst, when I get to Berlin, if Albert is what we think he is and he believes my performance, we expect the German secret service will approach me to be useful to them."

And now Trask's declaration struck me as it almost did in Buffington's basement, that this recruitable German agent being the mother of a very effective enemy of Germany made her even more interesting to them.

I was so unaware of cursing in response, I could not even say, exactly, which curse it was that I'd used.

She said, "When a son replies to his mother with the exclamation 'Fuck me,' she is faced with a choice of several interpretations, none of them pleasant."

"I'm sorry, Mother," I said. "Your first 'useful' act for the Germans will be to try to lure me into a trap. You understand that, don't you?"

You could see the same stopping of breath in her that I had felt over my father's eyes. She was silent for one beat and another and then she said, so quietly that I could barely hear it above the clack of the train wheels, "Fuck me."

"That's the right interpretation," I said.

"Mr. Trask surely knows this," she said.

"Of course he does," I said. "And it's what we have signed up for, you and I. You understand that too."

"Yes." Another pause. And she added, "He'll have a plan."

"*We* will have a plan," I said. "We all will."

She nodded.

And we both watched sightlessly for a few moments as the Kentish landscape rolled past.

It was time to get to work. I said, "Have you been to Stockman House?"

"Not yet," she said, squaring her shoulders to me. "But 'house' is British understatement, I'm told. It's a castle. Just not a terribly old one. Built in the middle of the last century by his grandfather."

"Is he all inheritance? Or does he have his own dough?"

"He's got plenty of his own. He's an industrialist, he says. Metals. But if you push him—and I quickly learned not to—it's all milk cans and Oxo tins and dustbins. He's the Industrial Titan of Milk Cans, and he's a bit touchy about it. For some years now, of course, he's a member of Parliament, and that's who he thinks he really is."

"Does he have family?" Though I tried hard to keep a just-trying-to-get-the-facts tone in my voice, even I could hear the fidgety undertone.

She looked at me for a beat, sizing up my intention with that question. Which was, at least in part, to understand the extent of his romantic availability to her.

Does the punk kid you once were ever fully vanish, especially when it comes to your mother, especially when she's the only blood family you ever had? And when that mother keeps casting you in his role, as she'd done ever since we'd boarded this train, and when you and he and she are sharing serious personal risks, his child's issue takes on a new relevance. She had to get close to this man, but not too close.

"A daughter in Scotland," she said. "He's a widower." She paused, waiting for me to openly become the young man with an inappropriate interest in her private life.

I declined. I fed her no cue. She still had the stage.

She said, "His wife died a couple of years ago. An accident."

She paused again. I made a little wide-eyed chin dip to ask for more.

"She fell off a cliff," she said. "He lives on a cliff."

"An accident?"

"Officially."

"Unofficially?"

"I asked our Mr. Trask that very thing." The ham in my mother came suddenly to a sizzle: she paused and let it roll on.

I finally asked. "And?"

"He shrugged."

"Be careful of this Stockman guy," I said.

"I just have to keep charming him. You're the one who'll need to be careful."

"Is this how the boss did it?" I executed Trask's little shoulder lift and head tilt.

She answered with a similar exact replica of Trask's shrug. "*That* way," she said, as if it were different from mine. It wasn't.

I didn't debate the point. I was finished bantering with my mother. We had more important business together. I looked out the window. The apple trees had become cherry trees. Far beyond them a church spire rose against the gray sky in a grove of village roofs.

Mother thought she sensed my mood, though she was a step behind now.

"Just so you know," she said. "Sir Albert's crazy about me."

I kept my eyes on the flash of cherry trees and, flickering among them, baskets and ladders and figures reaching up. The trees were fruiting.

"He'll probably touch my elbow." She paused.

I concentrated on the cherries.

"Or put his hand on the small of my back."

I thought about picking sour cherries one summer day in my childhood. Somewhere in upstate New York. It must have been near a summer theater.

"I will take his arm. Do you understand?"

I turned to her. I nodded. I made myself say, "It's all part of the job."

As soon as I said it, I believed it.

And my mother leaned forward, reached out, took my hand, and squeezed it.

6

Albert sent a Silver Ghost to meet us at Broadstairs Station. The liveried driver stood on the platform with feet spread, his hands clasped behind him, as we emerged. He recognized us at once, coming to attention. I almost expected a salute. He took our bags from the porter and handed them off to a man in well-worn blue serge who'd been doing a respectful cringe behind him, and he led us to the Rolls-Royce parked just outside the station door, a landaulette with two leather armchairs and a couple of jump seats in the tonneau, an open driver compartment, and that long, long Rolls hood ending in the marque's nickel and bronze mascot, the Spirit of Ecstasy, a beautiful woman bent toward the onrushing road with her nightie billowing up along her arms like wings.

We drove south down the coast, clearing Broadstairs, and we approached Dumpton Gate, the "gate" being one of the rare, narrow gaps in the otherwise unbroken white chalk cliffs of the Kentish coast. The road had gradually been gathering a loosely intervaled but considerable traffic: dog cart and carriage, Brit-blue Model T and Daimler landaulette, and folks on foot as well, singly and coupled up, buddied up and in families. We followed a dense grove of sweet chestnuts parallel to the cliff line, showing an iron fence flashing within the trees and farther glimpses of go-to-meeting-size tents. Something more than a weekend house party was happening at Stockman House, at least for today. Then the trees ended abruptly and the iron fence emerged and turned toward the sea. So did we, and so did the other travelers on this road.

We all entered a macadamized access road. The fence uprights were taller than a man and spiked at the top. They'd run through the tree line, no doubt all the way from the gap, and also bordered this southern side of Stockman's property, surely to the edge of the cliff. He had a serious security perimeter. And through the fence's transparent blur, beyond the cluster of cream and blue-striped tents set up on the wide, flat green, Stockman House showed itself.

Mother leaned across me to look. For now the place was simply vast—but much wider than tall—and it was black, and this west side of it, away from the sea, gaped open in its center, three long wings around a courtyard.

Mother withdrew, sitting down hard in her seat. My hand lay on the chair arm between us and she immediately put her own hand on mine and squeezed. I looked at her.

"Stage nerves?" I asked.

She stretched out a tight little smile for me.

I turned my hand upward and clasped hers.

As we neared the house, an iron-arched entryway appeared in the fence, with a couple of uniformed local constables pulling the gates open for us. Only for us, for now, as the travelers were simply gathering on the south side of the road, parking their vehicles, waiting to enter the grounds. We slowed and turned in.

The main inner road headed for the courtyard, but the driver shortly angled off into a side road toward the cliff. We entered a driveway circle and went the long way round, to the right, and we stopped, presenting Mother's door to the center of the south face of the house. The driver jumped out and galloped around to open it.

He was a hulk of a man with a thick neck, but he moved quickly and lightly. If he were an American I'd take him for a Wolverine half-back. Since he was a Brit, a rugby footballer. Since he was Stockman's man, though, however he'd acquired his skills, I was willing to bet he was more than a driver. A tough guy. I slipped from my side and stepped clear of the car. I looked at Sir Al's abode.

Sometimes a man's castle is his home. His was well fortified and he was the only family member residing in it, up here high above the Strait of Dover. I glanced that way, at the cloud-begrayed water laid out against the horizon, just beyond which was Calais and the shooting war. If he was a German agent, he was well placed.

The house was Victorian-Elizabethan-Eccentric. Seventy-five years old at most, but it was of quite another era: this wide facade—at least sixty yards, maybe more—was an Elizabethan profusion of glass, two dozen vast window casements transomed and mullioned into hundreds and hundreds of panes on this south face alone.

To my right, at the wing's eastern end, rose a parapeted tower that was more King John than the Virgin Queen. This Gothic tower lifted a full two storeys above the slate roof, its only window a cruciform loophole. And from the top of the tower Stockman House rose higher still. On another two storeys of flagpole flew a whopping Union Jack, nearly as wide as the Silver Ghost was long. Including the cliff on which everything stood, that flag waved a good two hundred feet above the shore. The pole was high enough and big enough that it was even anchored against high winds by four guy wires lashed to the tower parapet. Such an extravagant declaration of Britishness struck me as Stockman wrapping himself in a big flag to hide his treachery.

A striking thing about the house itself—a vaguely intimidating thing—was its stone. Ashlar-worked black flint. An odd contradiction to my eye, this darkly craggy stone, usually found rusticated, made smooth and slick and polished. And even as that thought passed through me, Sir Albert Stockman's polished baritone filled the salty air, booming and yet mellifluous.

I could understand Mother thinking she needed to warn me about her putting her arm in his. Outwardly he was her kind of guy. He was a tall man, taller than me by a couple of inches, bareheaded but wearing an unbuttoned single-breasted day-wear tailcoat with striped trousers and sporting a flash of pink silk in his breast pocket. He had a fine, angular face, chipped and polished from a craggy white stone. He was graying lightly, probably Mother's age but having arrived in his fifties beautifully, in the way she loved, envied, and despised in males. He was a leading man.

I began to move toward the point between them where they were about to meet, him striding to his Isabel Cobb, she taking her own step toward him, and another. They arrived. He caught up both her hands. He bent to her and they bussed on each cheek. I stopped.

They finished bussing and stood back to look at each other. They kept holding hands. I was watching him closely enough to see his eyes not quite leave hers but register me, as I was comfortably within his line of easy peripheral sight and only a few steps away. I tried to portray a respectful deference, slumping a little at the chest, lowering my chin ever so slightly.

"I am so happy you are here," he was saying.

"I am happy to be here," my mother said.

"You'll have time to rest a little," he said. "Today the grounds are open to the good people of Ramsgate and Broadstairs. We will host and feast some of my constituents. You don't mind appearing for them?"

"Of course not, Albert. I am happy to be hostess of Stockman House tonight."

Albert straightened to full height in overplayed joy at this. He bent again, this time toward her hands, one of which he lifted and kissed, somewhat lingeringly.

Mother lowered her face and watched.

Albert rose. "Thank you, my dear," he said. And then he turned his face to me.

"And this must be Mr. Hunter," he said. Warmly. Convincingly so, I had to admit. This was good. I needed to appear useful to a man not only whose heart and history but also whose active, secret allegiance might be to Germany.

"Yes," my mother said, turning to me.

Not "my mother." *Isabel*, I thought. I had to play this role inside my head as well.

Stockman let go of Isabel Cobb and took the three steps to me as she said, "This is Joseph W. Hunter . . ."

He offered me a hand, which I took, prepared for a firm grip. I got one. Luckily I wedged my own hand fully into his and gave him just enough back to let him think I was a substantial enough man but not a rival. Meanwhile, my mother was saying, "Sir Albert Stockman."

He and I were locked in at the eyes. Perhaps it was just the dulled light of the cloudy day but I could have sworn his eyes were almost precisely the shade called *feldgrau*, literally field gray, the color of the German army's fighting uniforms, gray but cut by green, the combination perfect for camouflage in the European countryside.

"Sir Albert Stockman," I said.

"Mr. Hunter," he said. "I am delighted to meet you."

He lifted his chin just a little. I was wrong about his eyes. I stopped indulging my impulse to see him, in every detail, by the light of our suspicions. This wasn't a feature story for the Sunday edition. That newswriter reflex was bad for my present line of work. His eyes weren't *feldgrau*. They were grayer than that.

He said, "I get the newspapers from the United States. We are all very attentive, as you may know, to your country's attitudes. I've read you with great interest."

The locution he used was not uncommon. But he paused, as if to let that soak in. That he'd been reading *me*. Not just my stories. But I got the strong sense he meant more.

"I hope I didn't cause you any offense," I said.

He lowered his chin and gave me a careful look. "Why would you think that?"

"You are English. Perhaps the stories I write are too willing, from an Englishman's point of view, to understand the German side of things."

Stockman gave me a slow, nodding smile. He said, "Perhaps I am trying to understand your President's reluctance to become more involved."

I let my Mr. Hunter show his nerves at all this, looking briefly away from Stockman in a deferential shrug. "Just so," I said. "That's my concern on your behalf. If he no longer heard the voice of those Americans who favor Germany, he might be more willing to help you."

I was back to Stockman's eyes and he was focused intently on me, assessing me. He smiled. "Don't worry about that. You are a welcome guest in my home."

"You're too kind," I said.

"Besides, I understand you are doing a story on the estimable Isabel Cobb."

"Indeed," I said.

"You see? I don't hold her appearance in Berlin against her," Stockman said, and he initiated a gentle, socially reassuring laugh. The estimable Isabel Cobb and I joined in.

When the laugh faded into a comfortable silence between us, he said. "I remain interested in your views. We can speak later."

"I look forward to it," I said.

"You are invited for the weekend, of course."

Without giving me even a moment's chance to reply to this, Stockman did an about-face and quickstepped to Isabel. Without a look at me, she tucked her hand into the crook of his offered arm and the two maundered off toward the house. I followed.

7

This brief passage toward the castle door surprised me in the claw-scrabble of unease it started up in my chest. We entered the castle through a reception hall with twin suits of armor flanking the door, helmets closed, occupied by a couple more of his tough guys for all I knew. Stockman stopped Isabel and half turned to me and said, "Martin will show you the way." His driver loomed up beside me and extended an arm toward the inner door and swept it to the right. I went where I was told, while my mother and her leading man swept out to the left.

I heard her voice and footfalls fading into stone-echoes behind me, and I realized this was what my unease was all about, my mother and me separating in this place. If Stockman and his boys were what we suspected they were, she could well be in over her head. Alone here, I could be too. I always figured I could handle anything. I wasn't so sure about her.

But it was all very polite. Even Martin was polite, in a silent way. Nonchalant even. If he was a hired tough guy, I had no sense he was under orders to intimidate me or even to keep a special eye on me. He led me along a corridor hung with fox-hunt Aubussons, and ahead was a massive stone staircase, which we were approaching from its great, gray, triangular wedge of a side. As we reached it and began to turn, Martin flipped a forefinger toward an open doorway at the base of the steps. "Billiards," he said. "You can play."

His English—these four words were, I suddenly realized, the first I'd heard of it—was not British in accent, was oddly not accented at all but clipped and precise. I thought: *a carefully trained German.*

We'd made the turn now and the staircase was simply a wall face beside me, but my mind went up these steps. The castle was complex in its layout and I knew I had to simplify what I took in, what I memorized of the layout, or I'd get lost. This staircase seemed worth noting. I reckoned that it ascended within the five-storey parapeted tower.

Martin said, "The stairs lead into the private family wing of the house. I am sorry that guests are invited no farther than the billiards."

His seeming to read my mind was vaguely unsettling, but his treating me like a regular, well-intentioned guest was vaguely reassuring. If I were an ill-intentioned guest his comment would only be an invitation to snoop. As, indeed, I was and it was.

We passed through the Great Hall, its abrupt three-storey lift to a vast hammer-beam roof giving it something of the same heady kick of a big-league church. But Martin was talking again and I focused on him. "That's the library," he said, motioning to a door in the east wall. "The billiards and the books. These are for you to enjoy until we collect you at about five. You may dress casually tonight, as the public will be here for festivities and we will be serving high tea alfresco."

"Are there other guests for the weekend?" I asked.

"A dozen," he said. "Many are here now. You'll have competition." I assumed he meant at billiards.

At the far end of the Great Hall we entered the arched colonnade of a screens passage and turned left into a staircase. We climbed to the second-floor bachelor corridor of the castle, laid out over the kitchen and pantries.

When we reached my room Martin opened the door and stepped back for me, as if in deference. He even pulled his hat off, showing a spiky crop of wheat-chaff tan hair. He was consciously playing a role. As I passed him, I played my part in his little scene, giving him a nod of gratitude-to-a-servant, but catching and holding for a moment those eyes, which were as opaquely gray as the Strait of Dover.

The room had a narrow set of mullioned windows and was furnished with the simple straight lines of the Arts and Crafts movement: bedstead, wardrobe, hard leather-seated chair, small break-front writing desk.

I sat in the chair and I waited for the cringing man from the station. He and the bags were coming by a separate vehicle. The Rolls was not a touring model and didn't have an elegant way of transporting a great deal of luggage. But I figured Stockman might have arranged that so as to do a quick check of the contents. Certainly enough time was passing.

At last the luggage man arrived, and I took my bags at the doorway and closed him out at once and I laid them—a leather valise and a Gladstone—on the bed. I opened the valise and lifted out books and a toilet case and a notepad. But for this weekend these were mostly just filler to cover the false bottom I was now prying out of the valise.

Stockman's boys might have searched, but they didn't find my Mauser pocket automatic, a rock-hard bantamweight of a pistol with a .32 caliber punch. I pulled it out of the false-bottomed depth of my valise. It was tucked inside a left-hander's leather holster with the flap cut off, so I could wear it in the small of my back and draw it with my right hand.

I laid the holster on the bed, and I freshened up in cold water in my small bathroom and changed my suit from sack to brown mohair, with a fresh shirt and tie.

I slipped the Mauser and its holster onto my belt and centered it in place.

They didn't find my leather pouch of lock-picking tools either. This I put into my inner coat pocket. Or my six-inch tungsten flashlight, which I snugged into my side pocket. Or my Luger, which I left in the comparable false bottom of the Gladstone.

I sat down on the edge of my bed and retied my shoes.

What sounded distantly like a small salon orchestra had arrived, out on the green, and was tuning up.

I was ready to begin.

I wasn't interested in books or billiards. I wanted to look around. I'd carry my notebook and keep only Joseph W. Hunter notes in it, as if the grounds of the castle was local color in the Kent part of my feature story on Isabel Cobb.

I stepped out of my room and closed the door quietly behind me. The corridor was empty. I went along it and down the stairs and emerged in the screens passage. A scullery maid in white uniform and mobcap brushed past me with her face cast down and a quiet "Pardon, sir."

I emerged into the Great Hall.

Though the windows here were limited to the west wall and looked into the courtyard, the place felt bright, for it was faced in white granite. The floor was covered by a single Persian rug large enough to define the foundation of a Sears ready-made bungalow. In its dense weave, hunters on horses leapt and gazelles fled.

A young Queen Victoria—the Stockmar family's benefactress—was on horseback, as well, rendered massively in oils above the white ashlar walk-in fireplace. Beyond her was the doorway into the library. I was sanctioned to go there. Books and billiards. The things I needed to really learn about Stockman were in the unsanctioned places, but it was daylight and Stockman House was preparing to receive the public and Albert's men would be prowling around, so for now I had to interpret what I could from the things I could access. A library was as good a place to start as any.

I set out across the Persian hunting ground, thinking of books. Early in my previous assignment I'd discovered at least a temporary Rosetta stone for one of the Germans' methods of secret communication: a book called *The Nuttall Encyclopaedia of Universal Information*, the placement of whose words were the basis for numbered codes. Not that Al's *Nuttall* would be kept on the library table off the Great Hall. But if they weren't simply tony wallpaper, I was interested in his books.

I approached three Brits in summer tweeds and spats drinking tea and talking low on red-velvet Jacobean chairs before the fireplace.

Middle-aged gents, all of them. Other guests for the weekend, no doubt. One glanced my way as I approached and then back to the discussion, the voices clipping phrases and extending vowels in that toffish, fixed-jawed upper-class British way. The reporter in me thought to slide into their conversation and find out what they knew about Albert. But a young American, out of the blue, asking the kinds of questions I'd need to ask to make it worth my while, would only create suspicion. My real work required that I remain mostly unnoticed.

I passed them by and stepped into the library.

The place was chockablock with wainscoted shelves full of books in great, uniform runs of sets, the blues and reds and browns and greens of their spines coordinated carefully into a variegated but orderly panorama. The east wall held a twenty-foot-wide bay window looking out to the strait.

I strolled along Stockman's books, the sets a patchwork of writers and subjects. A dozen volumes of *Illustrated World Geography* running in green into fifteen umber Sam Johnsons into twenty tan Bulwer-Lyttons into a couple dozen French Shakespeares in black and gilt. I stopped here and saw, on the shelf below, another complete Shakespeare, in English, and then next to that a twelve-volume set of the Schlegel and Tieck German translation. *Shakespeares sämtliche dramatische Werke.*

I looked more closely at the Schlegel Shakespeare. They were placed in evenly at the front edge of the shelves. All the books in the library were arranged like this. Not quite flush. There was about a quarter of an inch lip between the edge of the shelf and the spine of the book. And that quarter inch was gray with dust. I pulled one of the Schlegels out. The shelf was instantly wiped clean in a band the width of the volume in my hand. I replaced it.

I continued on, more slowly, looking at the ubiquitous layer of dust. He was not a reader. Not from this library at least. And I also kept an eye out for the German works. There weren't many and they were scattered along. The collected Goethe. Schiller. But Stockman's books were mostly English. Still, if he was trying to make an impression, he didn't mind showing at least some of his Germanic origins. Not that he was reading the English-language books either. Not lately.

I finally reached the wall of stuffed shelves at the far end. I stood with my back to the rest of the room and found twenty-two volumes of a German writer I did not know. Johann Gottfried von Herder. Two of the volumes had been pulled from the shelves recently. By Sir Albert or by an invited guest. I drew one out. The end board was marbled in blue and brown and cream. I opened the cover. The volume was from 1820. *Die Vorwelt.* "The Primeval World."

I lifted my face from the page.

Perhaps he'd made some small sound. Or, if he'd quietly drawn close, perhaps there was some kinesthetic clue, a displacement of air perhaps. Whatever it was, it registered on me so quickly and subtly that I could not trace it. But I knew someone was in the room with me.

I turned.

Stockman was only a few strides away. He stood with his arms folded over his chest, changed from his tailcoat into more relaxed day wear, a three-piece gray linen suit.

I kept the book open in my hand.

Stockman unfolded his arms and moved to me, saying, "I'm happy you're exploring the library, Mr. Hunter."

"It's impressive," I said.

He stopped just a bit beyond arm's length away.

He glanced at the volume in my hand. "Do you read German, Mr. Hunter?"

"Pretty well," I said. "Do you, Sir Albert?"

"I do," he said. "How are you with the Fraktur?"

Fraktur was the broken-angled, heavy black letter typeface Germany had used for nearly four hundred years. His identifying it only by its esoteric name in the question struck me as part of what was likely to be a subtle, ongoing test of my Germanic credentials.

"I should read it more often," I said. "I do all right, but it still strikes my eye oddly."

He smiled. "Of course. Were your parents born in their homeland?"

"Yes. They came to the United States when I was very young."

"My family background is German as well," Stockman said. "As is the case with a great many Englishmen."

"Your present royal family . . ." I began, hesitating only for a fraction of a second.

He finished my sentence. "Is Saxe-Coburg and Gotha."

He looked at me for a moment. Though it was very brief, I felt certain it was filled with a serious, subtle, rapid assessment of me. He made a decision and said, "Some might say that a royal family by any other name would be a different royal family."

"Would not smell as sweet," I said, bringing his sly joke closer to the Shakespeare quote and to the political point we were quietly deciding to share.

He laughed out loud, a bright, sharp bark of a laugh.

He flipped his chin at the book in my hand. "Do you know von Herder?"

"I don't."

He smiled. He nodded to the shelf behind me. "May I?"

I stepped aside. He moved forward and removed a volume of von Herder and searched its pages for a moment. He found the passage he wanted and handed the book to me, taking *Die Vorwelt* from me. "Beginning of the second paragraph on the right-hand page," he said.

I read it. Another little test. I struggled with the wildly angled letters of the Fraktur and then with the German itself. He watched patiently. But he did not let me off the hook. A few moments along he said, "Apropos of our recent observations."

Then I had it. Though it probably took less than a minute, it felt like a very long time. But I knew that for the circumstances, I'd done this fast. I lifted my face from the page and smiled at him. Just in case he was open to the suspicion, I let him think for a moment that I'd overstated even my modest declaration of proficiency in German and I was about to confess. It would be all the more impressive when he realized I was, indeed, far better than I'd claimed.

"Shall I translate?" I asked.

"Please," he said.

"The heart of it," I said.

"I'd be interested in your selection."

I let go of the literal enough to make it read smoothly in English and I went to the heart of the message: "The English are Germans, and even in recent times the Germans have showed the way for the English in the most important matters."

Stockman slowly unfurled a small, one-sided smile. I could easily read approval into it. For a clever boy passing a tricky test.

He said, "Can I have your assurance that my personal views and sympathies will be strictly omitted from any story you write?"

Though the context was almost mellow in tone, I'd never heard the word "strictly" spoken with such bite. It leaped from the sentence as if he'd flashed a pistol and threatened to use it. Perhaps he had.

"Of course," I said. "I understand the delicacy of your position. I often feel it myself."

I sounded convincing.

He made one more brief, evaluative pause.

I'd passed another test.

"I have a few minutes," he said. "Perhaps the only ones for the rest of this day. Would you like to sit for a time?"

"Of course," I said.

He led me across the room and into a cluster of modern overstuffed reading chairs before the bay window. Beyond were a hundred yards of dense, manicured grass. Very simple. No garden. A fieldstone path to a waist-high stone fence. I wondered if that was where Lady Stockman went over.

Beyond the fence lay the wide stretch of the Strait of Dover, its surface gray starting to mitigate, becoming the vague blue of slate now, as the clouds were beginning to break.

Stockman pointed to one of the wingback reading chairs. I sat.

He didn't. "Brandy all right?" Stockman asked.

"Of course," I said. "Thanks."

He went to a drinks table beneath the apron of the far right segment of the bay window. That part was a casement, I could see. And the baronet himself poured us snifters and carried them over. He sat in the companion chair—the two were at a slight angle toward each other—and he handed me a snifter.

"A fine Armagnac," he said. "I prefer it." Meaning, I presumed, to the more popular Cognac.

"To Armagnac," I said, lifting the snifter in a toast.

We touched glasses.

The brandy was a deep red sunset on the tongue and a noonday sun going down.

"You do understand German quite well," Stockman said.

"We spoke it in the family," I said. "I had sense enough to keep it up afterwards."

He said, "You understand, of course, that I am thoroughly British."

"I understand," I said.

"But I find that compatible with a regard for Germany and a regret over this animosity that has sprung up between us."

"The English are Germans," I said.

"Just so."

"Strictly speaking," I said, "the United States is not yet allied to one side or the other, but I feel the same tension at home."

"I do love my country," he said.

He had turned his face to the window. No eye contact. He allowed the ambiguity but would not overtly share it: which country was that?

As frank as he'd become with me, it sounded as if this was as far as he would go. He might well have decided I was no threat and, indeed, a friend of Germany. The declaration of his Britishness and the rhetoric suggesting a compatible Germany and the wrongness of the war were undoubtedly risky for a Brit, given the anti-German war fervor felt by most of his countrymen. But this was no doubt a position quietly kept by a number of other Englishmen, who nevertheless remained loyal by the light of a democracy's highest belief in the freedom of thought. He didn't have to be an active German agent to be talking like this.

He intended to show me no more.

I thought: *He has just run an automobile-size Union Jack up a castle-roof flagpole.*

Which led me to gently prod him. "That enormous flag above us," I said, "flying over a British castle on the way to the mouth of the Thames. Isn't it a sharp stick in the eye of a Zeppelin commander, daring him to drop his first bomb here?"

"Their realm is the night," he said. I knew the answer, of course, that the flag was invisible when the Zeppelins typically came. But it was the hint of a hush, the tinge of a tremor in his voice over this subject that I'd wanted to evoke and listen to. Just for starters. And all of that was clearly there in his voice. A good actor would kill to render that vocal nuance at will.

"They are impressive, aren't they," I said.

"They are the future," Stockman said.

I said, "The Londoners stiffen their upper lips and elevate their bravado, but I think the Zepps unsettle them."

"Terrify them." Stockman inflated the verb I'd deliberately diminished. Intensely so.

"The airship war is getting stronger," I said.

He drained the rest of his Armagnac.

He was saying no more.

I thought to press on. To probe his feelings about the poison gas attack at the Second Battle of Ypres, about the lesson felt in London and Washington and Paris and Berlin from that battle: the Allies still weren't ready to effectively fight a war. And it wasn't just about the gas. Or a shortage of artillery shells. Kitchener was struggling to properly train his million promised troops. The Anglo-French army had no near prospects of breaking the German line. Germany was growing fearless. And the Zepps would soon rule the night.

I wanted to work Stockman up, now that he was comfortable with me. But my credentials with him were too fresh. I risked undoing them if he sensed I was baiting him.

He stood up, moved away. The bottles rattled at the drink table. "Would you like a refill?" he asked.

"No, thanks," I said.

He returned with a renewed snifter and sat.

He drank. He said, "What do you know about Isabel Cobb?"

I hid in a sip of my brandy. I could easily have seen this as ominous. I'd tried to finesse him into showing me signs of his allegiance to Germany in a weapons-and-havoc way. He could well be doing likewise, looking for a conspiratorial connection between me and this woman he was wooing.

"What sort of thing?" I said.

"I'm interested in her background. You're writing about her. Something I might not know."

It was one of the Kaiser's own precious Prussians who formulated "the best defense is a good offense." So I said, "Since you read American newspapers, you may have seen a Cobb byline. Christopher Cobb. It's not well known, but that's Isabel's son. They broke off contact more than a decade ago, as I understand it."

I watched Stockman's face. It didn't register much of anything. Old news, maybe. "I've heard about him," he said. Nothing more. No follow-up question. He was simply waiting for something he *didn't* know.

Okay, I thought. Maybe it actually was my mother he was assessing now. As a potential spy. Or a potential lover.

"I didn't realize this till recently," I said. "She sings."

"She's singing tonight," Stockman said.

"Sorry. I haven't been working the story for very long."

Stockman stirred in his seat. Sipped. Looked out to the late afternoon sky, which was brightening.

He did indeed want to know about her men, I thought.

I drained my Armagnac. I wished I had another. I'd slug it down quick. But for what we needed to accomplish, my mother and I, Stockman had to stay interested, and this opportunity would not last.

I lowered my voice. "Man to man?" I said.

"Yes," he said, keeping his eyes out the bay window.

"From what I can gather she has no . . . affiliations."

He turned his eyes to me. Me, who had become his mother's pimp. In service to their country.

His look was man to man. He was grateful for the news.

Then he glanced away, toward the library door, responding to a cue that I had missed.

I looked too.

Martin was standing there, changed from his chauffeur livery into a two-piece gray suit.

"I'm afraid it's time to attend to my beloved constituents," Stockman said.

He rose. I began to rise as well, but he stopped me with the flash of his right palm. "Enjoy the books," he said.

I sat back down.

"Help yourself to the brandy," he said, and he turned abruptly and strode across the library floor. He reached the door and paused, speaking a few words to Martin, whose eyes slid briefly to mine as he listened.

Either I'd passed all my tests, as I'd thought, and he was telling his tough guy I was okay, or I was dead wrong and he was issuing a warning. Or a nasty instruction.

But as Stockman pushed past, Martin lingered for one small moment and looked to me, seeing that I'd been watching, and he gave me a slight nod. I nodded back.

I figured I might be all right for the time being.

Then Martin vanished and I was alone in the library.

I stayed where I was. A thing had lingered in my head, from the words unspoken. The matter of the unprepared Brits. Night before last I'd sat in a reading chair next to Trask's in Buffington's bomb shelter and we'd gotten around to our own unpreparedness. The United States had a hundred thousand troops and about that number of National Guardsmen. The Germans alone had two million in uniform, well trained. And Wilson was still twisted around trying to find his backbone, even with a hundred and twenty-eight dead Americans on the *Lusitania*. He'd issued no call to arms, instead offering tardy, mealy-mouthed, diplomatic pipsqueaking.

After we'd fallen for a time into a brandy-begot, brooding silence, Trask had leaned to me and said, "He won't do this on his own, you know."

He meant Wilson. I nodded.

"These machines are getting better," he said.

He meant the Zeppelins. I nodded.

"All of them."

Airplanes too. The tanks. The artillery.

"The nasty stuff as well," he said.

The gas.

"I know what you mean," I said.

"We are important," he said. "You and I, and Buffington's boys too. They understand. That's why we're helping out, you and I."

I thought I knew what he meant. But I leaned closer. "Explain that," I said.

"Easy," he said. "*We* are driving the . . . what? The cart?"

"The cart," I said.

"No," he said. "Too humble. The train."

"The train," I said.

"No," he said. "That's got a track heading in a certain direction already. I wish that were so."

"The bus?"

"Sure," Trask said. "The bus. A sixty-horsepower bus and we know the route. You see?"

I did. "The *secret service* is driving," I said.

"Yes," he said. "The secret service. We'll find out the real stuff about who's our friends and who's our enemies and we'll make it so clear that even Woodrow Damn Wilson will have to do what's right."

I sat back in my chair. My glass was empty. I understood.

I rose now from the reading chair in the library of Stockman House and moved toward the drink table. But when I arrived, I put the empty glass next to the bottle of Armagnac. I looked to the library door. It was empty. I was alone. I put my hand on the latch of the casement and I turned it. But I left the window closed. My mother was singing tonight. Everyone would be watching, including her would-be lover. I now had a quiet way back into the house.

8

The salon orchestra began to play. "Songe d'Automne," a sad little waltz.

Did Stockman arrange this song deliberately, having his covert joke on us all?

Surely not. Only those of us in first class knew what had been on the musical program in the grand dining room on the *Lusitania*'s last voyage. I'd heard the song myself. I'd heard it again in Istanbul. This time I froze at the library window. It was a popular tune for these little strings-and-piano salon orchestras. But the song had found me twice since the torpedo, and that felt a little excessive, as if it were a Siren singing from the bottom of the North Atlantic, wanting to take another crack at me.

I stepped away from the window.

The Stockman House event was starting. I needed to be visible. I hoped to catch Isabel Cobb for some reportage. And perhaps some private words in a cloaking crowd of constituents.

I crossed the library and entered the Great Hall. The Brits by the fireplace had vanished. At the far end I passed through an arched doorway beneath a music gallery and into the courtyard entrance hall. The yard itself lay before me, shadowed from the reemergent sunlight, and I recognized Martin, even from the rear, even wearing a gray trilby. He was standing just outside. I'd get a better reading on my status shortly.

I straightened in a reflex of stage nerves. I wanted to feel the reassurance of the Mauser lying solidly against the small of my back. It was there. I certainly did not want to use it tonight.

I stepped through the door.

Beyond Martin was another tough guy, watching the far end of the courtyard. He was also in a gray suit and trilby. A serge suit just like Martin's. They were in uniform, these two. Stockman's little army. Martin heard me, turned to me.

He nodded again.

I figured a guy like Martin wouldn't make the show of another nod to a guy he was supposed to be keeping a suspicious eye on. He'd be playing it close.

"It's clearing up," I said.

Martin grunted. But it was a grunt of agreement.

I moved on by him and across the fieldstone courtyard and onto the verge of the castle's wide, western green. It held three of the big, blue-and-white, open-sided canvas tents that the Brits called marquees. The nearest was off to the right, next to the service wing of the castle, and it bustled with bodies setting up the high-tea food service for the public. The marquee directly ahead of me, due west, about a hundred yards away, was the source of the waltz, the salon musicians dimly visible at the far end, on an elevated platform. To the left was the third tent, set with folding chairs, and flowing past it was the vanguard of the public, now unleashed upon the grounds, some peeling off to sit, some moving on toward the music, others veering away to prime places on the grass and beginning to spread blankets.

I was glad for the hubbub. Martin and all the other Gray Suits would be the watchers tonight, stationed out here, keeping an eye on the unsorted public wandering the grounds. They'd have their hands full. Stockman would be working his constituents, with Isabel Cobb on his arm. I needed to be patient. And careful. But I figured I'd have a chance to look around inside. For only a limited amount of time, however. I needed to think this out. To make a plan.

Something moved at the right periphery of my sight.

I looked.

The other Gray Suit had stepped up even with me, a few yards away. He had a boxer's battered-and-mended nose and close-cropped dark hair.

He did not look my way. He was watching the flow of townspeople.

I strolled into the green.

I tried to reason things through. If Sir Albert spent much time at Stockman House—and it seemed that he did—the confirmation of his connection to the Germans was somewhere in the castle. The most likely place was wherever he did his personal work. An office. I kept moving toward the music marquee.

But I was mostly thinking about the house behind me.

"Songe d'Automne" dipped and rose and dipped again, to a finish.

I was nearing the tent. The elevated musicians were silhouetted against the now sunlit distant tree line.

Men in seersucker and women in percale were flowing into the chairs set before the music.

The ensemble struck up "Maple Leaf Rag," the song's brothel-born syncopations sounding odd with all the inappropriate strings. But the smattering of gathering crowd applauded in recognition.

I stopped and turned to look back at the house.

My eyes instantly were drawn to the flapping of the British flag up its high pole on the Gothic tower. The wind was brisk. The sun was shining.

All of this registered on me as stage whiskers and greasepaint, this elaborately fortified flag and the high-society orchestra putting on music hall airs. Stockman was trying hard to be English, and a man of the people, no less.

Where was his office? Not on the kitchen and bachelor side of the castle, surely. Perhaps over the library. But more likely in the south wing, the family quarters. It was formalized as private. Visitors knew never to wander there. And he no longer had any family residing with him. I'd go there first, when I had the chance.

I turned away from the house but wished, as well, to distance myself from the music. I walked north, toward the cliff edge along the gate, passing the marquee next to the service wing. The black-and-white-liveried kitchen staff was laying out food on a long row of folding tables. At the end of it, three men in blue serge were setting up another row at a right angle. Two of these boys were heading toward a stack of collapsed tables a few yards outside the tent while the third was unfolding the legs of the next table in the new line.

I realized these guys were dressed not only like each other but also like the baggage handler who met us at the station. These were indeed de facto uniforms. The blue suits were the privates in Stockman's army. I thought all this and slowed a step or two as I did and it all happened quickly: as I was about to turn my attention again toward the cliff, the man in the tent popped the last leg of the table into place and looked up.

I stopped.

He turned his face to me.

It was the stage-door lug from the Duke of York's.

9

Of course he was Stockman's man.

I broke off our look and kept on toward the cliff.

Stockman had been keeping a watchful eye on this woman he was interested in.

The first flash in me was that this guy was an immediate danger. He knew who I was.

I neared the stone fence at the cliff's edge.

I stopped a few yards short, expecting he might be following me. I didn't want to put the cliff in play if there was a struggle.

I turned.

No one was near.

I looked to the tent. He was blocked from my sight by his two colleagues depositing the next table in front of him. Here were two able-bodied boys carrying one table at a time from a pile fifty feet away. Stockman's privates lacked a certain sharpness and motivation. Which threw an odd light on the lug. This same guy setting up folding tables had been entrusted to slip in quietly backstage, armed, and keep an eye on Isabel Cobb. Had he fallen out of favor?

And it occurred to me: my special fear of him now was based on my having been at the theater in my own persona. But he didn't know that. He didn't know Cobb from Hunter from some other guy who just happened to see a play and give him some dirty looks. Maybe this would be okay.

The other two Blue Suits headed back to the pile of tables. My man was unfolding legs and not looking my way.

Okay.

I turned and moved to the stone fence.

The cliffs separated here at the shore and curved inland, the beach running into a narrow valley. Along the path to my right, out in front of the east wing of the house, the cliffs were high and sheer, heading down to Ramsgate.

I looked over my shoulder. The lug was standing behind a table he'd just set up. He was leaning there, looking out at me.

I turned fully around to him. I thought to take out a cigarette and light it, but the wind had brisked up a bit and I was afraid I'd have trouble with the match, which would, of course, ruin the effect. So I just leaned and stared back. And then I took a page out of Sir Martin the Gray Suit's book of etiquette. I gave the guy a nod.

He returned it.

I had no idea what it all meant.

But I figured I was free to stroll along, which I did, casually, like a house guest out sightseeing, following the curve of the fence and watching the waves on the Strait of Dover. What a swell day. What a swell castle. What a swell host. What a swell guest I was. I wanted to see if there'd likely be any problem sneaking in tonight through the window I'd unlatched.

I looked back. I was out of sight of everyone in the tents. I looked at the castle. This eastern wall held three massive bay windows. The library was behind the central one, directly before me. No doors anywhere on this side the house. No need for a Gray Suit to stand guard. All very reassuring. The flag flapped and drew my eyes up to it high on the tower to my left.

I turned and looked out east toward Belgium, seventy miles away beyond the horizon. Occupied Belgium. Ravaged and brutalized Belgium. Stockman's true countrymen—I was thinking of him definitively this way, guilty now until proven innocent—Stockman's boys in *feldgrau*, were in control over there. If he was working importantly on their behalf, how did they communicate?

The last German agent I'd dealt with, in my recent adventure on the *Lusitania* and beyond, relied on telegrams. That and his *Nuttall* handy one-volume encyclopedia.

The wind gusted up and the flag whopped behind and above me.

I turned one more time and looked at St. George's Cross laid over St. Andrew's Cross in our own red, white, and blue. And I looked at its pole lifting the flag to a point as high above the sea as a Chicago skyscraper. And I looked at those guy wires. And I realized what they'd been reminding me of without it reaching my conscious mind, the kind of thing that would have come to me only if I'd been in the white, metaphorizing heat of writing a story about this place. *The guy wires held the flagpole steady on the tower of Stockman House as if it were the telegraph mast on a great ship.*

Between antenna wires in the guys and wires in the pole, at this height, Stockman had plenty of telegraphic juice to make it to Brussels, if not all the way to Cologne and beyond.

The Union Jack thrashed at me. I knew I was looking at Sir Albert's wireless to Germany.

His office—his real office—had to be below, in the tower.

Now all I had to do was wait until the night came and my mother began to sing.

10

At twilight Stockman fed the throngs. By then upwards of five hundred people had been drifting around and lolling around or gathered around listening to the salon orchestra and, in the adjacent tent, to a dialect comic, after watching jugglers and a magician. A two-ring music hall. At the call to high tea they'd all queued into the lug's tent and emerged with substantial enough food on paper plates to make a working-class last meal of the day, which they took to the chairs or the picnic blankets or to the grass or the stone fence. I suspected the area east of the house, before the library, was now populated. I counted on my mother drawing them away when the time came.

As for the house guests—Isabel Cobb and Joseph W. Hunter included—we were gathered and brought to the courtyard and we took our high tea alfresco at temporary tables covered in linen behind a barricade of half a dozen Gray Suits. Pickled salmon and soused mackerel and sliced beef. Boiled eggs and cucumber sandwiches and radishes. Scones and marmalade and sponge cake.

Al and Isabel were side by side at the head of the table nearest the house. I was down the way, at a separate table, surrounded by a London banker, an Edinburgh banker, a Zurich banker, and their wives, who had much to say to each other, not knowing what to make of an American journalist. Which was fine with me. As the daylight waned I waited for a chance to have a few moments with the subject of my story.

I forced the issue as the dozen guests were in the midst of their sponge cake. I knew my mother would not be taking sponge cake. Particularly before performing. I rose, notebook drawn, and I crept toward her table. She was listening to one of the three Brits I'd passed in the Great Hall. He was bloviating about the French trying to run the show on the Western Front. She listened with her elbow on the table, her chin on her fist, declining to play the absolute lady, even in her role as Stockman's hostess. She knew her business. Stockman must have liked her this way. Stockman was also focused on the man, and I crept some more, letting my notebook show in my hand.

I drew near enough and she was bored enough that the movement drew her eyes. I stopped. She turned to Stockman and leaned to him and whispered a few words, in the midst of which he glanced my way. He nodded assent to her—making a pucker-mouthed, veiled-eye show of how *of course* it was all right—and she rose and came to me.

"Mr. Hunter," she said.

"Madam Cobb," I said.

"I'm sorry to have neglected you this evening," she said. "You could use some impressions for your story."

"Just a few," I said. "Before you perform tonight."

We said all this in our best stage whisper. Stockman heard it, though he was looking at the still-rambling speaker.

Isabel took me by the arm and guided me away, out of earshot of both the tables and the line of Gray Suits. We turned our bodies, however, toward Stockman. Nothing to hide.

I would take notes during every word she spoke. Scribble.

I said, "I have a pretty good hunch where to look in the house."

"He's nervous about something," she said. "He and his cohorts."

"About us?"

"I don't know. Maybe. I don't think so. He doesn't try to hide it. The demeanor of it."

"The public?"

"He talks offhandedly about *them*. No. The public's been here before. *This* he doesn't talk about. Not around me."

"Be that as it may . . ." I began.

"Do what you have to do," she said.

She was right about my gist. ". . . Tonight is likely my only chance," I finished.

"Where?"

"The tower."

"Doesn't surprise me."

"You see it?"

"Only the staircase," she said. "I didn't climb it, but I had a chance to look up and down."

"A guard?"

"Not that I saw. I think our man's comfortable in the house."

"Keep the show going tonight for as long as you can," I said.

"You know me when I sing," she said. "Keep applauding, I'll keep encoring."

"Keep encoring even if they don't applaud," I said.

She did a stagey spine stiffening. "You just do your job. I'll do mine," she said.

11

Night came without a moon and without stars as well, a high cloud cover sweeping in from the North Sea. The grounds fell dark. Stockman ordered standing torches lit, and he worked the spectators as this went on, sensing a trepidation in each newly lit set of faces and then encouraging them loudly. "These infernal machines will not darken our land!" he cried. He spoke to their fear of the Zeppelins, their hesitation to violate the local blackout. "Let us defy them tonight!" he cried. He repeated this appeal again and again, up close to them, to those who watched each torch flare into defiance. He was the British hero standing up to the Huns. He was with them, palpable in their midst. Whoever was within earshot of one of Stockman's miniature outbursts of patriotic oratory listened, rapt, and then cheered. And the word was circulated, as well, that a special surprise entertainment was imminent in the central marquee. His constituents, who'd dispersed for high tea, began to coalesce into a crowd and move toward the music tent to turn into an audience for Isabel Cobb.

I used this movement of many bodies from all parts of the ground to casually make my own way toward the eastern side of the house, where news of the entertainment had recently arrived. The lawn here was mostly empty now, only a few young couples left, tearing themselves away from the cliff edge to go to the show.

I drifted toward the house and stood for a time in the grass, watching the last of the lovers disappear around the corner. I looked all around now, peering hard into the darkness, seeing no one. And so I was also invisible.

I moved to the casement in the library bay window. I pressed at the sash. It opened. I climbed inside, pulled the sash closed, and stepped at once into the deeper darkness before me.

I stopped. I stood still for a moment to listen. In this room it was quiet enough for the silence to buzz faintly in my ears. My eyes were adjusting. A vague mitigation of the blackness came from outside, from the seepage of starlight through the clouds, from the nearby outglow of torchlight on the other side of the house. I could discern the door to the library. It was closed.

I moved to the door and opened it gently. I looked out. The Great Hall was empty and it was dim, lit only by the glow of the lanterns through the high west windows and by electric light spilling from the kitchen wing through the screens passage. I approached the wall beneath the music gallery, put my back to it, and eased along to the edge of the archway. I peeked into the courtyard entrance hall.

It was empty. The only person in sight had his back to me ten yards or so into the courtyard, beyond the open front doors. One of the Gray Suits. From his stature it could have been Martin.

The crowd outside cheered and clapped and fell silent.

No music yet.

I imagined Stockman making a little speech. He'd probably just mentioned the great Isabel Cobb.

I passed silently and quickly through the hall.

I drew my pistol and my flashlight and started up the wide, stone staircase, making myself take the steps one at a time with a soft, careful stride, holding back my impulse to rush, flashing my light onto each floor at the last moment of approach, pistol ready.

But there were no guards. Not at the second floor, not the third, not the fourth. Each floor was the same: immediately before me a carved oak door with a warded lock, a long corridor to the right along the wing, a blank wall a room's length to my left.

Now I was at the foot of the staircase to the fifth floor—the top of the house proper—and then I reached its landing. If my suspicion was correct about the tower, Stockman's office could very well be at the top of these last few steps, where it could easily wire up to the antenna. If a Gray Suit remained in the house, he'd be here.

I took the turn, and I could see nothing but pitch darkness at the top. I crept up, holding pistol and flashlight at the ready.

Distant now as if it were a memory, I heard another upswell of applause and hurrahing as the salon orchestra struck up the introductory bars of "Keep the Home Fires Burning." Mother was about to sing.

A clock started ticking in my head. I had to be back in the midst of the crowd before she took her last bow.

With the next step and now one more, I was ready for the light and I switched it on and shined it straight in front of me as I rushed the last few steps.

There was no guard.

And this time, no doorway before me either.

I scanned the light to the left.

There was the door, a couple of paces down the way.

This was the room directly beneath the tower. Before I moved to it, I shined the light way off to my right, down the long, empty corridor, and then back very near me, expecting the staircase to continue into the tower.

It did not.

Instead, where the staircase had turned on the floors below, here a stag's head hung on a wall over a vase sitting on a pedestal. There was no staircase going up.

So this door to my left was very likely Stockman's office. Which provided my best chance to learn something useful in this vast house with my limited time.

I moved down the hall and confronted the door. Like the ones below, it was oak. But it was not carved. A new door. A good sign. And it held a modern lock. Pin and tumbler. My favorite.

I holstered my Mauser, put myself before the lock, switched off the flashlight, and took out my packet of tools. A torque wrench and a pick. Though strictly speaking I no longer picked most locks. I raked them. I located the keyhole in the dark and bent to it and I slipped in the wrench, turned it gently to the right, worked the pick in all the way to the rear of the keyway. I levered the inner tip. Up went the back pin. And then I raked carefully but quickly along the other pins, pushing them into their columns. I felt most of them yield on the first pass. It was all feel now. No thinking. All about the fingertips. I delicately increased the wrench pressure and raked again. And the lock yielded. The door opened.

I pushed in, closed the door, put my tools away. The room was large. The footprint of the tower, I figured. The mullioned casement windows faced east and south, mostly filling those two walls, and were dim with the moonless night. I had to be careful about my flashlight.

But I did need it.

I let my eyes adjust, let them prepare to use what little outside glow there was. I could see the form of a massive desk set parallel to the wall that held the door to the room.

I moved to its opposite side, faced it, putting my back to the southern windows. The guards were more likely arrayed in that direction, with the south facade holding a major entrance to the castle. I was standing well away from any possible sight line from the ground. With my body blocking the beam, I switched the flashlight on.

From its top, the desk certainly seemed to be a working desk. Neatly kept, but it was in use. There was an electric table lamp; a crystal ink well with a dip-pen holder; a large, leather-edged desk pad with a blotter surface and the intense hieroglyphs of backward, superimposed, blotted words. In a wire basket sat a dozen pieces of mail addressed to Stockman, some of them by way of the House of Parliament, most of them to Stockman House or simply to his name and Margate. Or Broadstairs. Or Kent. One was stamped but addressed only to Sir Albert Stockman. A hodgepodge of hands, some elegant, some seeming barely literate. There was a comparable, empty basket. One for incoming mail and one for outgoing.

I circled the desk. I sat in the massive, polished oak rotary chair. I shined my light on the desk drawers, opening them one at time. They were filled with everyday things. Pen nibs. A staple fastener. A stash of mailing envelopes, unused. I looked in each, though from the first pull I knew I'd find nothing of importance: the drawers were all unlocked.

I rose. I stood away from the desk.

Of course this wouldn't be easy.

This was the MP's desk. His constituent desk.

His serious stuff could still be hidden elsewhere in the office. He saw this as a secure room, on a secure floor, in a secure house with a private army. I shined my light toward the western wall. Half a dozen four-drawer filing cabinets. Wooden. Clearly also unlocked. He had a file on everybody in his constituency. He had files on his other MPs. Whatever else. And a set of files in there somewhere, perhaps, revealing his unholy ties to Germany but hiding in plain sight. It could take all night to find them.

Applause and cheers wafted faintly into the room from far away.

And the music again. Some damn music hall ditty. Mother would play that one to the hilt.

I turned my light to the wall behind the desk. I'd noted vaguely that it was full of books. My light went to these high shelves, to the top, at the far left, and I began quickly to scan, my hand doing this almost on its own, disappointed from the library downstairs. Codes still in my head, I supposed.

More sets. Sets and sets. Law books here. And then some other sets. Kentish matters no doubt. Sets on agriculture. Sets about hops and cherries and cattle and fish and whatever else.

I was scanning down the center section now, directly behind the desk. Sets. Sets. I needed to look elsewhere.

And then the books abruptly changed.

Not sets. Odd volumes, a whole row of them, directly behind and slightly above the desk chair.

I circled the desk again.

I looked at titles.

The British Almanac and Family Cyclopaedia.

Appleton's Annual Cyclopaedia.

The Dictionary of English History.

The New International Year Book for 1913.

I had not seen a set of *The New International Encyclopaedia.* Even if there was one somewhere, its yearbook was separated. These were all books that made finding words easy. They all went from A to Z. Code books for telegraph messages.

My flashlight moved on. Quickly. Past several volumes. I knew what I was looking for. And there it was.

The Nuttall Encyclopaedia of Universal Information.

The books were set in here as they were downstairs. And on that quarter of an inch of exposed shelf in front of *Nuttall* was a thin layer of dust.

Since I last knew it to be the book of the week or month or whatever the interval of use was, the Huns had moved on from this *Concise and Comprehensive Dictionary of General Knowledge* edited meticulously by the good Rev. James Wood. It was my first German code book and I felt a little nostalgic for it. How sad for its dusty lip.

I went back and wrote all these titles in my notebook. The German library of telegraphic code books. This was a good night's work in itself.

The second time through, something finally registered on me that I'd rushed past looking specifically for *Nuttall.* An empty space.

After recording all the titles, I returned to it. By the width of one volume, the shelf was wiped clean all the way through the outer lip.

A recent withdrawal.

One code book wasn't here.

And now the obvious thought, delayed by my focus on documents, finally struck me: the wireless set wasn't here either.

Its antenna was directly above me.

I looked up into the dark.

There had to be a room above this office.

The question was how to get there.

And something else struck me at last. I turned my light back to the western wall and the line of filing cabinets. I'd assumed the entrance door to this office was farther east than the entrance doors on lower floors because this room was larger. It wasn't. That wall my white light was drilling into was too close. This room was not a footprint of the tower. It was too small.

I rose. I moved to the end filing cabinet. It was set six inches or so from the wall, as were all these cabinets. I shined my light behind them. Solid wall.

I moved to the door. But before I opened it, I looked back to the western wall. I put the heel of my foot at the edge of the doorjamb and did a yard-stride to the corner. Five paces. About fifteen feet.

I went back to the door. I put my hand to the knob.

I turned stupid. I opened the door and stepped out and immediately before me the shadows had bulked up into the form of a man.

Before I could even twitch I felt the barrel of a pistol press into the dead center of my gut.

Outside, the crowd cheered.

1 2

"This is just to keep you from being stupid," a cigarette-blasted British voice said, pushing a little on the pistol.

"Too late," I said.

"Very well," he said. "From *carrying on* being stupid."

"That's big of you," I said.

"Very slowly upend that light of yours and have a look at me," he said.

I did. The beam came at a sharp angle from below, turning him into a chiaroscuro: a wide, central, corpse-white stripe of a face surrounded by a night-black skull.

It was the lug from the Duke of York's.

"Mr. Catwalk," I said.

"Mr. Front Row," he said.

"You prowl for your boss, I take it," I said.

"And who do you fancy my boss to be?" he said.

"Stockman."

"You are mistaken, Mr. Cobb," he said, his voice pitched down and sounding convincing.

I tried to place this guy in the class system. He sounded, at turns, cultured and working class, never quite either, which meant he was the latter with extended exposure to the former.

It struck me. "You're Buffington's man."

"Lord Buffington," he corrected.

"You're the guy in the vicinity."

"Very near," he said. "Thanks to the baronet's need for a bit of outside assistance."

"At the theater then, you were what?"

"Watching over Isabel Cobb. You and I are on the same side, sir."

"I'd be more inclined to believe you," I said, "if you'd take the pistol off the center of my gut."

"I'm terribly sorry," he said, and the barrel end vanished at once in a twisting of his body and a ruffling of his suit coat.

"You seem to be doing well," he said.

"Did you know about the tower?"

"No sir. I just followed you through the window."

"Bloody hell," I said. "If you don't mind my borrowing a phrase."

"Please," he said.

"Another case of stupid. I wasn't even aware," I said.

"Not at all. I had the advantage of knowing exactly who you are and what you're up to."

"Which I need to resume," I said.

"Of course. But I had to let you know who I am and that I'm at your service."

"And who are you?"

"Sorry," he said. "Jeremy."

"Kit," I said and we shook hands.

"Unless you have a specific task for me," Jeremy said, "I think I'd do better to linger downstairs. If someone is to get caught at this, it should be me. You need to keep your identity intact."

"But no getting caught," I said.

"I'll do my best."

Jeremy half turned to go and then had a thought. He stopped and squared around to me again. "I am obliged to stress, however. If things do get rough, you are to take the opportunity to endeavor a quiet retreat. On no account intervene on my behalf."

I didn't like that thought. If we were on the same team, I was reluctant to duck out on him.

"This is imperative," he said.

I knew I'd be saying the same thing in his place. "All right," I said. And he was gone. As quietly as he'd followed me.

I was left with a tower above me and no staircase to get there.

I returned to the doorway of Stockman's office. I put my heel at the door frame and paced off the five yards. I kept my foot on the spot and took note of where it was: directly across from the left-hand banister.

I paced on, doing the stride I knew to equal about a yard. Seven more to the door of the next room. A little over twenty feet.

I expected this door to give itself away with a pin and tumbler lock. I was wrong. The room had one of the carved oak doors with a simpler warded lock. I drew out my tools. I had half a dozen skeleton keys. On the second try I had the right one. The locking bolt gave way and I opened the door.

I stood beneath the lintel while I shined my flashlight toward this room's left-hand wall, which should have been shared with Stockman's office. Then I leaned back and looked down to the banister opposite that western wall in the office. I didn't need any more measurements. I stepped inside this room, closed the door. The wall before me should have been twenty feet away. It was maybe half that. Against it, left of center, was a massive wardrobe of plain, squared oak built flush to the floor and taller than a man, its only ornamentation being large, beaten-iron hinges and drawer pulls. Of its wide facade—a good twelve feet—the two outer sections were drawers and half-cabinets.

The major center section was a pair of doors. Their small ward lock yielded quickly and I opened them to a thick atmosphere of cedar and moth-balls. Inside, the space was wide enough and tall enough to hang the longest ball gown, but in spite of the smells to protect clothes in storage, it was empty. I had little doubt what was next. The back of the wardrobe was hung with a black cloth.

I stepped in. The cloth split in the middle into a pair of drapes that ran easily open on metal hooks along a heavy curtain rod.

And they revealed the doorway to the tower. This was unconventional castle architecture. Sir Albert's granddad had been either paranoid or up to something covert himself. The door was what I'd expected for the room. It was like the one on Stockman's office, and with the same sort of lock. Made by the same locksmith, I figured, for it felt familiar to my fingertips and the pin tumblers all jumped at my first bidding.

I opened the door inward to blackness. I closed the wardrobe behind me, and I stepped into chilled air smelling of damp stone and of all the spores that grow in the dark. I ran the drapes together and shut the door. I shined my light onto a metal staircase commencing immediately to my left and circling its way upward.

I climbed.

About ten feet I reckoned, and I came to another metal platform. The staircase continued up, to the roof of the tower, no doubt, but I stood before a rough-hewn wooden door. No more picking. This one had no lock. No knob either. Just a latch, which I lifted.

And now I stood in the upper room of the Stockman House tower and searched with my flashlight, keeping it angled low to prevent its being visible from outside, straining my eyes to see into the dim edge of spill from its beam.

On the eastern wall, directly before me, was a single, centered, cruciform loophole, which was used in a functioning castle for safe viewing and medieval sniper fire, the shape to accommodate a crossbow, not the Christian God.

I knew all four walls had loopholes because I'd seen them from the outside, but only the one in the eastern wall was visible now in full. The west-facing loophole was in the well of the circular staircase. The other two, in this room, were each shuttered by a wooden door on hinges and a hook and eye. The shutter for the eastern loophole was open.

The shutters were probably a Stockman renovation, so he could work up here at night and not show it. The electric lighting was certainly his doing. A stand-up lamp stood in the center of the floor beside a library table big enough to lay out the corpse of even the tall Sir Albert.

The wireless telegraph setup was certainly his doing.

There it was, as expected, a jumble of condensers and transformers, tuning coil and induction coil, ammeter and helix, antenna switch and spark discharger. And at the uncluttered front edge of the table were the two things the jumble served: the transmission key and the head phones.

This was where Sir Albert Stockman transmitted and received coded messages with his bosses in Germany and his underlings wherever they were lurking.

In considering the wireless, the object that had led me here, I'd taken some steps toward it at an angle past the library table. I knew there were other objects of interest on the tabletop, and I turned my beam to them now.

A stack of books on the near end.

That much I'd seen out of the corner of my eye and I expected more. There was a stray volume near the center, but the table was otherwise clear.

I stepped to the wireless table, hoping to find a notebook or a scrap of paper with a message. There was nothing. The key block was even squared up to the edge of the table; the headset's wire was neatly coiled.

I knew Al, understood his ways. I needed to be careful to leave everything precisely as it now was. And this thought made me visualize his next visit here, which reminded me of the clock ticking in my head.

I clenched off the next breath.

I could not hear the orchestra. Had they finished? Had Stockman shut this thing down quick?

But I was, after all, in a flint tower six storeys above and five hundred feet away from that plinky little sextet and that middle-aged voice. Still, all I could hear was the accelerating beat of my heart and the heavy hiss of the silence in Stockman's aerie.

I moved to the northern loophole and opened the wooden shutter. I leaned in, as if to fire an arrow, and turned my ear to the opening.

And yes. The sound of strings faintly drifted this high and slipped in through the slit in the stone. I could not hear her voice, but she was out there singing. At the moment, about how long a way it was to Tipperary.

I closed the shutter, strode to the eastern loophole, and closed its shutter as well. I returned to the table in the center of the room. I switched on the reading lamp, extinguished my flashlight, stuffed it into my pocket, sat on a bent-wood chair.

I put my hand to the stack of books, which also had been squared up to the edge of the table.

I took up each, one by one, thumbed them, looking for marks. All that they yielded were their titles.

The System of British Weather of the British Islands.

The Weather of the British Coasts.

The Fourth Report on Wind Structure published by the Authority of the Meteorological Council.

Surface Wind Structure Analysis. This one from His Majesty's Advisory Committee for Aeronautics.

And another big seller from the Brits' meteorological boys: *The Beaufort Scale of Wind-Force, Being a Report of the Director of the Meteorological Office upon an Inquiry into the Relation Between the Estimates of Wind-Force According to Admiral Beaufort's Scale and the Velocities Recorded by Anemometers Belonging to the Office.*

I restacked the books precisely.

And then, the one stray book near the center of the table: *The Britannica Year-Book 1913.* Not stray, really. Simply separate, for it too had been placed with a squared-up kind of precision.

This book I understood at once. It was the present code book for the Germans.

I carefully noted its position, its orientation, and I pulled it before me. Not much larger than a novel, dusky green, twelve hundred onion-skin thin pages. I opened it and thumbed for hand notes. No words. But occasionally the first two or three or last two or three letters of a word were underlined in pencil. On page 27, about the Balkan War: *ag* was underlined in *against*; *ste* in *step*; *ity* in *inability*. The Germans' numbered codes—indicating page and line and word—probably had a way to indicate whole words, but they could also spell out words in a pinch or a rush. I tried to fit these underlinings together, forward and backward, just to make sure, but my suspicion was soon confirmed: they were simply highlighted here for quick use.

I put the book back exactly where it had been and, unaware I was even doing it, I stretched out my left leg. I heard a soft clatter onto the floor. I got up, circled the table.

Several pieces of wide, heavy paper, rolled together, were lying on their side near where they'd no doubt been sitting on end, beneath the table. I picked them up, spread them carefully in the light on the tabletop.

They were three contiguous ordnance survey maps, tracking the Thames River from the Isle of Thanet, County Kent, to London.

No marks.

Precious little else here.

I rolled the maps together once more and placed them standing on the floor beneath the table where I reckoned they'd been.

I returned to the chair, set it in its previous place, put my hands on the top of its cane back, and leaned a little against it.

Had I missed something in this room? I looked around. It was bare but for the two tables. I imagined Stockman sitting in this chair alone, shut off from the world, high above the sea, in this circle of pale yellow light, in his wooden chair, reading. These books. Other books that were gone now. Deciphering telegrams from Berlin. Happy in the quiet. Fussily keeping the edges of things straight. Planning. Planning what?

Winds and weather didn't quite add up.

If there was nothing more than this, I could think on these things later. I needed to go. Joe Hunter needed to be protected.

I switched off the stand-up lamp.

I moved to the eastern loophole, unhooked it, opened it, as it was when I arrived.

Though it was still a very small sound, I heard it at once. Coming through the loophole from the east, from out in the strait.

The sound of an engine.

From *over* the strait, I realized.

I could hear the distant drone of gasoline engines. I was willing to bet they were Maybachs, two-hundred horsepower each, attached in fours to Zeppelins. Stockman's bravado at the torch lighting buzzed into my head along with them. He knew they were coming. They knew where he was. He was lighting their way into the mouth of the Thames.

I went out of the tower room, but I did not descend. I went up the inner staircase and emerged through an upright metal door set in a stone enclosure built into the courtyard corner of the parapet. I moved toward the eastern wall, passing beneath my daylong landmark, the massive Union Jack. I looked up as I went by. The flag hung straight down, barely stirring. It was a perfect night for the Zepps. No moon, a high ceiling, the air gone almost still.

I stood at the parapet and looked into the thin gruel of the night. I could hear the orchestra again, distantly, from up here in the open. It was directly behind me, playing "There's a Long, Long Trail." Mother was still working on the wartime standards. She hadn't even begun to encore.

She and the crowd were about to get a fright.

I strained to hear the engines above the music. And there they were. Nearer now. The drone had become a hammering, the piston fire itself almost distinguishable. I strained to see them. And then the stars were moving and then I realized with a quick grab in my throat just how low the Zeppelins were and how near, and they were rushing this way, still only a few dollops of light, perhaps from their undercarriages, but also a vast thickening of the dark above.

Though the Zepps would not drop a bomb on Sir Albert's house, though we were their beacon, their allies, though we were Albert's big show, my hands pressed hard against the stone of the parapet with a terrible realization. These vast flying machines hammering our way, invisible against the dark and carrying a ton of incendiaries, these were the ghosts of future warfare, death from the sky, death that one day could reach to every home, every parlor, every crib, in every nation on the planet. This was mankind's fate pounding its way toward us on a moonless night.

All these things were what my hands knew as they clung futilely to a rock.

And now I felt a quick stirring of the air as a dark mass drew very near, its palpable invisibility pressing against my eyes, and I began to lift my face as it came, no more than a hundred yards above where I stood, and it was quick, it was over the beach and then the cliff and then I was looking up, up, and the air was thrashing, sucking the breath from me, and I was looking directly up as the sky vanished in a grimy dark and then a gondola with lit windows slid over me and the engines combusted in my head and the propellers clacked, and the Zeppelin passed over the castle and passed and passed and passed, as long as a steamship on the Atlantic, and the rear gondola drew its lights over me, and I turned to watch, and the flag was lifting a bit in the currents of the Maybachs, as if the Union Jack were actually thinking of waving for this infernal machine. But it was Stockman's Union Jack, of course.

And the band stopped playing abruptly and there were cries from the green and now another pounding, behind me, and I turned and a second Zeppelin was approaching, slightly to the north, and I could see the lit windows of the commander's gondola as it passed and I could see figures moving there.

Wind structure and the system of British weather and the path to London along the Thames. This was what Sir Albert Stockman was about. These machines. And the second Zepp droned on by and the orchestra started up playing. I recognized the tune. "Nearer, My God, to Thee." The song the newspapers all reported the *Titanic*'s salon orchestra played as the ship sank. Courage is an odd thing. In this case, given the actual circumstances, it could seem a foolish thing, a hysterical thing, a cheap imitation, a grimly ironic joke. Except these boys didn't know the circumstances. They were trying to calm a crowd's panic in the face of disaster. It was probably irritating the hell out of Stockman, whose carefully prepared, courageous oratory was being drowned out by some hired musicians stealing his thunder with a hymn.

I needed to rouse myself from all this. The time was right to get downstairs as fast as I could and slip into the crowd during all the uproar.

I crossed the tower, entered the stairwell, circled downward. I caught myself rushing. I couldn't put haste over caution. I slowed as I neared the bottom platform, made my footfalls soft. I stepped back and away as I pulled open the door from the wardrobe. Gently.

I was glad I did.

I heard voices.

I pocketed my flashlight and drew my Mauser.

Muffled still, these voices. Not moving. I drew back one side of the curtain to the inner darkness of the wardrobe. I did not trust the wooden floorboard to take my weight silently. I leaned in as far as I could, turning my ear to listen.

Martin's voice.

Jeremy's voice.

They were both speaking German.

13

The button to release the Mauser's safety sat right beneath my thumb. I pushed it.

Joe Hunter may have to die so that Kit Cobb has a chance to live. I'll shoot my way out.

The button and the thought happened instantly, simultaneously, before I could make out the German words being spoken.

Then there was a scuffling of feet.

The voices were closer.

Jeremy said, "You and I are on the same side."

He'd said the same thing to me, in English. I tried to decide in which language it sounded true.

Martin didn't seem to be buying it. "Let's look upstairs," he said. "Through the wardrobe. Move."

The words and the tone made it clear he'd disarmed Jeremy and was holding a pistol in his back. If Jeremy was indeed working for the Huns, he was covert enough that Martin hadn't been apprised. But maybe Jeremy was like me. He had this skill. He knew German. I'd tell the same lie if Albert's henchman got the drop on me while I was trying to delay him.

I backed out of the curtain, softly slid it shut, closed the door. I went up. Quietly. Quickly. To the tower room? There was nowhere to hide in there. There was no way to take out Martin when they entered without almost certainly losing Jeremy anyway. And Jeremy said not to intervene. I'd promised not to intervene. Rightly, given his mission and mine. But I wasn't comfortable with that either. Still, the wireless room was a losing hand.

And if Jeremy was telling the truth to Martin about working for the Germans, in the wireless room I'd have to figure that out in some very unpleasant way I could not control.

I went up farther, all the way to the telephone booth-size access enclosure on the roof. I stepped into the space beside the door and listened down the stairway well.

Footsteps on the stairs. No attempt to move quietly.

Martin didn't seem to expect to find a cohort up here.

He wanted to check to see if anything had been disturbed in the wireless room. Signs that Jeremy had been in there.

Footsteps now on the landing below, a door opening, no sound of a door closing, a muffled shuffling of feet receding into the room, a brief murmuring of voices.

I straightened, leaned back against the stone wall.

If Jeremy was truly working for the Huns, he would've done something other than what he did when he'd caught me. He had his pistol in my gut. He sent me on my way. It was his confrontation with Martin that was a problem for him.

I had to assume Jeremy was Buffington's man.

But there was nothing I could do to help downstairs.

He expected that I was escaping right now, with Martin diverted into the wireless room.

I should have been. But that choice had passed.

If the two went back down the steps from there, I could wait for a time and then slip out. I'd have to let Jeremy manage his own fate, as he'd signed up to do, as he'd insisted I let him do.

Martin clearly had the drop on Jeremy.

I realized how little I actually knew of Buffington's operation. Or, of course, Stockman's. Trask probably knew less than he thought, as well. Maybe Stockman had let Jeremy this far into his operation in order to trap him. His fate might already have been sealed.

In which case, Martin could be bringing him to this roof to take care of things. At least to hold him till the crowds went away.

I had no play down the stairs.

I thought of the roof.

I became aware of the wall I was leaning against.

And now voices rose through the stairwell.

"Up we go," Martin said. In English.

Jeremy didn't respond.

I unlatched the door to the roof, the sound masked in the clatter of their footsteps, and I stepped out and closed the door behind me. I circled around to my right and pressed my back against the outer wall of the enclosure. I laid my shooting hand against my chest, the Mauser barrel lying upon my heart.

I waited.

The Zeppelins were barely audible now, flying away up the Thames. The crowd was silent. Stockman was probably orating. I just hoped the music would resume.

Footsteps rasping now onto the stone floor of the enclosure.

I held my breath.

The door latch clacked.

I lifted my Mauser.

Over the past few minutes my eyes had grown accustomed to the dark. I turned my face to the left.

I heard the door open and close.

"Go that way," Martin said. "No quick movements."

And Jeremy appeared, moving off to the right at an angle heading inward onto the roof, toward the flagpole.

Now Martin followed, his right hand lifted into Jeremy's spine. I saw the side of his face from a sharp angle to the rear.

I turned away from the wall and made one quick, soft step forward and another and I pressed the muzzle of my Mauser against Martin's occipital bone.

"No movement at all," I said.

He stopped.

Jeremy did not give him time to figure out the situation. He spun off from the pistol and grabbed Martin's shooting wrist while I pushed the Mauser at the Hun's head just for good measure. Albert's boy wasn't going to do anything stupid, even if he cared about his mission. He was figuring Jeremy and I would have our hands full downstairs. Which we would.

Jeremy had Martin's pistol now and he stepped back in front of him.

I kept my Mauser where it was.

Martin still hadn't gotten a glimpse of me, but I regretted letting him hear my voice. At least I should have spoken German. He probably knew who had the drop on him. I had to assume he did. Which was why I was supposed to have simply slipped away into the night.

Jeremy gave me a look. He shifted the pistol to his left hand, and he drew back his right leg, his body angling that way into a boxer's stance. I knew what was next.

I pulled my pistol away.

And Jeremy threw a hell of an overhand right into Martin's jaw.

The Hun flew back hard and was out cold even before he slammed down in front of the door.

The salon orchestra began to play.

Jeremy and I both briefly turned our faces to it.

"This will make things a little easier for you," he said, lifting his chin toward the music.

"And for you."

"We shall see," he said.

He looked my way again, and I said, "Nice right hand. Were you a pro?"

He nodded a small, slow nod of regret.

"I bet you were good," I said.

"I once went sixteen rounds with Tommy Ryan."

"And?"

"He was prepared to go seventeen."

"Jeremy what?"

"Miller."

"Did you fight in the States?"

"You bet," he said. "For a couple of years. Philly and New York and points west."

This made sense of a little bit of American that sometimes crept into his mix of accents and phrasing and lingo.

"Chicago?" I asked.

"Never made it there."

I liked this guy Miller. He stirred the reporter in me. I wanted to sit him down and talk a while and do a story on an ex-boxer who gave one of the greatest middleweights of all time a run for his money and then turned into a British spy. And I'd have bet good money that his family name was once Müller.

But he and I had other work to do.

"What about our boy Martin here?" I said, nodding toward him.

"How compromised might you presently be with Stockman?" Jeremy said.

"Remains to be seen," I said. "There's a big crowd. He's got his own agenda. If he didn't go looking for me and if I wasn't observed sneaking around, I could have innocently been out of his sight all this time."

Jeremy nodded. He looked down at Martin. "He knows too much about both of us." He stepped nearer to me, and his voice turned as serious as that right hand. "You need to slip back into the crowd now, and then make certain Stockman sees you. After the music ends, stay visible and be patient. I'll divert any possible suspicion from you."

He paused.

He was waiting for my assent. I wondered what his plan might be, particularly for himself after an effective diversion. I thought about trying to help.

He figured that out. "You defied me once, Mr. Cobb. I won't say I was not grateful. But we have to be professional now."

He gave me only the briefest moment of silence to respond before saying, "We have no time for this."

"I understand," I said. I did.

Jeremy tucked his pistol away and moved past me to Martin. He bent and grabbed the Hun by the coat and shirt and lifted the man half off the ground, twisted him around, and flung him down again as if he were a gunnysack of lettuce greens.

I stepped to the door and opened it.

"Mr. Cobb," Jeremy said.

I turned.

"Kit," I said.

"Kit," he said. "I'm grateful."

"As am I," I said.

And I was into the stairwell and circling downward.

14

I made it all the way into the Great Hall without seeing anyone. I wouldn't chance crossing the courtyard. I needed to give the appearance that I'd been on the grounds throughout Isabel Cobb's concert. I would trust that Sir Albert had delegated any suspicions to Martin and the boys and was keeping his own attention on his actress and his acting.

I crossed to the library, which remained dark. I slipped in and went to the casement and opened it gently. I looked out. This eastern lawn seemed empty. Jeremy had somehow kept himself hidden here. But he'd had inside information.

I climbed out and pulled the window to.

I strolled now. Casually. I went to the stone wall at the cliff's edge. I followed it north, and the only Gray Suits that gradually became visible were far away, guarding the north entryways to the house. A distant passerby was nothing they would automatically care about.

I followed the curve of the wall past the service wing, past the high-tea tent, and walked toward the music.

The marquee was lit inside by electrical light, the seats packed and the place ringed by standees. Mother had begun her encores. The orchestra was playing a song she could overact to her hammy heart's content. "Some of These Days." It was ridiculous, accompanied by strings and a salon-tempoed piano. Her acting talent was being challenged, no doubt, so as to hide her murderous feelings toward her accompanists.

I could see now, above the heads, the back of the pianist and his upright in front of him. Not Mother, who would be at the center of the stage.

But I began to hear her voice.

Not the words quite yet but her voice, floating out of the tent on a cloying cloud of strings and trying to keep its honky-tonk edge. The torches were blazing still.

The standees were a welcome sight. The crowd was large and disorganized at the edges. Stockman surely was in the middle of all that. From his limited vantage point he might be willing to believe I'd been around all this time.

My mother's voice clarified now, as she moved into the chorus. She sang, "Some of these days, you'll miss me, honey."

I hesitated in the dark, just outside the torchlight.

"Some of these days, you'll feel so lonely."

I looked along the tent line in both directions. No Gray Suits.

"You're gonna miss my huggin'. You're gonna miss my kissin'."

I moved past the torches now and approached the backs of the standees who were even with the stage.

"You're gonna miss me, honey, when I'm far away."

I peeked between the heads and there, in a front row center folding chair, sat Stockman, his face lifted to Mama.

I didn't even have to shift around to see her. I knew she was singing straight to him.

I backed off, beyond the torches, and I waited for the show to come to a close, not really listening to the music, my mother's voice familiar in the way that a twenty-year-old memory that hadn't come up for about nineteen years would be familiar. Jeremy came and went in my head. He was a pro. He was doing what he knew best to do in the way he wanted to do it. I didn't have to think for him, didn't have to save him. Stockman wanted to come into my head, wanted to rehearse my imminent encounter with him, but if I started scripting myself for Stockman, I'd end up *sounding* scripted, sounding like a liar. I needed to improvise. As if with Mama and me on a train. I stood and waited and now the crowd was applauding and some of the standees were starting to peel off.

I slipped forward, took a standing place at the edge of the tent but a few rows behind Stockman.

Mother was bowing.

I thought: *If they keep applauding, she'll keep singing.*

But Stockman stood up as he clapped. She saw him. She recognized her cue to ring down the curtain. I saw her hands flip down a little. She'd been on the verge of raising them to stop the applause and cue the orchestra and keep on going. But she knew this was Sir Albert's show.

A Blue Serge had appeared at Stockman's side and handed over a bundle of red roses. Stockman headed for the steps up to the platform.

Isabel Cobb rolled her head to project the rolling of her eyes over the applause and she flared her hands, aw-shucksing to beat the band.

Others in the audience were rising too, especially the swells in attendance, seasoned theatergoers accustomed to giving a standing ovation to a famous actress. A small handful of the other folks were starting to slip away, just on the fringes. An outer-edge chair opened up in front of me, still to the rear of where Stockman had been sitting. I stepped forward and slipped in before the chair, as if I'd been there all along.

I applauded.

Stockman presented the roses and the applause surged and Isabel Cobb did her flourishing bow to the crowd, the one with a touch of the forehead and then a rolling hand salute descending as she bent deep.

All this good feeling went on for a while. Then at last the applause waned and Stockman stepped forward, the expert emcee, and just as the clapping stopped he announced in a throbbing tenor projected effortlessly as far as the very back row, "Thank you again, one and all, for coming tonight. Before we part, I ask everyone to rise to your feet so that we might honor our king and our country."

Stockman motioned to the orchestra—this had clearly been arranged beforehand—and they began to play "God Save the King."

As everyone rose, Stockman strode to the front edge of the stage and began to sing loudly, guiding the lyrics to the slightly different, earliest version of the song, from 1745, having his ironic little joke on his constituents, sounding as if he were a rabid British patriot, as if he were restoring the original words to personally address King George V, as if he were singing to this present monarch leading the country in its war with Germany while in fact he was singing to George II, born in Hanover, the second German king of England.

"God save great George our king," he sang and the crowd joined him as one vast voice.

This had not, however, been arranged beforehand with Mother.

"Long live our noble king."

She gave Stockman one small, unveiled glance: *You bastard, whose spotlight do you think you're stealing?*

"God save the king."

The crowd was joining in boisterously now, singing in defiance of the Huns and their gas bags.

"Send him victorious."

The Huns' secret gas bag smiled as he bellowed, even as his voice was absorbed into the crowd's.

"Happy and glorious."

Isabel Cobb was back in character, singing along, smiling all around.

"Long to reign over us."

The orchestra was slowing the tempo. This was the big climax.

The voices filled and stretched at the tent like hydrogen in an air-ship: "God save the king."

The music stopped, the voices stopped, the place light-switched into silence, and then, one beat later, flared into cheers.

Stockman lifted both his hands high above his head as if the adulation was all for him and then bloomed them outward like a chorus girl as he took a deep bow.

Perhaps no one else could read her as I could. Certainly no one was particularly aware of her at that moment. But Mama gave this guy a look that laid bare her true, undramatized desire: to put her foot in the middle of Sir Albert Stockman's backside and launch him off the platform and into about the fourth row.

15

I kept standing where I was as the cheers faded and the applause smattered to a stop and everyone politely took their cue and shuffled away into the night, where they were no doubt watched and herded by suits both gray and blue. I kept standing and applauding, though more slowly now, softly, head angled smilingly to the side to portray the personal accolade of an insider.

Stockman had hastened back to my mother as soon as the crowd began to disperse and was no doubt praising her lavishly. He was no fool. And great actress that she was, she showed no trace of her recent—and surely still lingering—feelings.

She was the first to notice me, turning her face my way and showing, to the extent she dared, her get-me-the-hell-away-from-this-man pleasure at my presence. Her turn prompted Stockman to turn.

I lifted the mimed applause to him and nodded in deference. He gave me a noblesse oblige smile that warmed my heart for the moment. This did not strike me as the smile of a man who regarded me with newly formed suspicions.

I was wrong, however, to feel safe quite yet.

Something slithered its way out of him as the three of us walked from the marquee together, heading toward the courtyard and the house, the other weekend guests following loosely behind, the straggler constituents floating past us in the dark, bowing in quiet thanks and deference toward their host.

Stockman ignored them all.

He said to me, "I looked for you during our little interruption."

"I'm a reporter," I said. "I heard the engines before most everyone else and I knew what they were and I slipped into the night to see the airships and capture them in words."

"Indeed," he said.

"Don't forget who you're supposed to be writing about," my mother said.

Stockman and I both looked to her.

He chuckled.

I said, "But of course."

I still was not quite sure Stockman accepted my absence. A few minutes earlier I'd prepared for this. At the foot of the stage, Stockman had broken half a dozen steps away to speak to the Gray Suit with the boxer's nose, who'd suddenly appeared. I wondered if they were speaking of Martin, and I worried, for a flash, about Jeremy, but I'd put that aside to have a quick word with my mother. I asked her for a sentence or two from his declamation to the crowd upon the arrival of the Zeppelins.

I played that card now. "I didn't go so far away that I missed your eloquence," I said, and I quoted him. "'We will shake our fists at the sky and we will not run. Our courage will not be shaken.'"

Stockman looked at me. He smiled. "I'm happy you recorded that."

"Naturally," I said.

He was reassured about my attendance, but I recognized the tightrope he walked in public. It was possible he'd be a little apprehensive about his local attitude being portrayed abroad.

Quickly I added, "Not that I would quote you for my American readers. Your eloquence was to quell a panic, not to legitimize a foreign policy."

"Quite so," he said.

We were approaching torchlight and he and I exchanged a glance that lingered an extra beat, and another, as if we had an understanding.

Beneath my feet the grass abruptly became macadam as we entered the drive in front of the courtyard.

I turned my face to the house.

I'd done what I needed to do. I figured I was square with Sir Albert. Jeremy didn't know that.

The macadam turned to fieldstone and we took our first steps into the courtyard and my gaze was ahead but my attention was on my thoughts, and so it came into my sight simply as movement, quick movement from above, off to the right, a mass plummeting downward and then the heavy thud of it, the thud and cracking, and my mother let out a sharp bark of a scream and I looked now directly at what had fallen and I saw a body hunched into the ground as if it had been trying desperately to dig into the earth but had failed terribly and was resting now, the head twisted sharply away, however, its neck snapped. The body wore a gray suit and was hatless and its hair was spiky and yellow in the electric light. It was Martin, of course.

Martin, Stockman's head tough guy, dead now, but by a hand that was other than mine. That diversion of suspicion was what Jeremy had just given me. Martin was a dead man as soon as he'd seen Jeremy's face and heard my voice.

Stockman turned around at once to the rest of the weekend guests, who'd bunched up close behind. "Stay away," he commanded and then he strode off toward the body.

Two Gray Suits were hustling from the house in his direction.

As Joseph W. Hunter it was better for me to hang back. I was just a guest.

And Isabel Cobb needed me now.

I stepped to her.

Her bundle of roses was lying at her feet.

I put my arm around her shoulders. She was trembling.

"What have we gotten into?" my mother whispered to me.

16

For a few moments we just stood like that. Neither Joe Hunter nor I knew what to say to Isabel Cobb.

She trembled on.

Finally I whispered, "It's all just melodrama. You've played this a thousand times."

"Don't be a fool," she said.

She was right.

"Okay," I said. "It's life. But we're acting in it. We can do this."

She nodded.

She lifted her face. But not to me.

I felt a shudder pass through her.

And her trembling stopped, as if the curtain had just risen and she was on.

I followed her gaze.

Stockman was heading this way. He was looking at me as if through rifle sights, me standing with my right shoulder tucked behind her left and my arm enveloping her, pulling her close. I was very lucky that I'd not actually taken her into my arms, even in the chaste way I would have, as any son might have when his mother was suddenly terrified. This tableau was bad enough, as far as Stockman was concerned, as far as his intended woman and this snoopy journalist were concerned.

Mother knew the look. She broke away from me at once, rushed forward to meet Stockman, whose body paused for her, whose arms opened for her, even as his severe gaze remained on me.

She threw herself into his arms with a flurry of words.

"Oh Albert, what's happened to that poor man? Is he dead? And where did you go? It's a good thing Mr. Hunter was nearby. He held me up when I was about to faint. I was swooning away."

She looked back to me from Stockman's chest. "I'm sorry to have frightened you like that, Mr. Hunter. Thank you."

She was a pro. She was convincing.

She laid her head on his chest again. "Can you take me away from this now, Albert?"

His gaze upon me went more or less neutral just before he looked down at Mother. "Of course, my dear."

For good measure, she wobbled suddenly at the knees, threatened to slide from his arms.

Stockman held her closer, held her up. "Be strong," he said. "My people will take care of this. We can go in now."

"Yes," she said. "Please." She pulled away from him just enough to put her arm in his and begin to turn him.

He gave me one more look. Grudging. I'd touched his woman, even if it was innocently. But he seemed ready to overlook this.

I nodded at him.

He did not return the nod, but he looked away as if I were not an issue.

That was good enough.

The two of them moved off toward the door into the house, Mother clinging to Stockman's arm, her head against his shoulder.

A Gray Suit instantly filled the space where they had stood. "Please come with me," he said to all of us weekend guests. "Stay together and follow me quickly."

We complied, and he and another of his cohorts, who met us in the Great Hall, hustled us to the north end of the house and up the stairs, one of them leading us solitary denizens into the bachelor wing and the other taking the couples up to the next floor.

Our hallway was lit with electric bulbs on sconces. The Gray Suit made sure we all went into our rooms and closed the doors, telling us, as we disappeared, to be sure to turn the lock after us.

I did.

I waited in the dark.

I paced.

I waited, and then I softly undid the lock and eased the door open.

I looked out into the still-lit hallway.

"Please," a voice said sternly. "We must insist. It's for your own safety."

I withdrew instantly.

I was stuck.

But it was just as well. My own instincts needed to be reined in now. I had nothing to do but wait until the morning and hope for a few private moments with my mother. And hope that Jeremy Miller had made good use of Martin's gray suit and was rushing safely through the woods or along the shore by now.

I went to my casement window and undid the latch and pushed it open.

I listened. The action was likely to be on the far side of the house.

The clatter of feet. The sound of struggle. These things would never carry as far as this room. Not through a window looking north.

I lay down on the bed.

One thing would carry, however, and about ten minutes later I thought I heard this thing: the pop of small arms fire. Once, twice. Perhaps a pistol or pistols. The sound was very distant. Perhaps Jeremy Miller had just been shot dead. Or he'd just shot his last pursuer dead. Or everyone had been shooting at shadows. Or perhaps an automobile had simply backfired on the road to Ramsgate.

But now there was silence.

And there was nothing to do about it.

I got up. I took off my coat and my pistol and my shoes. I would make no further concession to my confinement.

I thought to turn on the light at the writing desk.

But I did not. The dark was better for now.

I lay back down.

Like Jeremy out there in the night, I started running from my pursuers. Thoughts. I was running in my head from thoughts. Small-caliber ones, which were harder to deal with. The big things to worry about, the fundamental things, seemed easier somehow. That was why I figured I was cut out for the work I'd done over the past six years of my life. At first, I'd dodged bullets and watched men die and I wrote about that. Lately, I'd risked myself in ways that made bullets from a bunker seem reassuringly predictable. I'd learned to kill in service for my country. To kill in unpredictable ways. Dealing with that was simple and it was deep. It was merely how this roughneck planet we all lived on was put together, and so the way to cope was already imprinted in our muscles, was coursing in our veins. But this whole thing about my mother and her men, which was whining after me in my head now: that was all just niggles. Of no consequence to me. Long ago I left off needing to give a damn about how she lived her life. Which was the way it should be for any son and mother. You have to leave, and she has to let go.

So I slept.

And I woke. I didn't know how long had passed or what had awakened me.

I rose and crossed to the window.

Before me was barely differentiated darkness. The dark of a lawn. The deeper dark of the miniature canyon of the Dumpton gap. The dark of the woods beyond.

And a sound.

I closed my eyes and listened.

This sound may have been what drew me: the distant revving of an engine. I leaned out, looked, tried to catch its direction.

To the east, toward another darkness, was the fierce bratting of a runabout engine, moving away now, diminishing. Out there, where I knew the Strait of Dover to be, I could see a cluster of lights. A larger vessel upon the water. And someone rushing toward it.

17

Shortly after dawn I tried the hallway and it was empty. I went to the steps, descended into the screens passage, and emerged in the Great Hall. It too was empty. From the courtyard I heard a hammer pounding. Nails into wood.

A Gray Suit, framed in the courtyard doorway, began to turn at my step, and beyond him I caught sight of one of the Blueboys hammering the lid shut on a wooden box about the size of a hotel room writing desk. One more of the same size sat nearby, wrapped at both ends with steel bands. Half a dozen more, the size and shape of steamer trunks, were already done. A little apart were two more of these packing boxes standing upright, each about the size of a three-drawer filing cabinet.

The Gray Suit was the guy with the boxer's nose. He eclipsed the courtyard, putting himself square before me and close enough to try to seem intimidating. I wasn't intimidated, but I was still Joe Hunter the benign guest, so I kept my first impulse to myself.

"Please, sir," he said, straining to be polite when to be so wasn't the sort of order he'd been hired to execute. "Guests are to stop in their rooms or in the dining room until transportation."

"Transportation?"

This guy was looking at me a little more closely now.

"Sorry, sir," he said, working even harder at his politeness mandate. "Plans have changed. You're Mr. Hunter, are you?"

"Yes I am."

"I am to give you this," he said, and he dipped into his inner coat pocket and withdrew an envelope. He handed it to me. "From Sir Albert," he said.

The envelope had my name on it. That is to say, "Joseph Hunter." But I knew the hand. It was my mother's.

"How changed?" I said.

"Sir?"

"The plans," I said.

"Breakfast is served in the breakfast room. The guests will then depart."

"And Madam Cobb? I am in her party."

"She has departed with Sir Albert."

The boat in the night, I assumed.

"Departed?"

"Yes sir."

"Where to?"

I'd reached the limit of Boxernose's authority to speak. "Breakfast is served in the breakfast room," he said.

"Thus the name," I said.

His brow furrowed.

"Thanks," I said, and I turned on my heel and beat it back across the Great Hall and up to my room.

I sat at the desk with the envelope and I opened it.

I unfolded a single sheet of writing paper and there was nothing of Sir Albert here, except, of course, the certainty that he had seen, openly or covertly, every word herein. She wrote:

Dear Mr. Hunter,

Sir Albert and I are very sorry to leave so abruptly. The accidental death of a member of the house staff has cast a pall over our weekend, and Sir Albert has decided to accompany me to Berlin. We would be happy to see you there if you can arrange passage, perhaps through your newspaper. I am anxious that the work we have done on your story will not be wasted and that my true intentions for being in Germany at this time can be accurately represented in the American press. Please wire your arrangements to me care of the Hotel Adlon.

Best regards,

Isabel Cobb

I folded the letter and replaced it in its envelope and slipped it into my inner coat pocket, doing all this almost fastidiously, aware of the small sounds of it—the creasing of the paper, the ruffle of the mohair. I was gathering myself to think clearly, calmly.

She was safe. For now, at least. She was not implicated. I was invited. Joe Hunter was still viable. For now. Or if the "for now" was as ominous as it might be, and if she wasn't, in fact, safe, and if Joe wasn't either, my actions were clear just the same. I'd go to Berlin.

18

The boys in gray made sure we went back to our rooms after breakfast and stayed there. And it wasn't till very late morning that one of the boys in blue knocked on my room door and invited me downstairs, luggage to follow, for my trip to the train station in Broadstairs. I carried the Gladstone myself. It was comfortably weighty, though its only heavyweight secret was my Luger. I'd kept the Mauser in the small of my back. From this point on, that would be my standard practice.

The Blue Serge led me past another of his kind who was to bring my suitcase. He led me out of the house by way of the southern door, as I'd come in, and strode ahead of me toward the Silver Ghost, which sat waiting. He opened the tonneau door. I approached and was about to enter when I had the impulse to look back up to the tower where all the action had been the night before.

The Union Jack was flying.

But the guy wires were gone.

I looked just long enough to make sure I was seeing what I thought I was seeing, and I turned and entered the tonneau without even glancing at the driver.

I sat down in the near seat.

"Your bags will be along presently," he said.

The door clicked closed beside me.

Now I knew what was in at least a couple of those boxes in the courtyard. The whole telegraph setup. The guy wire antennas were gone. The flagpole was no doubt gutted. The wireless itself was carted off somewhere in the night. Along with every other household shred of evidence against Stockman.

They were taking no chances. Even if they'd caught Jeremy and killed him, the guy's disappearance could trigger a search of the house. If nothing came of it, they'd set back up again. Buffington had only one shot at digging into the castle of a member of Parliament.

A short time later my suitcase ended up in the tonneau with me. Nothing and no one else. I seemed to have retained my privileged status even without Isabel Cobb's presence.

At the curb before the front doors of the station, the driver hustled out to open my door and then around to pull my suitcase from the other side of the tonneau. I circled behind him and he offered to find me a porter. I thanked him and declined. I made a bit of a show in presenting him with a crown, a very good tip for the service he'd just done.

He hesitated. Then he took the silver coin.

"Thank you, Captain," he said.

"And where's the Rolls driver from yesterday?" I said, the objective of my silver gambit. "I was expecting to tip *him*."

The driver looked at me a little wide-eyed with uncertainty. He'd been pressed into this job, given the unusual circumstances, and this was way outside of both his job responsibilities and his ad hoc briefing.

"Martin, I think his name is," I said.

"He was the one in the courtyard last night," he said.

"Oh no," I said. "What happened?"

The driver sniffed heavily and held his breath as if he'd just been shivved.

He didn't have the presence of mind simply to walk away. I waited, as if there weren't the least doubt that he'd give me an answer.

"He died," the driver said, still flailing inside.

Without giving him a chance to draw even one more breath, I said, "Did they catch the bloody bastard who did it?"

"Not yet," he said with a ferocity that seemed very personal, that made me wonder what kind of an okay guy our Martin might have been in a bar with his buddies. "But maybe in Ramsgate."

"You got him cornered there?" I said.

"I don't know, Captain," the Blue Suit said, as if I were suddenly a copper trying to squeeze him for a confession. "Thank you for the crown," he said, and he turned and moved off.

Too bad. He probably didn't know much more anyway. But I was left with nothing to allay my fear that Jeremy Miller was dead as a result of protecting me and my phony identity.

It wasn't until well past midday that I reached my room at the Tavistock Hotel. The train ride back through the same Kentish countryside my mother and I had traversed twenty-four hours earlier had filled me, of course, with an even more pressing fear. For her. Miller, indeed, hadn't been protecting my role in this present drama so much as he had hers. I was simply carrying a spear for the leading lady. And she'd been abruptly whisked away by her Othello.

So my bags were unopened on the floor of my room and my hat was still on my head and I was sitting at the desk where I'd been creating Joe Hunter for weeks and I was waiting as the telephone operator connected me to the American embassy.

After I was finally rung through to some inner embassy sanctum, a man said, "Sorry, Mr. Trask isn't here at present."

I left a message for him to contact me as soon as possible.

He hadn't expected me till tomorrow, of course. I went from stuck in a room at the Stockman House to stuck in a room at the Tavistock Hotel.

The only thing that made the next few hours bearable was to lay a pack of cigarettes and an ashtray next to my Portable Number 3 and to turn back into Christopher Cobb and write the lead paragraphs of a king-beat news story about a German spy in the midst of the British Parliament.

I restricted myself to the first three pages, the number I felt confident I could burn in the metal wastebasket without burning the hotel down as well. So those three pages were created slowly, each sentence being refined and rehearsed aloud before entering the Corona and emerging from its platen and then being honed to an Alexander Popeian extreme beneath my Conklin Crescent-Filler.

At last I received a call from the embassy and an appointment on the Waterloo Bridge, and I lit my front-page story with the butt of the last cigarette in my pack and hoped I'd have a shot at it for real someday.

19

I stood in the dead center of Waterloo Bridge and leaned on the stone balustrade as the western sky stopped bleeding and started bruising and the lights came on along the Victoria Embankment. Trask suddenly appeared at my side.

"Cigar?" he said, lifting a very good one before me.

"Sure," I said, and we each lit up a ninepence Vuelta Abajo and blew the smoke over the river, which was running about four storeys below us, black from coal tar and Thames mud and the onflow of night.

"I'm sorry I couldn't bring you a chunk of my steak from Simpson's," he said.

"This'll do," I said, taking a second draw. This was some fine stogie, with a heavy body and a taste of plantain and palm, of leather and earth, but with all that gone up together in flames so that you somehow knew all those tastes were there but they made a single new thing.

"I ate dinner tonight with your old friend Metcalf," he said.

I'd had quite a feed with my old friend Metcalf, my embassy contact who sent me off to Istanbul back in May. He took me to Escoffier's eatery at the Carlton Hotel. "Did you understand everything he told you about the food?" I asked.

"I don't care to know that much about a cut of beef," he said.

I didn't tell Trask I listened to every word.

Instead, we shared a nod and we each looked at the end of our cigar at the same moment. Somehow I'd always known to do this, having learned to smoke a cigar like an actor, from actors, but I never knew why it seemed so natural, even necessary. Maybe it was just to punctuate a conversation, which is certainly what it did for Trask and me, at that moment.

"You're back early," he said. Though this was a declaration, he clearly was asking for the story.

You would have thought he'd get a little worked up for that question. Something had to have gone seriously awry for me to be on this bridge with him tonight. But he was languid as cigar smoke. He was a cool customer, my old friend Trask, and in our line of work that was probably good. But I wondered if maybe in this case he already knew the reason.

He waited.

I decided to let him do it his way. I told him about Jeremy and Martin, about Isabel and Stockman, their coziness and their abrupt departure. I told him about the contents of the tower room, the code books and the wind books and the maps. And the wireless. I told him about Stockman's torches and his oratory and then the Zepps.

I'd kept my conclusions and my worries to myself in all this, just stating the facts for him, as starters.

We both seemed silently to understand that the facts part was done with.

We puffed on our Cuban cigars.

The first conclusion to draw from the facts didn't need saying: generally speaking, Stockman was everything Trask and Buffington had suspected.

The next piece of the puzzle begged for conclusions. I handed him my mother's note from this morning.

He slid a few feet away to the spill of electric light from one of the iron standards. He read her message and slid back again.

"The Adlon." He said the name with a sneer in his voice, as if its significance should be clear to me.

"Yes?"

"It's the Kaiser's favorite," Trask said. "Everyone of importance is put there. So the phones are tapped, and the place is crawling with agents."

"I'm worried about her," I said, nodding at the note still in Trask's hand. "That was written before they sailed away. Have you heard anything more from her?"

"Not yet," Trask said. "Even going in through Ostend, they'd still be in transit."

"Does the Adlon suggest anything?"

"If he suspects her, it's the best place to put her. But if he doesn't, it's still best for him."

So I had to live with that worry for a while. Probably for a long while.

I went on to the second one.

"Anything about Jeremy Miller?"

Trask shook his head no. "There's a lot the Brits didn't say, even after we agreed to help, as you no doubt have already gathered."

"I have," I said.

"This is the first I've heard of him," Trask said.

One more fact now. "They won't find anything if they search Stockman's house," I said. "When I left, his boys had clearly dismantled the wireless. They were packing it in boxes at dawn. I'm sure they did the same with anything else incriminating."

Trask grunted.

"The Brits probably don't know this, if Miller's still missing," I said.

"They'd have to assume it either way," Trask said. He looked at the end of his cigar again. It was burning, of course.

Worries were for civilians. I had to move on.

"Stockman seems to be about the Zeppelins," I said.

Trask took this in and then turned around, put his back to the balustrade. He lifted his face to exhale his smoke in the direction of the streetlight.

Only a few moments passed and he took another deep drag.

Trask was a cool customer all right. But I figured he knew how to treat a good cigar. We were smoking these things too quickly. His continuous puffing was a tip-off to his agitation.

And now he seemed ready simply to watch the evening traffic crossing the bridge.

I joined him. I've known a lot of guys like this. The worse things got, the less they said. I gave him a long minute. Then I said, "Don't clam up like the Brits."

He moved his face a little in my direction without giving me his eyes. "I'm just thinking," he said. "You're right about the airships. But this much they say about Stockman. He's smart. He's a *big idea* kind of guy."

Trask was smart too. He was already thinking what I now realized had been nagging at me all along. "Winds and weather and beacons along the Thames," I said.

Now he turned his eyes to me.

"Those aren't big ideas," I said.

Trask smiled. The smile felt personal. It was maybe the first personal gesture I'd ever gotten from him. He knew we understood each other easily.

"Those are matters for a navigator, an airship commander," he said. "At most an operations officer in Düsseldorf or Nordholz or Ghent."

He could have named any of a dozen other Zepp bases.

"It doesn't add up," I said.

"We need to find Joe Hunter a hotel," he said. "So you can answer this." He handed my mother's message back to me.

I put it in my pocket. We both looked at the traffic once more.

A double-decker bus rumbled past.

We didn't have to say it. We needed to drive the bus.

20

It wasn't until late the next afternoon that a leather portfolio and a brown paper parcel arrived by way of George, my familiar, aged bellhop. It wasn't until I'd closed the door and placed these things on the bed that it struck me: George was in the employ of one or both of the secret service agencies I was working for. Maybe the hotel management was too.

Indeed, the portfolio that had been entrusted to George's hand from lobby to room door contained all I needed to change hotels and then leave the country as Joseph W. Hunter. A room key at the Faulkner's Hotel in Charing Cross. Tickets and passport for Hunter. A piece of paper with a hotel name and address in Berlin, but a handwritten note at the bottom saying, "Defer to theirs, if offered." Letters of passage and introduction, these the cleverly wrought products of the ongoing irony of America's occupying the German embassy at the Germans' request and with their gratitude. We still officially represented their interests in London after they'd made a hasty departure in July of last year.

One was a letter of introduction on the letterhead of His Excellency Baron von Schwarzenstein, ostensibly by his own hand, granting the bearer official sanction to ask questions. Answers were, no doubt, optional. But at least I wouldn't have to open Joe Hunter's mouth to the force-feed of German propaganda.

And I had an alternate set of papers for a German military identity, a full colonel attached to the *Auswärtiges Amt*, the Foreign Office, including an authorizing letter of introduction over the apparent signature of the foreign minister himself, Gottlieb von Jagow. The colonel could be played as a spy, if need be. I also instantly knew what was in the paper parcel. This man's uniform.

I saw my face on his passport, a picture taken without my close-cropped beard and showing the long, white scar arcing across the center of my left cheek. A perfect replica of a German university fencing scar. A *Schmiss*, the sign of youthful bravery and high breeding. In my case, it was an inadvertent souvenir of my work in Mexico. A useful thing that I despised. In his case, it was a result of aristocratic breeding and education. The name on the passport was Klaus von Wolfinger.

I put those papers back in the portfolio for now. They would soon reside in the false bottom of my Gladstone, along with his clothes. That wasn't me yet, and if that face didn't absolutely have to be mine, I didn't want anything to do with it.

A note on generic American embassy letterhead was written in the same hand that accompanied the Berlin hotel information. Two words: "Good luck." No signature. But no signature meant Trask. No signature was him looking at the end of his cigar.

I was nearly finished packing when the telephone on the desk rang. I answered.

It was the front desk. "A woman to see you, sir."

I went down.

In a corner of the lobby, rising from a red settee framed in two palms, was the pretty-like-a-farm-girl suffragette from my mother's dressing room. She was wearing the dark skirt and white shirtwaist uniform she'd had on the other night, though she'd come with her tricolor suffrage ribbon discreetly omitted from her ensemble and a straw boater with a blue bow on her head.

I moved to her. But it beat me how she knew I was here.

"Mr. Cobb," she said when I'd drawn close.

She offered her hand for a shake.

I took it. I remembered her shake being a meek thing the last time. Now her grip had a little spunk to it, befitting a woman ready to chain herself to an iron fence in Piccadilly Circus so she could vote.

"You've been working on your handshake," I said.

Her cheeks bloomed quickly.

"Now you have to work on suppressing the blush," I said.

We were still shaking and she withdrew her hand quickly at that.

"I don't mean to be critical," I said. "I share my mother's convictions about your cause."

"Good," she said, looking down.

I had to admit to myself, particularly on this late afternoon, that this woman stirred me. I liked a woman trying to be strong. Better still, I liked a woman already strong. Strong even beyond seeking the right to vote. But trying was also attractive to me. I'd been bred into a sympathy for suffragism. How could I not, with a mother who lived her life, always, as if she could be anyone, could do anything.

I put the tip of my finger gently beneath her chin and lifted it.

"I didn't mean to embarrass you," I said.

"It's not just them has to change," she said. "It's us too."

"Neither is easy," I said.

She fixed her eyes on me—they were the color of horse chestnut—and she set her jaw and she smiled a downright comradely smile.

I matched it. Her blush was gone.

And then she abruptly disengaged her eyes and let go of her smile in the flurry of almost having forgotten what she was there for.

She dug into her small brown suede bag and withdrew an envelope. She handed it to me. "From your mother."

The envelope was sealed. It had upon it my full name in her ornate hand: *Christopher Marlowe Cobb*.

"When did you see her?" I asked, too sharply, the tone driven by my surprise and by the reflex assumption that the chronology of delivery was the chronology of composition.

But she stood her ground, this suffragette whose name I'd avoided asking and still did not know. "Thursday night," she said. "At the closing party."

The night before we went to Stockman House.

The lesser mystery resolved itself as well. This was how I'd been found by a virtual stranger. Mother had known all along where I was. It was she who'd sent the play ticket, and now she'd dispatched her suffragette as a courier.

I gentled up my voice. "She must think highly of you," I said.

My sharp tone had braced her. This tone caught her way off guard. She fluttered into the self she was trying so hard to leave behind, and she cast her eyes downward.

"I was honored to help," she said.

"What did she ask you to do?" I struggled to keep her from hearing the sense of urgent business that I felt.

She lifted her face again. I couldn't read her mood now.

I added, "If I might ask."

"She said if I hadn't heard from her by three o'clock on Sunday to come here and wait for you and give you that envelope."

If the weekend had gone as planned, we were to have returned by noon today. And presumably I wouldn't have received this.

My hands went itchy to tear the thing open. I wanted to do that alone. But I found I also wanted to spend a few more minutes with this suffragette, who smelled of something nice but appropriate to the woman she was trying to become. Patchouli and musk and maybe some sweeter things too but only in the background.

"Can I have a few moments with this?" I said.

"Of course," she said.

"But don't go entirely away yet."

She braced up again, as if I'd spoken sharply to her. That sweet, wide mouth moued a little, but it was an ironic moue, an amused moue.

She glided away toward another settee across the lobby.

I tore open my mother's envelope. She wrote:

My Darling Kit,
If you are reading this, things may have gone terribly wrong. I fear you
will never see me again. "Accurst be he that first invented war."

The quotation was from the playwright for whom she named me.
Though my present worries for her were, of course, rooted in the
very risk she invoked, the fact was that she was very much alive. That
she had, however, contrived to speak to me from the grave turned
this all into an overplayed Isabel Cobb performance in a second-rate
melodrama.

I am sorry if ever I have wronged you, by things I have done or by things
I have failed to do. "Mountains and hills, come, come and fall on me,
and hide me from the heavy wrath of God."

Marlowe again. She was at the edge of the stage in my head, playing to the back row though I was in the front row and able to see the
tears, which she was so adept at producing, run through her makeup.

I have come to this end from love of country. I write this letter from love
for you, my son. I have always loved you. Always. From wherever I am
now, I love you still.

The words ran instantly in my head: "The lady doth protest too
much, methinks."
And she too turned to the words of the character she'd recently
portrayed. His death scene, of course:

If thou didst ever hold me in thy heart, absent thee from felicity for a
while, and in this harsh world draw thy breath in pain, to tell my story.

Though this too was a quotation from her recent performance,
she had removed the quotation marks, had made the words her own,
had become, herself, the tragic figure. And since she assumed that my

own mortal risks on the same mission had proved to be not as great as hers, I was spared in order to tell the tale of Isabel Cobb's sacrifice for her country.

I have done my best, which is all anyone can do. The rest is silence.
   Your mother

I folded the letter and placed it in the envelope and then into my coat pocket.

She played Hamlet's death more convincingly than her own, in spite of the liberal quotations from two masters and a little bit of quasi-plagiarism.

I looked across the lobby.

The suffragette was already striding my way.

Perhaps she had thought over our conversation so far and regretted the moments when she seemed a little intimidated, a little weak, a little too traditional in her femininity.

She arrived.

"I saw that you'd finished," she said.

I held up my two empty hands to confirm her impression.

"You didn't wish for me to go away," she said.

"That's right."

She waited for a beat to see if I would carry on from there. I chose not to fill the brief silence, interested in what she would do.

She filled it almost at once. "The skies are clouding up, but not much. It is a Zeppelin night. My friends gather to eat and drink and wait and take shelter. Would you care to share the event with me?"

This all came out in a rush, perhaps even a single breath. Yes, this woman yearned for enfranchisement beyond the vote.

I liked her.

"Yes," I said.

"Good."

She handed me an address on Brook Street, Number 24, just off Hanover Square, written out on a scrap of paper.

"Can you come at eight or thereabouts?" she said.

"Yes."

She did what she'd worked herself up to do and she turned away, as if to stride off.

"One other thing," I said.

She turned back to me.

"Should I know your name?"

Her eyes widened. "You don't know my name?"

"I don't."

She humphed softly. Then she stuck out her hand once more. "Millicent Gibbs."

I took it. She was putting all the muscle she could behind it. "Kit Cobb," I said.

She looked hard into my eyes. "I like you, Kit Cobb," she said. "And you like me. Just don't patronize me."

She let go of the shake, turned on her heel, and strode away.

I figured, in spite of her little lapses, she was doing pretty well with her project. She was right about what had been wrongly creeping into my attitude about her. I liked her even more for tweaking my nose for it.

I beat it back upstairs, finished my packing, and an hour later I'd moved into the Faulkner's on Villiers Street, a modest, four-storey, brick-faced hotel on the Strand side of Charing Cross Station. Its street front split its space with Faulkner's Hosier and Hatter. Just the sort of place for a minor journalist, and no doubt another discreetly government-friendly establishment.

I wouldn't be here long. The tickets put me on the steamer tomorrow night from Folkestone to Vlissingen and then the train onward through neutral Holland to the German border and then to Berlin.

I went out at once and into the Strand and found a telegraph office. I wired Isabel Cobb at the Adlon of my presence at the Faulkner's and my travel arrangements to Berlin. I was vague about my accommodations, saying I planned to stay at a *Residenzpension*, a boarding-house, common in the city.

In fact, Trask had put me into the Hotel Baden, a comparably modest hotel on Unter den Linden, near the Russian embassy and a five-minute walk from the Adlon. I didn't want Stockman to know exactly where I was if I could avoid it.

I wrote at the end: *Am eager to see your performance in Berlin. The play's the thing.*

A covert, needling little joke with my mother. As soon as the telegram was sent, however, I worried that I'd unwisely gotten caught up in whatever it was that always went on between my mother and me and, as a consequence, I'd endangered her. Stockman would surely be monitoring the telegrams to her through the Adlon.

I tried to talk myself out of the worry: he would understand the *deutschfreundlich* reporter's reference to her performance as being about Hamlet, not an American spy; he'd understand the quote as referring to the play being the central feature of her visit to Berlin, not "the thing wherein I'll catch the conscience of the King," the King being Sir Albert himself.

But I walked back to the hotel unsettled, eased only by the thought of an enfranchised Miss Gibbs.

21

The sun was just vanishing when my taxi slipped along the lilac hedges of Hanover Square and stopped before a flat-roofed, brick town house half the width but just as tall as my hotel. It was a private residence but without apparent servants and without a clear owner, at least on this Sunday night, the door being answered by one of the other women from my mother's dressing room, the one wide enough to be the cellist in that string quartet of suffragettes. She recognized me at once and led me up a single flight to the parlor and I was introduced at the door as Mr. Christopher Cobb to a dozen or so of Millicent's colleagues, about half of whom had also invited men. Most of these guys struck me as dandies, though I didn't look at them very closely, simply registering among them more than one frock coat, apricot tie, waistcoat the color of the Hanover Square hedges in bloom. The women murmured at me sweetly. The men displayed indifference.

Millicent presented herself before me.

"I'm sorry I'm a little late," I said.

"I remember using the phrase 'or thereabouts' with the time," she said.

"So you did."

"I will feed you now," she said.

And she led me to a table set for high tea and I grazed a bit. Between the cucumber sandwiches and the dandies in the room I felt as if I'd been cast in an Oscar Wilde play.

Which made me appreciate Millicent Gibbs all the more intensely. She and I drank a pretty good red wine off in the corner. The men kept their distance, and the suffragettes made solitary, hope-I'm-not-intruding pilgrimages over to us to chat briefly, mostly about how they felt nothing short of adoration for my mother.

When the air raid whistle blew in the street, the room upswelled in conversation and bustle like a theater crowd responding to the call to seats at the end of an intermission. "To the basement," a woman's voice cried out, and the group made for the parlor door.

I had no real interest in joining them and merely shifted my weight in our standing position, but Millicent's hand went straight to my forearm to keep me where I was. She had her own plan.

When everyone was out of sight and clattering down the stairs toward the cellar, Millicent took my hand and we left the parlor and approached the staircase. But she and I climbed upward.

Two flights more, in darkness. By my count this was the top floor, but she led me around the banister and toward the back of the house and onto a narrower staircase leading up still farther.

She had not spoken a word. She had not let go of my hand. We reached a small vestibule and she released her hold on me and opened the door.

We stepped out onto the roof.

She closed the door behind us and stood beside me, our arms touching, and she said, "I've been longing to do this. Your mother is intrepid. I know you must be as well."

The warden's whistle was still piping somewhere along the street.

And now the six-pounders began to pop off in futility, out east.

I felt a shudder run through her. My first thought was that she was afraid.

But before I could raise my arm to put around her and before I let the obvious thing back into my head—she couldn't be afraid because she'd deliberately brought us up here—she said, "Come this way," and she took my hand again. The rush in her voice and the firmness of her hand both spoke not of fear but of some sort of dark exhilaration.

We neared the front parapet of the roof and she stopped us. "Here," she said and she knelt, pulling at my hand, bringing me down beside her, and she let go of me and lunged forward. My knees were resting on a soft thing. I put a hand down. A blanket. My eyes were seeing enough now, adjusting in the dark. A searchlight flashed overhead and away. I could see Millicent there, stretched out on her back on the blanket, looking up into the sky.

"Please lie beside me," she said.

I did, placing myself so our bodies touched from shoulder to foot. She did not ease away. Indeed, she gently pressed her shoulder and her hip a little closer. But I sensed this wasn't about sex. Not at the moment, at least.

I was right.

"Do you think they will pass over us?" she said, and she slipped her hand into mine, our fingers intertwining, our bundled hands coming to rest upon our joined hips.

"Do you think they will drop a bomb on us?" I replied.

It was the cue for us to turn our faces and look at each other in the dark, on this open roof, beneath a London sky, on a Zeppelin night.

This we did. And as soon as our eyes met, we laughed.

We turned our faces skyward again and we did not speak. We waited. We listened. The six-pounders soon stopped. I had lately been quite near a Zepp or two on a rooftop. I wasn't looking forward to another. But I was quite happy to be tagging along in Millicent Gibbs's journey to an intrepid self.

We strained to hear the hammer of the Maybachs. I would tell her about these fine engines if she would like. But all we heard were the distant blackout whistlings. A brief spatter of small arms fire. A siren somewhere. And then a long, persistent silence, underscored by the silent scan of a searchlight and another, showing, however, only clouds.

At last the lights stopped and so did the sounds.

She said, "They are elsewhere, I suppose."

"Or perhaps they did not come tonight," I said.

She sighed.

"It makes no difference," I said. "Your courage is the same."

"Thank you," she said. "But I wanted more."

This seemed another cue. Even if she hadn't consciously intended it. I turned to her on my side.

She looked at me.

I kissed her.

And we began.

She was strong and she did not mind my being strong and somewhere in the midst of the clutch and crash and cling I began to realize something that made me wish the Zepps had come and that they had been enough for her. I pushed the thing from my mind, but when this woman and I were done and lying side by side again and looking at the dark sky above, I could not help but think: Mother carefully chose this woman for me and arranged this very act, her being dead and her having that dark and ironic and utterly tormenting sense of drama that made her the actress and the mother that she was.

I kept my mouth shut.

But Millicent went straight there: "She said I'd like you."

I was ready to bolt.

"And I do," Millicent said.

22

I did bolt. Politely. She was not terribly disappointed, being strong. My mother was still very much alive and had miscalculated this whole thing. Or perhaps she hadn't. Perhaps she was even now amused at the thought that her posthumous message had been delivered and had thus set in motion this very sort of playlet for two. She'd relish the irony, given her own two-hander at the Hotel Adlon.

But my playlet had ended its run. I was glad for that, glad to focus now simply on risking my life for my country as a spy in Germany. The irony with *that* being I had to wait to hear from my mother to actually get started.

Word came early the next day. She was happy to receive my telegram and Sir Albert was absolutely insistent that he put me in the Adlon near the two of them. *Still working on my performance*, she said. *Every other night it is in German.*

I vowed never again to engage her in innuendo. But I knew the vow was futile.

I met with Trask one last time, at the A.B.C. café on Duncannon Street just opposite Charing Cross Station. It was a tea and pastry shop mostly (the A.B.C. once having been the Aerated Bread Company) but it was a guy's place, for all that, with severe dark wood tables and chairs, a checker-tiled floor fit for a bar, mirrors on the wall, and a roomful of men.

Trask and I ordered coffee, however, to the faint distaste of the waiter.

We drank, we spoke of its mediocrity as coffee but of its superiority, even still, to yet another cup of tea. At least we were among *men* drinking tea. Trask made this last point; I had not, out of deference to Millicent Gibbs.

Then Trask and I leaned toward each other and lowered our voices to only what was necessary, though the conversational welter at teatime that surrounded us was plenty of ground cover for our conversation. Our business was brief.

"Our English friends will give you some help over there, in case you need it," Trask said.

"You've spoken to them, I take it."

"I have."

He took a folded piece of paper out of his pocket and passed it to me. "This is where and when."

It read: *Thursday night. Nine o'clock. Zum Grauen Köter. South of the Stettiner train station on* Borsig-Strasse. *"Too much smoke and noise."*

The place was called the Gray Dog. The "help" would identify himself by speaking of the smoke and noise.

I looked at Trask.

"It's a cabaret," he said.

"One of their people inside Germany?"

"Yes."

"We don't have anyone inside?"

"That would be you."

"How will he know me?"

Trask's hand came low across the table once more.

He put an object in my palm, small but with a little weight. I opened my hand and glanced just before I dropped the thing into a side coat pocket.

A brass *Reichsadler*, the Imperial Eagle, with a blunt-ended pin attached to the back.

"Your boutonnière," he said.

"Any other news from the Brits?" I said.

"Nothing."

"Did you ask?"

"I did." Trask nodded at the piece of paper in my hand.

"You have that in your head now?"

"I do."

He extended his hand and I gave the paper to him. He stuffed it into his inside pocket. "Now," he said. "What was the word?"

I told him the details of the telegram from Isabel, and I asked, "Should I take Stockman up on the offer of the Adlon?"

"You will have no secrets in your room," he said. "The place is an anthill of German spies."

"To refuse him on this . . ."

"You can't," Trask said. "Perhaps it'll be useful for you, as well, as long as you can keep your act going."

"I can do that."

"You need to deal with your extras," Trask said, meaning my weapons, my alternate credentials.

"I told them I'd stay at a boarding-house. Unnamed."

Trask instantly knew what I was driving at. "Good," he said.

"I take it the Baden is safe?"

"Relatively. The clientele is assumed to be of little interest. The German operation along the Unter den Linden is high-level stuff."

"I'll check in at the Baden before the Adlon," I said.

"Tonight I'll send round a tool or two," he said. "The base of a wardrobe is pretty useful. Just in case."

I nodded.

I kept silent for a moment and he shifted needlessly in his seat, as if there was a touchy thing he needed to say but he hadn't figured out how to work it in smoothly.

He said, "Unfortunately we don't presently have an equivalent of Metcalf in Berlin. But if and when you need to leave the country abruptly, make your way to the embassy and invoke my name. They can take care of you."

"All right," I said.

Trask and I looked at each other for a moment. I figured we'd said all that we had to say. But just as I thought to lean back in my chair and finish my coffee, Trask gave me a final thought for my trip. "It's come to this now," he said. "If they think you're a spy and you can't get to our boys at the embassy on your own, they'll assume you're a Brit, take you to Spandau Prison, and shoot you the next morning."

23

I left Trask and checked out of the hotel and caught the train from Charing Cross to Folkestone, the night boat to Vlissingen, and a Dutch train to the German frontier. The first test of my Joseph William Hunter credentials came in a wooden customs hall in Bentheim.

My passport was being scrutinized before a Kaiser Wilhelm mustache. The owner of the mustache was an apparent *Bratwurst* and lager fiend of serious proportions, which no doubt was why this infantry captain was in a customs hall and not a trench on the Western Front. He was settled behind a heavy wooden table, and half a dozen times he glanced from the face in his hand to the face standing before him.

He knew I spoke German, from the few words we'd exchanged so far.

I was prepared as a next step to present a fine forgery of a letter of passage and endorsement full of high praise for the bearer, Joseph W. Hunter, from *seine Exzellenz* Baron Alfons Mumm von Schwarzenstein, the Foreign Office minister who manipulated propaganda abroad by manipulating journalists from neutral countries. But before I had the chance, the mustache rose, not a preferred task of the body it was attached to, and the captain moved off and disappeared through a door at the end of the hall.

I did have my Mauser beneath my coat, but with German travelers all around and armed guards on the platform outside, I did not see a good outcome from a breakdown of my credentials.

The captain returned and did not sit. He was breathing heavily. My passport was not visible.

Now he caught his breath.

"Herr Hunter," he said, smiling a little. Kaiser mustaches sometimes made it tough to read a smile. He was being either friendly or sardonic. "I think that has not always been your name," he said in German.

If he had *Cobb* in his head as an alternative, things would shortly get hot. He had not immediately brought anyone back with him, but maybe he was waiting for a couple of boys from the platform to make their way through the crowd.

I played the other alternative. "You are shrewd, Captain," I said in my own best German. "I was born Josef Wilhelm Jäger."

He nodded, keeping that little smile. "I suspected so," he said.

Then he dipped into his breast pocket and removed my passport. He handed it to me. "Welcome home," he said.

After a whispered word from my new German pal, the baggage inspectors gave my suitcase and Gladstone only a perfunctory look and I left the hall and boarded the train to Berlin. I suspected the *Kapitän*'s question about my name was indeed a shrewd guess. Clearer to me was that Joseph W. Hunter was on an approved list in a back room in Bentheim, and that only could have been arranged by Stockman.

Ten hours later, with evening coming on, the train pulled into the Bahnhof Friedrich-Strasse and I stepped out onto the platform, beneath a great, steel-trussed vault of glass, and I heard the sound of men singing. The other platform was loading a regiment of soldiers wrapped in cartridge belts and knapsacks, their rifles slung over their shoulders, their field gray uniforms blending into the twilight. Their voices rang to the high vault above them.

The tune was what struck me first. It was straight from the marquee on Stockman's lawn, straight from his little stage show with Zeppelin accompaniment. These German soldiers were singing a melody that would chill any Brit with national pride: "God Save the King." But the tune had its own words here; it was also used in the unofficial national anthem of the German Empire, *"Heil dir im Siegerkranz."* "Hail to thee in victor's crown."

These boys were deep into the song already as they queued into the train carriages along the platform, heading for the Western Front. *"Heilige Flamme, glüh', Glüh' und erlösche nie,"* they sang. *"Fürs Vaterland!"* "Holy flame glow, glow and extinguish not, for Fatherland."

I strode off down the platform while the boys sang on, dewy-eyed warriors, "standing valiant for one man"—Willie the Second—"gladly fighting and bleeding for throne and empire."

I went down the stairs and out one of the vaulted south doors and into a Benz landaulette taxi. I paid the driver well to do an odd thing: go just a few blocks, let me check one bag into a hotel while he waited with my other bag—I didn't want the Baden people to see me walk in with two bags and then out with one—and then drop me with the second bag at a second hotel less than three hundred yards away.

The Baden had the same profile as the Faulkner's, four storeys and six bays, with its own commercial enterprise sharing the frontage, in this case an international newsstand advertising my Chicago rival, no less, the *Daily News*, above the door.

I left my suitcase in the waiting taxi and checked in with the Gladstone. As soon as I was in the room I opened the bag and took out the contraband in the false bottom. Included now was a branded, compact combination tool, consisting of a handle with four screwdriver blades and a flat-edged metal end to tap a small nail.

The wooden wardrobe Trask recommended I utilize was sitting against the wall. The Baden, the Faulkner's, the Tavistock. I suspected the Anglo-American spy boys had a hand in all these for their own select clientele. But neither could they fully trust the staff. I pried the baseboard loose on the wardrobe with the thinnest of the flat screwdriver blades, put the Luger, its holster and box of shells, and the German officer credentials and his tightly folded uniform inside. I replaced the board and tapped it in securely.

The Mauser stayed in the small of my back. A very bad thing to be caught with, but a necessary thing to perhaps keep from being caught.

The tool went with me. I'd put it into my toilet case. It was an innocent enough object in a room where nothing hidden could be found by using it.

And then I was pulling up to the front of the Adlon, a vast neo-classical box with a mansard roof of green slate. The doorman was uniformed in Prussian blue, the bellhops and page boys in lighter livery of Egyptian blue, one of the latter toting my suitcase behind me with white gloves as the former swept an arm toward the revolving door, where I spun through into the marble and gilt lobby.

My first thought was of Trask's words. The Kaiser's favorite hotel was crawling with agents. Just making my way to registration I noticed some serious candidates. Conversing by one of the sienna marble columns, a couple of guys with the wrong kind of tough-guy faces for their linen suits and patent leather shoes let their eyes slide my way; lounging in one of the settings of brocaded chairs in the reception area, two more broad-shouldered boys done up in tweeds gave me the quick once-over; standing isolated a few paces off the front desk, a close-shaved, hollow-cheeked, lean-and-hungry-looking Johnny wearing a dark gray three-piece and a wing collar openly stared at me. I had to stop looking at the boys who were looking at me so I wouldn't look suspicious to them. Whoever was an agent in this joint was going to do his job and I had to do mine.

I merely spoke my name to the frock-coated boss of the rosewood front desk and he turned instantly to the wall of pigeonholes behind him. This stirred up my wariness again, though their knowing me at once could have been a reassuring sign, suggesting that my coming here at the arrangement of Sir Albert—who surely had the blessing and good wishes of the German Foreign Office—made me a trust-worthy guest.

The frock-coat withdrew my key and an envelope and handed them both to me with a nod of the head. I hoped for something more from my mother. But my name on the outside of the envelope was not in her hand. It was written with a heavy, broad-nibbed stroke. A man's hand. I tucked it away until I was in my room.

Which was on the top floor, the fourth. The floor attendant bowed his way out of the two-room suite and I locked the door and put down my bag. The place was done in Empire style with the furniture in the sitting room all standing on animal paws, from the scroll-armed chair to the divan to the side table to the desk beside the bedroom door.

I stepped into the bedroom, where, fortunately, the mahogany bed, with gold Etruscan helmets on the headboard, had no mammalian touches. For decor I definitely preferred the Baden, which had been done in unpretentious German vernacular.

The drapes were open. I crossed to the glass door, which opened onto a narrow balcony, a wrought-iron balustrade, and the Unter den Linden beyond. *Under the linden* indeed. The street's wide median was thick with linden trees. I angled to my left and gazed upon still more Empire.

The Brandenburg Gate. The Germans' vast sandstone version of the entrance to the Acropolis, its half dozen passage walls fronted with Doric columns and bearing up the bewinged goddess of Victory— *Victoria*, appropriately enough—standing in her chariot, driving four chargers, and hoisting a standard of the Imperial Eagle and the Iron Cross. It was lit with electric light from below, its copper turned victoriously gold but splashed with black shadows. I figured Willie must make a frequent pilgrimage the thousand yards west from his palace at the other end of Unter den Linden to see his own fate writ large up there on the Brandenburg.

Beyond the Gate was the vast linden canopy of the Tiergarten, once the private hunting ground of the prince-electors but now Berlin's centerpiece public park.

I closed the drapes, sat on the side of the bed, and switched on my own, small, night-table splash of electric light. I opened the envelope that had been left for Joe Hunter. It was signed *Sir Albert*. It read: *Dear Mr. Hunter, I will ring you in your rooms in the vicinity of nine this evening. I would be pleased to have a drink with you in the lobby bar.*

At nine o'clock exactly, the phone rang.

24

At five minutes past nine I was sitting where Stockman instructed me to sit, arriving there in the way he instructed me to arrive, by speaking his name to the bartender, a clean-shaven elderly man in an Adlon-emblemed dinner jacket and black tie. The man immediately left his post and led me to the end of the room that looked onto Unter den Linden. We turned to the right and went to the farthest corner, beyond the last window. I sat in one of a pair of facing armchairs, my back to the wall. The chairs, like all the drink-and-conversation-facilitating furniture in the place, were dark Spanish leather with cabriole legs and curving crests and arms.

"*Ein Joppenbier, bitte,*" I said, ordering a fine, odd German beer made in Danzig, and he nodded and disappeared.

Stockman had arranged for us to be private. This dim, far-corner setup seemed designed for that. At the nearest cluster of chairs and table, before the windows, four young German officers sat huddled close, drinking. Their *feldgrau* was fresh. From that and from the intensity of their drinking and the bloom of their cheeks it was clear they'd not yet seen battle but were soon to be shipped out to the front.

I watched them talking low, laughing a couple of times, but in a subdued way, and then talking again, and now they sat back, first one and then the others, thinking quietly, inwardly, and drinking for a moment as if they were each alone, and now they resumed talking.

A few minutes passed, and then Stockman's towering figure swooped into the bar and headed in my direction. He was dressed in a German-style informal evening suit with silk-faced lapels and a double-breasted waistcoat. I rose to greet him and we shook hands with a nodded hello. He'd arrived before my beer did. As soon as he and I settled onto our chairs—he with his back to the young officers—the bartender showed up, though empty-handed.

"What are you having?" Stockman asked.

"A *Joppenbier*," I said.

He looked at the bartender, and with a soft little nod he held up two fingers. The man vanished instantly.

"You know the beers," he said.

"Some."

"A German will order a *Joppenbier*. Not so often an outsider."

"I am German," I said.

He made exactly the same small, familiar nod he'd just used with the bartender. "Are you not an American as well?" His voice was as gentle as the nod.

"Yes."

"Is that possible?" he said.

I needed a good answer for that and a quick one, to seem sincere, and I tried to think fast. The bartender rescued me by appearing with our beers.

He put two white, lidless steins on the small, polished mahogany table between the chairs. The beers had come very quickly after Stockman's order. Which meant the bartender had deliberately kept mine back until Sir Albert arrived. I was right about the familiarity between them. Not to mention the barman made the delivery himself, even as a couple of black-coated waiters were working the rest of the room. Our Sir Albert was a celebrity here.

Stockman leaned forward and took up his stein as the bartender vanished. I picked up mine as well. Its only decoration was the hotel crest in gilt: the planet earth, upon which sat the Imperial Eagle of the German Empire and below which, in an unfurled banner, were the words *Adlon Oblige*.

He offered his stein across the table and I touched his with mine. We neither of us spoke a toast.

The beer was dark—very dark, nearly black—and it had a pretty stiff kick, and it was heavy in the mouth, almost like syrup.

Stockman put his stein down, as did I.

"So?" he said.

I was unsure enough of my true standing with him that the monosyllable seemed ominous, as if he were trying to bluff me into a confession of something he suspected but could not specify. I'd used that trick myself with some of the stupider Chicago politicians.

I had no choice but to proceed as if everything was just fine between us. "Is it possible to be both American and German?"

"That is my question," he said.

"Can I speak honestly?" I said.

"For as long as we sit in this bar tonight, I would like that to be the rule for us both."

That he would assert this—and with a quickness and vibrancy that seemed utterly sincere—made my breath catch in its ambiguity. Either trust was growing between us or he was laying a trap.

He leaned near. "How much of a journalist are you?"

This didn't sound good. But once more I had no choice.

I said, "I am a journalist whose intention is to properly represent a country, a *Kultur*. What is the measure of such a journalist?"

Stockman considered this for a moment, his eyes intently fixed on mine. He said, "Forgive me for speaking as I am about to. But we are being honest."

"Of course," I said.

"I say this not from a distrust of what you have just declared. But perhaps a concern over what you might include in such a story, no matter how noble its intention." He paused. He let this soak in.

He didn't say he trusted me as Joseph W. Hunter, but I liked his disavowal of distrust. Still, I knew his method. I waited for the threat. I was interested to hear it.

"I am a powerful man," he said. "Here and in England and abroad, even in America. I have associates in all those places. Friends. And they exercise my power on my behalf." He paused to let me work out the implication. I figured his next step was to clarify what offense on my part would engage his friends.

It was clear enough already. I decided it would be a good strategy to anticipate him. "Sir Albert," I said, "I will never publish, never write, never repeat a word you say to me unless doing so is explicitly discussed and agreed upon between us."

"I am glad to hear it," he said.

He sat back. He laid his elbows on the arms of the chair. He intertwined his fingers before him and rubbed first one palm and then the other with the opposite thumb. His hands came to rest.

He seemed satisfied.

"You were going to say," he said. "Honestly."

We'd returned to the question of being both an American and a German.

I had to be very careful now. I'd said the right things so far. I sensed the possibility that I'd won his trust. At least for this evening's conversation. There were things on his mind. He wanted to talk, even still sober, though I had to figure he'd already been drinking this evening. But something about him seemed almost needy. *Careful*, I said to myself. His commitment to Germany and its interests would be fine to hear. But I needed to know his *plans*. I was tempted to try to guide him there directly. Incrementally but directly. But even in this state of mind, even if he'd had a few drinks, he wasn't a dirty alderman ready to brag about his doings. This man was dangerous.

So was I. But I had to be careful.

"I like America," I said. "I grew up there. You cannot help but feel a certain allegiance to the place where you are reared, particularly if it rewards you in many ways. Rewards and even nurtures you."

"Like a benign stepfather," Stockman said.

"Like a benign stepfather," I said. "But there are stronger bonds than those."

"It is not his blood in your veins," he said.

I nodded. He'd leaped in to finish my thought, seemed to want to answer this question himself.

But he said no more. He leaned forward and took up his stein and sat back again. He drank.

I did likewise.

"Eventually you have to choose," I said, to finish the thought.

He took the stein away from his lips. "Do you like this special German beer?" he asked.

"I do," I said.

"Some would say it is too strong in its taste, too thick on the tongue."

Stockman seemed in an odd mood. I wasn't sure if it was just beer he was talking about.

I said, "I don't acknowledge the idea of 'too strong.' It does things the beers of other countries cannot. This is good. No other beer in the world tastes both of the earthiness of malt but also of a sweet something that reminds one of nothing other than a fine port wine."

This made Stockman straighten a little, consult his palate. He smiled. "So it does," he said.

We drank some more.

"Blood is stronger than nurturing," Stockman said, following an associative track in his head that surfaced and submerged and surfaced again.

"Blood is stronger," I said.

"Blood," he said, "does not make itself new with each generation. It is perpetual. It is eternal."

I nodded. He fell silent, working out his thoughts inwardly. I was tempted to again affirm my agreement with him, but I kept my own silence. I didn't want to interrupt his process.

"Civilization is borne onward by a current of blood," he said.

He was speaking German now.

He stopped again. But he did not seem inward. He was watching my eyes, as if waiting for me to comment. Was he testing me?

"The truth you just spoke," I said, also in German. "Is it a quotation from von Herder?"

He smiled.

"Someone else?" I asked.

"My own thoughts," he said.

"Excellent," I said. "I'm sorry I'm not taking any of this down."

"Nor should you," he said. "When I am commenting for the public record, I will tell you."

We were speaking only German now.

"I am eager," I said.

The officers beyond him laughed.

Stockman glanced over his shoulder.

"They go with joy," he said. "Our young men."

He paused. He heard himself. *Unsere jungen Männer*, he'd said. *Our* young men, not *their* young men. As if he had already chosen between his two countries.

So he added now: "That is to say, they *all* go with joy. The young men of both sides."

I nodded. Strictly speaking, his correction remained ambiguous.

He took a long pull on his *Joppenbier*. I could sense his mind freely associating as he did.

He lowered his stein. "Do you know there are three million socialists in the German Empire? The other sixty million Germans detest the beliefs of socialists."

He paused and let me take that in.

I kept quiet.

He said, "No doubt the socialists detest the beliefs of all the rest of us."

This time he did not pause to ambiguate his pronoun.

He said, "So do you know what the socialists are doing, now that the country is at war?" He began to raise his stein, but he immediately lowered his hand again, letting go of the rhetorical question. "You must understand. These are *German* socialists. This is the German Empire we are speaking of. The three million German socialists have joined together with the rest of the country. They are sending their sons to fight. Their sons are going to war for Germany. With joy."

Now he took the deferred drink.

The stein came down lightly. Empty. He leaned forward and put it on the table between us. He lifted his face to me without sitting back.

"There are beliefs," he said. "And there are overarching beliefs."

Glaube and *Überglaube.* I'd never heard the second word. I figured he'd made it up by piecing two words together. The people of Willie's empire loved to do that, with two words and sometimes with even more. To my mind this was a *Sprachenperle* of German. A pearl of the language. A lollapalooza feature of this *Kultur.*

I realized my stein was empty and I leaned forward and placed it beside his.

He was still suspended over the table.

We were very near each other.

"Blood," I said—*Blut*—to identify the trumping *Überglaube* the German socialists and nonsocialists shared.

"Blood," he said.

"*Blutweltanschauung*," I said. Bloodworldview. I'd expanded Immanuel Kant's famously invented word even further.

Stockman laughed.

He and I pulled away from each other as a waiter arrived and set two full steins of the black, strong Danzig beer on the table and vanished at once, without a word.

The refill had been automatic. They'd been watching and knew what Sir Albert expected.

"You have *Kneiperuhm*," I said. Tavernfame. It was entirely my own word. He laughed again.

We focused for the moment on a long, warming pull of the beer. I'd said the right things so far. I'd made him laugh, and I'd done it by acting German. I could simply keep that up. But it would get me no further. Exploring the *Weltanschauung* of his allegiance to the Germans was way short of what I needed. I needed to know what he was *doing* about it.

At any moment he could reach his limit, either in time or in number of drinks, and call this off. And he could reach a certain point, as drinkers often do, when he would turn from talkative to silent. It was time to push him a little, even at the risk of making him suspicious. It was my work in Chicago for the *Post-Express* to get local prosecutors and lawyers, criminals and politicians, working stiffs and working girls to talk about things they'd rather keep to themselves. A bar and a strong drink were as useful as my notepad and my Conklin. Those and Polonius's good advice, spoken at the Duke of York's just the other night, "By indirections find directions out."

I stuck to German. I said, "I have lately asked myself what I will do if the United States enters the war on the British side."

Stockman lowered his stein. "What did you answer yourself?"

"I would leave the United States," I said.

He nodded.

"I think it is the right answer," I said.

He stopped nodding. He kept his eyes on me but he did not speak.

I could not read him. This could be a sympathetic stare. It could be critical. I doubted the latter, but there were attitudes on a continuum between those two—several of them bearing risks—that would influence what I said next. I was improvising. I was tempted to ask him outright if *he* had now left. If he was in Germany to stay.

Not yet.

"I have no close relatives here," I said.

"That does not matter," he said.

"I have to confess," I said.

I took a bolt of beer. I let him wait for the rest, as he'd done with me a few times already. Then I said, "I was exhilarated by the Zeppelins flying over us on Friday night. I knew where they were going and what they intended to do, but nevertheless . . ."

I stopped again, as if I did not know how to express what I wanted to say. That the bombing of London did not lessen the exhilaration.

Stockman said, "Nevertheless." Not to prompt me to say more but to permit me to leave the thing unsaid. We already understood each other.

But I nudged him. "Do you disapprove?"

"I do not," he said.

"Please don't mistake me," I said. "I admired your speech."

He smiled just a little. "You were very shrewd to understand." And he said in English, quoting my own words, "My speech was 'to quell a panic, not to legitimize a foreign policy.'"

I said, "I find myself thinking about the Zeppelins. How they might end this war quickly."

Stockman leaned back deeper into his chair. His mouth tightened, its line vanishing beneath his mustache.

I thought: *He's withdrawing now, for my mentioning this.* But then the alternative: *He's thinking of his own mission somehow.*

With his mouth still tight, he made one small nod.

And I knew my second thought was right. *My* mission in Germany was entirely about whatever was in his head at that very moment.

I said, "They are beautiful and terrifying but something still seems missing. The English close their curtains and go to the basements and have polite conversation."

Stockman made a short, sharp smile that came and went so quickly that I could consider it only after it was gone.

And now the young German officers cried out as one for another round of beer. Politely. *Vier Biere, bitte.* They laughed at their harmony.

Stockman swung his face toward them, showing his chiseled profile, watching them in his periphery. Or watching me.

I had to back off.

Stockman looked my way again.

He lifted his stein, pausing it before him, pushing it ever so slightly in my direction. He was saying it was time to take a drink and change the subject.

I lifted my own beer in exactly the same way, saying, *Okay.* Saying, *Of course.* And we quaffed.

When our steins were down, Stockman squared his shoulders a little and said, "Madam Cobb is resting from her journey."

He said this in English. On this subject we would speak English.

"She asked that I instruct you to visit her rehearsal at the Lessing Theater tomorrow morning," he said.

I worked hard to understand his suddenly flat tone. Perhaps he was still suspicious of my arm around Isabel Cobb. But if that were truly a serious thing between us, surely this whole conversation would not have gone as it had so far.

He paused. But he had the air of a churning mind. Maybe he had to get a certain number of quaffs in him to stir all that back up.

Then he said, "She had an unsettling moment on Friday."

He was focused on the scene I feared was still working in him, though his lead suggested a different concern from mine.

"She nearly fainted," I said, glad to gently reinforce my excuse for touching her.

"She has died a thousand times on stage," Stockman said, "but she has seen very little of that in real life."

I heard my mother's words in this. She'd been working on him.

"This was particularly difficult," he said.

I nodded. I kept my mouth shut.

Stockman looked me in the eyes. I did not see suspicion. I saw him standing before his constituents, needing to act.

"Martin was a brave man," he said, with an unmistakable tear-stifling tremor in his voice. He paused. It sounded convincing. He was a good actor.

I caught myself. He could be acting, but he could have legitimate feelings. In this present job of mine—in my job as a reporter, as well—I had to stay alert to the complexity of the human mind and heart. You tell yourself that your subject or your enemy is unremittingly bad, and you will fail. More than fail—you'll compromise the value of what you're doing, of who you are.

"Too brave sometimes," Stockman said. There it was again in his voice, the snag at the man's braveness, the breathy slide to finish the sentence.

He looked away. He took a moment.

He didn't have to put on real feelings for me about a hired thug, not in this situation, not in any situation. He wasn't acting.

"He fell from the tower," Stockman said, composing himself with a statement of the obvious.

It was he who had initiated this further explanation of the death to me. That was Stockman the spy. I'd gotten near to his secret self a few moments ago, touching on the Zeppelins, and it prompted him to forestall any suspicion about the other big event from Friday. But he was sorry now he'd brought it up. He really couldn't explain it anyway.

"He'd become careless," he said, with a soft but clear thump of finality.

I could let the silence drag on to put the pressure on him to explain it further. But I knew the answer anyway. I said, "I'm very sorry about your man."

We took another drink. Stockman said, "But it's put Madam Cobb in a state."

"It's good she has her work," I said, finishing the sentence in my head: *nailing you.*

"I suppose," Stockman said.

And the four young German voices that had harmonized to call for a beer, the voices of these newly minted officers about to go to war, took up together once more, singing. "*Heil dir im Siegerkranz, Herrscher des Vaterlands.*" The beginning of the anthem for the German Empire. "Hail to thee in victor's crown, Ruler of the Fatherland."

Stockman did not turn to them. He closed his eyes.

The enlisted men's voices at the train station had rung to the rafters. These officers sang softly, thoughtfully, as if to a child, or to a fiancée. Even the next lines. *Heil, Kaiser, dir.* "Hail, Emperor, to you."

Stockman, of course, had himself sung this very tune on Friday night in the wake of the Zeppelins. "God Save the King." But this time the song's lyrics flowed with pure German blood. His eyes still closed, Stockman began to sing. "*Fühl in des Thrones Glanz . . .*" "Feel the throne's great glow . . ."

Other voices from throughout the bar also began to sing. ". . . *Die hohe Wonne ganz.*" "Fully the highest joy."

Stockman opened his eyes, and he rose from his chair.

I rose too. I was in character. I was Josef Wilhelm Jäger. And yes I sang, my body suddenly prickling into gooseflesh. "*Liebling des Volks zu sein.*" "To be the people's beloved one."

The bar was filled with voices now, rising together in blood and empire. "*Heil, Kaiser, dir!*"

And when we had done, the bar fell into a ringing silence. The silence held for a moment and a moment more and still another moment, and then bodies began to rustle and settle.

Voices resumed, low and murmuring.

A glass clinked from the bar.

Stockman sat down.

I sat down.

My chest was still swelled with the Zeppgas of a Bloodbonding.

I was far from home. The further irony struck me hard now: the precious melody for both Brits and Germans was also the melody for "My Country 'Tis of Thee." Sweet land of liberty, of thee I sing.

As the sole American sitting in a German hotel bar, I came to this thought with no gooseflesh, no urge to sing. I'd already sung tonight. You can call it blood. You can call it nationhood or empire or Fatherland or family. All of it was, at its heart, the terrible, deep, human yearning for an identity. You find it by being part of something larger. Even an impromptu gathering of voices in a bar.

"You must be tired," Stockman said.

"Yes."

"As am I."

We'd sung together. There was no more to say tonight.

We rose.

I reached into my pocket for my wallet and he waved away the gesture.

"Thank you," I said.

I circled the table and he stepped from behind it to face me. We shook hands.

But before I could move away, he put his hand on my arm. He leaned near me. He smelled of *Joppenbier*, as no doubt did I. He said, in German, "They bring only isolated neighborhood disruptions. Commonplace, soon enough."

25

I slept and woke and slept and woke again, working Stockman's curtain line over and over in my head. I assumed this had been his response to my leading comment about the Zepp attacks missing something. He'd initially been quite professional and had clammed up. Maybe he and I singing together about the joy of the German Empire had made it personal. The thought that followed his fleeting smile kept working in him, and he finally said a little something. I'd gotten a glimpse at his mission, though it was as fleeting as the smile.

Too fleeting. So the problem with the Zeppelins he'd been studying was that their attacks were too isolated? True enough. Smart enough. But everyone in London knew to fear the day when the attacks were carried out by thirty airships at a time instead of two, when the fires and crumbling buildings would appear all over the city instead of in a few isolated neighborhoods. The Germans simply had to build more of these machines. Which they presumably were gearing up to do.

This was a big idea but an obvious one. I couldn't figure why it would require their secret ally in the British Parliament to come to Berlin. The trip certainly wasn't about being with my mother. Whatever he felt for her, that was a useful ruse. He'd discovered that the British secret service was sniffing around, but his boys scrubbed down the castle overnight just fine. He didn't have to take off in the middle of the night. Indeed, it would have been swell for him if the authorities had stormed in and found him reading a book in the library of a house that didn't hold a single shred of the evidence they sought against him. Perhaps he would have waited another day to depart if Jeremy hadn't shown up, but it had already been planned. He was here for something crucial. This wasn't about building more Zepps faster.

My mind gave out somewhere near dawn.

I woke for good a couple of hours later and headed for the Lessing Theater.

It sat in massive isolation on an odd wedge of land, pressing up against the *Stadtbahn* railway viaduct on one side and looking out onto the River Spree on the other. It resembled a cathedral more than a theater, with twin, flat-topped towers and a central dome. Fronting the building was a portico with four sets of double columns and four more sets above, holding a gabled roof.

I passed through the portico and into the lobby. It was dim and cool inside, for a late morning in August, and I was immediately stopped by a vaguely uniformed old man stationed on a chair. The mention of my name drew an instant nod toward the doors directly ahead of me.

I crossed the lobby floor and went up a short flight of stairs and stood before the center door into the auditorium. My hand hesitated at the handle, as I heard a familiar voice projecting not just to the back row but beyond.

I opened the door very gently and only far enough to slip through and step sideways into the shadow of the aisle behind the last row of the orchestra seats. The house lights were off but failed to shroud the auditorium's golden rococo flourishes on its proscenium and on the facings of the side balconies and loge boxes. The stage was uniformly bright from the electric utility lights. Downstage center was my mother.

She was to-being and not-to-being. A few rows before me, a man with broad shoulders was standing with his head angled backward sharply, as if looking into the dark above. Concentrating. *Herr Regisseur*, no doubt. The director. The estimable Victor Barnowsky, the rival of Max Reinhardt and the creative director of the Lessing, who was personally guiding the acclaimed Isabel Cobb's Shakespearean adventure in Bard-loving Berlin.

My mother was dressed for rehearsal in knickers and a white shirt. She rolled to the end of her soliloquy, and as soon as she heard the fair Ophelia approach, Barnowsky lowered his head and said in good English, but with a heavy German accent, "Sweet prince, may I stop you now, *bitte?*"

My mother gracefully fell from character, moved the few steps to the very edge of the stage, and bowed toward her director. "Of course, *mein Regisseur,*" she said.

Barnowsky bowed in return.

A blond actress in shirtwaist and skirt—the fair Ophelia, no doubt—who had appeared upstage, quietly withdrew.

Barnowsky said, "If, please, we may hear this speech in your German. Our German cast will join you tomorrow, but I was hoping to listen just a little. Yes?"

Mother bowed once more, returned to her place, lifted her face, closed her eyes, took a deep breath as she slid back into her Hamlet— her Schlegel-voiced Hamlet—opened her eyes again, and began: "*Sein oder Nichtsein; das ist hier die Frage.*"

Barnowsky watched her for a few lines more and then lifted his face once again to the theatrical heavens, simply to listen.

She was good. The only significant German she knew were the lines in plays. But she could mimic anything. Anyone. Any feeling. Any nuance of any feeling. No matter what the words were. I knew the language well enough now to hear and think and feel in German, and she was very good. And I was struck by this: in the German language, Hamlet's infamous hesitation to kill his murderous uncle was even harder to swallow.

But she would pull off that actor's challenge too, I had no doubt.

She ached and agonized and yearned on until at last she said, "*Still. Die reizende Ophelia. Nymphe, schließ in dein Gebet all meine Sünden ein.*"

She fell silent.

Barnowsky began to clap. Slowly, heavily, and then faster and faster. My mother became my mother and she beamed from the stage. She bowed. She curtsied. She put her hand on her heart.

"Excellent," Barnowsky said. "Now let us have an interval to rest and to eat."

My mother slipped offstage right. Barnowsky moved to the stage-right aisle and started down it. I figured he would surely lead me to her. I stepped through the center entrance to the orchestra and hustled along to follow him. From an opening just this side of the orchestra loge, my mother emerged. She and the director embraced in the way famous directors and famous actresses who were not sleeping together but felt a legitimate warmth for each other during the lifetime of a production typically did.

I slowed. I was watching them in profile, though my mother was turned slightly toward me. She would see me soon enough. I stopped only a few feet away.

The embrace ended.

As Barnowsky was saying, "You are everything in this great adventure that I imagined and still more," her eyes flitted briefly to me and then back to her director.

"As are you, *mein Liebling*," she said.

And now she made a little bit of a show at noticing me.

"Ah, Victor, may I introduce you to my chronicler," she said.

He was turning to me.

"The man I mentioned to you," she said.

I stepped forward, extending my hand to him.

He took it strongly.

Barnowsky had a square face and heavy eyebrows and seemed on the surface to be a roughhouser, reminding me of Ike Bloom's boys from the First Ward. I liked this about him, seeing as he was also one of Gorky's boys and Strindberg's boys and Shakespeare's boys.

"Joseph Hunter," I said.

"I am Victor Barnowsky," he said. "Welcome to the Lessing Theater."

"I don't mean to intrude on your lunch," I said.

"Not at all," he said. "I have matters to attend."

My mother said, "I told Victor you and I needed to catch up. Your deadline approaches."

Barnowsky turned to his Hamlet. He clicked his heels and bowed.

Mother led me in silence back the way she'd come, past the wings staircase and along a corridor to her dressing room.

There were two places at the makeup table and mirror. She sat at one of them and motioned me to an overstuffed chair next to a lacquer dressing screen inlaid with mother-of-pearl cherry trees and geisha girls.

Her first words were abruptly *in medias res*, either from her flair for the dramatic or from a gathering fright at what we were doing; I could not tell which. "I had no choice," she said. "He woke me and said to pack and we steamed away into the night."

"I got your note that morning," I said.

"Good."

"Are you okay?"

She sat rigidly erect and clapped her hand onto her chest. "Okay? I *wish* my flesh were too too solid to melt and thaw or drown or be shot or however you spies deal with each other."

Flair, not fright.

"You sound okay to me," I said.

"I sound terrified," she said.

"We need to talk straight," I said.

Something seemed to let go in her. Her uprightness in the chair eased abruptly. She looked down. She looked back up. "Of course," she said. "Forgive me for actually enjoying all this."

"Are you?"

"Yes." This came out softly. Almost tenderly. Self-reflectively.

I was afraid I knew why.

Before I could ask about Sir Albert, she slipped into what I took to be another place in her mind: "What happened to that man in the courtyard?"

"The dead man?"

"Of course the dead man."

She had no need to know about Jeremy.

"He fell from the tower," I said.

"How, for heaven's sake?"

For a moment I found myself in the same fix Stockman had been in with me on this subject. How to explain it without explaining it. But of course, invoking *him* was my solution.

"I don't know," I said. "I asked Stockman the same thing and all he'd say was that the man was careless."

She nodded. She looked away from me. Something had come over her I couldn't identify.

I said, "He was a tough guy in Sir Al's employ."

Then it struck me.

I *did* know what was going on in her.

I said, "Did you ask Stockman about it when you were alone?"

Mother looked back to me.

"Yes," she said.

What a life I'd lived with this woman. No wonder we couldn't say anything to each other straight. If it was about anything of importance, I could not hear even a single word from her without trying to read its subtext, hear the persona behind it, figure out if that was really her or somebody she'd simply decided to portray, figure out if there was ever a difference between those two things. *Yes*, she'd just said. And my first reading, my first hearing, my first figuring all told me that she was in love.

Or thought she was.

Or was playing at being.

Or just trying to test me. Or torture me.

Or all of that.

"And?" I said.

"He wept." The tone in her voice was familiar. From her two recent *yes*es. Soft. Not a whisper, but only a few vibrations above one. That tenderness again.

I thrashed about for something to say but nothing was coming to mind.

Then she said, still softly, "Is he an actor, do you suppose?"

Worse yet. She asked this as if she feared it. Her feelings for him were real, not put on out of a sense of drama.

I asked myself the same question. Last night seemed to offer a clear answer. But I was reluctant to admit it.

"Some sort of actor?" she said, pressing the question gently.

I didn't speak.

"I know what you sometimes think of me," she said. "But you said we should talk straight."

I did.

I saw something in her eyes that I'd seen often before about some man or other. But did I really? How do eyes say these things? There seem to be so few variables in eyes. I'd seen this supplicating look, this longing look, this I-need-you-to-believe-me-and-approve look, this I-need-you-to-look-the-other-way look. And in that lifelong, complex, recurring look I also could usually see her own recognition that those feelings I was seeing were, in her heart of hearts, put on. But this look now, in her dressing room at the Lessing Theater in Berlin in a time of war, though it showed all those old familiar things, also showed what seemed to be a new thing.

I would not label it.

Should I talk straight?

"He's acting to his constituents," I said.

"Yes."

"He's acting to Parliament and to his government. He's acting when he says he is loyal to Britain."

"Yes."

She waited for more.

She knew and I knew and she knew I knew that she was asking this in another sense.

Should I talk straight?

"No," I said. "I don't think he's an actor."

Tears filled her eyes.

We sat before each other like this for a long moment.

"One more bad guy," she whispered.

I certainly didn't expect her to leap to this. I didn't remember if I'd ever accused her. Of course I must have. It wasn't just leading men she had a weakness for. It was the bad ones. The drunken ones. The abusive ones. Or so it always had seemed to me.

She tried to shrug. "Of a different sort."

She turned to her mirror. She picked up a makeup towel and dabbed at her eyes.

She looked at me in the mirror.

"I'm an American," she said.

"I know you are."

"I'm a loyal American," she said.

"I know," I said.

She turned around to face me again. "But this isn't America's fight yet," she said. "Is it?"

I didn't say anything to that. Not for the moment.

She was mulling it over.

Then I offered, "That's what you and I are trying to help our country figure out."

That didn't exactly sound straight, even as I said it. Not fully. But it wasn't untrue.

We still didn't know what Stockman was up to, exactly. What he believed about country, about blood, about loyalty: these were just beliefs. He lived in a democracy. Mother and I lived in a democracy. We were working on behalf of a democratic society. In a democracy you can have any goddamn belief you want. When does having an idea make you an enemy?

But his beliefs were apparently in service to a country that was at war with a democracy.

What the hell was Stockman up to? With Germany. With my mother.

"What are you saying?" I asked her.

"I don't know what I'm saying. Except he wept for that dead man in the courtyard and I felt something for him. He is a hard man. I've seen that too. But he is equally a soft man. A vulnerable man. Do you know what that does to me?"

"You can back off from straight talk now," I said.

She stopped.

"I'm sorry," she said. "But this is all very difficult in ways I never expected."

"Then the best thing is to figure out exactly what he's doing here," I said.

One moment of silence passed between us, our eyes on each other, our circumstance settling in.

Then she said, "Yes."

This one was not soft.

She said, "He's meeting someone at four o'clock this afternoon. I wrote down what I know."

She dipped into the pocket of her knickers and handed me a piece of note paper with the Adlon crest. It read: *11 Schlesische-Strasse, Osthafen, Heinrich Reinauer Gewerblicher Einführer, 4 pm.*

I stared at this for a moment.

Heinrich Reinauer, Industrial Importer. An address in the East Harbor district.

Mother said, "He spoke German. That was all I could get."

I lifted my face. I didn't say anything as I shifted my gears. She was trying to make clear to me that she'd been a diligent spy, in spite of her feelings for our quarry.

I hesitated another moment.

She said, "He wrote that down and I had a chance to see it. Then I wrote it for you later. I didn't touch the note he made to himself."

"Spoke where?" I said. "To whom?"

"I don't know to whom. On the phone. He received a call late last night."

She didn't have to add "in the hotel room." His room or her room or their room. He received a call late. She was there. She was still there even later, when he stepped away, giving her the opportunity to read what he wrote.

Did he think he was in love with her, as well?

"I need to get as close to this meeting as I can," I said.

"You've come to the right place," she said. "Sit here." She pointed to the wooden chair next to hers.

I knew how to do this for myself, more or less, but it had been a long time and she was very good at it.

I rose. I sat.

She motioned and I turned the chair to face her.

The table and the mirror were a good seven feet long, the mirror rimmed in electric bulbs. She reached behind her to the far end of the table and pulled her makeup case in front of her. It was the shape of a miniature steamer trunk, the sealskin rubbed and scuffed and stained by thousands of nights at the theater. The case was an object of wonder from my childhood.

I needed this done. It was her case, her art. I could not refuse. How old was I when she first opened this case for me and made me up into some other child? I could not remember. I could not refuse. I waited with delight and with dread.

She lifted the lid and squared her chair around to me. With the tip of a forefinger she tilted my head to one side and then to the other, lifted my chin, lowered it. "We should do as little as we can get away with," she said.

"I agree."

"You may have a near encounter. We have to balance naturalness with a large enough adjustment he won't find you familiar."

"The meeting is near the docks."

She hummed a soft assent.

"You could use a different nose," she said. "Wash up."

She nodded me to the sink at the far side of the room. I took off my tie and my shirt. I washed with Castile soap. The water was warm. I dried.

When I returned and sat, she was bending into her case, looking hard at her choices. Her grease sticks were new and bought in London, with the English theater system of numbering.

While she pondered, I faced the mirror and rubbed on a thin coat of cold cream to my face and neck. When I was ready and facing her again, she'd made her choices. Using her left palm as a palette, she stroked down a large amount of Number 3, a skin color slightly darker than medium. Then she took up a stick of Number 13, reddish brown, and she began to incrementally blend and blend and blend it into her hand, darkening the Number 3.

"We'll give you some extended sun," she said. "It's August on the docks."

And she put her right hand to my face and began to apply my new skin, her fingertips working at my forehead, my cheeks, my chin, my eyes, my throat.

I thought: *I should have put on my own stage face. But the makeup has to be done well. I need to remember what she's doing, in case it needs doing again. For now, though, there's limited time and a lot at stake. She needs to do it.*

I clung to the necessity of it.

I hid in *thoughts*, in that chattery, abstract voice that you can talk with on the surface of your mind.

But the straight thing was: I didn't like her touch. Not this much of it. Boys have to come to that, at some point, where they stop their mothers from grooming them, dressing them, fussing over them, remaking them. And they have to stick to it. At some point it's all or nothing: I am what she wants me to be, or I am me.

I tried not to flinch.

I expected her to be talkative. She said nothing. I was grateful for that.

I thought about the Chicago Cubs.

Then she was rubbing mascaro into my beard, cutting its blackness with auburn, making it the color of certain black cats if you see them up close in the bright sunlight. This was done with a small toothbrush, for which I was also grateful.

She'd left my nose for last, which she'd been thoughtfully glancing at since the beginning. Now she built me a broken one with paste.

She said her first words through all of this. "I'm giving you the nose of a boxer," she said. "You wanted to be a boxer once, when you were thirteen and skinny."

I didn't reply.

She said no more.

She finished with the nose paste and blended it with my new skin tone, and she put a light coating of powder over everything she'd touched.

She sat back. She nodded at the mirror.

I turned. She'd made me into someone else. A half brother she birthed in some dressing room somewhere along the circuit before I was born and she gave it away. He'd boxed some but not well. Maybe he'd just brawled in bars. Not surprising.

I turned back to her. "Thanks," I said.

She nodded.

And then she said, "Look. You're a big boy. You know the score. However things turn out, I figure I had to do this." I knew at once she was talking about Albert. She said, "I'm either doing it for love or I'm doing it for my country."

26

Mother didn't expect that half brother of mine to have straightened himself out. She was ready to go off to the costume room for some stevedore's clothes. I thanked her for the offer and for the new face and I wished her well for her rehearsal, but I returned to the hotel, figuring to change into a two-piece blue-gray flannel suit Trask's boys had given me with the label of a Berlin tailor. Stockman hadn't seen Joe Hunter in this one. And it befit the way my brother had gotten on in the world, in spite of the knocks that gave him his nose. In the taxi back to the Adlon I settled into this character I'd become. What was his name? What was *my* name for the next few hours? Isaac. The hardworking stagehand and his wife knew whose baby he was, of course, receiving him straight from her hand. They called him Izzy, thinking of his mother by blood.

I slipped into the Adlon lobby, keeping my face down, and I went up to my floor and approached my room. It was early afternoon. The floor was quiet. Most everyone was out doing what they were visiting Berlin to do. I unlocked my door and pushed through.

A man was standing in the center of the sitting room.

He was my Cassius of the lobby, the lean and hungry, hollow-cheeked, staring man. He was facing the door, his hands folded before him just below his rib cage, as if he'd been waiting for me, though my actual impression of him was that only moments before I confronted him he'd sprung into this posture at my imminent entry.

I had no doubt he was discreetly searching my room. He was probably attuned to just such interruptions and had assumed this position at the first faint whisper of my approach along the corridor.

I made this rapid assessment in a comfortable, self-assured frame of mind, which vanished instantly when I realized I was standing before this guy with another man's face.

Hollow-Cheeks had even tilted his head a little as he contemplated this vaguely familiar but unexpected visage before him.

I had too many factors to think out—what should I say about my nose, if anything? could he see it was fake? what was this guy's frame of mind in being here? routine because of my connection to Stockman? staunchly suspicious, that being the attitude of the Foreign Office operatives at the Adlon no matter who the guest?—so many factors to think about that to hesitate long enough to think effectively would itself make me seem guilty of something. I recognized all this in the briefest of moments and I chose to wing it.

"Who are you?" I asked, faintly aggressive, in the most formal German I could muster.

"I am with the hotel," he said.

"I am staying at the hotel," I said. "In this room."

He hesitated a beat. He was doing the thinking now.

But it was about my nose, my complexion. He'd seen me pass through the lobby last night. He tilted his head again, in the other direction, and looked at me carefully.

"May I ask what brought you to the center of my sitting room floor?" I said.

His attention snapped from my nose to my eyes. I thought I saw a flicker of uncertainty in him.

Give him a punch, give him a pat. I stepped to him and offered my hand, making my voice go warm. "I'm Joseph Hunter."

He took my hand and shook it, still looking at me, still hesitating behind his eyes. Mother's makeup was good. He was trying to accept what he was seeing before him as me, given his impression from yesterday, when he'd directly seen my face only briefly and from ten or fifteen yards away.

I knew I'd eventually have to pay the piper if I didn't address this issue now. Izzy's face would vanish by tomorrow. The question was when I'd encounter this guy again.

"I am the assistant manager," he said.

We ended the handshake and I gave *him* a quick, overt once-over, saying, "*Herr* . . ." and leaving it for him to fill in his name.

"Wagner."

"Herr Wagner," I said. "What can I do for you?"

"I am here to make sure everything is correct in your room," he said.

He did not twinkle at the ambiguity. He kept his little joke to himself.

I did not let him know I was in on the gag. "That is very kind of you," I said. "Everything seemed to me to be in order."

He clicked his heels, but his eyes stayed fixed on my face. And then he said, "Good day, Herr Hunter."

I stepped aside for him and he went out of the room and closed the door softly behind him.

27

I did not check the room. Thanks to the Hotel Baden, I had no secrets here. I regretted showing my altered face; I could have used the chance to think a bit before reacting to Wagner. I was suddenly afraid I'd winged it into a threshing machine. I probably should have dealt immediately with the whole issue of my appearance, one way or another.

But it was done. I changed my suit and slipped watchfully through the Adlon lobby again, more than an hour before Stockman's appointed time. There was no sign of Herr Wagner.

Outside, I put on a charcoal-gray, snap-visored golf cap, and I stepped into a taxi and told the driver simply to drive down Unter den Linden till I said otherwise. I watched out the back and made sure we were not being followed, and then I directed us to the address on Schlesische-Strasse.

The street ran parallel to the Spree near the old Silesian Gate, which was now an elevated railway stop. Number 11 was a large brick building on an even larger lot at a corner, and I instructed the driver to pass it by and drop me at the next corner, at Ufer-Strasse, a hundred yards farther on.

I stepped out of the taxi. At my back was the harbor's train-track-laced jumble of grain elevators and package freight terminals and petroleum tanks, the whole area oddly pristine for a dock, having opened only a couple of years ago. Before me, Schlesische-Strasse emerged from the upriver shadow of the massive brick Oberbaum Bridge, which carried the elevated across the Spree.

The street was a little sleepy at this hour, only a few local boys passing through on foot. Both sides were lined with variations on Reinauer's joint, blood-clot-red brick boxes holding trade offices and light warehousing.

I pulled my Waltham.

A quarter after three. Forty-five minutes to go.

I crossed the street to approach his building from the opposite side. I had to find a way to watch the building, for now and maybe for later. And just in case, I had to find a way in.

The frontage was all private business with simply a narrow stoop in the center going up to double slab doors. The facade's array of windows suggested a very high ceiling on both the first and second floors, and two more standard office floors above.

I walked past, crossed at the intersection, turned at once to the left and crossed Schlesische-Strasse, heading south, away from the river, on Cuvry-Strasse. This western side of the building had the same pattern of windows as in the front, though without a doorway. I approached its southwest corner and slowed my walk after I could tell in my periphery that I was just clear of the building.

I stopped and pulled out a cigarette, and I twisted away to light it, before looking where I wanted, just in case I was being observed. Before me was an alleyway that ran along the back of this block of buildings. The big brick box immediately at hand had half a dozen sixty-gallon galvanized refuse cans lined up at the closer of two alley doors.

My cigarette was lit and I casually straightened and turned around, waving the flame from my match. As if incidentally, I looked toward Number 11. The alley had ended at my feet. On the other side of the street was a large, macadamized delivery lot. It lay behind Reinauer's building, which comprised two wide bays of loading docks, with raised concrete platforms and metal canopies.

On the nearest platform a couple of Reinauer's boys in overalls slouched against a stack of pallets. They were also taking this moment to light up, sharing a match.

They hadn't noticed me yet.

I'd seen enough for now.

I turned back the way I'd come, in the direction of the river, and strolled off.

At Schlesische-Strasse once again, I realized I'd been so concentrated on Number 11 a short time ago that I'd walked by without noticing the ongoing enterprise in the corner storefront. The signs along the Cuvry-Strasse wall spoke of keeping an orderly line and detailed the hours for work calls. I stepped around the corner. The place was an employment center for temporary day laborers on the docks.

The daily calls finished at noon. This was a reasonable place for a guy with a job handing out jobs to take a slack-time break to have a smoke. I leaned against the cornerstone, putting my profile to the front doors of the Reinauer building. I had plenty of Fatimas and a fretful, let's-get-on-with-it need to do some uninterrupted smoking.

I didn't like the daylight. There was no effective way to get into the building. I was beginning to think this was a waste of time, though I'd had no choice but to come down here. Stockman would arrive, the real stuff would happen inside, and I'd be a futile, distant observer of bricks and mortar. But it was all I had.

I smoked the pack down low but kept a few back for props and I gave my watch fob a workout, and then it was four o'clock, and on the dot a taxi pulled up and Stockman got out.

I nipped my cap down a bit on the right side and watched him in my periphery. He was focused on the stoop and then the door and then he was gone.

I shuffled my feet and waited some more. And some more.

And then I was reconfirmed in my faith in sometimes just hanging around and waiting. Muttering its way up Schlesische-Strasse from the docks came a three-ton Daimler truck. It approached, and its gears ground, and it turned in front of me, into Cuvry-Strasse.

This was a late model with high wooden sides on its bed and a canvas top. I looked around the corner and watched it turn once more into the back lot of Reinauer's building. He rated, this import guy, to command a truck like that in wartime Berlin.

I strolled along after it.

One quick glance to the left: the truck was backing up to the near bay; Reinauer's boys continued to slouch and smoke.

I turned right, into the alley, and hustled a little into the closest doorway, which was recessed and provided the refuse cans to run interference for any casual glances in this direction.

I leaned back against the door, took off my cap, slid down to a touch more than refuse-can height, and I leaned forward just enough to put one eye on the loading dock.

A hundred feet away, the slouchers were unslouching as the Daimler stopped at the platform edge. One of them flipped his cigarette butt and disappeared into the back of the building. His colleague reslouched and the driver appeared on the platform and the two men spoke casually, the driver bumming a cigarette. I leaned back into the doorway for a few moments.

New voices now, and I leaned forward carefully once more to look.

Stockman had appeared on the platform with a short wisp of a steel-haired man in a three-piece suit. Heinrich Reinauer himself, I presumed. The two loading dock boys disappeared into the bed of the truck, and the driver approached Reinauer and made a stiff little bow. He presented a clipboard, and Heinrich signed.

The boys emerged.

Stockman took a step toward them.

They were carrying one of the packing boxes I'd seen in the courtyard at Stockman House. One of the two upright boxes the size and shape of a three-drawer filing cabinet. They were keeping it upright.

Stockman stepped to them, stopped them, patted the box, and spoke a word. They sat it at his feet. He examined the label, the steel cord binders, the four sides.

He nodded at Heinrich, who spoke a word, and the two boys took up the box again and carried it into the building.

Stockman and Reinauer spoke and the driver came down off the platform.

The two loading boys reappeared and disappeared into the truck. The second box came out, got a once-over from Stockman, and vanished into the warehouse with its twin.

And that was it.

Stockman and Reinauer followed. The driver circled his cab, and he and the Daimler ground gears and rolled into Cuvry-Strasse and away.

I stood up, put my cap on, leaned against the door, and lit the last Fatima in my pack.

I didn't have much.

But at least I knew my next move.

Only these two boxes from the castle were involved in this rendezvous with Stockman and the importer. He'd seen to them personally. The truck was sent away, but the boxes remained. This late in the day I figured there was a chance they'd stay till tomorrow. Surely there was no good reason to offload them here at this hour otherwise. If they didn't remain, I was helpless anyway.

When the dark came, I'd have to pay another visit—a more intimate visit—to Number 11 Schlesische-Strasse.

But first I had a rendezvous of my own. At the *Kabarett* called Zum Grauen Köter.

28

The Gray Dog. South of the Stettiner train station on Borsig-Strasse, it was twenty yards down a side alleyway, in the cellar of a *Braten und Bier* joint. A perfect place for a Zeppelin blackout party.

My brass eagle boutonnière in place—my actual face restored as well, with cocoa butter and Castile soap—I descended into too much smoke and noise, in a room that would fit on the stage of the Duke of York's and was jammed with tables and Berliners. Some rooms demand you read their bouquet like a wine, and this one was beer and roast meat and sweat and mustard and tobacco and lavender perfume and even a waft of femaleness, coming, I guessed, from the line of half a dozen kicking chorines in negligees who had to work hard not to fall off at each end of the tiny stage.

A pianist banged away in the far dark corner and the girls were singing about a lusty husband dancing around a rose bush with his wife. The headwaiter in a tux took a look at my lapel and guided me to a small back row table and sat me down, pressing the second chair tight into place. The girls kicked high and belted out an untranslatable "*KlingklanggloriBusch.*" They were loud and shrill in the way chorus girls often seemed to think was alluring but they were competing with a few dozen ongoing conversations in the room.

A girl came to my table in a tux and asked what I was drinking. I had work to do later tonight, so I ordered what the Berliners called a *kühle Blonde*, a cool fair maiden, a wheat beer that Germans used for sobering up. The girl gave me a sly look as if to ask what I'd been doing the last few days. She brought the *Weissbier* in a pint-sized stone bottle and poured the contents into a massive, half-gallon-size glass goblet, which the pint of beer nevertheless filled to overflowing with an inordinate amount of foam.

I paused to watch it froth away and I became abruptly aware of a presence beside me. Before I could look up, a man's voice said in German, "That is Monday beer. No authentic man should drink wheat beer on a Thursday."

I knew the voice.

I lifted my face to look into the boxer's mug that belonged to Jeremy Miller.

I was very glad to see him alive, but I repressed the urge to jump up and clap him on the shoulder.

"What if I had a bad Wednesday night?" I said.

"Then you should stay away from a place like this," he said. "Too much smoke and noise."

I nodded him to the other chair.

He sat.

The girl in the tux came up and bent to Jeremy and took his order, which I didn't hear.

We leaned near each other and spoke in English, audible to each other but walled in by the noise of the Gray Dog.

"How'd you get away on Friday?" I asked.

"Briefly I joined the search for myself," he said.

"Your blue suit," I said.

"My blue suit. There were several lately hired Blue Suits that evening. I had a convincing reference."

"Are you sure?" I said. "I thought perhaps they'd let you in on purpose to trap you."

"The thought did occur."

"And?"

"It still occurs."

Jeremy's drink arrived. A stone bottle and a glass goblet. He was drinking light too.

"We're a couple of fine dudes," I said, nodding at his wheat beer.

"I look forward to someone reading us wrong and picking a fight," he said.

The girl finished pouring and slipped away.

"How do we toast with these?" I said, thinking of the awkward shape and size of the glass.

"It's hardly a toasting sort of drink," he said. "Perhaps to recuperation."

I looked at my own glass. "There seems to be no safe alternative to two hands," I said.

"You are correct," he said.

So we agreed together, on the occasion of this fortunate reunion, to accept a milder meaning for two-fisted drinking.

We sipped through the foam and it was light and it tasted more of banana than of malted wheat; I presumed from the yeast.

"The headwaiter seemed to know you were coming," I said, thinking of his meaningful glance at my buttonhole adornment resulting in what seemed to be the only available table in the place and then his securing the second chair.

"We have friends here and there."

"Pro-Brits in Germany?"

"Ask me again when we are alone," he said.

"We have an opportunity for that tonight," I said.

"Good," he said. "Does it involve our friend?"

"Our baronet. Yes."

We sipped again at our cure for a hangover as the chorus kicked its last kick and its girls fluttered away through a side door off left. While the crowd still applauded, the emcee bounced onto the stage in monocle and tux.

As soon as he was squared around to them, the applause died and most of the conversations died and the emcee cried, "*Gott strafe England!*"

God punish England.

And the crowd roared back, "*Er strafe es!*"

May he punish it.

I'd heard this already several times in the street. It seemed universal in this town. No doubt in the country. Part quotidian mutual greeting, part liturgical call and response.

The emcee seamlessly rolled on into his introduction. He was sorry, he said, but the next scheduled singer had died last night from a broken heart. The crowd let out a moan, but it was instant and exaggerated and as the emcee went on in faux eulogy, the curtain at the back of the stage, which to the eye seemed flush against the wall, opened in the center and a woman in cadaverous whiteface and a tight black dress emerged.

The crowd made a collective sound once more, part horrified gasp, part incipient laugh.

Jeremy leaned toward me. "You mentioned an opportunity?"

The crowd was laughing outright now.

I leaned toward Jeremy. It was well past sunset outside. "I did."

29

We emerged from the Gray Dog without any further word until Jeremy pointed south on Borsig-Strasse with his chin and we walked off in that direction.

"I have a motor car," he said.

"Glad to hear it," I said.

A few steps later I said, "You don't strike me as a cabaret type of guy."

"I didn't choose," he said. "You were right about our having friends in the place. The orderly minds at the Foreign Office see the threat there from Bohemians, not foreign agents."

"Hide in plain sight."

"There was a time," Jeremy said, "when the woman in black would have sung her death-by-boredom from the idiot speeches of a parody Kaiser. A *Quassel-Wilhelm*."

The constructed German word meant a "gibberish-Wilhelm."

"Now," he said, "the censors only have to worry about keeping the girls' private parts hidden."

The political satire period of the *Kabarett* ended more than a decade ago.

"Were you a cabaret type of guy back then?"

"Back then I was already a British pub type of guy."

"We are alone now," I said. "I asked you inside about the pro-Brits."

Instantly, flatly, he said, "There are no pro-Brits in Germany."

We went another couple of steps, with me waiting for him to elaborate.

He stopped.

But he simply said, "This is it." He nodded to a Model T tourer, its canvas top latched in place, sitting at the curb. Henry Ford, quietly conquering the world.

Jeremy made no move to get in. He lifted his face a little, looking away from me briefly, finding words. "Not in the way 'pro-Brit' sounds," he said. "Those who would help us here are not disloyal. They are not working *for* the British. They are working *against* the gibbering Kaiser and the world-conquering *Pickelhauben*."

He identified the German military leaders by their ridiculous, polished-leather, brass and silver-trimmed, spiked helmet—the *Pickelhaube*—that sat up over the ears, protecting very little except the feelings of inadequacy of the officers beneath them.

"Is that you as well?" I said. "Aren't you pro-Brit?"

The question lifted him up by the chest just a little. It had taken him by surprise.

"I *am* a Brit," he said.

"Born?"

"No," he said. "But naturalized."

"Do you have people in Germany?"

"I boxed as an Englishman. Every professional fight."

"Then you are English," I said.

"My mother lives in Spandau," he said. "For her, the Kaiser can do no wrong."

He was speaking softly now. Making no move to his Ford. "My brother, who has lived with our mother—she is a widow—my brother is now an artillery lieutenant. His mind is fiercely opposed to the gibbering Kaiser and the world-conquering *Pickelhauben*. But he thinks there is no other way to be a loyal German."

We thought about this, both of us, for a few moments.

I said, "Didn't you have to become an Englishman to truly fight the Kaiser and his generals?"

He did not hear me. We had each come to a thought. I had merely spoken mine first. Breaking his own separate silence, he now said, "In spite of our past, we are capable of a republic."

I heard the *we*. I did not challenge him on it. I didn't have to. I trusted this man. In spite of his blood.

"Where do we go from here?" he said.

I was not sure which *we* he meant.

"The East Harbor," I said.

"In our American car, imported through London," he said. "Pre-war. It's had a few years of hard use, but it will be loyal to us."

He circled to the driver's side, reached in to the coil box, and switched the battery into its chattery readiness.

"I'll crank," I said, heading for the front of the Ford.

At the steering wheel levers, he retarded the spark and advanced the gas just a little. I bent below the radiator and clutched the crank with my left hand, carefully tucking my thumb alongside my fingers. I gave the crank of this worldwide symbol of American industry a sharp tug, and it rattled into life.

On the way to Reinauer's, I briefed Jeremy on my afternoon. We crossed the Spree and approached the East Harbor on Schlesische-Strasse, passing under the Oberbaum Bridge.

"Slow now," I said, and we rolled by the front of Number 11. I saw no lights.

I directed Jeremy around the block and we approached on Cuvry-Strasse, from the south.

We parked and shut down in front of the building at the edge of Reinauer's delivery lot. We could see the left-hand loading dock from where we sat.

There were no lights at the back either.

I said, "I'm guessing he's got a man inside."

"Probably," Jeremy said. "Tonight at least."

"But if he's in there, I'd rather confront him on our terms."

"Agreed."

"I'll be right back," I said. I opened the door. "A little reconnaissance."

I closed the door and beat it softly across the macadam toward the loading dock. The air smelled of grain and diesel and creosote.

I pulled my tungsten flashlight and went softly up the side steps. I cupped the beam end with my other hand and shined it low, though I was very aware now of my Mauser and of any sound from inside, just in case. I shined the beam all around the dock surface, starting where I watched the two mugs smoking this afternoon. The stack of pallets was gone and so were any butts they might have dropped.

I moved along past the big steel-slat rolling entrance, and as I neared the access door at the end of the dock I started scanning the light in front of me.

I found what I was looking for. I crouched to a couple of cigarette butts. Flattened but unscuffed. Unswept.

I beat it back to the Ford.

"We need your good right hand," I said.

So we set up to wait with Jeremy at one side of the door and me just down the steps at the other side, my Mauser drawn, in case things went wrong somehow. His fist was our first choice. Which he got a chance to use pretty quick. I was looking off the other way when the door clicked and its hinges chirped and then there was a little choked what-the-hell sound and the crack of bone and a major thud.

I went up and Jeremy was already coming around to drag the guard's body back inside. I followed.

The place was deeply shadowed, but across the main floor the guy had turned on the electric light in the windowless shipping office.

Jeremy slipped off in that direction. I closed the outside door and took a little tour. The main floor was mostly empty, but beyond a row of packing tables, my flashlight found an arrangement of wooden boxes and crates and shipping drums. All large. Bigger than Stockman's two boxes. I was convinced this wasn't the part of the haystack we should be looking in anyway.

I returned to Jeremy, who had the unconscious guard on his face and was binding his ankles and wrists behind him. "Not much of a bout," I said.

"He was fighting out of his weight class," Jeremy said.

He said it dry, so I kept my laugh and even my smile to myself. The guard was out of Jeremy's class all right; he was a good twenty-five pounds bigger, all of it apparent muscle.

"Did you look in the shipping office?" I said.

"Just the packing tables." He cinched the hog-tie tight.

"The office is the most secure spot on this floor."

He nodded and finished with a gag job using a couple of oil rags, and we strode across the warehouse floor to the office.

Not only were the lights on, the guard had left the door standing open. He had easy access to the office. It wasn't promising as a place to stash Stockman's precious boxes.

I stepped in first. Jeremy lingered just outside.

A desk.

File drawers.

A safe. But it was half the size of even one of the boxes we were interested in.

A work table with ledger books. A small bookcase.

Nothing.

I wasn't surprised.

I stepped out. "Not secure at all, really," I said.

We both thought for a moment in silence.

"The boxes aren't that big, really," Jeremy said. "They could be anywhere in the building.

"How special are they?" I said.

A rhetorical question.

Jeremy nodded and I said the thing we were both thinking. "We should find this man Reinauer's office."

At the end of a corridor on the third floor was a mahogany door and a brass plate: *Heinrich Reinauer, Geschäftsführer.*

Our man, the managing director.

"Shall I assume you can deal with this?" Jeremy said, in that cultured British tone he sometimes put on.

"You shall," I said. I handed him the flashlight.

He illuminated a friend of mine from the Great Fraternal Order of Tumbler Locks, of which I was an honorary member. I took out my tools and raked this one quickly and I opened the door for Jeremy as if I were his butler, finding myself very pleased to have shown him my own good right hand.

He grunted admiringly.

We went in and closed the door behind us.

Jeremy immediately switched off the flashlight.

Pitch black.

"Good drapes," I said.

He lit the flashlight and found the electric light key next to the door. Reinauer's corner office, secreted away in a bland brick warehouse building at a come-lately urban river dock, was paneled in oak with glass-doored bookshelves and an oil portrait of himself hung behind a West Wing–size desk. Each of its four windows was draped in a black single panel with a massive gold Imperial Eagle in the center sinking its claws into the planet earth. All befitting a *Geschäftsführer*.

But the most striking feature of Heinrich Reinauer's office was the pair of steel-band-strapped wooden boxes sitting in the middle of the floor. Once again I was struck by their size and shape. They were standing with their long side upright. I half expected each of them to contain a three-drawer filing cabinet, the drawers filled with every German secret known to Albert Stockman.

Jeremy and I approached them, however, as gingerly as if we expected them to contain ticking time bombs. We stood side by side before them, silently, without moving, for one beat and then another.

In the center of each of the facing panels was a shipping label. The two labels were set at slightly different angles and showed fragments of previous labels beneath.

Jeremy and I each moved to a box and knelt before it.

The label was an *Umladungsformular*. A transshipment form. The new address was written by hand.

Jeremy read his aloud. "FVFB. Kalk. MDH."

I read mine. "Krupp. Essen."

30

We looked at each other.

We didn't need to speak.

Krupp, of course, meant steel. The House of Krupp was what Lord Kitchener and the Brits desperately needed, a homegrown industrialist producing more artillery shells than the rest of the world combined.

Jeremy squared himself to the box, crouched, put his arms around it, and lifted.

Only six or eight inches.

He put the box down again.

He nodded at me to do the same.

I did.

The box went up very heavy, but it didn't feel like a three-drawer cabinet full of files. Not nearly heavy enough. And the distribution of the weight didn't feel right. And, of course, there was the matter of its destination.

I put the box down.

I said, "So either Sir Albert is getting Krupp into the milk can business or Krupp is getting Sir Al into the artillery business."

We took a step back.

Then Jeremy had a thought. He crossed to the box before me, crouched, and lifted that one as well.

He put it down, nodding, and stepped back. "The same weight."

"A couple of shells," I said.

"Likely," Jeremy said. "Empty ones."

"Then they're a special design. Stockman, the idea man."

Jeremy nodded.

We both turned our eyes to the box going to FVFB. Or to MDH.

"Where's Kalk?" I said.

"Near Cologne."

The question now hung in the air between us: what was our next move? Which pushed a question on stage that had been lurking in the wings. I said, "My man said the Brits were sending me some help. What did your people say?"

"I was the help."

For a moment I wondered how Trask had negotiated his way into our running this British show.

Then Jeremy said, "I'm to help the two of you."

Mother was how. Her crucial access to Stockman was what Trask brought to the table.

But I said, "As far as I'm concerned, you and I are simply in this together."

Jeremy gave me a single, sharp nod.

I said, "For the record then. We want to figure out the full extent of what Stockman is up to and stop him. Agreed?"

"Agreed."

We both looked at the boxes.

"They're nailed and steel-banded," I said. "Can we look inside and then restore them so Reinauer won't notice?"

It was a rhetorical question.

We stared at them some more.

"We open them, that's all we're going to get," I said.

"I think we have a good notion what's in there," he said.

I was glad to have Jeremy along for this. I kept thinking aloud with him. "How clever can that design be? Is looking at it worth putting these guys drastically on their guard?"

The silence of Reinauer's office hissed softly around us.

And then I finally put two and two together. I said, "Not an artillery shell at all."

I'd forgotten it until this moment, but I'd dreamed last night, in my mahogany bed at the Adlon, about the great whirring beasts passing over me in the night, as if I were sleeping on the ocean floor and these were vast creatures of the deep.

"The Zepps," I said. "He's about the Zepps and he's dealing with Krupp. Those are aerial bomb designs."

Jeremy looked at the boxes as if to confirm this and then back at me.

"No doubt improved," he said.

I asked the big question. "How badly do we need the design?"

We quietly consulted the boxes again.

They weren't talking.

"Essen is Krupp's main foundry, isn't it?" I said.

"Yes."

"This is where they'd turn out a million of these."

"It is."

"So what's in Kalk?" I said.

"That's our more interesting question."

"I think I was getting pretty close to Stockman last night at the Adlon bar," I said.

I considered that for a moment. My reporter self had indeed caught a whiff of something. Things were roiling in Albert.

I said, "I can't shake the feeling he's up to more."

Jeremy and I let my hunch hang between us for a moment.

I nodded at the boxes. "The first dud they drop and our bosses have this much. You and I grab these now, Stockman still has his designs, and we can do no more."

"Then shall we let this be?" he said.

This needed no answer. Together we turned and crossed the room. He switched off the lights, and I reset the lock on the door.

On the way to the main warehouse floor we devised a little ruse for the guard, who could have recovered his mind by now.

And so Jeremy and I ransacked the shipping office, arguing in German about which of us stupidly suggested the money would be in something other than an actual safe.

I'd earlier noticed some cases of what looked like a pretty damn good bock and we stole one of those, for appearances sake, and we argued some more—out of the hog-tied guard's line of sight—with me insisting on searching him for cash so we'd at least leave here with a little ready money and with Jeremy talking me out of it, saying this guy was just here doing his job and his aching jaw was enough trouble for him for one night.

Then we beat it out the loading dock door and back to the Ford with our case of beer.

We stopped at the curb a block before the hotel. From the wide median, the streetlights were shining through a scrim of linden trees.

"How do we meet again?" I said.

"You still have a room at the Baden?"

"I do."

"I can leave a message there for you," he said.

"And if I need to get *you*?"

There was an odd hesitation in him, which I wished I could read. But it was dark inside the Ford and he turned his face away. Whatever it was passed quickly.

"For the next few days you can reach me at this telephone." He reached quickly inside his coat. If he were anyone else I'd be drawing my Mauser.

His hand emerged with a piece of paper, which I took from him.

"They listen in on the phones at the Adlon," he said.

"I know."

"The lobby of the Baden has a telephone kiosk. You can call from there. Say as little as possible."

"Let's decide on a place that need never be mentioned."

"Yes," he said. "Make it the Hindenburg statue in the Tiergarten."

"But we speak of beer."

"Or brat, depending on the time of day."

"One other thing," I said. "I don't know who you are."

"A pretty good middleweight who once upon a time almost beat Tommy Ryan."

I'd meant around Berlin. On the phone. This answer came quick and dry. His German sense of humor. Or his German *Angst*. Or both.

But he played neither, giving the line only a brief beat before appending, "I am Bruno Obrecht. A Swiss businessman."

I started to get out of the still idly quaking Model T.

He put a hand on my arm. "But not for the next two days."

I sat back down.

"I am Erich," he said. "Erich Müller."

"Was that your birth name?"

"It was."

I stepped out of the T, and he said, "You want a couple of our bocks for your room?"

"Take them all," I said.

He pinched the brim of his hat to say good-bye and drove off.

I looked at the paper in the streetlight. His telephone number. *Spandau 4739.*

He was going home to his mother.

31

I stood for a moment on the street. An El train was softly clacking through the median lindens. I considered this roll of the dice, the opportunity we'd just left behind. Perhaps the content of the two boxes was all I'd come to Berlin to find. What we felt certain was in there could be everything there was to know about the sotto voce declaration I'd finessed from Stockman last night. If the bombs the Zepps were dropping could somehow be improved, made more accurate, more effective, the airship attacks might become far more than isolated, neighborhood disruptions. They might bring the war-changing terror to London that many people on both sides felt was possible from these machines. The Brits deserved to know the details of what they were up against as soon as possible. They needed to start making their own.

So why weren't those two boxes on their way to the American embassy right now?

Instead, I'd stolen some beer.

"Shit," I said.

No. "Shit" was what was in my head, certainly. But what I said aloud there on the Unter den Linden, what rang in the silence following the passing of the El, was *Scheiße*.

I was thinking in German and maybe I was just a little too close to this place right now.

However.

The British had no aerial attack of their own. They'd see plenty of this design long before they'd have their own airship. Surely it was better for now to keep the Germans confident about their security inside the Fatherland.

And I still had a reporter's niggling hunch.

I instantly questioned even that. Maybe that hunch was simply the feature writer in me. Stockman intrigued me. I wanted to get into his head. I had one foot in already. But maybe the only hard news he had in there was still sitting in Reinauer's office.

I tried to shake all this off.

I made myself walk. I let the blandly neoclassic, granite ashlar face of the Education Ministry scour my mind clean.

Spinning in the Adlon's front door I left the doubts behind. I had no choice but to play my hunches now. And I played one more.

I turned to the left and stepped into the doorway of the bar. In the far corner, drinking alone in an evening suit, was Sir Albert Stockman. He was sitting where he'd sat last night, his back to the rest of the bar.

I began to cross the floor, and he turned in his chair. It was an odd moment; I felt, chillingly, that he somehow sensed my approach. But he was actually seeking the bartender's attention. I drew near and now he did see me and he instantly rose, turning to face me. He said, in German, "Please. Yes. Come sit."

We shook hands.

I sat in the chair where I'd sat last night.

Stockman motioned to the bartender and sat down as well.

On the table before him was an empty whiskey glass.

Stockman saw me looking at it.

He said, in English, "They have a splendid American rye. Not to the taste of most Germans. They don't drink whiskey. But I have acquired some British tastes. I wanted this tonight."

The glass was empty, but now that Stockman was sitting and speaking, an afterwhiff of spirits floated past me. He'd been drinking for a while.

Last night's bartender appeared.

"Don't feel obligated," Stockman said.

"Not at all," I said. "I'll drink American with you."

"The bottle, Hans," Stockman said to the bartender, who nodded with a click of his heels and did a smart about-face.

Stockman instantly asked, "Were you with Madam Cobb?"

I still found it difficult to trust how I stood with him. I had a quick pulse of worry. This morning she had made me up into another man so that I could spy on Sir Albert. But he'd delivered the message himself, that I was to see her. Then why was he asking?

"This morning," I said. "At the theater."

"So. Yes. She and I had dinner tonight." He was speaking German again. "An early dinner before she returned to the theater. Were you at the rehearsal?"

"Not this evening," I said. "They are very busy. Working late. She has two casts to deal with, you realize. One German-speaking."

"I know," he said. "It wearies her."

Hans the bartender appeared beside us.

He put a glass in front of me and poured two amber fingers of rye in mine and two in Stockman's glass.

He put the bottle down between us.

A Pennsylvania whiskey. *Sam Thompson Old Monongahela Pure Rye*, with an etching of Sam's riverside distillery in Pittsburgh.

Stockman and I touched glasses.

"To the hardworking Isabel Cobb," I said.

"To Isabel," he said, putting as much into her name as my mother had put into her eyes about *him*. He was in love.

At that, I took the bolt of rye gladly, took it in full, relishing the burn down the throat, like a Pennsylvania summer noonday sun. And it bit with the spiciness of a pure rye, this particular one mixing cloves and pumpkin and cracked pepper.

When I lowered my glass and my face, I found Stockman looking at me. He'd sipped his. He was smiling a little half smile at me. "Were you ever a soldier, Mr. Hunter?"

"Can you call me Josef?" I said.

He cocked his head.

I said, "When I was brought as a child to America my name was Josef Wilhelm Jäger."

He smiled. "Of course," he said. "Josef."

"Never a soldier," I said.

"And if you'd stayed?" he asked.

"In Germany?"

"Yes."

"Perhaps not for the sake of the colonies. But for this war, I would have been in a trench in France by now. There is no doubt."

He nodded.

"With joy," I said, picking up on his observation from last night.

He lifted his glass to me and shot the rest of his rye.

He put three fingers in each of our two glasses.

I'd take this one slow.

We both lifted our glasses.

No toast this time. We were just two guys doing some serious drinking together. I liked that.

I sipped.

Off to my left, there was movement. I let the rye slide down my throat and I casually looked.

A German officer and a woman were arranging themselves at a table. His field gray tunic had a high turnover collar, and his shoulder boards were cornflower blue with two pips. A cavalry captain. I saw him in left profile. His cheek was imprinted with the crescent scar of his university fencing days. A *Schmiss*.

The scar caught my eye and held my gaze for longer than I'd intended. I could see, in my periphery, Stockman turning to look as well.

The woman was a peach, wearing a green silk and organdy evening gown with a high waist that lifted up and presented her ample bosom as if on an invisible platter. She was in the process of stripping off long, white kid gloves.

I looked at Stockman and he was still watching the couple. Then he turned back to me. He leaned across the table and flipped his chin to have me bend near.

"*Nicht Gesellschaftsfähig*," he said. He caught himself. For this observation, he hadn't meant to speak German. He shot the couple a quick glance. They only had eyes and ears for each other. He returned to me and said it again in English, speaking even more softly, translating the euphemism literally. "Not fit for society."

I looked at her.

Perhaps.

As I watched her—they too bent near each other—Stockman said, "Not that I criticize him. He has earned this privilege."

The captain said something and the woman smiled softly. She lifted her right hand and brought it to his cheek and gently began to trace his *Schmiss* with the tip of her forefinger.

"She is his fiancée," I said. I looked back to Albert. His face was blank. He wasn't used to being contradicted; I feared I was overplaying our growing rapport. I angled my head for him to look. "The gesture."

He looked.

She was still moving her fingertip over her captain's scar.

Stockman chuckled softly, and he and I turned to each other, still leaning near. "You're right," he said. "But he will never have a moment of peace when he is apart from her. For fear her tenderness may stray."

I thought: *Like you with my mother.*

I nodded in agreement.

And then he surprised me. He lowered his voice still more. "Nor will she," he said.

Briefly I thought he was still talking about sex. But he said, "So many good men will die."

We took up our drinks. We sat back. This time I was the sipper and he immediately took the shot.

I knew if I was to justify those two boxes remaining in Reinauer's office, I'd have to get closer still to Albert. I'd never do that if I started thinking out each move. As he lowered his whiskey glass after his emotional bolt, I understood all this. And so I stopped thinking. Which allowed me to say, "Can I tell you a secret?"

Stockman leaned forward again. Rather abruptly. "Of course," he said.

I leaned in slowly.

I said, "I too have a *Schmiss*."

His eyes moved slowly, deliberately, to my bearded left cheek and then returned to mine.

"I think I told you I grew up in America," I said, leading us back to German. "My father made sure that I spoke the mother tongue. I was not allowed to say even a single English word in our house. And he wanted me to have an education. I also wanted that, but I dreamed of the University of Michigan. My father had other plans. He insisted I go *home* to university."

I paused very briefly, to let the *home* sink in. Stockman said, "He is a good man, your father."

"So I came to realize," I said. "In 1902, when I was eighteen, I packed a bag and I came to Heidelberg and they welcomed me and they disciplined me and they allowed me into their inner circle and I took up a saber and I earned my badge of honor."

He glanced at the place of my presently invisible scar.

I'd said my piece.

He looked at me closely for a long moment, reassessing me one more time. Then he said, "I must ask you why is this a secret. Why do you cover up this mark?"

I said, "For the same reason it is necessary to write newspaper stories for the people of America to explain the real Germany. This is something not in their blood."

"I understand," Stockman said.

He leaned back. He palmed the ends of the chair arms. "But you are in Germany now," he said.

"I am."

"Josef," he said. "Would you do a favor for me?"

"Yes."

"Would you go upstairs to your room, right now, and shave off your beard?"

This took me by surprise. But the reflex feeling I would have had even a few minutes ago did not occur. I did not for a moment hear this as the calling of a suspected bluff. He was mellow, avuncular even, in his manner and tone. He was encouraging me to come even closer to him.

"I will," I said.

"Good," he said. "You must wear this scar with pride. It is a rare thing. It is a precious thing."

"I shed my German blood for it," I said.

He smiled.

32

I stood before my mirror. The last thing he said as I'd risen to go was that he would wait, that he was looking forward to speaking this evening with Josef Wilhelm Jäger.

I found my hand severely steady as I worked the lather into my beard, as if I were about to pull a trigger. This was a badger-hair shaving brush, not a .32 caliber Mauser, but my body had invoked my conditioned response to a spy's stage nerves. It had been bad enough this past spring, confronting the scar for the first time since the wound had healed and I'd let my beard cover it up. Now this second revelation was odd indeed: I was fully asserting my cover identity to a German spy by showing him my actual face, which was, however, forever altered by the first German spy I'd ever confronted. And rubbing the cream into my cheeks summoned up my mother from this morning, her hands rubbing color into this beard, turning me into my battered doppelgänger to disguise me from the very man who was now waiting downstairs to see my naked face. Which would convince him utterly that I was someone I was not.

I'd had no idea spy work would be as unsettling as this.

I stropped the razor and I cut and I cut and I was clean and I was scarred and I was Josef Wilhelm Jäger.

I went back downstairs.

I expected that Stockman had continued to drink. I half expected this whole shaving event to have been in vain, that he would have reached his limit, that he would have forgotten even sending me upstairs.

He was sitting very still when I approached and he heard me and turned. The level of rye in the bottle had receded no farther since I'd left, and a cup of coffee was sitting before him on the table.

He rose.

He extended his hand to me. He spoke, of course, in German. "Herr Jäger, I am Albert Stockman."

He had shaved himself as well, by offering his first name without the title. Given who he was, it was an odd and unsettling thing for me to feel—as I now briefly did—a twist of barroom affection for this guy.

But I held off from using "Albert" to his face, though I'd thought it a number of times already, in disrespect. "Herr Stockman," I said. "May I ask a question?"

"Of course."

"Was your name once Stockmar?"

He threw back his head and laughed, and when he was done, he cuffed me on the shoulder. "You are a shrewd man, Herr Jäger. You are correct. It was done before I was born, however."

"That makes no difference," I said. "In your blood, you are still a Stockmar."

He laughed again and nodded me to my chair.

When I sat, I motioned for the bartender to come. He did, briskly. I said to him, "I'll have what he's having."

"Coffee?" the bartender said.

"Coffee," I said.

The man vanished.

I faced Stockman now, as the truly revealed Josef Wilhelm Jäger.

His eyes moved to my scar and lingered. "Please?" he said, lifting his hand, waving it as if turning the page of a book.

I turned my face to the right, fully showing the *Schmiss*.

I felt grindingly uncomfortable, but I understood my job would be made easier by all this. Nevertheless, the examination, though probably brief, felt endless. I focused on the thought that it was a good thing I would never know my own father. At our first meeting I'd be subjected to this same ordeal. *Here, let me take a look at you, my son.* To hell with that.

Then Stockman said, "Thank you."

I faced him once more.

"You did not pack it with horsehair?" he asked.

The dueling sword of the friendly, prearranged duels, the straight-bladed *Korbschläger*, had a blade as fine as my straight razor and did not bruise when cutting. Some duelists packed their cuts with horsehair to irritate them and keep them agape as they healed so as to create a more prominent scar. Mine was plenty striking on its own.

"I did *not*," I said. "That would be a lie and a sacrilege."

"Good," he said. "It's interesting how those of us who have grown up in exile sometimes have a purer sense of these things."

"Perhaps this war will refocus all Germans," I said.

"I greatly envy you, bearing this mark," he said. "I was in a different circumstance, of course, going off to university. My father had complex commitments. His son could go nowhere but to Oxford."

He paused. I had the impulse to keep improvising onward. I even thought to say: *A true German soul bears this mark invisibly from birth.* But even without thinking it out, I knew I was on the verge of going too far, of turning this into melodrama.

So I simply nodded sympathetically and was glad to find the bartender suddenly beside us, giving us pause, presenting my cup of coffee and topping off Stockman's from a carafe.

After the bartender had vanished again, Albert said, "Of course, it is the same with the British as the Americans. There is so much they do not understand."

I sipped at the coffee, hot and bitter, and I remained plausibly silent. Let Albert follow his own internal path.

He lifted his coffee, cup and saucer together, and looked at it steaming before him, and he said, "I'm afraid the British will *never* understand."

He sipped. But his voice had already turned hot and bitter.

"Not by reason, they won't," he said. "Not in a civilized way. They are waging this war against us by using their navy to starve Germany slowly to death, every man and woman and child. *That* is the act of terror. And they do it with their damnable outward restraint, as if its incremental effects civilize it. But they are not rational. They are cold-blooded, which is a different thing. Civilization cannot exist without passion."

He'd placed the cup back onto the saucer, but kept them both suspended before him. The cup was chittering lightly.

His hand had begun to tremble.

He seemed aware of it. He looked at the cup.

And the sound abruptly stopped.

He returned his eyes to mine and said, "I still have hopes that the Americans will come to understand."

"It's why I write," I said.

"I admire that," he said.

We drank our coffee for a time. Stockman seemed to turn inward. But whatever he was aware of in himself, I was apparently the point of reference. He would sip and think and look at me and look away and then do it all again.

Finally he said, "I am meeting a German scientist tomorrow who has created a process that will eliminate famine from the face of the earth. He did this six years ago. You do not know his name. I have read essentially every issue of your most important newspaper, *The New York Times*, for the past decade. His name has never appeared. Not once. Nor his discovery."

Stockman paused. Inside my head I'd paused several sentences ago. This guy had a way of veering off and surprising the hell out of me. He seemed to want me to comment now.

"What is his name?" I asked.

"Fritz Haber."

I had always read very widely. I possessed a very good memory. But Stockman was right.

"I have never heard his name," I said.

"You see?"

"What is this process?"

"He can convert the inaccessible nitrogen in the atmosphere into ammonia, which contains extractable, usable nitrogen. Do you know what this means?"

I knew some science. The air was mostly nitrogen. But I'd never heard of anyone figuring out how to use it.

"Perhaps," I said. "But tell me."

Stockman said, "Nitrogen is in everything we eat. Meat, bread, anything with protein. The nitrogen comes from the soil, through the crops. The wheat, the corn. The rye you and I have drunk together. But there is only so much nitrogen. The earth can be sucked dry. Fertile land can become exhausted from use, and it is the nitrogen that vanishes. Before the Haber Process, the only way for man to create large quantities of nitrogen to put back into the soil was by using the nitrogen in saltpeter. No one has saltpeter but the country of Chile, and even there, the supplies are finite. But you can make fertilizer from nitrogen-bearing ammonia, and if you can turn the air into ammonia, you have an infinite amount of fertilizer. The world has nearly two thousand million people. This is nearly twice as many people as a hundred years ago. It will not take another hundred years to double again. Already millions starve. But Germany will never starve. America need never starve. No one need starve. A *German* will feed them all. Fritz Haber will feed them all forever."

I sat in silence with that abrupt, vast, visceral feeling that a reporter gets when he picks up on a story that nobody has reported.

About the feeding of millions, now and into the future, of course. But the thing Stockman wasn't saying was that nitrogen was also essential in making explosives. Nitrogen created from the air meant *killing* millions as well.

The Allies controlled all of Chile's saltpeter.

How much did our government and the European Allies' governments know about this?

"This was six years ago?" I asked.

"Yes, when he demonstrated the process."

"And they're doing this now on an industrial scale?"

"Twenty-five tons of ammonia a day. For two years already."

I wanted to ask where. But I flipped the crank on my reporter's instincts and they started up instantly. I knew this was a fragile moment. An inappropriate, pointed question could shut Stockman down.

The links forward from where his mind had started were clear, from his having hopes that America will come to understand Germany, to his admiring my journalism in pursuit of that very aim, to his abruptly waxing rhapsodic about German nitrogen someday feeding a hungry world. He had it in his head to arrange for me to do a story. A grand one. The one with a humanistic face. I needed to be careful.

"If only America knew," I said.

"Perhaps that can be arranged," he said.

"I'd do the story full justice," I said.

"Have you seen Baron Mumm von Schwarzenstein at the Foreign Office?"

I had that phony letter from the baron who controlled the press, courtesy of the American-occupied German embassy in London. I had to assume whatever Stockman might have in mind would run afoul of the bureaucracy. It was still unclear to me how much high-ranking, maverick authority Albert actually had. Or how naive he might be about the ways of the German publicity machine. I had to ask a delicate question.

I created a warm little insider laugh. "Do you know the baron well?"

"Not at all," he said.

I tried not to show my rush of relief. "I've had my obligatory *Kirschwasser* with him from his crystal decanter," I said, improvising the details. "And all is well."

"Good," he said. "Meet me here in the bar at two tomorrow afternoon," he said. "Wait for me if I am late."

"Thank you," I said.

"And now," he said, "I must take a pot of coffee to my rooms to await Hamlet's entrance."

I had nothing to say to that.

I rose and offered my hand.

He rose and took it.

He inclined his head toward my scar. "This is who you are," he said.

33

I told Stockman I wanted to finish my coffee before I left and he bade me good night and consulted with the bartender—I presumed about having his pot of coffee delivered—then he walked across the floor, pretty steadily for all the drinking he must have done tonight, and he vanished into the lobby.

I gave him a couple of minutes to negotiate the elevator, and I emerged into the grand reception lounge of the Adlon ground floor. I stepped clear of the overhanging mezzanine, held aloft by square columns of yellow sienna marble, and I moved into the center of the lounge, with its frescoed ceiling vaulting high above me.

I carefully checked the scattering of people in the lobby. No eyes turning to me. No Herr Wagner.

To my left now was the reception desk, and there were empty settings of overstuffed chairs before it, but I moved on to the nearest chair and table of the Palm Court at the south end of the reception lounge. I sat in the center of three chairs closely arced around a small round table. I faced north across the central floor with a clear view of the stairs from the Unter den Linden doors. I ordered a pot of coffee. And, just in case, two cups.

The coffee was still warm when Mother swirled through the revolving door. She was surely tired after a long day of rehearsal, but she could do nothing other than make a dynamic entrance into such a public space as this. I knew that she would instantly, though covertly, assess her effect on her impromptu audience. I rose from my chair and began to applaud in broad, smooth undulations, though making no sound whatsoever. She was still fifty yards away and the sound was irrelevant anyway.

She saw me.

She fell out of the *Grande Dame* role and strode my way. To a viewer she was simply another woman walking across an open space. But I knew that this throttling back on her stage star aura meant she was all business.

She arrived.

"I'm having coffee," I said. "Would you like some?"

"Good evening to you as well, my darling Christopher," she said.

She used my real name but she spoke it low. When she wanted to be all business with me, she had to be the one who initiated it. Thus her umbrage at the missed niceties of greeting.

"Good evening, Madam Cobb," I said, also low. "Who are you thinking of, may I ask? I am still your humble and eager scribe, Joseph Hunter."

She stiffened. I realized she'd been unaware of the name she'd used.

And now I stiffened a little from the same twist of fear she'd just experienced. Her lapse had not been heard, much less understood. But she was capable of forgetting like this in a crucial moment, a crucial circumstance.

"I'm so sorry, Mr. Hunter," she said. "What did I call you?"

"Christopher."

She laughed lightly.

"Well, you see," she said. "That's my son's name. He's been much on my mind lately."

"You may have good reason not to recognize me."

"I'd say so," she said.

We were speaking very low now, and it was safe, but she kept up the pretense a little longer. She said, "When I last saw my son, he had stitches in his cheek in that very place."

"Did he indeed," I said. "I got this from my college days in Heidelberg."

"You went to Heidelberg, did you? You never mentioned this."

"I revealed it only tonight, to Sir Albert," I said.

"I'm sure he was impressed," she said.

"He's having coffee himself at the moment," I said. "We can chat for a few minutes if you like."

She began to sit on the chair to my left but glanced again at my scar and circled the table to sit on my right so as not to see it. I settled into my center chair and we leaned toward each other.

I could smell the orange blossom and violet of her Guerlain perfume. And the familiar musk of my mother herself, from her dozen hours on the stage, which the French scent was intended to cover. And the licorice bite of her Sen-Sen, covering the whiskey, which she always took in true moderation after a long day of rehearsing but for which she always felt guilty.

She looked with seeming casualness around her. So did I. As I'd thought, no one was near enough to have heard a syllable of this. And we were clear of the vaulted ceiling, so the acoustics remained local.

We could speak privately like this.

"He drinks too much," she said, gently.

"For which I am grateful," I said.

"It must make you look like a real pal sometimes," she said. There was a cat-tongue rasp to her tone, as if I were being a hypocrite, taking advantage of him.

I leaned closer. "Do you remember why we're risking our necks?" I said.

She sighed.

"What the hell is that sigh all about?" I said.

"You're right, is what it's about."

I never could quite figure out how she was able to switch me from irritation to guilt in the time it takes for an electric light bulb to go from dark to bright.

"How was rehearsal?" I asked, trying to soothe things.

"This is terrible, wearying work," she said. "A never-ending assault on your mind and heart."

It was never like that when she was still perceived to be a leading lady. I didn't say this. "Two casts at once, in two languages," I said.

She looked at me. "Not the theater, child."

She'd flipped on another light. She meant the spy work.

"You got into this all on your own," I said.

"I'm not blaming you."

"You didn't have to fall in love with him," I said.

She turned her face from me, as if she were hiding something.

"Are those real tears or fake?" I said.

She plucked a handkerchief out of her lizard skin bag and dabbed at her eyes. "Both," she said.

"Look," I said. "I'm sorry this has gotten complicated."

"I need to go," she said.

"Have you gone through his things?"

She turned her face sharply to me. "It hasn't gotten that far," she said.

I wasn't sure what distinction she was drawing.

"I don't have a key," she said.

"I'm not prying," I said.

"I know you have to ask."

"I'm asking if you can do this, given your feelings."

"I'm gathering as much information as I can."

"I appreciate that."

"I can do this," she said.

She was no Hamlet.

She said, "How was your adventure at the docks?"

I had to make a decision now about my mother and this role she'd taken on. The more she knew, the more she could inadvertently reveal, especially to a man she had feelings for. But the less she knew, the less she might recognize as useful information. I stalled for thinking time by leaning forward and topping off my coffee cup from the *Adlon Oblige* pot.

Her feelings for men. They came and they went. Readily. How deeply could this Albert possibly be touching her?

"Coffee?" I asked.

"Yes, dear," she said.

I filled the second cup as well.

She knew what was at stake for her and for me and even for the country she wanted to serve.

She took up her cup and sipped. As did I.

She was a smart woman. Trask trusted her with Stockman. I could use her help.

So I told her most everything that had happened on this day.

Among the omissions: I didn't tell her about the cadaver act at the *Kabarett*. She didn't need more ideas on how to reinvent herself.

When I'd finished, she said, "I should go now. I have things to listen for."

She rose.

I rose with her. "Just be careful about asking leading questions," I said.

"I understand," she said.

She turned, but she paused and turned back. She touched my arm. "Thank you," she said. "For trusting me."

"Even when you're in love." I said it as a declaration. In fact, I said it to try it out, to try to hear if it was true.

She said, "Love only makes me stupid in one way. My *mind* is always untouched."

And with this, she whisked away as if she were making an entrance into a swank hotel through a revolving door.

34

I sat where I was.

I thought of what my mother had said, about Albert's drinking helping me to befriend him. He was a common figure in a profession that was still figuring itself out for the twentieth century. He was officially in the employ of the German Foreign Office, certainly. Secretly so. He was powerful, clearly. But he seemed an amateur at heart. The Huns hadn't sufficiently accounted for people like my mother and me being able to get this close to a man like him. That was good for us. But I realized his amateurism made him less logical, less predictable, more dangerous in his work.

It had been a long day.

I stopped thinking.

I had two places to sleep.

It was too late to call Jeremy's mother's house.

I chose the Adlon.

I rose, crossed through the reception lounge, and neared the desk on the way to the staircase behind it. The steps led to the mezzanine and the hotel elevator.

Just before passing beneath it, I glanced up to the mezzanine.

Grasping the ironwork balustrade there, standing upright with his arms straight, his eyes fixed on me, was Herr Wagner.

I did not hesitate but nodded at him and went up. It was time to try to deal with him.

I emerged on the mezzanine landing. He had already turned around to confront me.

I was well aware that I was showing him my third face in two days. But I made sure he got a good look at the scar on my cheek as I approached. He was working hard at maintaining the opacity of his own face.

"Good evening, Herr Wagner," I said.

He nodded. I was no doubt a unique challenge for him. From the intensity of his gaze, from the faint, incipient shaping of his mouth, which waxed and waned and waxed again, I knew he was struggling to find words to say.

I was concerned, however, that if he failed to find any words for me, he'd decide to leave the task for some boys in a back room at the Foreign Ministry.

"I am sorry to keep confusing you," I said.

He stiffened a little. "Sir?"

"Do you know what I'm doing here?"

He stiffened some more. "Doing?"

I could only play the cards in my hand. I said, "You are no doubt aware that a special and powerful friend of Germany, Baron Albert Stockman, is staying at the Adlon. And that he is accompanied by the great American actress, Madam Isabel Cobb."

I paused. Wagner was keeping his face blank and his mouth shut. I waited him out.

Finally he said, "I am aware of them."

"I daresay you know that Baron Stockman arranged for me to stay at your lovely hotel. I am here to write a major story for the American newspapers on Madam Cobb's performance of Hamlet. As part of the story, I am—in my ignorance of these matters—experiencing some aspects of the life of an actor. Putting on makeup, for instance. Changing a face to become a character for the stage. Do you understand?"

"I'm not sure, Herr Hunter."

"The face that puzzled you yesterday afternoon. It was not mine. It was makeup that Madam Cobb herself put upon me so that I might experience, for a few hours, what the actor experiences. Being inside another person's skin. I regret making you an unwitting part of our little experiment."

Wagner struggled to take all this in.

His eyes moved sharply now to my scar.

I said, "The *Schmiss*, however, earned in Heidelberg, is real. I write for American newspapers. I am technically an American citizen. But I am, in fact, German."

His eyes remained on the scar.

"Would you like to touch it?" I said.

He flinched his eyes away from my cheek. "No sir," he said.

"To verify its reality. Go ahead," I said.

"No thank you, sir," he said, growing as uncomfortable as I'd intended.

"The experimenting is over, Herr Wagner. I will cause you no more confusion."

He summoned the power of his formality. He straightened. He clicked his heels. He said not a word. He moved past me and down the steps.

This might all have gone well.

This might only have bred distrust in him, and therefore, as well, in the men he worked for.

I could only hope my own work would go swiftly in Berlin.

I waited and watched Wagner shortly emerge from beneath the mezzanine, stepping smartly, his backbone flagpoled into his butt, his chin lifted.

I thought, *A goddamn Hun.*

The elevator door opened on the fourth floor, and I padded along the dense Ushak hall carpet to my room.

Huns, I thought. It was a little too easy for me to use the epithet. It was just a word. But I had to make sure it didn't induce a reflex *feeling* about the Germans, as well, or I could miss their equivalents of Mother and me. Or Jeremy. Stockman was no simple Hun.

And twenty minutes later, with my balcony door open to the upspill of street light and to a wisp of a night breeze, with the linen top sheet draped over my bare feet, the Huns lingered with me. The irony, of course, was that Kaiser Willie himself stuck the label on his people. As I drifted off to sleep, the quote—suppressed in the German press at the time, but lately resurrected among the Allies—rattled around in my head, words he spoke fifteen years ago to his troops heading off to China to crush the Boxer Rebellion. *Prisoners will not be taken. Whoever falls into your hands will be put to death. Just as a thousand years ago the Huns, under their King Attila, found a glory that shines even today, may you exalt the name "German" so that no one in China will dare to look askance at a German again.*

Which was just fine as an American spy's lullaby, a drifting away on a reminder of why I was here, doing what I was doing.

I woke to light and automobile horns from beyond the balcony. An hour later, braced with its good coffee and fresh eggs, I went out of the Adlon and headed for the Baden, walking briskly, though I immediately turned off Unter den Linden onto Wilhelm-Strasse and then turned again onto Behren-Strasse. I stopped immediately in front of the National Bank and lit a cigarette, waiting to see if anyone came around the corner following me. No one did. I went on east and made my way back to Unter den Linden and the Hotel Baden.

And finally I stood in an enclosed wood and glass telephone kiosk in the Baden's lobby. I asked the hotel operator to put me through to Spandau, number 4739.

A woman answered the phone. "Müller," she said.

His mother. "Mrs. Müller," I said. "May I speak with . . ." I hesitated very briefly. I had three of him to choose from. ". . . Erich?"

"Who is it calling?" she said.

"Josef Wilhelm Jäger," I said.

"Please wait, Mr. Jäger." She spoke German very formally, with every *r* carefully trilled.

The phone clunked, onto a tabletop no doubt, as the line stayed open.

After a few moments Jeremy's voice said, "Josef. Good morning."

"Good morning, Erich."

"I'm sorry I am in Berlin only briefly," he said. For his mother's consumption, I figured.

"We should have lunch," I said.

"What time?"

"To meet, let's say eleven o'clock."

"Good," he said.

And he hung up.

I stepped from the booth.

I went to my room at the Baden and found the fragment of a matchstick, which I'd left wedged, unseen, halfway up in the jamb of the door, still wedged there.

I lay down for an hour, resting better than I had all night at the Adlon.

At about ten o'clock I walked the three hundred yards back to the Kaiser's favorite hotel. For the hell of it, I gave my room a careful look. Wagner or his boys had done a pretty slick job with their search. But the last item I checked showed their hand. My portable combination tool had been laid back into my latched toilet bag a hundred and eighty degrees off. The two ends were reversed. I wondered when this had been done. Sometime before or sometime after my confrontation with Wagner on the mezzanine? Was this a bit of clumsiness on his part? Or was Wagner sending me a little message that he was still watching?

Either way, I'd done all I could, and I would continue to be mindful that I was surrounded by some of Willie's best Huns, who'd reserved a place against a wall at Spandau for guys like me.

Ten minutes later a note in a hotel envelope skiffed its way along the carpet and into the room at the bottom of my door.

Before picking it up I opened the door and looked right and then left and I saw a flash of Egyptian blue turning the corner at the end of the corridor. An Adlon page boy.

I closed the door and opened the envelope.

Stockman worked fast.

I was to meet him at four o'clock, not two. And I would go with him to see Fritz Haber at the Kaiser Wilhelm Institute for Physical Chemistry.

35

The lindens of the boulevard before the Adlon flowed like German blood into the vast forest of the Tiergarten. I entered through the Brandenburg Gate and along the Charlottenburger-Chaussée, which was lined with plane trees and marble statues of the Brandenburg-Prussian rulers, the Margraves and the Fredericks and the Joachims. All of these monarchs were dramatically outranked, however, when I turned into the Sieges-Allée.

He asserted his authority at once, though he was still two hundred yards away and though another goddess Victory floated behind and high above him on a red granite column. This was a military monarch, four storeys high, shaped from khaki oak, the massively square-faced Field Marshal Paul Ludwig Hans Anton von Beneckendorff und von Hindenburg, in great coat, leaning on his sword, and facing down this "Victory Avenue."

I approached him.

He was a Nail Man. He was the latest in an odd German revival of an old Austrian custom of putting up a heroic wooden statue and then ceremonially driving nails into it for luck, for a blessing, for charity.

Hindenburg was brand-new, dedicated only recently and with the wooden platforms still girding him up to his waist to facilitate the first assault of nails. Berliners were asked to drive nails into their military hero for charity, the rehabilitation of East Prussia, overrun by the now expelled Russians in the first months of the war.

I began to circle him. The nails were mostly iron but with a noticeable scattering of silver-plate and very occasional spots of gold-plate. The kiosk by the front of the marble base had displayed the donation rates. Iron was one *mark*, silver was five, gold was a hundred. For your hundred *mark* you got a lapel pin, replicating the iconic German Iron Cross, done in onyx with gold-plated trim and a golden **H** in the center.

I paused at Hindenburg's backside, where he'd already been nailed a good hundred times. All in iron.

"That's where I'd put one," Jeremy said from behind my left shoulder.

Still pondering Hindenburg's backside, I said, "You figure those hundred guys had that German sense of humor about it?"

"Of course," he said.

I turned to him now. "Good morning, Erich," I said.

Very briefly his eyes went as wide as they might have when Tommy Ryan caught him with an unexpected shot to the ribs. He recovered fast, but now he was driving a nail of a gaze into my *Schmiss*.

"I had no idea," he said.

"So what's your idea now?" I said.

"I still don't have an idea."

"It's a war story I'd be happy to tell you over lunch."

"It looks like . . ."

"So they say. That's why I'm showing it to my new German pals." I glanced back up at the oaken Field Marshal. "You know, it just occurred to me. That Chicago journalist I once was had a pretty shrewd strategy when interviewing local dirty politicians. He always made a point to wear the lug's buttonhole campaign pin when he wanted to finesse incriminating quotes out of him."

Jeremy had stopped looking at the scar, but his usually stoic face was still furrow-browed with puzzlement.

"Trust me," I said.

"Carry on," he said, briefly dropping into English.

So we circled back around to the front of the statue. I gave the Field Marshal a last glance before taking him on with a hammer. He had a faraway look and the stiff posture of a man with hemorrhoids. But maybe it was just the hundred nails in his ass.

I asked the elderly, bristle-haired attendant for a hundred-*mark* golden nail. He clicked his heels and bowed, and I paid him two ten-dollar gold liberty heads from the money belt I'd worn since I'd first gone to war as a correspondent. Once newspaper money, now government.

With elaborately grateful heel clicking and bowing, he gave me a hammer and a gold-plated inch-and-a-half nail.

I clicked my heels and bowed a thanks, and Jeremy followed me to the foot of the scaffold.

He said, "The British have had their way with me, I'm afraid. My first thought was you are a fool to pay such a sum. But the German in me looks at that pin and I know what you're doing. That says you opened your heart and gave to them in difficult times. They have warm hearts, the Germans. They will count you as one of them."

"For that, given what we've got to do, twenty bucks is cheap," I said.

And I went up the first level to stand as high as Hindenburg's knees and the second to reach his waist. His arms were crossed loosely before him, parallel to the ground, resting on the sword, and I climbed up onto the railing of the scaffold and grabbed his left elbow and hoisted myself up and crawled into his arms and I hammered a golden nail into the center of Field Marshal Paul Ludwig Hans Anton von Beneckendorff und von Hindenburg's chest.

Applause rose up to me from a gathering of passersby.

When I came down, Jeremy met me at the bottom of the scaffold. He clicked his heels and bowed.

Then we walked away, past the southern edge of the Reichstags-Gebäude, the Hall of the Imperial Parliament, the legislators inside as ornamental as the building's Italian Renaissance flourishes. We left the Tiergarten and found a café along the Spree and we had our beer and brat and I told him about the scar and my late drink with Stockman and the upcoming interview.

"Have you heard of this guy Haber?" I asked.

"Fertilizer?"

"You have. How?"

Jeremy shrugged. "The German newspapers. It's been a while. He's respected. They try to make him a bit of a hero, but fertilizer doesn't play a big part in the German mythos."

"So this afternoon Sir Al wants me to mythologize manure for the Americans."

"German manure."

"The critical thing is the conversation those two boys will have after they kick me out of the room."

"Bombs starve without nitrates too," Jeremy said. "If Stockman's working on big-scale bombing from Zepps, Haber's process is critical."

True enough. But things still didn't quite add up, a thought I voiced with a "However" that I let stand on its own for a moment. And then I said the thing I couldn't get straight: "Haber's active role in nitrates for bombs is long since done with. Why the personal meeting?"

Jeremy nodded. "So how do we listen in?"

Over the rest of lunch, he and I failed to come up with a plan for that. All we could conclude was that more improvisation would be called for.

He did stop me, however, as I turned to leave him outside the café. "Remember this about us," he said.

He heard himself. Us.

"About the *Germans*," he said. "They are difficult to fool. But they are often easy to bluff."

36

I took the elevator to the lobby of the Adlon a few minutes before four o'clock and emerged next to the front desk. I expected to meet Stockman in the bar, but he was talking to the frock coat at reception. He saw me out of the corner of his eye and glanced my way to wave me over with a little tilt of the head. As I approached, he was giving instructions for the envelope he was holding nose-high between his face and the clerk's. Both men's hands were still on it. Stockman hadn't let go yet, a gesture of emphasis to accompany his wishes.

"I want this delivered to Madam Isabel Cobb at the Lessing Theater. Personally. By hand." He paused dramatically after the "Personally." And even, briefly, after each word to follow. No mistakes. *Persönlich. Mit der Hand.*

"Absolutely," the clerk said, clicking his heels and bowing.

Stockman released the envelope to him.

"You may rely on the Adlon, Baron Stockman," the man said, still speaking to the English baronet in German.

The meeting time with Haber must have altered his dinner plans with my mother.

I'd trained myself as a reporter to take in every detail with a fresh eye and ear. Trask and his boys had only sharpened that. But sometimes it took a few details to pile up for me to finally notice. What I'd just witnessed had to do with a delivery. A delivery of something important. And it had to do with the mode of delivery. Stockman's emphasis clanged again in my head. And again. *Mit. Der. Hand.* And then I got it. MDH. The box to Kalk, near Cologne, the box to FVFB, was to be delivered personally. *With the hand.*

Stockman was clicking back at the frock coat. Of course he'd trust the Adlon. Now he turned to me and offered his hand. I shook it. And I wondered: *Mit dieser Hand?* With *this* hand? Given his obvious connection to the device in the box, I figured it was likely that the answer was yes. Stockman himself was going to deliver the Zepp bomb to Kalk.

We were soon in a taxi and heading toward Dahlem, a villa colony eight miles southwest of the city center. It was also the home of the Kaiser Wilhelm Society for the Advancement of Science. Four years ago Willie lent his name and gave big money to do a grander Berlin version of the Institut Pasteur in Paris. Instead of just biology and medicine, Willie's little *Gesellschaft* was hiring the big dogs—the German ones—to set up separate institutes in all the major sciences, where they could do what they damn well pleased without having to teach students or answer to bureaucrats or politicians or other government operatives. I figured maybe that last principle was getting a little shaky now that Germany was at war, which maybe was why Stockman was having this meeting.

The Tiergarten had barely vanished from the back window of our Daimler taxi when Stockman squared around toward me a little in the seat and said, "There are a few things we should talk about." He said this in English, the first English we'd spoken in quite a while, I realized. Though the driver's compartment was separate from the tonneau and the engine noise was loud, the partition window was partly open for the summer heat.

I shifted in my seat to match his angle toward me.

He said, "I am accepting Madam Cobb's faith in you. But I will be frank. From our conversations I can fully understand that faith."

He paused. Sober, he had nothing of the sentimental, the vulnerable about him. So I understood that this restrained pause and these somewhat indirect words were significant in Stockman's unintoxicated range of emotional expression.

"Thank you," I said.

"Your story with him must regard his process *only* as a benefit to humanity."

I heard the command and so I filled the brief silence that followed: "But *not* to include the benefits to humanity of our quickly ending the war."

He laughed. "You understand my full meaning."

"That's my job," I said. Indeed. I repressed that thought, however, a reflex sense of irony being a dangerous trait for a spy.

But he heard it the way he needed to. "If only all journalists had that gift," he said.

"I understand your *intended* meaning," I gently corrected. Surely he didn't want even a trusted journalist to know his *full* meaning.

He got it. He laughed again. "So if he volunteers anything else . . ."

"I will treat him as I do you," I said. "Nothing will ever appear in print that would embarrass him or Germany or will reveal anything that will aid Germany's enemies."

"I have already given him that assurance," Stockman said. "Now, a few incidental but problematic things, as you might naturally be inclined innocently to make small talk or to enhance the human elements of your story."

"As indeed I may," I said.

"Little more than three months ago, Doctor Haber's wife took his army-issued revolver into their garden and shot herself to death."

He said this flatly.

He said no more for a moment.

"So no questions about his family," I said.

"Best not."

The Daimler shifted gears and so did Stockman. He said, "Doctor Haber is a Heidelberg man, like yourself. And like yourself he bears a scar on his cheek. But I understand it is not a scar of honor. Forgive me. As the bearer of a true *Schmiss*, you no doubt would have recognized it for what it is. But I thought I should mention it."

"Yes, thank you," I said.

"He is a Jew," Stockman said.

He let me absorb that for a moment. The haters of Jews—often those who have leaned close and revealed this sotto voce—assumed the following moment of quiet was filled with an agreement on the subject that needed no further expression.

But Stockman said this as uprightly and flatly as he'd spoken of the suicide of Haber's wife. I kept my manner and face as neutral as his. I hoped he'd show more of himself now. A man who, in his ignorance, showed his prejudice, about whatever sort of subject, was a man who gave power to others. He showed the way his mind tended to stop working, his sensibility tended to shut out the real world. That was always useful, to a reporter or to a spy.

And Stockman said, "He converted to Christianity more than twenty years ago. So he is a Christian the way I am an Englishman."

He let me fill in the meaning of that. Clear enough. He was still a Jew.

Stockman said, "He has been a German from birth. As was his father and his father's father. Do they not bleed? I am one of those who thinks that Shylock was justified in seeking his revenge. And that Shakespeare intended so. But the Jew has his own blood. His people were born to wander. As things are, the Jew who has a legacy like Doctor Haber is certainly a German. He overtly proclaims his strong allegiance to Germany. You and I will take pride for America to learn what this German has done for humanity. Doctor Haber is my stepbrother, Josef. Certainly that. But does one trust a stepbrother as he does his brother by blood?"

Stockman shrugged, as if in answer to his own question.

I did not reply.

Stockman looked away briefly, at the passing shops along the Kaiser-Allée, and then back to me.

"I don't know what you should make of that," he said. "Perhaps just to understand the man."

Once again, he looked beyond the taxi that carried us.

He said, still looking away, "I suppose I trust a loyal German Jew more than any London Christian."

This ended the conversation between us for the last few miles to Dahlem.

Haber's Institute for Physical Chemistry was a large but only lightly ornamented four-storey, nine-bay Greek Revival building, its central three-bay section sporting mid-floor Doric columns holding up a bare-bones pediment, which was adorned with nothing but a central, circular window. The one striking feature, however, was hardly classical: a circular tower attached at the building's northern end with a *feldgrau* metal dome and a high-spiked spire making the thing look unmistakably like a massive, field-officer *Pickelhaube*.

The place was surrounded by barbed wire. It had two soldiers, draped with Mauser G98s, flanking the central door beneath the Doric columns. These boys were not features of the institute when it was pursuing the hundred-year quest to pull nitrogen out of the air so the plants could grow.

A soldier led us up the two central flights of marble stairs to Haber's office. At each floor I glanced right and left and there was a quiet, ardent urgency about the place: white coats flashing, intense words from the end of a hall, a canister rolling on a hand truck with a gray-hair in a three-piece suit hovering over each turn of the wheels.

You walk into an institute of chemistry, especially a bustling one, and you expect the place to bray in your nose from the smells of things whose names are unpronounceable and whose purpose can be understood only in formulas. But the place smelled like a Boston Brahmin boarding school, all floor wax and ozone.

I did not have a chance to walk down one of these laboratory corridors. Immediately at the top of the third-floor staircase we turned into a short hallway back toward the front of the building and were ushered straight into a conference room with windows looking into the tops of the plane trees on the Thiel-Allée. I figured Stockman would get a grander tour when the interview was over and I was beyond the barbed wire.

The room had an oak table for ten and was hung with Holophane reflectors and tungsten lamps, illuminated now, in the afternoon light, for the sake of the wall facing the windows, which held a twelve-foot blackboard festooned with equations. If the corridors of the institute smelled like those in a boarding school, this was the faculty lounge, redolent of chalk dust and tobacco smoke.

Stockman and I sat down next to each other along the lengthwise center of the table, facing the blackboard. The soldier vanished.

We both stared at the equations for a moment, the flow of constants and unknowns, coefficients and parameters. As if on cue we looked at each other.

I said, "We needn't worry so much about his saying something he shouldn't. I just hope he says something we can understand."

Stockman glanced once more at the equations, but only briefly. "I know some basics, from metallurgy," he said. "But far downstream from this. Far enough so I could make useful things in the world."

Like milk cans and Zepp bombs, I thought.

We nodded knowingly at each other.

Then we had one of those silently agreed upon shifts in a conversation where the two parties understand there is nothing more to say about the current subject but aren't ready to stop talking. We had to wait here together, so we consciously turned our minds elsewhere.

In so doing, Stockman's eyes fell to my lapel. "I meant to say earlier. I admire your pin. I'm sure there's a story behind it, which I'd like to hear sometime."

Stockman didn't know about the Nail Man, or at least about the reward for a big donation, and the Iron Cross was a powerful icon for this country. Good.

"The story's a simple one," I said, making it sound like humility masking bravado.

And Fritz Haber strode into the room.

He was a stocky man, wearing a bespoke summer wool suit, a high wing-tip collar, and a necktie knotted tight. He had a round face, with a pince-nez clamped to his nose, and was determinedly bald, having shaved off every last hair, slick as a chemical canister. The scar on his left cheek was of the South Chicago saloon-brawl variety, too short and too severely curled at the end ever to be rendered by a saber stroke.

Stockman and I jumped to our feet.

"Please, gentlemen, please," he said. "We shall be informal with each other, yes?" Nevertheless, he placed himself across the table from us to reach and shake our hands. "Can I have my assistant get you some coffee?"

Stockman and I declined with thanks and we all sat.

Haber had known from the jump-off to speak German with this Brit and this American.

"It is a pleasure to see you again, Baron," Haber said to Sir Albert.

"For me it is an honor, Privy Councilor Haber," Albert said, using the honorific *Geheimrat*, an open acknowledgment that Haber had the ear of the Kaiser or at least of his high minions.

Haber turned his face to me.

I thought, for just a molecule of a moment, that the mysteries of chemistry were no greater than the mystery of the pince nez hoop-spring, which held the damn fool thing in place.

"And Mr. Jäger, I am pleased to meet you," Haber said. "Baron Stockman has told me very good things about you. That you should find it as preposterous as I do that your country has ignored what we have accomplished here, this is encouraging for me."

"I have a forum to dispel that ignorance, Privy Councilor Haber," I said.

He smiled. "I appreciate both of you recognizing my status, but please call me *Doctor* Haber."

He said this with a magnanimous flare of the hands, as if he'd just sanctioned *Fritzy.*

I took out my notebook and my Conklin, and *Geheimrat Doktor* Fritz began, no initial question necessary. He talked for a while—lectured, more like—about the challenge of the locked nitrogen molecules in the air: the delicate balancing of very high temperatures and very high pressure for extraction; the need for an effective catalyst for the project; the frustrating search for precisely the right one, with Haber eventually moving from osmium, which was good, to uranium, which was more abundantly available, and then, when BASF made an industry out of it, finally arriving at iron, though iron alone was a failure and needed a subtle blend of the oxides of aluminum and potassium and calcium to make it work. He called what he'd done a kind of alchemy, as if he'd figured out how to make gold from the air. These limitless nitrates meant, after all, that *Geheimrat Doktor* Fritz had saved the world from starvation.

I took dutiful notes.

And all the while, my mind sought the delicate balance of heat and pressure so as to extract, from the rush of highly charged molecules of air in this room, a fertilizing clue or two about Stockman's full intentions.

Haber wrapped up his lecture and folded his arms, in satisfaction, upon his chest. "Those are the basics," he said. "Perhaps you have some questions, knowing better than I what it is that Americans have failed to grasp."

"Thank you, Doctor Haber," I said. "What you've said is very clear to me and very compelling. Please understand that Americans in general have not even had the chance to grasp any of this. The failure has been among a very small group of Americans. The journalists."

Haber nodded his head at the validity of my point. To his credit.

"And journalists," I said, "need a catalyst. They are—on their own—simple iron. May I seek now, for a few minutes, the aluminum, the potassium, the calcium oxides to mix with them?"

Haber smiled and nodded as I appropriated the terms of his mini-lecture for my request, as if he were a teacher and gave a damn about his teaching and a student from the back of the lecture hall had raised his hand and made a smart comment.

I had a fleeting sense of him. Not so much what he was as what he wasn't. Or didn't seem to be. In mourning. He was nothing like a man whose wife blew her brains out with his own pistol a couple of months ago. He seemed animated without mitigation. He gave off energy and focus and devotion.

Either this was one hard son of a bitch or his anguish was so strong he'd dug a hole for it and threw it in and all this energy was him shoveling dirt. I hoped for the latter. That would make him even more eager to talk about what was presently preoccupying him.

It was time now to suppress my scoop-seeking reporter's gag reflex. Which I did. And instead I recited my already twice-refined Stockman Doctrine, my fawning assurance to this guy that he could say anything that was on his mind and if it was the last thing in the world he'd want to tell a newspaper reporter, it was okay because I was there to protect him against himself.

In the midst of this, Haber had glanced once at Stockman, with a little flex around the eyes that appealed for reassurance. I'd kept my own eyes on Haber, and it was clear from the abrupt relaxation in his face that Stockman had come through for me.

When I finished, Haber said, "You may seek."

"Thank you," I said. "First, I'd like to return to a phrase you used—and naturally so—a few moments ago. 'Your country,' you said to me, referring to the United States of America. You are, strictly speaking, correct. But now I ask that you grant me the same assurance I have given you. I will tell you a thing meant only for the three of us. *My* country is Germany. It was the country of my father, and of my father's father."

I paused.

I did not need to say *Just like your father and your father's father.* I could read his face. The ever so slight firming of his mouth. The minute nod.

226

"That is perhaps the aluminum oxide," I said. "The American reporters who came to hear about your discovery lacked the . . ." I hesitated very briefly to find just the right word.

Haber intervened. "Promoter," he said.

I cocked my head at him, and he elaborated.

"These compounds are called *promoters* of the catalysis."

"Thank you," I said. "Yes. These journalists lacked the promoter of an existing connection to our country. I come to this story able to energize it for my readers by my pride in Germany."

Now it was time for a little catalytic self-deprecation, with an embedded appeal for him to spill his own beans. "I confess I'm intimidated interviewing such a great thinker as you, Doctor Haber. But at this moment in history, great thinkers need to step forward. I hope I'm saying all of this precisely. Am I making sense?"

"Perfect sense," he said. "During peace time a scientist belongs to the world. But during war time he belongs to his country."

I took a sudden, deep, seemingly admiring breath. "May I write that down?"

"Of course."

I did.

"Your discovery will help feed our country," I said. "Particularly in the face of this barbaric blockade of food by the British."

"It will help," he said.

"'Barbaric,' of course, is our private word."

"An appropriate word for our private use," Haber said.

"Are you continuing to refine the Haber Process for agricultural uses?"

"It is no longer a matter of science," Haber said. "It is a practical matter, for industry. They are the ones who seek refinements, mostly to do with increasing output. You should speak to the people at BASF in Oppau."

"The war must be making very heavy demands on them," I said, walking a high wire now with Stockman next to me, trying to lead Haber by rhetorical indirections.

"Carl Bosch, for instance," Haber said. "At BASF."

"Excellent idea," I said.

"Very heavy demands," Haber said.

He was circling back.

"It frightens me, in retrospect," I said. "If it were not for your process, our dear Fatherland could be running out of all that it needs."

I was referring to explosives, of course, not food. Ammunition. Bombs. I kept it vague, to keep Stockman quiet for as long as possible. But Haber instantly knew what I meant.

"We would have run out six months ago," Haber said.

Stockman jumped in. "We are all frightened of that in retrospect," he said. "But we have come through. And the subject of explosives falls outside of the story we wish to do."

He was staying vigilant.

"Sorry, Baron," I said. "These are emotional issues."

"I am well aware of that," he said.

I turned back to Haber.

I was glad to be in my reporter's frame of mind. I knew if you couldn't get something out of the guy you wanted to expose, you might at least get him to rail at his enemies. Whose names you made careful note of.

I'd even had a whiff of collegial conflict from that earlier quotable proclamation.

I figured it would take Stockman a little time to assess this line of questioning. And that he wouldn't hold it permanently against me. It was worth the risk.

"Doctor Haber," I said, "your fine observation still sings in my head. The responsibility of a scientist during war. Do all of your colleagues feel the same way?"

"Some. Most."

I could see him stiffening. Not against me. Against somebody in his head.

"I'm sure you of all people could persuade anyone who would waver."

"Not always." His face was turning red. Catalysis.

"If they are German," I said.

"German? Yes, German."

"And loyal."

Haber turned to Stockman, put his hand onto the tabletop in his direction. "I've spoken to you of this man," he said.

I could feel Stockman stirring.

This was a touchy issue between them as well.

Haber's face swung back to me. "Albert Einstein," he said.

37

This was another scientist whose name I did not know, but from the tone of Haber's voice I was expected to.

"I myself brought him from exile to the Institute," Haber said. "I overlooked his personality for the brilliance of his mind."

Fritz was going red in the face again.

I had to assume Stockman was about to intervene. Haber was in the grip of a powerful desire to talk.

"That exile was self-imposed," Haber said. "Though he was born in Germany, as was his father and his father's father."

He paused, letting this irony sink in.

I looked to Stockman, who was poised to speak. He glanced at me. I furrowed my brow and nodded to him, fleetingly, a gesture of reassurance. I lifted my notebook from the tabletop, while still looking at Stockman, and I turned to Haber and closed the notebook before him and put it back down, making a little show of it, more for Stockman, of course, than for Fritz. Though Fritz took notice.

"How distressing," I said.

Haber said, in crescendo, "Perhaps you are unaware, from living presently abroad, that ninety-three important figures in German science and culture, ten Nobel Prize winners included and more surely to come—Max Planck, for example—and even including a great figure from the world of your other subject, Isabel Cobb—I refer to Mr. Max Reinhardt—we all signed a manifesto declaring our support for our government and our opposition to the lies and calumny being spread about us abroad. Doctor Einstein was invited to sign. Not only did he refuse. He signed a scandalous counter-manifesto that gave credence to those very lies."

Haber was nearly shouting now. Shouting and quaking. He stopped. He calmed himself.

"Forgive me," he said. And then, almost gently: "Albert is fortunate that his position was so ludicrous. Only four of the invited hundred intellectuals signed, and the manifesto was never published. He was spared."

Haber removed the handkerchief from his breast pocket and patted his head. "I otherwise admire his mind greatly," he said. "However, for what one may call a cosmological physicist, he knows very little about the real world. How sad."

"Perhaps," Stockman said, matching Haber's abruptly subdued tone, "it is time for us to excuse Mr. Jäger and for you and I to discuss our business."

Haber pulled a watch on a fob from his vest pocket. He said, "I told Colonel Bauer four-thirty."

It wasn't four-thirty yet and Haber clearly had more steam to let off. But Stockman was getting nervous. "There are a couple of matters to discuss before he arrives. You have enough for the story, Josef?"

It was still critical that I appear eager to obey Albert. I stood up at once. "Of course, Baron Stockman. You know I am here simply to serve you. I can do a fine story with what Doctor Haber has officially given me."

"Excellent," Albert said. I remained his man. He even shook my hand at once. This led to Haber's offered hand and bowings and heel-clickings all around.

And so they were done with me.

The soldier was summoned and I was respectfully but efficiently escorted from the Kaiser Wilhelm Institut für Physikalische Chemie, placed in a waiting Daimler taxi beneath the plane trees, and sent away.

I got out at the Adlon and lingered on the sidewalk long enough for the taxi to drive off. I turned west and walked the three hundred yards to the Hotel Baden. I strode through the lobby and straight into the telephone kiosk. I'd barely gotten the receiver into my hand when somebody knuckled the glass pane directly behind my head.

I turned.

It was Jeremy.

I replaced the receiver and opened the door. "I was just calling you," I said.

"I supposed," he said.

"How are things in Spandau?"

"The factories never rest, thanks to your man Haber."

"They make shells?"

He nodded.

"Are they Krupp's?"

"Government factories."

"Your mother is well located."

"She is. I keep my eyes open. How was your improvisation?"

"That remains to be seen."

So we sat in the Baden coffee shop, in the corner farthest from the Unter den Linden windows, and I brought Jeremy up to speed, from Stockman at the Adlon reception desk to the taxi at the Adlon front door.

He said not a word till I'd done. Then he went straight to my interpretation of the writing on the second box in Reinauer's office. "I've not seen it used before, but your reading of MDH seems spot on."

"You agree it's likely mit *Stockman's* hand?"

"Seems so."

"Ever hear of Einstein?"

He shook his head no, even as he tried to think. "I don't believe."

"We need to find him."

"Around the Institute, perhaps." As soon as Jeremy said this, he shook his head again. "But how to approach him there."

"And this Colonel Bauer?"

"About him, I've got people to ask," Jeremy said. "Berlin is densely populated with colonels and 'Bauer' is common. No first name?"

"It wasn't spoken."

"If he's a third party to Haber and Stockman, maybe we can sort him out."

"How late can I call your number in Spandau?"

"Very late," Jeremy said. "My mother takes a long while going to sleep. What's your next move?"

"I have a hunch I can find Sir Albert tonight."

38

Jeremy and I went our ways, and I had dinner alone in the Adlon Pariser Platz, the red walnut-walled à la carte restaurant off the lobby, and then I retired to my room to give Albert a head start on his drinking.

At nine I entered Stockman's favorite watering hole. I strode automatically toward the far corner and in a few steps I could see past the end of the zinc bar to his table of choice. Three strangers in evening suits were confabbing there, two with Willie mustaches and one with a fez.

I stopped, roughing myself up in my head for not trying to formalize a drink with Albert for tonight.

But then a familiar voice said my name. "Mr. Hunter. Join us."

Even Mr. Hunter immediately recognized Isabel Cobb's voice.

I looked to my left.

Along the full width of this western wall ran a Bacchanalian mural, an unbroken, dancing, leaping, swooning, embracing flow of naked flesh and diaphanous gowns and goat parts under which were three arrangements for drinkers, two chairs each, their backs to the bar, a table before them, and a two-seat settee against the wall. In the center of these settings, nuzzled up shoulder to shoulder on the settee, were my mother and Sir Albert Stockman.

He was dressed in his evening suit. She was wearing a front-buttoning shirtwaist with intricate sylvan lace inserts and an apricot silk scarf thrown round her neck. She was straight from rehearsal, I presumed.

I approached.

As I did, a man rose from one of the chairs before them.

It was Madam Isabel's director, Victor Barnowsky.

He turned to me.

"*Herr Regisseur*," I said.

"Mr. Hunter," he said.

We exchanged another strong handshake. I was reminded of my first impression of him, how like a roughhouser he seemed.

"Won't you stay?" my mother said.

"Alas, I must go, Madam Cobb," Barnowsky said, sounding very formal. I figured they knew enough to hide their stage-star-and-present-director warmth in the presence of her beau. "A pleasure to meet with you, Baron." Barnowsky bowed to Stockman, who nodded at Barnowsky but said nothing. I figured Albert wasn't quite buying all this formality between his beloved and this theater director.

Barnowsky vanished and Albert loosened a little and motioned me into the empty chair.

I sat.

This wasn't going to be easy.

I had a front row seat before a very small stage with two lovebirds snuggled up and a great deal at stake and some messy personal issues in the script.

One of which was: *I may someday need to put a bullet between this guy's eyes.*

Another of which was: *He might need to do the same to me.* Indeed, the only thing that was keeping his finger from squeezing a trigger was his ignorance about me. The only inhibition for me was knowing too much about him. His restraint was more apt to change abruptly than mine. That put me at a severe disadvantage in any likely showdown.

We all looked at each other for a moment in a sort of dazed silence. I didn't know if I could talk about the Haber meeting in my mother's presence. Had their intimacy gone far enough for that to be okay? She didn't know what had transpired between us two men since last night and she was smart enough to let us set the tone and pace. Stockman had his airship überagenda mixing with his jealousy over his woman.

We were relieved by the bartender, whose arrival I realized by Albert's eyes shifting abruptly up and over my shoulder. He looked back to me. "What are you having?"

I looked down at the table.

It was Sam Thompson again, though if this was still the first bottle of the evening, the two of them were drinking their way forward quite moderately, judging by the amount of whiskey remaining. Their glasses were presently empty.

"There seems to be plenty of rye left," I said.

"A third glass, Hans," Stockman said to the bartender.

And we were silent for another moment.

Stockman was going to have to start this.

I took out a Fatima and gestured the pack to the snuggly couple.

Stockman waved it off with a thanks and dipped into his evening suit inner pocket and took out a silver cigarette case, going after his own brand.

My mother also declined the Fatimas, with a little shake of the head and a focusing of her eyes on mine and a surging of something in them that I read as, *Well, here we are, my son, in quite a melodrama together.*

Stockman lit his cigarette and offered his match across the table. I bent to it and sat back, as did Stockman, and we blew smoke together.

"I was telling Isabel about our impassioned Jew at the chemistry institute," Stockman said.

So they'd gone *that* far in their intimacy.

Then he made his more important point: "She has her own Jew to deal with."

Barnowsky was still weighing heavily on him.

I glanced at Mother. She was no doubt grinding her teeth, but she was a fine actress, after all, and, indeed, since she was already pressed shoulder to arm to hip to thigh against Stockman, she even crossed her free right arm over her body and placed her hand gently on his forearm. While wishing, instead, I would've bet, that she could slap him in the face.

But maybe not.

She was, indeed, quite convincing. Maybe she forgave him this attitude. She was, after all, presently in love with him.

"Herr Barnowsky is a sad, driven man," Isabel Cobb said.

Stockman took another drag on his cigarette, turned his face sharply away from us both, and blew the smoke toward the door, apparently releasing his jealousy, for his face swung back to Isabel and he put his hand over hers. "You work very hard for your art," he said.

"Don't I though," she said. She was looking into his eyes for this line, but I decided she was talking to me, telling me not to worry, she wasn't so smitten as to lose her secret way with him.

He patted her hand again and looked at me.

"This Albert Einstein was a touchy subject for our impassioned Doctor Haber," I said.

Stockman nodded.

I deliberately slowed down.

I took a drag on my cigarette. I blew the smoke.

My glass arrived.

"May I?" Hans the bartender said.

"Sure," I said, and Hans poured me a couple of fingers of rye.

Only when all this was done and the bartender had disappeared did I say, "You know anything about Einstein?"

"He's a Zionist," Stockman said. "I believe in the sincerity of Doctor Haber's allegiance to Germany, as far as it is possible for that to go, but this other man is a dangerous man. Made even more acutely so by his apparent genius."

"Albert was asking Herr Barnowsky about Herr Einstein," my mother said.

Stockman turned his face sharply to her. "Are you sure this director isn't a Zionist?"

"Of course he's not," she said. "He is a citizen of Shakespeare and Ibsen and Shaw."

"This Einstein likes his Shakespeare as well, apparently," Stockman said. "That doesn't prevent him from despising the land that gave him birth."

My mother patted his hand. "Victor Barnowsky is no Zionist, my darling."

"I say you deserve better, is all," said darling Albert.

She patted him some more. "I've dealt with this all my professional life."

Stockman's voice mellowed a little. "How difficult for you."

He turned to me now. He was, of course, trying to make a case for *himself*. As her exclusive lover. Perhaps even as her husband. I was his foil. I was the jury. I was the impartial public in obvious, silent agreement with him. He said, "This is widely overlooked by lovers of the theater, the terrible sacrifice a great actress must endure for her art. That she must inevitably surround herself with actors and directors and other men of that world, unprincipled men, emotionally tumultuous and unreliable men, morally weak men."

I could see her jaw clench at this, great actress though she was. Her hand stopped patting, but it stayed on his forearm.

Man oh man, was he ever trying to make a case. He even started to swerve back to Einstein.

"And these revered scientists. These outsiders."

He paused dramatically.

She must have said something admiring about scientists along the way.

He said, "This Einstein has a wife and two children. They were with him when he came to the Kaiser Wilhelm Institute, and he drove them away. She fled to Zurich because he began an affair with his own cousin in Berlin. This cousin was no doubt the reason he returned to his despised Germany. Not his vaunted research."

He paused to present us a moue of pained disapproval. Even Stockman could not miss the blanching of Mother's face. He just didn't have a clue what was behind it.

"I'm sorry to mention these scandalous things," he said. "But there are many men of this sort in the world who can be very attractive to women. I just believe in a different way of living."

As different as Stockman felt himself to be from the men of the theatrical world, he was, however, their kin. By something stronger than blood. By an instinct for self-performance. Little did he know. And little did he know that it was perhaps the deepest hook he had in my mother.

I could sense her gathering her actor's strength now. She said, "This is why I've come so quickly and strongly to rely on you, my darling."

He put his hand on hers. "I know," he said.

She grew urgent. "Must you leave me next week?"

"We've spoken of this," he said, lowering his voice a little. This was something he *didn't* want to discuss in front of me.

Mother was playing her own, woman's version of Albert's earlier strategy. A man used the public setting to display his plumaged worthiness. The woman reopened a private argument with her man. I was foil. I was jury.

Of course, Mother was also doing her job. She was giving me information.

He'd told her he was going away.

This was, I assumed, the *Mit der Hand* trip.

"I know we've spoken," she said. "But you have only reminded me now, with your characteristic eloquence—oh how I would miss that too, for even a few days, your lovely words—you have reminded me how bereft I will be."

"You must rehearse," he said.

"Opening night is still two weeks off. I can take a few days."

"It's strictly business."

"I won't interfere," she said.

"I'm not sure how long I'll be needed."

"But at least I could come for a few days."

"There are complications I cannot speak of."

"I will happily stay out of your way, in any nearby hotel you wish. Just come to me at night." She put her head on his shoulder.

He glanced my way, lifted his eyebrows to me.

I smiled a comradely smile.

He rolled his eyes.

Women.

He and I understood about that.

"I might be out until very very late," he said.

"I will rest."

"And your days will be empty as well."

She lifted her head. She made a show of trying to think of a solution. She came up with one and brightened. "You have spoken so warmly of Mr. Hunter. Perhaps we can bring him. During the day he can finish our story for the American papers. And he and I might even find a chance to discuss my memoir."

Stockman did not reply to this. His lover's head returned to his shoulder.

He looked at me.

I leaned forward and poured two fingers of rye into his glass.

I offered it to him and he took it with his free hand, in exchange giving me a muted reprise of the comradely smile.

He drank it down, not in a quick shot but in a steady, uninterrupted draft.

I took the empty glass from him and put it on the table.

He gently extricated his right arm without letting her raise her head and he put it around her shoulders. She snuggled in. "We'll discuss this later," he said.

She lifted her face to him.

If I were not sitting across from them, they no doubt would have kissed at this juncture. As it was, they goo-goo-eyed each other long enough that I was forced to look away and concentrate on my Fatima for a drag and blow.

I hoped she hadn't overplayed her hand. In spite of my encouraging Sam Thompson to help out, Albert would confront all this soberly in the morning.

They'd begun to murmur things to each other.

I thought, hopefully, about Albert Einstein's love for Shakespeare. I figured there might be a way to approach him.

I checked out the loving couple, and Stockman was withdrawing his arm. He'd suddenly turned downright shoulder-rollingly, tie-straighteningly furtive. He seemed finally aware of the public setting. Maybe he wasn't all that akin to theater people after all. Maybe it was just the power of my mother. The spell she put on any man.

He reached for the bottle and began to pour.

My mother sat herself up straight. She arranged the bodice of her dress. She looked at me. *Calm* she was, or she was simply portraying that. *Confidently in Control.*

Okay. She'd pressed all this forward. I'd come a long way with Albert myself. I thought I, too, could push him a little. Carefully.

"Did the rest of your meeting go well at the Institute?" I asked, while reaching for my own whiskey glass.

Maybe he'd talk a little more readily about this because it offered a clear shift away from the wheedlings of his lover.

I grasped the glass and looked at him.

He lifted two more fingers of rye. I straightened and offered my glass for toasting.

He leaned to me and we touched our Sam Thompsons. "It did," he said.

We sat back. I sipped. He took his whiskey in one quick shot.

"I hope Doctor Haber calmed down for the colonel," I said.

There was a brief stopping in Stockman, a flicker of something. I was afraid this was about me crossing a line. I hoped it was still about Haber. Maybe Albert had to remember how I'd learned about there being another person in their meeting. A colonel, no less. Whatever it was, it seemed to pass.

"Max wouldn't tolerate it," Stockman said.

Max. Nothing like a good bolt of whiskey sliding down your throat to get you to speak familiarly about your pals.

But the burn of the rye cooled and he corrected himself, made things properly proper. "Colonel Bauer," he said.

"Is he someone I should meet?" I said.

"I can't imagine why," Stockman said. Quickly and firmly. I was afraid *suspiciously*.

I'd gotten careless.

"Sorry," I said. "I'm just increasingly frustrated, wanting to help our cause and not knowing how."

Stockman waved this off.

But he said nothing.

I hoped it was the apology that he'd brushed aside and not the explanation.

He was staring at the bottle.

"Can I pour for you?" my mother said.

Stockman looked at her and then at me and then at her.

"No," he said. "Let's retire."

"All right," she said.

I waited for some look, some gesture, some word from him that could reassure me he'd not become suspicious.

But he rose and she rose and she hooked her arm in his and they turned to go.

"Good night," I said to them both.

"Good night," my mother said.

Stockman said nothing.

39

I left the Adlon bar soon after the retiring couple, and I went out of the hotel and headed for the Baden. I worried every step of the way that I was starting to lose Stockman. But I'd needed to press things forward. I had to let this play itself out.

I rang Spandau from the lobby telephone kiosk. The mother answered instantly. "Müller."

"Hello, Mrs. Müller," I said. "It's Mr. Jäger. May I speak to Erich?"

She said nothing, but the phone clunked and then Jeremy answered.

"Is your mother all right with me calling?" I asked.

"Don't mind her," he said "We've been talking about the Kaiser."

"Is she disaffected?"

"Far from it."

"How's your brother doing? I meant to ask."

"He's presently alive and unwounded."

We both fell silent a moment.

Then I said, "Max."

"Max?"

"His first name. Colonel Max Bauer."

"That will help," he said.

"I have a thought to find the other gentleman."

"Good."

And we both reminded ourselves that a telephone was still a telephone, even in the lobby of a relatively safe hotel.

We bade each other good night.

I hung up and hesitated only a moment before going out of the Baden and back to the Adlon.

In the lobby, Wagner was nowhere to be seen. In my room, nothing seemed to have been reexamined.

My laundry was waiting on the foot of the bed, wrapped in brown paper and folded neatly therein and giving off the faint, fresh, broken-rock smell of Persil. I had a clean set of summer-cotton BVDs and I put them on to sleep.

I opened the door to the balcony but pulled the drapes closed.

I put my Mauser in the drawer of the night table, went to bed, and fell instantly asleep.

And I awoke abruptly in the dark to a knocking.

My bedroom door was open to the sitting room and the knock had come from in there, at the door to my suite.

It was soft.

And then it came again, a little less soft.

I rose.

I switched on my bedside lamp.

"Please," a voice said outside. A heavy, feminine whisper.

A stage whisper.

I brisked across the floor and looked through the peep hole.

It was my mother.

I opened the door.

"Quickly," I said.

She slipped in.

She was wearing her shirtwaist but not her scarf. All the button-to-hole matches were off by one.

"You shouldn't be doing this," I said.

"I didn't know when I'd get to talk to you. No one saw me."

"There's a floor attendant."

"He's sleeping."

"German agents on staff."

"I'm telling you I wasn't seen," she said.

"I need pants," I said.

"I'll wait," she said.

I left her in the dark and disappeared into the bedroom, pushing the door partly closed. I put on my pants from the wardrobe, cinched the belt tight, and took one step back into the sitting room. "Come in here, away from the door," I said.

She entered the bedroom.

She sat at the dressing table and I sat in a side chair.

Her hands were clasped tightly in her lap, fingers intertwined. Her upper arms were drawn tightly against her.

"You dressed in the dark," I said.

She looked down.

She looked at me. She said, "He travels to Cologne on Monday."

"He told you the details?"

"Yes. Of course. He didn't think I'd make that fuss in public."

"Did that compromise his trust?"

"I don't know for certain. I don't think so."

"It was worth trying," I said. "You did well. And Monday to Cologne is very good information."

Her hands unclasped, her arms fell away from her lap. Her tension drained instantly, completely away, a tension I'd assumed was over her secret visit to my room under the sleeping nose of Albert and all the rest of the German secret service at the Adlon. In fact, she was tense because she was afraid I'd disapprove of her handling of his declared trip. I'd applauded. So all was right in her world.

Now she had to make a swift exit.

But I did need to speak with her privately, and here she was.

"Are you sure you weren't seen?" I said.

"It's three in the morning," she said.

"Mother . . ."

"I know. I know. I'm sorry. But I was careful. I came up the stairs. I saw no one."

"It's not just strangers I'm worried about," I said. I nodded at her skewed buttons and holes. Dressing in the dark meant one thing. "Did you come from *his* room?"

She didn't answer.

"You did," I said.

She stayed silent.

"How did you expect to get back in?"

She shrugged a so-what shrug.

I repeated the question with a tilt of my head.

"I have a key," she said.

"You took his?"

"No. That would be risky."

I clucked at this.

"I have one of my own," she said.

Of course.

"This whole complication is dangerous for us," I said.

"'O time, thou must untangle this, not I,'" she said. "'It is too hard a knot for me to untie.'"

Whenever she began to speak with lines from her favorite roles—this one Viola from *Twelfth Night*—I knew the topic would drag on. But this conversation was not worth the clock tick of risk. I needed to say the critical thing quickly.

"Look," I said. "This guy Albert Einstein may have some crucial information. He's a Shakespeare fan. He may be an Isabel Cobb fan as well. Your man Barnowsky may know him. I need for you to see Einstein and I need to go with you and we need to do this as soon as possible. Before your Albert heads for Cologne."

I was just trying to keep the Alberts straight. Mostly. But she played the phrase big, to tweak my nosiness. "*My* Albert hates that man," she said. "If he found out . . ."

"He won't. You won't let that happen. It's worth the risk."

She looked down again.

She started to unbutton her blouse.

"Look away," she said. "I need to fix this."

I rose and turned my back on her. I walked to the bed and I sat down on the edge, very near the night table.

"He has a dinner tomorrow night," she said. "At the Ministry of War. He's talking that openly to me."

"He didn't want you on his arm?"

She didn't reply.

I had to be careful how I spoke of him.

She cursed low. About the buttons.

I rephrased. "You're not going?"

"I tried," she said. "Boys only. You should come to the theater around seven. I'll see about the other Albert."

And from the dark at the far of end of the sitting room came four swift, hard knocks at the door.

I jumped up.

The following silence rang in the room. Only briefly.

Another two knocks. And Stockman's voice. "Josef."

I turned to Mother, who had succeeded merely in totally unbuttoning her shirtwaist, exposing a lacy vest brassiere.

She was wide-eyed. Her hands had fallen straight down at her sides.

I put my forefinger to my lips.

I looked in the direction of the door.

Two more knocks, louder still. "Josef," he said, in English. "I'm sorry, but I must come in."

I thought of the Mauser.

I turned to the night stand.

No acceptable solution presented itself in the maelstrom of my brain that involved my pistol and this hotel room at the Adlon in the middle of the night. I figured it would be best not to have that option.

"Sir Albert?" I called. "Is that you?"

"Yes."

"Give me a moment."

I looked at Mother.

She was standing now. I wondered if she'd played this scene before in one of those theatrical tour hotels.

She blew me a kiss, with a death mask face.

I breathed deep and stepped through the bedroom door, closing it behind me.

I turned to the desk, found the table lamp, and switched it on.

I moved to the suite door.

I looked through the peep hole and reared back. He was standing very near.

His hands were not in sight. But if he was holding a weapon, surely he'd have stepped back a little so he could at least raise his arm in preparation.

I opened the door.

Stockman had dressed in haste and only partially: his black evening suit trousers with a braid stripe; his white shirt, properly buttoned, but no collar.

At his side, fisted in his left hand, was Mother's apricot scarf.

I'd already observed that Albert was right-handed. To carry this in his off-hand was a conscious act. Was he keeping his pistol hand free?

"May I come in, old man?" he said.

A very friendly phrasing and tone for a presumptuous request at this hour.

Stockman felt very dangerous to me.

But the slightest hesitation would only make him more suspicious.

I stepped back instantly, opening the door wide.

"Of course," I said.

He stepped in.

I watched his eyes. He rapidly checked every corner of the room. His gaze lingered for a beat on the closed bedroom door.

I shut the suite door behind him.

"Drink?" I said. "The Adlon attendant has kept the side table nicely stocked."

"No thanks," he said.

We were standing in the middle of the floor.

"Would you like to sit?" I motioned to the divan and the chair.

"I'm sorry to bother you like this," he said, still in English.

I nodded at his left hand. "Isn't that the scarf Madam Cobb was wearing tonight? Is she all right?"

His eyes had fixed on the bedroom door again. At my voice, he looked at me.

"I don't know," he said. "May I step into your bathroom?"

It was the one place where she could hide outside of the bedroom.

"Of course."

As soon as he looked away and began his first step past me, I focused on the pockets of his trousers. Left front and then, as he crossed the floor, both back pockets.

He vanished into the bathroom.

The prime pocket, right front, had eluded me for the moment.

Water began to run in the basin.

It would be quickly obvious that she wasn't in there.

After only a few seconds the water shut off again. He'd made a cursory attempt to hide his suspicion. But his patience had quickly run out.

He emerged from the bathroom. One step and he stopped.

He looked at the scarf in his hand. An anguished little gesture.

If he was not still actively drunk, his head was surely pounding with the afterclap of rye.

I had to believe, from the look of his right front pocket, that he was indeed armed with a small pistol.

He drew near me.

I knew he would have to search the bedroom.

I had two thoughts. If I let him initiate the search, he might draw the pistol first. And whatever my mother was planning for this situation, she was ready by now.

"Sir Albert," I said, very gently. "My friend. You will not insult me if you'd like to look in my bedroom."

His eyes focused on mine but in that restless way of darting back and forth, back and forth, from one eye to the other.

"Yes," he said. "Thank you for understanding, Josef."

It had been the right thing to say.

He moved past me.

I turned.

In my periphery something caught my eye on the floor, where he'd been standing. He'd dropped the scarf.

Stockman wanted both hands.

He opened the bedroom door. The light was still on.

He stepped in and I followed, as quietly as I could.

He went first to the wardrobe. I stopped in the doorway.

He twisted the handle and opened the wardrobe door. Slowly now. He was using his right hand, his pistol hand. Good. It would mean a few moments of delay for him to be able to shoot.

I took another small step toward him, determined not to seem threatening, ready to lunge at him.

The door was swinging wide.

No rustling in the wardrobe.

No words.

He closed the wardrobe door and turned.

We looked at each other.

I offered him a gentle smile. "Whatever you need to do," I said.

He turned away from me. Looked across the room.

I followed his eyes.

The drapes at the balcony door.

He knew. I knew. The other likely place.

He moved past me once more.

I edged my way toward the night table and the Mauser.

He reached the drapes, hesitated.

The temptation in my fingertips was to ease the drawer open. But the room was quiet. The sound would make him turn and what he would see could be understood in only one way.

I stayed put. If he stepped out and there were sounds, I could have the Mauser pretty quick anyway.

He put his hand to the drape. Still he hesitated. He loved her. He did not want this to be true. But he loved her. So the possibility of this was roaring in his head.

He wrenched the drapes aside.

The door was open.

He stepped out.

He vanished to the right.

There were no sounds.

He crossed by the open window and vanished to the left.

Nothing.

He appeared in the doorway.

Even across the room I could sense the quaking in him.

My own mind was roaring now. There was only one other possible place. But could she even fit under the bed? I did not let my eyes go there. I knew that the sheets and the light quilt were untucked and hung low. I thought I even remembered a dust ruffle down to the floor.

Would Stockman go so far as to get down on his hands and knees to make sure about this last possible place?

He stepped into the room.

He stopped.

I tried to read his body. There was an aura of release about him: his shoulders had gone slack; his hands, which were prepared moments ago even to kill, hung limp at his sides.

"Can I get you that drink now?" I said. Very softly.

He hesitated.

Surely he wanted to believe what his hands and his shoulders already believed.

My last gesture of innocent confidence would be to step out of the bedroom before him. If he did energize his hands in a final burst of suspicion and he got down on his knees after I left, there would be sounds at the discovery—Mother would surely engage him—and only then would he come after me. I could maybe get back into the room in time to prevent his weapon coming into play.

"Yes, you can," he said.

I turned. I stepped from the room.

The drink table was against the wall just to the side of the bedroom door. I put my hand to the bottle of Scotch. I did not take the top off. I turned my hand and grasped it by its neck. A weapon.

But almost at once I heard Stockman's footsteps approaching from inside the bedroom.

I let go of the bottle and he emerged and passed on across the floor.

I glanced over my shoulder.

He was collapsing into the scroll-armed chair.

I poured two sizable shots of whiskey and crossed to him.

He took one with a murmured thanks.

I sat on the divan.

We did not toast. He shot his down. I sipped only a very little bit of mine.

"She's in her room," he said.

I waited for more.

"She must be in her room," he said.

"I'm sure she's safe," I said.

"She left my bed," he said. "We can speak as men together, you and I, can we not?"

"Of course," I said. Now I shot my whiskey down, and before he could say any more I rose and moved toward the side table. I needed a refill.

"For me too," he said.

I awaited Albert's men-together talk in much the same mood as his when he approached the balcony a few moments ago. I had to throw the drapes back but I really did not want to find what was on the other side.

I picked up the bottle of whiskey, a fine old Dundee, though it could have been a Chicago-saloon, two-bits-a-shot, squirrel whiskey for all either of us cared at that moment.

I returned to Stockman and poured us some more and I sat down.

My only revenge was that she was probably in the next room listening to every word.

"I woke," he said. "We had been man and woman together, you understand."

I understood. I pushed him along. I said, "She was gone?"

"She was."

I glanced across the floor to the apricot-colored pile of silk.

I had an inspiration.

"If she were going to another man, she would have taken her lovely scarf," I said.

He looked over his shoulder and then back at me. Then back at the scarf. Then he looked me in the eyes as if he'd suddenly realized it was *me* he was in love with.

"Josef," he said, in a commensurate tone of voice. "You are *right*, my friend."

I realized how tightly coiled a metal spring there'd been in my chest, because it now suddenly eased. I didn't have to hear his man-talk so he could convince himself he was still okay in bed with my mother.

"Of course," I said.

"Thank you."

"It was simply evident," I said.

"She is in her room. But she must be angry with me."

"Which is why she did not answer when you knocked."

"Exactly," he said. He looked at the drink in his hand, which he'd not yet touched. He took about a third of it now, as if it were his own choice and not a physical necessity.

"Yes," he said. "She must think she has cause to be angry."

He lifted his shoulders and let them fall as if to say, *What can you do?*

"You heard the issue tonight," he said. "I have to go south for a while. I don't know for how long exactly. A few days. A week. She has her play, after all."

I took a good bolt of my whiskey. Maybe half of it. Not from choice but from necessity. So I wouldn't choke on the irony of having to now say the things I needed to say. "But she has something more important to her than *Hamlet*."

His drunken brow furrowed in puzzlement. The dope.

"She has you," I said.

I wanted to keep on drinking while he figured this out. But I was already feeling a little too warm in the face, a little too reconciled with the stuff that had to come out of my mouth.

I looked for a place to put my glass down.

I may even have remarked at this point at the inappropriate absence of a table near this chair and divan.

If I did, the remark was lost on Stockman, whose face was crimped in thought.

I placed the glass on the floor.

All right, I thought. *Say it.* "She's a woman in love. When she told you she couldn't bear to be away from you, she meant it. She aches. You understand, Albert? She aches, my brother. For you."

I'd raised my voice for this whole proclamation. Grandly. So she could clearly hear that I knew what I knew.

I'd stopped drinking in time to manage the important things. I was coherent. I knew I'd remember everything we said. I was in control of my words and focused on their hidden rhetorical intent. Perhaps, though, the theatrical flourishes had a bit of a life of their own.

"She aches to be with you," I said. "And if there is any sense in her that this is an important trip you are making, that only causes her to ache more urgently. She wants to be there with you. Beside you. Don't you see?"

His face was uncrimping now.

"You are a lucky man," I said.

He nodded faintly.

"Chancellor Otto von Bismarck was a great leader," he said.

Ah, Albert, I thought. *This is your response to my invocation of Isabel Cobb's love? What the hell does she see in you?*

"Perhaps the greatest of all German statesmen," he said.

But what the hell did she see in any of them?

I was glad he was speaking nothing but English. I wanted Mother to hear him clearly.

"There would be no Germany, in all its present glory, if it weren't for him," he said.

I was tempted to pick up the drink from the floor, but I did not.

"He is the quintessential figure of diplomatic moderation and balance. And those qualities were often useful. But he had to learn a lesson from an American general. Did you know that?"

"I did not," I said.

"The great Union general from your Civil War, Philip Sheridan, dined with Chancellor Bismarck during the Prussian war with France. The critical last war that united us as a people. Sheridan said at table that the proper strategy of war consists not only in telling blows against the army of the enemy, but to cause the enemy's civilians—and I am quoting Sheridan now—'to cause so much suffering that they must long for peace and force their government to demand it. The people must be left nothing but their eyes to weep with.'"

At this he paused to drink. A natural pause for a man whose drinking was driven by a darkness in him that needed management, or encouragement.

"He had it in him, our dear father Otto," he said. "But he needed to hear that. He dealt properly with the French from then on. He had no further qualms to shoot every prisoner, burn every village, hang every man, dispose of any civilian at all who might conspire against us. And such measures ended the war far more quickly. Won the war. Allowed us to become the people that we are."

He paused again, looked at the empty glass. I thought to fill it, but I did not. Nor did he. He bent down and, with meticulous care, set his glass on the floor, beside the leg of his chair.

He lifted his face once more to me. "It's ironic," he said. "Our Kaiser himself dismissed Bismarck for failure to appreciate the call of God to create our German Empire. Wilhelm despised Bismarck's moderation. And yet the same flaw resides in him. Particularly with regard to England. I sympathize. There is blood involved. But his grandmother the queen's most powerful connection to all of us was her husband, and his pure blood did not actually flow in her veins. Her own Germanness, from her forefathers, was greatly diluted. Too much of England coursed in her. For our Kaiser thus to waver in his will because of his sentimental attachment to Victoria is madness. He will prolong this war. He will lose this war."

Stockman grasped the two knobs of his chair arms, straightened his spine, lifted his chin. "It is time for heroism in our Germany, Josef. Time for a new hero."

And the thing that was nagging at me, puzzling me, over this apparently drunken digression suddenly became clear. What leap had his mind taken from the adoring love of my mother to Otto von Bismarck and then to Kaiser Wilhelm? These men were the precursors for the new hero. The hero being Albert. The hero who needed a witness, a woman, my mother and her adoration.

I even bet that this chain of association had not yet snapped in Albert's head.

Softly as his own voice whispering inside his own whiskey-heated brain, I said, "She needs to be with you for this."

He lowered his heroically lifted chin and looked at me. "I should go now," he said. "I will let her sleep."

He rose. I rose. He was surprisingly steady on his feet. I was somewhat less so for a moment.

"*Eisen und Blut*," he said, the first German he'd spoken since he entered my rooms. I recognized it from Bismarck. His most famous speech. Not by speeches and majority decisions would the great issues of the day be settled, he'd said. But by *iron and blood*.

It would have been a good exit line, his *Eisen und Blut*. But instead, Albert moved to Mother's apricot scarf, bent, and took it up once more. He put it to his face and breathed deeply in. At *this* he grew unsteady, swaying a little until he lowered the scarf and blinked his way back to his purpose.

I, on the other hand, in witnessing this gesture, grew suddenly quite steady afoot and it was all I could do to restrain my right hand from fisting and knocking Stockman down.

But restrain, I did.

Indeed, I put my hand on his shoulder and said, "Don't forget what I've said."

"You are my friend," he said. And he was gone.

After the click of the door I stood in the center of the room and did some blinking of my own.

His declaration of friendship was the first thing to blink away.

Not so easy, I found.

But I blinked.

Then there was my mother.

I turned to face the bedroom.

And she was standing in the doorway.

She was not looking at me. Rather, she was studying her hands working at the buttons of her shirtwaist. She was half buttoned and I waited.

She did up every button to the top before she lifted her face to me.

I could not read her expression. I therefore assumed it was real.

"Where were you?" I said.

"Under the bed."

"How?"

"Barely," she said. And she looked down and took her two hands and fluffed her lately compressed breasts.

I looked away.

"Hamlet prepared me," she said.

I gave her a moment and looked back to her. She'd finished with her breasts. I said, "Hamlet has not prepared you for what's next."

"'I will screw my courage to the sticking-place,'" she said.

"Good," I said, though it didn't turn out so well for Lady Macbeth.

"Victor knows all the splendid Jews in Berlin," she said. "Especially the theater lovers. I will find this man Einstein."

40

And she did.

At six o'clock that evening I arrived at the Lessing and the old man on the chair nodded me through at once. I crossed the lobby and stepped into the back of an auditorium ringing with the sound of hammers. On stage the utility lights were lit and men in overalls were upstage center, building a wooden archway flanked by parapeted platforms. Barnowsky was no painted scenery man.

He was nowhere in sight. It was Saturday night. I figured rehearsal was finished already. I twinged in concern that she'd made no progress in finding the other Albert, but Mother had specifically said seven o'clock, and so I went along the side aisle and through the door that led past the wings staircase and down the corridor to her dressing room.

I approached the closed door. I drew near and laughter rolled into the corridor, my mother's familiar bray—the one laugh of hers I could never quite identify as real or fake—and a man's unfettered, alto laugh.

Was that the laugh of a man who faced down the mysteries of the physical universe? If it was and he was capable of this laugh, maybe things weren't so bad, cosmologically.

I knocked on the door.

The laughter stopped.

I heard a murmur of my mother's voice to her visitor, and then she called out, "Come in."

I opened the door.

She was sitting in her makeup chair in an informal dinner gown of pale-green taffeta. She'd been waiting for a while, having already changed from her rehearsal clothes. I wondered how long the guy in the room had been here. A while, certainly. The pervasive greasepaint and cold cream smell of the room was actually beginning to yield to his pipe tobacco, a bland but insistent blend of burley and Cavendish and something vaguely nutty.

He was rising to his feet to greet me, a trim, medium-sized man with upstanding, dense, faintly wavy black hair and an equally dense mustache that neatly shrouded his entire upper lip from laugh line to laugh line. His chin was deeply cleft and his eyes were nearly as dark as his hair but they came brightly alive as he rose.

"This is Doctor Albert Einstein," Mother said.

He offered his hand with my name on his lips even before she could formally announce it. "Mr. Hunter. I am very pleased to meet you." He spoke in English that was proper but German-accented as heavily as if by a ham actor.

I thought I saw his eyes flick toward my saber scar. But if so, it was so quick I could not say for sure.

Mother said, "I told the professor that you're working on a story about the Kaiser Wilhelm Institute and you need to speak with him."

"I am pleased to assist you from the urging of Madam Cobb," Einstein said. "She is pressing boldly outward our boundary of understanding. She tries to do for the immense William Shakespeare what a great physicist tries to do for the physical universe. So I comply with anything she asks."

He laughed that high, ringing laugh.

Mother laughed with him. Not the bray. His overriding laugh made hers harder to read, but I looked at her and her eyes were locked on him in appreciation.

"The story is narrower than the Institute," I said in German. "And I ask only to more deeply understand what I already know. You and your words will not appear in any newspaper. I ask for something perhaps like one scientist objectively testing another's work."

He brightened at my analogy, at my understanding of the process of scientific discovery. He laughed again. "A peer review," he said.

"Forgive us for speaking German, Madam Cobb," I said.

"Not at all," she said. "I want you two to communicate fully."

"As shall you and I," Einstein said, in English, turning to her. "Over some little food."

"Yes, Professor," she said. "I look forward to learning from you." And to me: "When you and the professor have finished, he and I will dine nearby."

Perhaps I showed a glint of concern in my face.

She said, "You will recall that our previously intended companion tonight is dining at the Ministry."

"I do recall that," I said.

She rose. "I'll leave the two of you alone so you can speak German without regret."

"You need not go, dear lady," Einstein said.

"I have to consult for a time with my director. I won't go far."

Einstein took up her hand and bowed over it and kissed it.

Mother shot me a look as if she blamed me for not regularly doing this myself.

As her physicist rose from her hand, he said, quite ardently, "*Soll ich dich einem Sommertag vergleichen?*"

And she shot me another look, this one approximately *You see how they adore me?* This look seemed unrelated to any apparent understanding of the words, though she was certainly correct about its intent.

She swooped from the room and the door clicked shut.

I said to Einstein, returning to German, as he'd just used with her, "You only asked to compare her. Are you saving the comparison itself?"

He laughed.

He had quoted Shakespeare's sonnet to her. *Shall I compare thee to a summer's day?*

"I am afraid," he said, "that I cannot remember the comparison. Only the request."

"Thou art more lovely and more temperate," I said. *Er ist wie du so lieblich nicht und lind.*

"I am indebted to you," Einstein said. "I shall finish the verse over dinner. Do you think she will understand?"

"She'll understand, all right," I said. "If not the words, certainly the intent."

He beamed and I smiled in return. I managed only a wan smile, however, as I felt once again, inevitably, inextricably—perhaps even cosmologically—drawn into my mother's flirtations and wooings and beyond.

Though I expected this Albert's intent was no more than courtly flirtation.

Einstein and I sat down on the two chairs before Isabel Cobb's makeup mirrors.

"May I?" he said, lifting his pipe.

"Of course," I said.

He drew out a box of matches from the side pocket of his tweed jacket, and as he did, he glanced at me. Brief though it was, I was certain this time that the glance had sought out my scar.

I knew Einstein had once abandoned Germany. I said, "My father exiled our family from this country, but he sent me back to Heidelberg for an education. When I was young and stupid," I said.

He smiled. "That is the state in which we all enter university," he said.

He tamped his tobacco with his thumb and lit the bowl and drew at it and lit again and finally was producing sufficient smoke for me to speak.

I knew he'd exiled himself, and I knew his politics. I tapped into them at once. I said, "I am writing for a syndicate of newspapers in the United States. These are newspapers whose readers are largely German-Americans. The gentleman Madam Cobb and I just referred to is an English baron with deep roots in Germany. Very deep roots. He feels the German cause is misunderstood in my country. He feels Germany is justified in this war. More than justified. Righteous. He wants me to write a story that will help advance that theory in America."

Einstein had just taken in a deep draw of his tobacco, and he turned his head a little away and blew the smoke to the mirrors. He turned back to me. Slowly now. The bright energy in him was gone.

He lowered his pipe.

A good reporter makes every person he questions think that whatever they say will be welcomed by a sympathetic ear, will be heard as true and persuasive and wise. Not only was this easy to do with Albert Einstein, it was a great relief. I'd been working in this way far too long and unrelievedly with Albert Stockman.

I said, "I have learned that you are someone whose sensibilities and values I might trust. Though given the people I've been involved with, I learned this about you indirectly, like an experiment where you cannot observe a thing directly but must infer it from its effects."

In spite of his sudden gravity, Einstein smiled at this.

"The English gentleman is named Albert Stockman. Baron Stockman is subtle in his approach. The article, as he has conceived it, will focus entirely on the great humanitarian accomplishments of your colleague Doctor Fritz Haber. I am to write exclusively and glowingly about the Haber Process feeding the hungry of the world."

I paused.

Einstein looked at his pipe, thinking, no doubt, to draw from it.

I said, "I will never quote you, Professor. But I feel as if things are going on that I need to know, and if I don't know them, I'll become part of a terrible deception."

Einstein stared at his pipe a few moments more and then gently placed it on the makeup table, watching it all the way.

He lifted his eyes from the pipe but did not move them to me.

I turned my head to the mirror.

We looked at each other there.

He was silent still.

We continued to look at each other, our directness an illusion, bent together by the silvered surface.

His silence worried me. I decided to lead him a little. I said, "I realize that the same process produces explosives. Without limit."

The face in the mirror looked away.

As did I.

And so our eyes met directly.

"Your intuition is correct, Mr. Hunter," he said.

He did not let go of my gaze but he searched for words. I had to be patient now. I held very still.

"I am indebted to Professor Haber," he said. "He brought me to the Institute. I have freedom here."

He stopped.

I wanted badly to challenge any sense of loyalty he might have to Haber. Did he know how Haber spoke of him? But I waited.

Einstein said, "Do you like an irony? At this institute that bears the Kaiser's name, within a country and a political system and a philosophy that reserves its right to repress whatever freedoms it chooses and that nurtures a violent disdain for the fundamental freedoms of anyone not of their nation, I am nonetheless free to think about what matters most. I suppose the deepest workings of the physical universe do not seem to them a threat."

He stopped once more.

I held very still.

And then he said, "This does not have to do with the Haber-Bosch Process. This does not have to do with explosives. All of that is a matter for the industrialists now."

He looked at his pipe, put his hand upon it. He said, "Fritz Haber has an excellent brain. But his nationalism is contemptible. He does not need a brain for that. The spinal cord would be sufficient."

His hand returned to his lap. His eyes returned to me.

He said, "You know what happened in France in April."

It took me only a moment. "Ypres."

"Yes."

"The German gas attack."

"Chlorine gas," he said. "A persuasive case could be made for the intrinsic moral superiority of physics over chemistry, judging them by their factors of risk, by the relative difficulty or ease of their doing terrible harm to humanity."

He picked up his pipe now and brought it to his mouth.

My mind at this moment was suddenly like those Allied troops in the trench as the first pale-green cloud of chlorine gas drifted toward them across no-man's-land. They knew this looked bad. But they had not yet been overwhelmed. They waited.

I waited.

He shrugged. "Ah, but no doubt physics will catch up someday. Humans will always find a way to pervert the beauty of knowledge. Our technology will soon exceed our humanity. No. I misspeak. It has done so already."

Einstein drew in vain on his pipe. He took it from his mouth and looked at it. And as if making this observation to the object in his hand, he said, "Fritz Haber was responsible for the beginning of modern chemical warfare. *This* is his science now. This is who he has become."

My own breath stopped. Briefly. I would put this all together later. Right now I had to focus on listening.

Einstein removed his matches once more and relit his pipe. "Do you know his wife committed suicide?"

"I heard."

"Do you know why?"

"I do not."

"She was herself deeply schooled in chemistry. She attained a doctorate degree in chemistry at the University of Breslau. She knew enough to adore Fritz. And enough eventually to despise him. She took her own life shortly after that unleashing of the beast in April in France. Against her pleadings, Fritz went to Ypres to person-ally observe the event. He returned exhilarated, unhappy only that the fools in command failed to understand this great opportunity. That they failed to have sufficient forces to take full advantage of the inevitable break in the front lines. Fritz thinks Germany could have won the war from this single, dramatic event if the military had been bolder."

Einstein paused. Then he shook his head, very slowly. "For him to think like that, more brutally than the professional brutes. Oh how he and I have argued. So much so that there is nothing for it now but to be silent before him, before the madness. He proposes that making wars more monumentally cruel will shorten their duration. And he makes the proposition to me that in war, death is death. If it is by the suffering of the eyes and the lungs and the brain and the heart from chemistry, it is no different than the suffering of limbs and head and torso from metallurgy."

Einstein drew in a deep draft of pipe smoke, taking it even into his lungs. He let it out slowly. And he said, "Clara put a bullet in her brain to advance the theory that Fritz was wrong."

We let the silence sit between us for a time.

I allowed myself to take a shallow breath or two of the toxic reality: Stockman and Haber were working together on a poison gas attack.

Einstein was considering Clara's theory. He said, "The isolated argument Fritz makes about the two modes of death is perhaps, in some ways, sound. Shrapnel and bullets and fire could be seen as already maximal in brutality. But he leaps to a ridiculous conclusion."

His next silence brought a calm draw on the pipe. He'd said all that he assumed he needed to say.

I needed more.

I said, "So Doctor Haber is no longer in the business of feeding the hungry. But his present business. How does it go?"

"I am no chemist," he said. "He and I collide at the Institute and interact and he always must tell me some little thing or other. I am afraid that in his mind my listening to him co-opts me into his work. But from respect to him personally, and from futility, I simply listen. He has moved beyond chlorine gas to phosgene. Phosgene is more toxic than chlorine. And it causes less coughing and so remains un-expelled from the lungs. He is quite proud."

My mind worked and worked at all this, even as I kept my attention on Einstein's words.

But I had to ask the right questions.

And I thought of the box in the export office.

"Has he spoken of bombs?" I said.

Einstein hesitated. He thought.

"Not artillery," I said. "Something that a Zeppelin might deliver."

He straightened abruptly. "More chemistry," he said. "Those infernal machines filled with a chemist's gas."

"Did he say anything?"

"Not that I can recall."

"In the light of Doctor Haber's philosophy of war, would an aerial bomb be an advance?"

He thought for a moment. "I am no military man."

"Just the science of it."

"Of course," he said. "The same wind sufficient to carry the poisonous gas across a battlefield also blows the gas quickly away. A bomb would greatly reduce the force of a necessary wind to a level just sufficient to stir things about."

"Would such a bomb need a special design? Would any bomb do?"

Einstein puffed briefly at his pipe, considering this, his brightness returning a bit, I presumed in the pure scientific puzzle of it. "Not any bomb," he said. "Certainly not. The perfect bomb would perhaps be something of a challenge. As I understand it, phosgene and similar gases boil at relatively low atmospheric temperatures, below the present summer temperature, for instance. So they will be transformed from the liquid inside the bomb to the killing gas immediately upon exposure to the air. However, there is the matter of the bursting charge. This would have to be carefully managed so that the shell will burst open but not, as well, consume the gas too quickly at the point of impact, which would greatly reduce the footprint of toxicity. And also so that the shell will not bury its striking end in the ground, trapping much of the liquid there unvaporized. The bomb maker would have to be very clever."

He paused, hearing his own implicit admiration. He clarified: "That is to say *despicably* clever."

"What would Doctor Haber see as the right conditions for an attack?"

In spite of the moment of self-awareness, Einstein leaned forward, bright again. "It would be at night, with cloud cover, to minimize the daylight-warmed ground from creating upward currents of air. These would otherwise quickly dissipate the gas."

I too found myself on the edge of my chair. I sat back.

I felt I had heard enough.

But Einstein added, "And of course the best target would be a large city. A nighttime crowd. The streets of a city would further temper the upward currents, and the buildings would tunnel any movement of air to its victims. The gas would linger to kill."

At this, my mind asked to shut down. His mind seemed to rear back from itself, abruptly alarmed at its own cleverness in working out this attack as a hypothetical.

He said, softly, "You see how we are all vulnerable."

41

Einstein and I made our good-byes and I rose and he rose and we shook hands. I offered to find Madam Cobb and I urged him to wait, as I knew where to locate her in the theater. He thanked me and sat down and I stepped out of the dressing room and softly clicked the door closed behind me.

I turned to head along the corridor to the auditorium.

Mother was standing a few paces away, alone, leaning against the wall and smoking a cigarette. She looked at me and hastily dropped the cigarette to the floor and tapped it out with the toe of her shoe.

I approached her.

We spoke low.

"It's been a long time since I've seen you smoke," I said.

"It's been a long time since you've seen me frightened."

"Are you?"

"Yes."

She said no more than that in answer to what she would usually take to be a juicy theatrical cue line. I believed her.

"What is it?" I said.

"I'm going with him."

"Stockman?"

"Yes."

"When?"

"Monday morning. Early. He asked me to go with the most tender of entreaties. Albert the vulnerable, the tortured, the needy. Then he swore me to secrecy with a whispered vehemence that scared the living bejabbers out of me."

I didn't respond at once. I tried to figure out how much I should tell her, in her present state, of my own recent fright. For *fright* it was quickly becoming. My mind had only just begun to work out all the implications of what Einstein had told me. Stockman was heading south to somehow expedite an aerial poison gas attack. And thinking this far now, I thought to add *against London.*

"He's not going to invite you," Mother said.

"He told you that?"

"Yes. I'm to play the *Grande Dame* to Victor *and* to you. The story is that I'm going away alone for a few days to a spa. I must. I'm not telling you where."

"Will Barnowsky tolerate that?"

"I'm ill. I need to go away for a time. He'll tolerate it. We're still two weeks from opening. I'm doing swell, my son. Swell. Let a stand-in rehearse with these locals. I can be ill for days and still play Hamlet in my sleep. In two languages? Not a problem for Isabel Cobb. You know I can do anything on a stage. Anything I want. My mind. My will. My heart. My mind. Did I mention my mind? It can do anything."

Abruptly she stopped speaking.

She heard herself. "What the hell was that little monologue all about?" she said. "That doesn't sound good."

"You'll be fine," I said. "The third act has begun in our play. That's all."

"Yes, my darling. Yes. You're right."

I reached under my coat and into the small of my back and I drew my pocket Mauser from its holster. I brought it out before her. Too quickly. She drew a sharp, lifting, stiffening breath and reared back.

"I want you to take this," I said.

"Is it necessary?"

"You tell me. It's to calm your fear."

She looked at it.

"Do you know how to use it?" I asked.

"Don't you remember my Lydia Justice in *A Woman Wronged?*"

I didn't. "Do you know how many plays I've seen you in?"

"Well, I learned to shoot for Lydia. And though on stage they were blanks, they were precisely shot."

"Fine." I offered the pistol.

She waved it away. "Do you actually think I could kill him?"

I'd even asked myself the same question not too long ago. The last ten minutes had given me my answer, I realized. I thought again to tell her about the gas. But after that one brief, clear-headed admission of her fear, she'd been thrashing around to deal with it in every way but honest. These much higher stakes might only frighten her more, and she could inadvertently betray herself to Stockman. She needed to know, but not now.

"You may not approve," she said. "You may not believe me. He may have terrible flaws. But I love him."

I clamped my mouth tightly shut and looked away.

She read the gesture. Partially. "Don't worry," she said. "I'll stop him. I know I have to stop him from whatever it is we're all worried about. I'll bring him down. But that's all I can do. There is no possible circumstance where I'd shoot him to death."

I said, "People other than Stockman could be a danger to you."

I offered my Mauser once more.

She looked at it.

"Believe me," I said, quite softly. "There are things we can't anticipate."

She took a deep breath.

She took the pistol from my hand.

She held it like she knew what to do with it. Like she was the wronged Lydia Justice six nights and two matinees a week.

42

Jeremy was waiting for me outside the Hotel Baden. He was a shadow and a flaring red tip of a cigarette and a plume of streetlight-gathering smoke from under a linden tree in the median. I saw him at once as I got out of the taxi.

I went to him.

"What are you smoking?" I said.

"Murads," he said.

"Close enough," I said. "I'm out."

He gave me one and a light.

"I have a feeling you know something," Jeremy said.

"You develop that intuition in the ring?"

"Doubt if it's intuition. You're telegraphing your punch."

"They call it the lead in my other line of work," I said. "Sir Albert Stockman, a member of the British Parliament, is masterminding a nighttime Zeppelin attack on London, employing a bomb of his own design filled with a deadly gas called phosgene. It will target civilians with the purpose of heralding enough terror to force a quick end of the war in favor of Germany."

That was the lead of our story.

I let it sit in him for a moment.

He took a deep drag on his Murad.

"It's all pieced together and circumstantial," I said. "But that's the business we're in. I'd bet my bankroll on it."

"I believe you'd win," Jeremy said.

"We have every reason to assume the attack will take place next week. And Stockman will try to put his own personal stamp on it somehow. He sees himself as a great German hero in the making."

"With the help of Colonel Max Hermann Bauer," Jeremy said. "What I've been told about *him* fits the puzzle. Last month Bauer was appointed chief of Section One in the German Department of the General Staff. His main task is to identify and test new weapons and tactics. Even before the official posting, he was the man who got Haber's gas to the front lines at Ypres."

"So he's being instrumental again."

"Bauer's also a political maverick," Jeremy said. "Despises both General Falkenhayn and Chancellor Bethmann-Hollweg."

"Then why did Falkenhayn promote him?"

"He probably figures shunting Bauer to new weapons keeps him on the fringe. So Bauer would be keen to counterpunch."

Jeremy let me finish the thought. "With a surprise strike by a new weapon that could win the war."

"Just so."

"He'd need a powerful buddy to get a Zepp to do his bidding."

"Erich Ludendorff would do," Jeremy said. "Bauer got his weapons credentials in artillery. He had a hand in the general's big-gun victory at Liège after the rest of the German command ate crow for two weeks at the start of the war. He and General Ludendorff are known to be very close."

"Our Albert would be drawn to a maverick," I said. "He was sharply critical of the Kaiser this morning."

"Most of the German high command is critical of the Kaiser."

"Willie's soft on the Brits."

Jeremy nodded. "Notwithstanding, he's duly tough after the fact. He never dreamed his U-boats would catch a target like the *Lusitania*. No one really did. But he was keenly vigorous in defense of its sinking."

"So Bauer and Stockman figure they can safely act on their own, as long as they pull it off."

"If you listen to Germans argue with each other," Jeremy said, "no one is ever wrong about anything. Collectively too. If the poison gas bomb goes off and England effectively suffers, then the High Command certainly was right all along. Every one of them, from the Kaiser on down."

"This makes sense of the tower at Stockman House," I said. "The wind studies. They were thinking about poison gas in British streets."

"My other bit fits as well," Jeremy said. "I decided FVFB had to be comparable to Krupp. I just couldn't sort things out in my head from the companies I knew. So I consulted the Berlin Stock Exchange. Farbenfabriken Vormals Friedrich Bayer. Pharmaceuticals. Dyes. Chemicals."

"I think we know what they make in Kalk," I said.

"Did Madam Cobb persuade Stockman to let her go along?"

"I persuaded him on her behalf, I think."

"And you?"

"Not invited."

"We need to invite ourselves," Jeremy said.

At this, we smoked for a few moments.

Across the street was the hotel where another identity awaited me behind the baseboards of a wardrobe. Colonel Klaus von Wolfinger. I'd already shaved for him.

"Time to bluff," I said.

"This is good advice."

"It was yours."

"I am never wrong," he said.

"Since you're so German, can your people fit you out as an officer? We're talking about getting very close to an army base."

"Yes."

"Trask has me set up as a colonel attached to the Foreign Office," I said. "Secret service."

"Your uniform complete?"

"The only officer headgear I could pack was a crusher," I said. "Can you get me a peaked field cap?"

"Size, if I have a choice?"

"Seven, British," I said.

"When does Stockman leave?"

"In about thirty-six hours."

"With that box, they have to be driving."

"As much as I'd relish the irony," I said, "I don't think your Ford will pass for a German staff car."

"I can arrange a car. But the people I draw on for support are all of them around Berlin. In Spich we'll be on our own. Any special needs you can anticipate?"

"In other words, what's our plan," I said.

"In other words."

I thought of what we knew about Albert and about Spich and about his wooden crate. What the likelihoods were.

Jeremy said, "I suppose the argument could be made that we simply need a bullet. For Stockman."

I shook my head *no*. "We let the boxes go in order to keep us in the game. And because those presumed prototypes are replaceable. The plans are somewhere. Several somewheres, I'm sure. But Albert's replaceable too, at this point. His work is done. The Zepps and the gas and the shell design already exist. What you learned about Bauer is the thing. We need to interfere in a striking enough way to prevent the maverick attack and also openly discredit the attempt. We need to get the half-British Kaiser's attention. The only cruelty he'll disavow is failed cruelty."

Jeremy nodded. "So what do you need?"

I was improvising now. Without a real plan. But from the realities I'd just voiced, there was a basic act that seemed to be called for. Indeed, I could think of no other.

I said, "I don't know exactly how to employ it, without our knowing Spich, but I think we need a bomb of our own. A portable one."

He thought a moment. About either what I had in mind or how to get one.

In case it was the former, I said, "If we can blow up the Zepp with Stockman's untested shell armed, either on the ground or very shortly into the flight, we can spectacularly poison an air base inside the Fatherland. The whole maverick plan will come out and look bad."

"I can arrange this," Jeremy said.

"And a dispatch case to fit the thing," I said. "I'd need to carry it close."

He dropped half his cigarette at his feet and stubbed it out. "I'll pick you up tomorrow at six. Here at the Baden. Dress like you are now and bring what you need for the south."

Jeremy pulled his pack of Murads from his coat pocket. He handed them to me. "In case you can't find Turkish tobacco in the hotel."

I took them. "Thanks."

Maybe it was the moment of leave-taking after a serious talk that suddenly brought this to mind, but I thought of Stockman in the Adlon bar.

I said, "That drink I had with Albert the first night in Berlin. He criticized the Zeppelins for bringing only isolated disruptions. That's what I was focusing on. But it was his other criticism that really mattered. *Commonplace*."

"This is anything but that," Jeremy said.

"Stockman is a terrorist," I said.

And I was letting him sleep with my mother.

43

When I got back to the Adlon, there was a note waiting for me, in a sealed hotel envelope slipped under the door. My mother had simply written *Hotel Alten-Forst. Spich.* Its brevity, its mode of delivery, the risks and suspicions of yesterday early morning, her place now, near the center of Stockman's plans, my exclusion from those plans: all this meant I should not—*dared* not—see her again before the time of my rendezvous with Jeremy.

Would I have tried to talk her out of all this? I wished I'd told her about the poison gas. But maybe it was better she didn't know. She was committed to her role. The most dangerous thing for her now would be to try to withdraw from him. Still. As a woman, would she continue to love a known terrorist? As a son, how could there be even a match-spark of doubt about the answer to that? But there was.

Spich.

I'd brought my Gladstone to the Adlon. I gathered the things I needed for travel and packed them. I stepped off the elevator and paused at the mezzanine balustrade and looked for Herr Wagner.

He'd kept his distance since I'd confronted him in this very spot, but I didn't want the Gladstone to set off any alarms in his head. He was standing just beyond the reception lounge, in front of the Palm Court. He was watching someone cross the lobby. I followed his gaze to a small man, dressed in a dark, three-piece suit. A Far

East Asian. Wagner openly observed the man as he marched with clear and oblivious purpose into the Palm Court. Wagner turned as if to follow.

I beat it quick down the stairway but emerged cautiously from behind the reception desk. Wagner was indeed following the Asian man, out the doors to the Goethe Garden. I strode away in the other direction, across the lobby and the vestibule platform, and then I was spinning through the revolving door onto Unter den Linden, feeling happier with each step to be leaving the Adlon behind.

I returned to the Hotel Baden and stopped inside the front door and asked the *Hausmeister* where Spich was. He touched the tip of his nose in thought and then led me to the front desk and a book of maps.

Kalk was just across the Rhine from Cologne; Spich was just nine miles farther south.

When I stepped into Jeremy's Ford in front of the hotel the next evening, *Spich* was still nagging at me in vague familiarity.

As soon as I'd closed the door, Jeremy throttled up the T and we drove off, and he said, "I didn't mean to be mysterious last night. I'm taking you to my mother's house in Spandau."

"I promise not to argue with her about the Kaiser," I said.

"You'd lose anyway," he said.

"What do you know about the town of Spich?" I said.

He glanced at me and then back to the street ahead. "It's a major army Zeppelin base."

Of course.

I told him about Isabel Cobb's note.

He glanced my way again. But he made no immediate remark.

He was thinking.

I was thinking. If Stockman was taking Mother along to share his triumph, then the choice of hotel was significant. It was in tiny Spich, not urbane Cologne. It was the hotel nearest the Zeppelin's ascent on the heroic day. She was going to be part of that. But the other witnesses—be they press or just a few influential people, including the greatest actress and most fascinating paramour in the world—these witnesses would hardly be present at the start of a secret military mission. The successful return would be another matter. And in that event, Stockman's standing as a hero would be greatly diminished if he was simply one of the crowd, cheering. Strategic advice and technological creativity and a place in the bedazzled crowd were not quite the stuff of statues in the Tiergarten. Not for the leading man. I bet he'd talked his way onto the Zepp for this thing. He was planning to step down from the gondola triumphant.

I looked at Jeremy. He sensed it. He looked at me.

"He's going up with the gas bag," I said.

It took him only one breath of thought. "Of course."

We kept quiet now as we drove through the linden forests of the Tiergarten, emerged on the broad central boulevard of Charlottenburg, and then passed into the villa colony of Westend. A few minutes later, with the northern sky striated in stack smoke from the arms factories and the western sky rimmed with the conifers of the Spandauer Stadtforst, we crossed the Charlottenburg Bridge into the narrow streets of Spandau city-center.

Jeremy's family was or had been well-to-do. His mother lived on Hohenzollern-Strasse in a stretch of very nice, scaled-down villas. Her two-storey house was stucco-finished with the window moldings cut into the rough stone in the German classic style. The place sat on an acre or a little more, thick with pine and birch. A beaten-gravel drive curved behind the house where we now parked the Ford.

Jeremy's mother emerged onto a flagstone veranda to greet us.

He stepped in front of me and bent to her and they hugged. Then he moved aside and she extended her hand and we shook. She was small and as sinewy-solid as corded wire. She had the grip of a retired bantamweight who once could throw a hell of a right cross.

"Welcome to our home, Herr Hunter," she said, her German formal in person as well, leaving no trillable *r* untrilled.

We went in and sat in her immaculate parlor, Jeremy and I on side-by-side matching wing chairs covered in unpadded leather and she on a plank chair before us with a cut-out heart floating behind her head. I imagined that she addressed her two sons on matters of motherly importance in this very setting. Her husband hung over the fireplace. I presumed it to be him. He was clean-shaven, a state far rarer in an earlier era, and I figured I could see his eyes in Jeremy's, though by this pose they would be the son's eyes only as he danced into the center of the ring ready to do some damage. And this guy's mouth was compressed hard, even as he sat for a portrait. A hard mouth and a harder gaze, such that it led me to recall: Jeremy's only allusion to his father was a reference to his mother as a widow.

The mother rose now and moved to a vast ebonized walnut buffet whose upper panel was laid with marquetry hunting scenes of leaping horses and fleeing elk. From the buffet she served us tea and buttered bread and we sat and ate and she spoke ardently about the price of the butter—two *mark* fifty a pound—and feared it would soon go to three *mark*. She took care to blame the British and the French.

And later she fed us a dinner of boiled beef with horse radish sauce and *Spätzle* in her dining room on a heavy wood table with a vast, spotless linen cloth that demanded every bite I took be an act of desperate carefulness.

As we ate, she asked me a little about the articles I wrote in America on Germany's virtues, but mostly she monologued, though with each bite of dinner she fell primly silent until her mouth was empty. Jeremy and I kept our own mouths closed while she chewed, digesting with our food each of her just completed segments of thought on such things as British iniquity and international ignorance and Wilhelmian inspiration and Bismarckian virtue, the breadth and depth of the latter winning, for the first chancellor of a unified Germany, a place at Martin Luther's right hand in heaven.

All this transpired with still another portrait of her husband looking down on us, this time standing with hunting rifle in hand and a brace of dead rabbits beside him and a look on his face that suggested he was, here in the dining room, as disapproving of the rabbits as he was of his sons in the parlor.

This I figured I knew: Jeremy's mother was a woman who not only acknowledged her son's father but enshrined him, lived with him openly every day in every room. A woman who was never touched by any man but him. A woman who played only one role forever. Nevertheless, in spite of our obvious differences in father and mother, Jeremy and I had been catalyzed into who we were by heat and pressure from a single unifying principle that would elude even Albert Einstein.

We sat on the veranda after dinner, Jeremy and I. The night had come and the horizon before us burned brightly from the munitions factories on the eastern bank of the Havel. He said, "She will drink *Kirschwasser* now until she can no longer pour it. And then she will sleep very soundly."

I thought to say something about his mother and my mother. But I said nothing.

I offered him a cigarette, from the pack he'd given me. He took one with a nod. We lit up and he said, "From the way we reckon it, this thing could go quickly, down there."

"If the weather is right."

"I'll make us a pot of coffee," he said. "Then we need to steal an automobile."

"Do you have one in mind?"

"I do," he said. "A few minutes' walk from here is the house of the longtime commandant of Spandau Prison. Colonel Walther von Küchler. He's shot more than a few chaps in our trade. He keeps a staff car. A good one."

I understood.

Jeremy took a drag on his cigarette.

And he added, in a voice that rasped away any sense of offhandedness, "He's also known in a few houses in the neighborhood as *Kuschelbär*."

Snuggle Bear.

That this colonel had executed some of the boys in our own trade was plenty of leavening for our little project. For Jeremy to add the man's exploits with the local women made me suspect I'd been wrong about his mother. Maybe I didn't have to look so deep for the familial chemistry I sensed he and I shared.

"Did you bring your lock-picking tools?" he asked.

"I did."

"Good," he said.

So when we were jittery with coffee and Jeremy's mother was kayoed from *Kirschwasser* and it was past midnight and the neighborhood was sleeping, he and I dressed up in our German uniforms—the peaked field cap Jeremy's boys got for me was a fine one, with red crown piping and a skull badge between the cockades—and with my Luger strapped to my waist and with our Gladstone bags in hand, we stepped out of his house.

Two guys with a common uniform have some kind of electrical charge between them. It might be low-wattage at times, but it's always there. The circuitry of an army. Of a police force. Of a baseball team, for that matter. This sudden thing between Jeremy and me made us stop just across the threshold and look at each other.

A dark energy was coursing in us. From our being Allied spies in disguise together, of course. But our uniforms also made us German army officers. So inevitably the German army crackled in us as well. That was a strange part of the personal bond forged by a uniform. You can be bound by blood. But also by skin.

And since we were military men, our eyes fell to the pips on our shoulders.

I was a colonel. He was a major.

Jeremy shot me a salute. With a wink.

I returned them both.

Then I introduced myself. "Colonel Klaus von Wolfinger." I offered my hand.

He thought for moment, finding a name for himself, and he grasped my hand. "Major Johann Ecker."

We shook.

We walked off briskly, heading north on Hohenzollern. A few minutes later we turned west on Pionier-Strasse, which was sheltered, even from the pervasive glow of the factories, by a dense run of plane trees. Almost immediately, across from a drill ground, Jeremy stopped us. He looked around. We were alone in this part of the street, and we slipped quickly up the lawn of a darkened, two-storey, half-timbered and gabled house.

We cut around the side and into the back yard, where we found a good automobile indeed parked near the door. As with most of the German staff cars, it was a civilian vehicle appropriated for military use. Dressed up in *feldgrau* camouflage was a late model Mercedes 37/95 double phaeton touring car, its cloth top unfurled into its secured place. This model was often called the "Torpedo" from the distinctive V-thrust of the radiator, which was echoed by the shape of the headlamps tucked inside the front fenders.

I found myself treading lightly now, as I approached. As befitted the most powerful production automobile ever built. Ah yes. Let us steal this fine thing. Especially from the spy-killing commandant of Spandau Prison.

Jeremy was a couple of steps ahead of me. I drew near and stopped. He peered in, put his bag into the back seat, leaning for a moment to open it and emerging with a leather portfolio case.

He lifted it so I would take note, and he stepped to the front passenger side and placed the case in there.

"We'll need your flashlight for the maps," he said.

I put my bag into the back seat and retrieved the light.

"But first, let me in at the back door," he said.

He was looking up to the darkened windows on the second floor.

Before I could reply, he added, "We don't want him to wake up."

We didn't. One way or another.

I did not clear up the ambiguity of his exact intentions, however. I would find out soon enough.

I put the flashlight in my pocket, took my tools from the Glad-stone bag, and led him to the back door, which had a tumbler lock. I opened the door.

He stepped past me, saying, "No need for us both."

Which seemed to me to clear up the ambiguity. Jeremy would arrange for Snuggle Bear *never* to wake up.

44

I stood in the yard, smoking a cigarette.

Jeremy was gone longer than I'd expected him to be. Long enough that I began to think about going in after him. But the house was quiet and dark, and I trusted Jeremy's skill at this. I wondered if he was having some preliminary conversation with the man, a necessary explanation of why it was keenly appropriate for Jeremy to be the guy who ended his life. I would do likewise, I figured, if I had his particular combination of motives and this opportunity.

Then there was movement at the back door. I straightened and took a step in that direction.

The shadow striding across the yard was Jeremy.

He arrived before me.

From the starlight and the glow to the east I could see him just well enough to read his state. At least roughly. He gave off a quietude, almost an inertness. He did not seem like a man who'd just killed another man. Anything but. Which made me all the more certain he'd done that very thing.

"I brought you something," he said.

He held out his hand and I received a palm-sized, cast-iron object. Flat with a pinback. I drew it up, away from the shadows of our bodies, and I could see the German Iron Cross, first class. The flare-tipped Maltese upright and crossbar were edged with silver.

"You deserve a better bluff than a phony lapel pin," he said.

I pinned it high up on my chest.

"The major drives the colonel," he said, and he circled the car to the right-hand driver's seat. I headed to the crank while he flipped the ignition switch. It took only a small, sweet pull to start up the immense engine, ninety-five horses worth.

When I slid into the passenger's seat, Jeremy said, "Someday, we'll need your lock-picking tools to steal an automobile." He reached outside the cabin—the gate change shifter was mounted to the car's body at the running board, just inside the upright spare tire—and he notched us into gear and we rolled away, the Mercedes' chain-drive grinding softly, deep inside its corridor of oil.

We doubled back down Hohenzollern-Strasse. I recognized his mother's house up ahead. It approached, it drifted past, he did not move his eyes from the road before us.

I took out my flashlight and thumbed the slide button. I opened the portfolio. It contained a sheaf of maps. I recognized them. They were part of the KDR 100, the *Karte des Deutschen Reiches*, the finely detailed set of large-scale maps of Germany done up over the past three decades for the General Staff.

"Our route to Cologne," Jeremy said.

I took out the first two we'd need. Map 268, *Spandau*, the thousand square kilometers of Germany in which Spandau was the major city. And Map 293, *Potsdam*.

We turned south on Wilhelm-Strasse and Jeremy throttled up and we surged ahead into the night. On an accommodating road, the Torpedo could do seventy miles per hour, could do a hundred with its chassis stripped down. Germany was fast asleep and dark, but shortly there were arc lights ahead and we flashed past a straight, cobbled road leading to a brick wall and twin, loopholed towers flanking a massive door that was as pale and jaundiced as a face from solitary. The main gate of Spandau Prison.

Then we were in the dark again, with just our headlamps before us. I thought we were on our way, but a few minutes down the road Jeremy slowed abruptly.

I looked to him.

"The last of our preparations," he said.

He pulled off the road and we rolled over gravel past a low wooden house with a kerosene lamp burning in the window. There'd been no hesitation, no searching to find our way here. Jeremy knew the place.

Our headlamps lit up a wide-mouthed garage. From within, the radiators and darkened headlamps of half a dozen vehicles stared out at us. A man in overalls emerged from the depth of the garage into our light. He'd been waiting.

We made a sharp right turn, passing an open-topped automobile stripped of tires and windshield and sitting on stone blocks. We stopped. Jeremy switched off the engine.

"Another good German," he said.

We got out.

I lingered by my door while Jeremy circled the car and strode to greet the man in overalls, who was carrying an acetylene lamp.

They shook hands and they turned their backs on me and leaned close to each other, speaking low.

I knew to stay where I was.

They had some intense, private matter between them.

I thought for a moment of the covert group Jeremy drew on, worked with, in Germany, wondered at the role he played for them, wondered how he explained his Britishness.

But they clearly trusted him. He clearly knew how to use them.

Then he and the man in overalls turned my way and I stepped to them.

He was Evert. Jeremy said just his first name. And he said, of me, simply, "Christopher."

I shook Evert's heavily callused hand. He smelled of graphite grease. He held his lamp low and his face was in deep night shadow. But his eyes were even darker than the shadow, were startlingly visible. "*Ein herzliches Dankeschön*," he said, bowing a little at the waist. He gave me heartfelt thanks, though he didn't elaborate. But I could surmise. He was working for a different sort of Germany. Jeremy was still very much a German in the eyes of men like this one, was furthering that cause. As, therefore, was I.

Evert turned to Jeremy now and said, still in our shared mother tongue, "I'll get your device. Do you need the lamp?"

Jeremy looked at me. "Do you have your flashlight at hand?"

"Yes," I said.

"See your own way," Jeremy said to Evert, nodding at his lamp. The man moved off toward the garage.

"Over here," Jeremy said.

I switched on the flashlight and followed him.

He'd stopped the Mercedes with its back end even with an upright gasoline pump.

I shined the light first on the pump, which Jeremy cranked, and then on its hose as he inserted the nozzle into the Torpedo's gas tank, which sat low beneath the rear-deck luggage rack.

As we topped off the tank, Evert arrived carrying a closed canvas bag. Jeremy looked up from his hose and they exchanged a nod and Evert put the bag into the back seat of the car.

The makings of our bomb, I assumed.

And now Evert had returned and Jeremy was replacing the gas pump hose. Evert kneeled at the back of the Mercedes and was working with a tool at the license plate. Off it came. And he was putting another in its place. The one removed and the one affixed were both prefixed with *MK. Militärkraftwagen*. Military vehicles.

At last we were ready.

Evert thanked me again. He said, "I would have expected no less from a German reared in America."

"Of course," I said.

"We will create a true republic in our country," he said. "Soon."

In response I pumped his hand a bit more vigorously and bowed a little at the waist, as he had initially done, and we broke off and I got into the fastest staff car in the world and we hit the road again. As we pushed south from Spandau into the deep dark of the heath country, I thought how the mission ahead of me was as vague and difficult as Evert's. And I wondered if the right thing wasn't to clarify the goal as Jeremy had done tonight and simply put a bullet in Sir Albert Stockman's brain.

45

Before the heath yielded to Potsdam we turned west. The road was accommodating and Jeremy throttled up the Torpedo and we raced on through the Brandenburg Forest, skirting the city, and we ran fast through the forest at Tucheim, and he said I should sleep, he was fine and the way was clear to him for a few hours. And though I'd had as much coffee as he and knew from other wars how to keep awake, I let myself sleep, and somewhere along the way I dreamed about drawing my Luger and shooting it into the dark. I couldn't see a target but I knew I had to keep shooting, and the clip in the handle kept feeding 9mm Parabellum shells, endlessly, and I fired and fired, and in the darkness I never saw who I was trying to hit or if he had fallen, and so I just kept firing.

I woke at dawn as we decelerated into a street of folk-tale houses and shops, bright-painted bossage or half-timbered white stucco, and with froufrou gables and roof edges. This was the Weser Renaissance style, born along the river that gave it its name, the style of the brothers Grimm. The city was Hamelin.

We were passing from the main street onto the bridge over the Weser before Jeremy realized I was sitting upright.

"You awake?" he said.

"I am," I said. "Are you?"

He was, but on Hamelin's western bank we stopped at a small café with the logical but unfortunate name *Der Rattenfänger*, the ratcatcher, from the name of the Grimm tale based in Hamelin and translated more vapidly in English-language books as the Pied Piper. We ate our breakfast—avoiding the *Wurst*, just in case they were having a joke on us all—and we received ongoing glances and bows of respect from the working men who ate there with us. We were high officers in their army. And I was more. One man with a vast gray mustache rose to full attention before me and saluted. He then inclined his head toward my Iron Cross. "Hail to your bravery," he said. I nodded in the supercilious manner of a son-of-a-bitch young secret service colonel, rehearsing the character I would need to play in Spich.

The owner tried to foot our breakfast bill but we declined, with thanks, and we stepped outside. Without having to say anything, we moved off fifty yards or so from the café where we could face the nearby upswell of mountains, the eastern edge of the Weser Uplands, and smoke a cigarette.

"About five hours to go," Jeremy said. "As long as the dirt-road bits stay dry and the cows keep to the fields."

"Spich has to be small," I said. "In a small town and a tight military community, these uniforms aren't camouflage. We're going to stand out."

Jeremy blew smoke toward the mountain. It was covered with a mixed-growth forest, pine and spruce, oak and hornbeam.

"So we'll have to strut," I said.

He looked at me.

"The colonel and the major have to be there with a purpose," I said.

Jeremy took in a thoughtfully slow drag on his Murad.

"They're in Spich about *him*," I said.

Jeremy exhaled sharply, in agreement. "Who do you expect knows his intentions?"

"The commandant has to."

Jeremy nodded. "And an airship commander."

"They could be the only ones," I said. "And I bet neither of them knows what the bomb contains."

"I bet you're right," he said. "But they do know the whole thing is on the sly."

We said no more for now. The point was to smoke and stretch our legs, and then we walked back to the car.

One last salute. A guy old enough to have fought for Moltke at Gravelotte was approaching the café. At the sight of us, he stopped and snapped us a brisk one. "*Gott strafe England,*" he said.

Jeremy and I answered in unison, "*Er strafe es!*"

And we drove off.

But at a garage on the southern outskirts of Hamelin, we topped off our gasoline tank to get us easily through to Spich, and Jeremy let me drive the Torpedo, breach of rank though it was, so he could sleep for an hour or so. She was another skin, my Mercedes, a great steel body about me and I was its heart, my own heart beating fast from the roar of the engine and the whip-grind of the chain drive and the sense of torque beneath me, the great unseen spin of things flaring out to the four wheels, hurtling us along.

I drove a stretch of the route that brought us through the center of small town after small town—Arzen and Reher and Herrentrup, Meinberg and Kohlstädt and Marienloh, Hemmern and Rüthen—and every time, I had to slow down for the narrow streets, the cobbled streets, the horse-cart and hay-wagon streets, and that was fine, for I could throttle down and shift down my Torpedo and then fire her back up again.

Jeremy got his hour of sleep and more, nearly two, and he woke and I let him have the Mercedes once again, and he was chest-puffingly pleased at the transfer of her; he was a man reunited with his mate after a trial separation during which she'd dallied with another guy. He forgave her. And he drove her fast.

It was early afternoon when we saw a wide stretch of factory smoke before us. Mülheim, with the Rhine invisible just beyond and Cologne nearby, south around a bend of the river.

We soon turned south ourselves, before Mülheim, and I said to Jeremy, "Time to start the bluff."

He and I were relying on the unthinkableness, in the heart of the Fatherland, that two Germans who looked and sounded like ranking officers of the *Deutsches Heer* could be anything but what they seemed. We all had the same blood. Even the three million socialists. So surely these two splendidly portrayed German officers were legit. Consequently, the more dramatic our public strut, the better.

So we stopped at the side of the road, surrounded by cabbage fields, and we lowered the cloth top on the Mercedes. Let the Spich locals and the air base army men know that two high officers from Berlin had come to town. Let those boys start to talk; let them start bluffing themselves.

The main street of Spich ran about a quarter mile along the highway, which had lately turned east-west. We slowed to a crawl and made our way through, the houses and shops bright with whitewash and scarlet geraniums in window boxes. We turned local heads, all right—at cobbler and grocer, at butcher and inn—and the military heads turned, as well, a couple of enlisted men wearing undress uniforms, who snapped to at once when they saw us. They saluted. I returned the salute casually.

At the eastern end of the main street we approached a town square with a four-spout fountain in the middle and a cobbled market area and a tidy three-storey, dark wood and white stucco *Rathaus*, the town hall. As we circled the fountain, a staff car passed us, heading in the other direction—a camouflaged Horch phaeton—and I exchanged a very precise salute with what seemed to be another colonel, out and about in his *Pickelhaube*.

"I wonder if that was our man," Jeremy said.

"I hope it was," I said.

We'd reached Spich's eastern-most cross street, Wald-Strasse. A sign urged us to turn left for the Hotel Alten-Forst. We did, and ahead was a great wall of pines, the southern edge of the Alten Forest, and notched into the trees was a clearing where the hotel sat, a white-stuccoed, hip-roofed building with two unequal wings joined in an L, the long wing at the rear, parallel with the line of trees. I twisted around to look down Wald-Strasse. South was flatland as far as I could see. The airship base was in that direction.

I turned back toward the forest.

Jeremy had slowed to a near stop.

Though we had not discussed it, I stated the obvious. "We're not checking in there."

I could not chance encountering Albert.

"Just reconnoitering," Jeremy said.

"Even if they come straight here, we've got a good six hours on them," I said.

Jeremy accelerated a little, and we approached the hotel, entering a circular driveway that curved around a tightly manicured lawn with a flower clock in reds and pinks and yellows, how time passed in a town where every window was studded with geraniums.

As the driveway bent back to run in front of the hotel, with the option of turning into its courtyard, we both focused on the settings of tables in a small, canopied *Biergarten*. We rolled on past and completed the circuit, and we headed back south.

Jeremy had noticed an inn on Wald-Strasse just north of the town square. The Boar's Head. It had two upper stories above the street-level bar. We'd passed it as I'd been looking south. We stopped there and parked our Mercedes off the street in a side yard.

We entered the ground-floor saloon. In the thick afternoon dimness that pressed against our eyes and seemed the same in drinking joints the world over, a young man, who was no doubt on the cusp of conscription, was wiping the long zinc bar. He took one look at us, threw his rag aside, stood up straight, and faced us. His Adam's apple bounced a couple of times. He was thinking to salute but was feeling unqualified and inadequate for the job. So instead, he turned sharply on his heel and beat it through a door at the back of the place.

A woman emerged. The young man's mother, I supposed. She was wiping her hands, working kitchen and front-of-the-bar both, and I would've bet her husband, the boy's father and boss of the inn, was off in the trenches already. She'd be running this place completely alone in a year or so, with husband and son in uniform, and she'd be waking in a sweat night after night, sure she'd lost them both.

Jeremy was speaking with her, as my subordinate, asking about rooms. She had only a single lodger on the second floor and the two other rooms were free there. Jeremy was about to engage them, but I intervened.

"And the third floor, madam?" I said.

She looked at me as if I'd leaped from the shadows.

"It is a longer climb, Colonel," she said. *Herr Oberst*. She was flustered, as intimidated by rank as was her husband in a trench in France.

"Is anyone booked there?" I said.

"No, Colonel. It is empty."

"How many rooms?"

"Three," she said.

"We will rent them all," I said. "And absolute privacy with them."

"Yes sir," she said.

The entrance was from the back garden of the inn. Jeremy and I climbed a tightly winding staircase and emerged in a musty corridor. He carried his Gladstone and also the canvas bag with the makings of our bomb.

Climbing, Jeremy asked, "Three rooms?"

"Our being at the inn instead of the hotel is suspicious," I said. "Renting the floor explains we did it for privacy. Any rumors about that would even be useful."

"*Der Bluff*," he said.

"*Der große Bluff*," I said.

The big bluff had begun.

46

Before I left him at his door I asked for the dispatch case I'd requested.

"I'll bring it to you," he said.

I moved off.

My room was high-ceilinged near the door but it followed the steep pitch of the roof so that I had to crouch to actually look out my window.

A man with too heavy a coat for the August afternoon was passing slowly by on the far side of the street. The coat was patched at the shoulder. His shoes were scuffed badly enough for me to notice the fact from this distance. As willfully costumed-up as all this seemed, he did not turn his face from the fountain square toward which he was headed, nor did he miss a step till he was gone from my sight.

A light knock at the door.

I opened it to Jeremy.

He handed me a russet leather vertical bag with a shoulder strap and a buckle fastener at the bottom of the weather flap.

"They will never see me without it," I said.

He nodded.

If and when the time came to do something with our bomb, I would carry it while appearing to be only what I'd always been.

"That little beer garden at the hotel," he said.

"I noticed it."

"In three hours?"

"Good."

We would rest. Then we would sit and nurse a few beers and wait to watch Stockman and my mother arrive. We had to know his vehicle. I had to know their room.

"Mufti or military?" Jeremy said.

"Military. Did Stockman ever lay eyes on you?"

"He did. A couple of times. But he'd catch me out only close up. In uniform, tucked away in the beer garden, we should be all right."

So we each slept our three hours and then we settled in at a table under the *Biergarten* canopy at the Hotel Alten-Forst. We ate, we drank, slowly, and the sky darkened and the electric lights came on in the hotel. We were sitting across from each other, Jeremy with the driveway before him, I with my back to anyone arriving at the hotel and able to turn my face away at his nod.

The nod came a couple of hours into our wait.

I angled my face past Jeremy's right shoulder, rendering myself unidentifiable to a passerby, but I moved my eyes sharply back toward his, watched him watching them. He tracked them past, and then he nodded at me again.

I looked out into the courtyard.

Albert's broad, tweeded back. My mother's darkly besilked body, her arm hooked in his. She seemed small. Very small. Had she always been this small? She could fill a stage. She seemed enormous on a stage. But tonight, as she pressed her body close to this man as they maundered toward the hotel doors, toward their room together, she seemed impossibly small.

I should have told her in Berlin. About the poison gas. I should have told her exactly what sort of man this was.

"I'll watch the check-in," Jeremy said, rising.

I rose too, swinging around to see the vehicles.

Two Opel touring cars, their tops up.

"They were in the lead car," Jeremy said. "He was driving. Just the two of them. But the car behind is with them."

Even in the night, in the spill of the electric light, I could see the lead car's deep red color. Dark-uniformed bellmen were pulling suitcases—mostly my mother's—out of the vehicle.

The Opel behind was in camouflage. A burly man in *feldgrau*, wearing a peakless field cap, was taking up a place to stand as a barrier to the tonneau door.

"We know what's in the back," I said.

"They didn't have time for Bayer. The thing is still empty."

"Watch the wall of keys," I said, turning my head a little bit toward him.

He slipped away to get me a room number.

I sat down in his chair, facing the automobiles.

The bellmen finished stacking a baggage trolley. One of them wheeled it up the courtyard while the other went to the red Opel, cranked it, and drove it off, heading for the parking area beside the hotel.

The guy in uniform guarding the camouflaged Opel remained at parade rest. Motionless. Waiting. Waiting for Stockman. Albert was going back out tonight.

You could bet he'd be heading for the poison gasworks in Kalk.

I looked out east, into the night sky.

The air was still. The sky was full of high overcast. The moon was down. Flying weather. The Zeppelin wouldn't go tonight, not this late. But if this weather held, if it was the same across the channel, then soon.

A few minutes later, Jeremy arrived.

The mug in field gray was still standing guard, and Jeremy gave him a last look before turning his back to the driveway and sitting in the chair I'd occupied for the past few hours.

I leaned a little across the table. I said, low, "Our man is gassing up tonight."

Jeremy nodded. He switched our steins, retrieving his own. Both of them still held some recently drawn beer.

He took a draft.

I didn't.

Jeremy said, "Notwithstanding all the reasoning we've done, as much as we trust it, I should go watch a piece or two fit into place."

He would follow to Kalk.

"Careful," I said.

"I'll wait ahead of them. Near Bayer. And then near the air base. Won't try to go the distance."

He rose.

There was one more thing. I figured he'd forgotten.

But before I could ask, he said, "Room 200."

47

Not even ten minutes later Stockman strode past, and the guard snapped to attention at the sight of him. As Albert approached, the man opened the passenger door. He stepped back as if to wait, but Albert waved him on to start and drive the car. Albert stepped in and closed the door, but before he settled, he gave a single, focused glance into the darkness of the back seat.

They drove away.

A grinding took up in my chest. I was anxious to do this next thing. I was grateful for the chance, the only one I could expect to have in Spich. But I feared this. For reasons I would have been hard pressed to fully specify. It was enough to say it was about *her*.

I drained the rest of my beer.

Warm and flat.

I rose.

I put money down and I walked into the courtyard and through the hotel doors and into a lobby of chestnut paneling and mounted elk horns. Inside, I walked as if I knew something secret and damning about every turning head and they had better realize it and keep to themselves. The heads turned quickly away.

The Alten-Forst had an elevator and I stepped in. The operator snapped to, a boy who would likely be inducted alongside the inn-keeper's son sometime next spring.

I stepped off on the second floor and went down the dim corridor to the door at the end. Room 200.

I was in character now. I was the American spy Christopher Marlowe Cobb playing the German spy Klaus von Wolfinger. I would maintain that role-within-a-role for the next few minutes, if I possibly could, focusing just on those two layers and not the full set, not little Kit Cobb, Isabel Cobb's forever-young son, playing Christopher Cobb the war correspondent playing that American spy playing that German spy. That was the grinding in me. Those *four* gears. Meshing now. Slipping now. Binding now.

I lifted my hand.

I knocked at the door. Sharply.

It yielded instantly, swinging a little away from its jamb.

It had been ajar.

I drew my Luger.

I pushed through the door and into the sitting room of a suite full of carved oak and leather furniture draped and stacked and strewn and be-vased with roses, dozens and dozens of roses, the place reeking of nostril-flaring sweetness, and in the midst of it Mother was rising up from a chair, still in her deep-purple silk evening dress, her head bare, her hair undone and tumbling down. And her hands were flying up and she was choking back a cry and she was wide-eyed from seeing, in this first burst of the sight of me, only my uniform and my pistol.

I stopped, lowering and holstering the Luger and whipping off my hat and saying, "Mother, it's me."

Her hands fell, her face twisted away. She slumped back into the chair.

I moved to her.

"Mother," I said. "I'm sorry. The door. I thought something was wrong."

I could see now that her face was wet, her eyes were red from weeping.

"It's all right," I said.

I kneeled before her, took her hand. The tears had long preceded my entry, I realized.

"What is it?" I said.

She was breathing heavily. She took her hand away from mine, pressed it to her throat.

She struggled to control her breath.

"I'm sorry I frightened you," I said.

She waved this away.

I stayed bent to one knee. I waited. She snubbed a long breath into her body. She let it out as if it were smoke from a cigarette.

She lowered her face. Took another slow breath.

She lifted her face once more.

None of this felt like an act. The tears were real. They'd been shed alone.

"It's all right," she said. "I should have known it would be you . . . That uniform."

"I had no choice," I said.

She waved me silent once again.

Tears were still brimming from her eyes.

They catalyzed in me.

I stood up.

"What has he done?" I said, my tone going hard, going nearly fierce.

She pressed back a little in the chair. Snorted softly, as if in scorn.

She wasn't answering.

She wasn't looking at me.

"What?" I barked.

She lifted her face to me, lifted her hand, swept it to the side, indicating the room, the flowers. "He has *done* all of *this*."

They were joyful tears. They were tears of goddamn love.

I backed a step off.

Two steps.

I made sure my Luger was seated properly in its holster. I thought of the suite door. I looked. I'd left it partly open. I turned and moved to it.

"Are you going?" she said.

I reached the door, simply closed it, as I had intended.

I stared at the closed door, putting space between myself and my mother, as I had also intended.

"You've always been like this," she said. A rebuke.

I turned now to her, taking it slow, deliberately taking it slow. I would not alarm her. Not by my actions.

"I love roses," she said. "Do you even know how much I love roses?"

I did. But she said it as if she knew the answer was *no*.

I said nothing.

"*He* does," she said. "I count at least five different cultivars in this room. Bon Silene, the dark pink here behind me," she said.

I said nothing.

"And Doctor Grill. Over there," she said, pointing with a nod of her head. "Pink tinted with copper."

I took a step now, to cross the room, to return to her, still taking it slow.

"Exquisite," she said.

With my second step she began to speak more rapidly.

"And Safrano. From the French for saffron. In its bud the color is the color of saffron."

Even moving slowly I was frightening her.

"Four Season Damask," she said. "And *Veilchenblau*. Can you believe it?"

I drew near.

"The nearest thing to a blue rose in this world. He found that for me. There are two dozen of those."

I stopped before her.

She lifted her face. "How did he find it?"

I said nothing.

"*Why* did he find it?" She said this as if I should know the answer.

"Don't you understand?" she said.

She seemed very small sitting there, my mother.

I crouched before her again, dropped to my knees so our eyes were level with each other.

"You must listen to me," I said.

She drew her mouth tightly shut. She straightened at the spine.

"He is a bad man, Mother. More than what we've always known. Much more. Bad in ways he's hidden from you."

She said, very softly, "You would have said this of everyone who has loved me."

"This is about Albert Stockman."

"They never had a chance with you."

"Mother, you need to listen now."

She stopped.

"He has come here to make a Zeppelin raid," I said.

She cut me off. "He's restless being so passive in the defense of his people. We may not agree . . ."

"Shut up now and listen." My hand did not move, would *never* have moved, no matter what, but I had the impulse to slap her across the face. For her own good. She would have done as much to me.

She reared back. The words were slap enough. I had her attention.

I said, "He will drop phosgene gas on London. Poison gas. Do you understand?"

Her face had gone blank.

"This is his plan," I said. "*His.*"

I'd never seen her face blank. Not just her face holding inscrutably still, making it impossible to read. Blank.

I said, "He's even built a special shell to hold the gas, to release it in the streets of London to kill as many as he can."

"Impossible," she said.

Her blankness shifted ever so slightly with this. How? Around the eyes. Just the eyes. *Something* there. They seized the blankness and slammed it into my face like a brick.

"I'm telling you the truth," I said.

"It's not possible," she said, each word enunciated like a boxing jab.

"Doctor Einstein told me."

"He doesn't even know my Albert."

"He knows Fritz Haber," I said. "At the Institute. He knows Haber better than anyone. Haber is the German father of poison gas. He and your Albert are working together in this."

I tried hard to read her face for some trace, some flicker, something, anything, to suggest she was at least opening to the possibility that this was true. I saw nothing.

"Has he spoken of London?" I asked.

She looked at me as if I'd not said a word.

I advanced the spark in my voice. "Has he spoken of London?"

"He loves London," she said, her face suddenly flashing alive. "Of course he speaks of London." She was going to seize on this sort of question as if it were the basis of my beliefs about him, typical of my flimsy thinking. "He loves the city. Loves the theater."

My breath caught.

"He fell in love with me in a London theater," she said.

"Has he lately spoken of the London theater?"

"You're not listening," she said.

"The theater *district*?" I said.

She leaned forward and slapped me across the face.

"You're not listening," she said.

I rose.

Of course. What they called "Theatreland" in London was still robustly defiant of the Zepps, the Huns, all of it. The streets would be full of people leaving shows at the prime striking hour. And there would be the spill of plenty of light.

I said, "Sometime soon. Perhaps tomorrow night, if the wind and sky are right, your Albert will bomb the theatergoers of London with poison gas."

She jumped up.

I retreated a step.

"Go away now," she cried. "Go away."

I turned my back to her.

"I can't do this anymore," she said.

I moved away, toward the door.

"I won't go on," she cried after me.

I approached the door.

"You're a liar, Christopher Cobb," she said.

I put my hand to the doorknob.

"You lie like a jealous lover," she cried.

And I was out the door and careening down yet another hotel corridor.

48

I walked to the Boar's Head and went in the front door and straight to an empty table in a far corner, sitting with my back to the wall. Not that I wanted to entertain the admiring glances of the half-drunks in the room. Jeremy would surely look in here for me when he returned from Kalk and I wanted to make sure he saw me. I avoided eye contact with the men in the bar and kept my left hand on the tabletop for a time, simply flicking it upward, from my still-planted wrist, to show my palm when anyone started to approach. A subtle gesture, really, given the context and the warm intentions of the inebriates. But I needed to do it only twice, and both times it worked instantly. The whole roomful, being German and quick to follow orders from on high, shortly understood and kept away. For this, I felt a warm feeling for these guys. An admiration even.

So I kept my stein awash in a nice black *Köstritzer* for an hour or more—the time sliding away after the boys in the bar learned to keep their distance—and then Jeremy was before me. He sat. Our innkeeper appeared almost instantly. Jeremy simply nodded toward my drink and she went away and shortly returned with the same for him.

We touched steins. He drafted long, and I drank not at all now but returned the stein to the table when he put his down.

"They met him at the gates of Bayer," he said. "Near midnight, but men in suits. They all went in. He drove out an hour later. Big event. Big, special, secret event."

He took another drink.

"Then to the air base," he said. "Then to the hotel. The drivers and the truck went away. Probably back to Berlin."

We sat in silence for a time.

Jeremy finally asked, "Did you speak to our actress?"

"Yes," I said.

I knew there to be only a few swallows of my *Köstritzer* left, and I finished them.

After that, I stayed silent long enough for him to prompt me.

"Anything?" he asked.

"Perhaps his target is Theatreland."

Jeremy humphed a that-makes-sense humph.

"I don't think we can count on her from this point forward," I said.

Jeremy fixed his eyes on mine and twitched his head a little to the side.

He wanted me to explain. I thought to say, *She's sweet on him.*

But that would have only led to more difficult explanations. Beginning with: *Don't worry. I cannot imagine her working against us.*

Which, I now realized, I couldn't entirely vouch for.

Instead I said, "I can't see her in any plan we might make from here on."

Jeremy shook his head faintly *no*, disputing my assessment. "Your man and mine in London think highly of her."

Hell. It even occurred to me to say, *She's my goddamn mother. I should know what we can and can not count on from her.*

But I said, "I've got a bad feeling about her."

"She seemed a tough bird."

"She's too much an amateur. Trust me on this."

Jeremy flipped his head a little. "Have it your way," he said.

Another of my mother's theatrical triumphs. Impressing tough guy Erich Müller.

I *would* have it my way.

"Thanks," I said.

And so we drank a bit more together, Jeremy and I, almost entirely in silence, and then we went up the back stairs to our rooms and we slept.

The next morning we sat at the same table and the innkeeper served us eggs and *Wurst* and black bread and her boy served us coffee. As we ate, Jeremy and I spoke of how short the hours had become. If the weather was right, this would likely be the night.

He said, "I'll spend the morning in my anarchist's workshop."

But before we could get to the matter of my next move, a figure appeared in the door, at first in dark silhouette backlit by the morning light on the threshold of the dim bar.

A man in uniform.

He hesitated there, squared around to us, and then he approached.

Two pips on each shoulder. A captain.

He arrived before our table, straightened smartly to attention, and saluted us.

Jeremy's hands happened to be free and he returned the salute, though casually.

I was lifting my coffee cup with my right hand. The cup had been rising when he arrived, and I continued on to take a sip.

The captain patiently held his salute.

I lowered the cup and placed it on its saucer.

I saluted.

He snapped off a finish to his.

"Colonel," he said, bowing his head to me. "Major." A bow to Jeremy. Then back to me: "I am sorry to have intruded on your breakfast."

"Not at all, Captain," I said. "Would you like to sit?"

"Thank you, sir, but I am simply to give you a message and wait upon you."

I lifted my chin a little to encourage him to proceed.

He said, "My commanding officer, Colonel Franz von Ziegler, commandant of the airship base, has taken note of your arrival, and he sends his warmest regards. He offers his personal assistance in any way that might be useful to you."

"Thank you, Captain," I said. "Perhaps I can visit with the colonel on the base at his earliest convenience."

"Of course, sir. If you would like to do so this morning, he has instructed me either to wait for you or to return for you."

"His schedule?" I asked.

"Is flexible at any hour till noon."

"Return in an hour," I said.

"I will wait outside with the colonel's automobile."

The captain straightened and clicked his heels and saluted once more.

I returned it. He did a sharp about-face, and he strode across the barroom and out the door.

Jeremy and I watched him go. Then we looked at each other.

"As we'd hoped," Jeremy said.

"The commandant's eager," I said.

"He expects to fear you."

49

The captain was leaning against the commandant's camouflaged Horch phaeton when I emerged from the inn with my Iron Cross on my chest, my dispatch case over my shoulder, and my Luger on my hip. He snapped to attention at my approach.

He made a move to open the front passenger door. I recalled his commandant sitting in that position when we passed yesterday on the main street. But I was an arrogant son of a bitch named Klaus von Wolfinger, a secret service colonel from the Foreign Office in Berlin, so I narrowed my eyes at him. He instantly recognized his mistake. He slammed the passenger door shut and opened the rear door in the tonneau. He would be made to act the proper chauffeur for me.

"Sorry, sir," he said.

I gave him a minute nod and climbed in.

The door clicked gently shut behind me.

We drove in silence down Wald-Strasse, across the railroad tracks, and out into the barley fields on the road to Uckendorf. Less than a mile later we turned onto a two-lane macadam leading into the air base, a thousand acres of flat, cleared, fallow farmland stripped empty for airship landing and maneuvering, but with a cluster of structures a half mile ahead, the centerpiece being a Zeppelin hangar, growing larger by the moment, clearly outsized, massive.

Measureable now: longer than the greatest Atlantic steamship and twenty storeys high.

We drew near. End on, the hangar was an octagon cut off at the knees and with a slight pitch to its upper edge, the squared-off frontal outline of an airship. The doors were shut. Along each flank sat wide, low, corrugated steel buildings. Storehouses and barracks. A telegraph station. And an administrative building, where we now parked.

As I stepped from the automobile and into the shadow of the hangar, its vastness seized my chest and lifted me. Like I once felt walking State Street in my Chicago, passing beneath the Heyworth Building and the Mandel Brothers Building, Marshall Field and the Masonic Temple.

The air base administrative building was steel and plain but it was smaller than the other buildings and had a brick chimney in the side wall. We went in. Two enlisted men at desks in an outer office leaped to their feet, shooting off salutes that the captain and I returned, and we went down a narrow corridor and straight into the main room of the place.

From behind a large, quartered-oak desk rose the commandant, a full colonel like me, but having arrived at the rank at a more traditional pace. He was perhaps sixty. He was clean-shaven except for a sword-blade gray Wilhelm mustache.

I waited for the office door to click shut behind me, and I stepped to the front of the colonel's desk, stopping between two oak chairs that were arranged to face him. He and I straightened and shared a simultaneous salute. I'd watched him take note of my Iron Cross as I approached. He did not have one or was not displaying it.

And then, as our saluting hands fell, we both glimpsed something that we now subtly displayed to each other, by very slightly and very briefly turning our faces to the right.

We each had a *Schmiss*.

This was good.

I offered my hand. "I am Colonel Klaus von Wolfinger," I said.

He offered his. "Colonel Franz von Ziegler," he said. "Commandant of His Imperial and Royal Majesty's Airship Station at Spich."

We shook.

Ziegler said, "Colonel, you have a fine medal there."

My hand moved to my chest beneath the Iron Cross. "Thank you," I said.

He smiled. "Of course that. But I meant your scar."

I returned the smile, though faintly. "And you, sir."

His was particularly wide, as broad as my thumb.

He figured he knew how to read my look. He said, "I drank foolishly long and much upon that night and inflamed it."

He was a purist. And he was solicitous of my goodwill. He did not want me to think he'd exaggerated the wound with horsehair.

"Mine was badly mended," I said.

We flashed a quick, comradely smile at each other.

"Bonn," he said, identifying his university.

"Heidelberg," I said. "Borussia?" I asked. The university fencers all were members of clubs, each school having a variety of these, differentiated in a de facto caste system by occupation or wealth or nobility of blood line. Borussia was Kaiser Wilhelm's club in his Bonn university days, the most elite in the country.

"You honor me by the question," the colonel said. "But no. Guestphalia."

"Also splendid," I said.

"And you?"

"Rhenania," I said.

"Excellent," he said.

We paused now for a beat.

This thing was forever shared.

He ended the pause with a deep intake of breath and a straightening. "I took the liberty of approaching you," he said. "If you are here for some purpose that is none of my business, I apologize."

"Not at all, Colonel," I said.

"It is early," he said. "But the occasion warrants. May I offer you something to drink?"

"It is early," I said.

"Coffee then?"

"No thank you."

He made a very small but abrupt lift of the chin, as if he'd been righteously rebuked. I was all business. He was a man who respected that, who was just that sort of man himself, and he regretted giving any other impression.

"Would you care to sit?" He lifted his hand only very slightly to indicate the chairs.

I sat in one. He sat. I opened my dispatch case and removed my letter of introduction from the foreign minister.

"My purpose here is very much your business," I said, extending the letter toward him.

He took it from me with a face gone grimly tight.

He opened it. He began to read.

The German foreign minister himself was vouching for me.

"Minister Jagow's introduction is general," I said, "because the specifics are for your ears only."

Ziegler took a short, quick breath at this.

He read on. He finished. He looked at me. "I'd *thought* you might be Foreign Office," he said, softly.

He was intimidated.

He began to fold the letter.

It was time to open the throttle on the big bluff.

"You may keep it for your files," I said. "If you have any concerns."

He finished folding the letter, slipped it back into the envelope, and handed it across to me. He would show no fear.

Good.

I opened the weather flap on the dispatch case once more and replaced the letter. I closed the case.

When I returned my attention to Colonel Ziegler, his hands sat one upon the other on his desktop.

His face was fixed in a stoic calmness. Placid, almost. This was his imminent-battle face, when all that could be done to prepare had been done.

"My people are not precisely clear as to what you know," I said. "But our inquiries reveal that you are a respected and trusted officer. No doubt that is why certain parties chose you and this base."

I paused.

I watched his calmness harden into a mask.

I said, "You and perhaps a single airship commander—and perhaps no one else—understand the unusual circumstances of the imminent mission to London."

I hesitated only slightly to give him a chance to leap in and clarify how many others knew of the mission. He didn't. I didn't press it. I said, "You are taking a civilian aboard. And within your arsenal on this raid, there will be a single, special bomb. For its very existence, the civilian is responsible, which is why he has been authorized to accompany it. I suspect you do not know the exact nature of that bomb's specialness."

I paused again.

Ziegler's face had not changed in the slightest.

I waited one moment more. And another.

He realized I expected something from him. The calmness collapsed into a brow-furrowed sincerity. "You are correct, sir," he said. "I do not know why this bomb bears its privilege."

"Good," I said.

It wasn't quite the word he'd expected. His eyes flickered with the temporary relief I'd intended: he'd said the right thing to disavow a conspiracy.

"I believe you," I said. I let him feel good for a moment and then I tweaked him again. "You met with him last night."

"Sir, he came to me as I was informed he would. I was instructed to receive the bomb from him and place it in safekeeping until its loading for the mission."

"Perhaps you do not know the irony attending him."

"I do not, sir."

I said, "He is an Englishman."

Ziegler lifted up slightly from the chest.

"You did not know," I said. "Good."

His eyes flexed in surprise. He understood that I'd read his reaction. He was not used to this.

And then he made a quick confession. "I knew he had an Anglicized name."

I waved my hand, absolving him.

He nodded his head faintly in gratitude.

"The man who directed you," I said. "I presume it was Colonel Bauer himself."

"Yes sir," he said. Very softly. This was *softly* from a man not accustomed to using that tone. "Though strictly by dispatch," he added. "I have never met with him."

"Colonel Ziegler, you do understand that our conversation here is strictly confidential."

"Yes sir."

"This is not a matter of treason," I said.

He stiffened at the mere mention of the word.

"Not strictly speaking," I said.

Ziegler launched a beseeching hand into the airspace above the desk. "I have only responded to orders."

I nodded.

He said, "Transmitted to me under the seal of the General Staff."

"I accept your innocently obedient role in this, Colonel. Otherwise, I would not be speaking to you like this. I am enlisting your help."

He withdrew his hand. Restacked both of them. He straightened as if sitting for a portrait. He was ready for further obedience. He was trained for this.

I said, "General Falkenhayn was himself unaware of the details of this mission. Though I do not suggest treason."

Colonel Ziegler braced himself.

"The Kaiser has *certainly* been unaware of the mission about to depart from Spich."

I could hear Ziegler's breath catch in his chest.

I said, "Though the officers in our High Command all yearn for victory over our enemies—and England is certainly the most heinous of these enemies—there is much dissension as to methods and targets. You are surely aware of this."

He nodded.

"This is very difficult for loyal and obedient officers in the field," I said. "Men such as yourself."

"I serve the Kaiser," Ziegler said.

"Just so," I said. "And we all serve our shared blood. The blood of the German race."

"Germany above all," he intoned. *Deutschland über alles.*

I gave him a paternal smile.

And then I made it vanish instantly. "This Englishman," I said.

The colonel's eyes narrowed a little. Yes, this Englishman.

"I do not suggest treason," I said. "The man is of German forebears. Though he is a prominent man in the English government, he works secretly for our cause."

I let this sit for a brief moment in Ziegler.

"Nevertheless," I said. "His blood is not purely ours. Do you understand?"

He did. He nodded.

"Should not our trust for a special mission be pure?"

One more beat to let the rhetorical question answer itself in his mind.

"He must not fly, this Englishman," I said. "Do you understand?"

"Yes sir," Ziegler said in his heel-clicking voice. "And this special bomb?"

I flickered now. I'd made a snap decision back in Berlin, in Reinauer's office. I'd compounded that decision later. To let this go forward. To sabotage Stockman's intentions in the riskier way, with the mission launched, so as to draw full, failed, discredited attention to it at the highest levels of the government. With the Kaiser himself. Otherwise I would only briefly delay things. I still believed that.

But the terrible moment I'd arranged was now upon me. The moment when I myself would order a poison gas attack on London.

"The bomb and its mission will go forward," I said.

50

"What would you have me do about the Englishman?" Colonel Ziegler asked.

I had two tasks now. Planting the bomb was one. But first I had to get Stockman out of the way. I briefly considered using Ziegler to accomplish this. But the crucial thing was to keep Berlin ignorant. Short of having the commandant arrest Stockman and prevent him from any outside communication, I had to expect Bauer would quickly become involved in any change of plans.

"I will take care of that, Colonel," I said. "In due time. Meanwhile, you can serve the Kaiser and our country by speaking to no one about any of this. No one."

"Of course."

"I may even allow the Englishman to proceed for a time in ignorance of our suspicions." I paused, leaned forward in my chair. And I added, "So we may be sure there are no matters of treason involved. Do you understand me?"

"Yes sir," he said.

"If there are, then we must determine how far the crimes extend. Both up the chain of command and down."

"Yes sir," he said, his voice gone tight. It was best to let him continue to worry about his own behavior.

Which he began at once to defend by going on the offensive, good officer that he was. He said, "May I say, Colonel, that I am relieved this man will not fly with our brave crew?"

"Yes, Colonel, you may say that."

"We choose to carry no parachutes, even though our airship has fixed launching hooks for the latest Paulus model. But each chute weighs fifteen kilos. We carry more bombs instead. And the men scorn even the temptation. If they cannot save their ship, they prefer to perish with it. But this man insisted on having a parachute."

I thought how this was Stockman, all right. He admired my *Schmiss*. He wanted to fight the war against England somehow. But his satisfaction was to have me shave and so to share the honor vicariously. And his fight was to sneak in and dose them with poison. Of course he'd figure out how to save his own skin.

"Just so," I said. "He is English." That was for Ziegler's consumption, but in my head: *Just so. This is the man my mother loves. Another professional pretender.* "Tell me, Colonel, what arrangement did you make with him last night? For his flight."

"We are ready each day," Ziegler said. "We await our final weather information. This comes to us by telegraph at about three o'clock each afternoon. If the weather seems favorable, I will contact him at his hotel."

Even as I improvised along now, new challenges were presenting themselves. The weather. As far as I knew, the weather today looked good for the mission. But I had no idea what it was in England, which was the crucial question. And the weather could quickly change, could stop the mission. If I eliminated Stockman and then the flight was suddenly canceled, his fate would quickly come to light—surely before the next opportunity for the mission to fly—and my only chance to expose the poison gas strategy in a bad light to Berlin would be lost.

Ziegler said, "We must be in the air by five to arrive in London at the target hour."

Another problem. Whenever I'd visualized planting the bomb on the Zeppelin, my mind had seen it as nighttime. But of course it couldn't be night. The flight to London was upward of five hours. I had to do my work in broad daylight.

Ziegler and I sat for a moment, fretting in parallel, showing none of it to each other.

"Will you load the bombs at three?" I said.

"Yes."

"But I presume the mission could be canceled in those last two hours."

"Yes sir. If the weather changes abruptly. We'd be advised of that."

So much could go wrong in all of this already. I didn't want to be forced to destroy the Zeppelin on the ground. I didn't know how far the phosgene would reach or how quickly from the larger explosion. Far enough and quick enough to be nasty. Far enough and quick enough, perhaps, to be inescapable. But if I'd already eliminated Albert and the weather changed and the Zepp didn't fly, I would have no choice.

First things first.

I had to be sure of access to him.

"Are you picking him up when it's time?" I asked.

"I am to telephone him. He wished to make his own way here."

I thought: *He's bringing her to see him off*.

I set that thought aside.

"You will telephone me first at the Boar's Head Inn," I said.

"Of course."

"There is no instrument in my room," I said. "You will make sure the innkeeper finds me. Leave no message. You must hear my voice."

"Yes sir." Colonel Ziegler punched each word.

I sat back in my chair.

I fixed my gaze firmly on him. I let him work all this over in his mind for a few moments under my steady scrutiny.

Then I said, "Perhaps it's not too early, Colonel."

His face muddled up. The gears ground in his head.

I gave him a faint smile. "To have that drink."

He fairly leapt from his chair. "Sergeant Götz," he boomed, happy to be back in command.

The door banged open behind me. "Sir!"

"Schnapps," the colonel said.

And so the colonel and I drank together for a time.

He grew intensely nostalgic and even sentimental about the military action he'd seen, regretting having missed, because of his age, most of the wars of unification; cherishing the bit he had finally experienced as a freshly minted, nineteen-year-old lieutenant at the Siege of Paris; doing his most ardent fighting later on, in the African colonies. I listened quietly and he talked volubly and when I felt we'd secured our bond of uniform and rank and shared secret mission, I asked to see a little of the base.

He was eager to comply.

We stepped out of the administrative building.

"Our airship is only lately delivered," Ziegler said. "The LZ 78. Modeled after the navy's newest."

And he led me first through a door in the freight-train-long row of contiguous lean-tos at the base of the near wall of the hangar—where maintenance supplies were kept and the ordnance and flying supplies were staged for the missions—and then through a sliding door into the hangar and into the presence of the Zeppelin itself, its long bullet-body darkly glowing from the massive bank of yellow-tinted windows in the ceiling.

The size of the airship staggered me even more than the hangar it sat in, as on the morning in New York a few months ago I was staggered by the *Lusitania* as I stood at the foot of its gangplank. These things were not simply vast, fixed objects. These things took you inside them and then raced upon the face of the sea or through the sky. This thing now before me, colossal as it was, actually flew. It was as if the Great Pyramid of Giza could suddenly lift up from the earth and soar away.

It seemed invulnerable, this Zeppelin. Even noble, somehow, intrinsically so. Apart from the terrible intentions its owners had for it, the airship itself seemed innocent. I was sad for what I had to do.

And terrified that I might not be able to do it. I was tiny in the world of this thing. The bag on my shoulder—more importantly, the single device I intended to carry in it—was tinier still.

The air smelled of hydrogen. Even here. Even with the Zeppelin at rest. It was filled full already, its twilight-gray skin stretched taut with two million cubic feet of gas, anticipating this night. LZ 78 was ready to fly. And I had to find a way to destroy it at the very last moment.

51

The doors at the upwind end of the hangar were partly open, about the width of the central guiding rails. Ziegler walked us in that direction. He spoke of the ton-and-a-half bomb payload and the four latest-model Maxim guns in the gondolas. I noted heavy-duty branch valves along the floor, bespeaking the deeply buried hydrogen conduits; wheeled distribution tanks for gasoline with heavy-duty pumps and safety cocks, the fuel itself also buried underground; two-branched water hydrants every hundred feet; three dozen ventilating chimneys in the roof; signs everywhere with warnings about smoking, about matches, about sparks; the dampness beneath our feet, the floor kept constantly wet by a sprinkling system. Everywhere around us were markers of the fear of fire. Fear of the explosive flammability of hydrogen.

"Good," Ziegler said. "Here's Major Dettmer."

We were passing the forward gondola, and ahead, standing in the center of the rails, arms akimbo, darkly silhouetted against the tall corridor of morning light at the open doors, was the commander of LZ 78.

We approached. He turned and took a step toward us, his face suddenly rendering itself, in the light from the windows, into clean-shaven, cleft-chinned stolidity.

He saluted us both.

Ziegler introduced me. And he explained me: "Colonel Wolfinger represents the Foreign Office. They have interceded about the civilian."

Dettmer's eyes cut instantly in my direction.

"He won't be flying with you," I said.

I patted my dispatch case, as if the written order for that was inside. I wanted the major to take note of the case so when I needed access to his airship, he would not question its presence over my shoulder.

I paused to let Major Dettmer reply if he wished.

He realized I was waiting.

He said, "It was not my idea to bring him, sir."

I smiled at him. "I did not imagine it was."

"I have clear instructions about his bomb," he said. "We do not need his presence to drop it where they wish."

To demonstrate my authority and validate my identity, I'd played the safest cards in my deck of deductions so far. I took a little gamble with one now.

"They do still light their theaters at night," I said.

Dettmer smiled.

I was right about the target.

"I would like to see you off," I said. "To see for myself that the bomb is secure," I said.

"Yes sir," he said.

"They have given you special handling instructions, I presume."

"They have."

"Have they told you why?"

I sensed Ziegler stiffen beside me. He'd answered this question already. I was checking up on him.

"We have speculated," Dettmer said.

Ziegler said, sharply, "He asked if they *told* you its specialness, Major. Not if you have a speculation."

Dettmer looked at his colonel and then back to me. "I'm sorry, sir. No, sir. They have told us only how to handle the bomb."

I said, "But that clearly suggests something to you, speculative though your thoughts may be."

He looked at his colonel once more.

I turned to Ziegler. I let him off the hook, mercy being as intimidating an assertion of power as severity. "You quite properly answered the question that I asked, Colonel. I am now asking for your speculation."

Ziegler said, "We assume the bomb contains a poison gas."

"Do you accept a war of terror upon a civilian population, Colonel?"

He straightened. But he was not composed. He had no idea what I expected him to say.

"I follow orders," he said.

"And you, Major?" I turned to him.

"Yes sir."

"Follow your instructions carefully with this device, gentlemen. We obey. We do our duty. All of us. As we must."

Including myself in the invocation of duty, I was reminded of the weather. How its fickleness could test that duty. Once I'd dealt with Stockman and planted the bomb, the Zeppelin had to fly.

And then I had a thought.

I turned to Ziegler.

"This matter of the weather," I said. "Once armed, this special bomb becomes even more dangerous. We should abort the mission only under extreme circumstances."

Ziegler did not reply.

I looked at the major. He was standing at attention.

The burden, the dangers, of what I was suggesting would fall on him.

Too bad.

And then my brain caught up with a thing I had been shunting aside, a thing I'd learned some months ago to shunt aside. I thought of the men I have killed, the men I had yet to kill, in doing my duty.

Unless I failed in my own mission, the man standing before me would not have to brave a flight into bad weather this evening.

He would be dead.

He and his whole crew.

By my dutiful hand.

I shunted this aside again.

I said, "This special bomb is very volatile. We do not wish to poison the air base and all of Spich."

"No sir," Ziegler said, his voice thick with what sounded like misery.

I looked at him.

This did not resemble war as he'd known it, as he'd relished it, for his long career. Not in any way.

I turned back to Major Dettmer. "I will not ask you to attack London if the weather is against you. But you must at least fly to the Strait of Dover or the North Sea and dispose of the thing. You must fly. Do you both understand?"

The commander of the LZ 78 executed a very slow, very precise salute and held it.

He was a good soldier.

This was necessary work, my work here. He was such a good soldier that he would otherwise poison London from his goodness. My work was necessary. Wretchedly so.

I looked at the colonel.

I lifted my chin slightly.

He snapped into a quick salute, also holding it at his temple.

I saluted them both.

And that was that.

52

Jeremy was waiting in what had become our place in the Boar's Head bar, the marble-top table in the far corner. He'd left me my preferred chair with its back to the wall. The man noticed things.

I sat.

He nodded.

I nodded.

The innkeeper arrived beside us. Before we ordered a little early lunch, I said to her, "I will receive a phone call this afternoon around three o'clock. I will be sitting here. Please find me. I want to speak to the man personally."

"Yes sir," she said, with the crisp snap of ingrained obedience, which seemed to be as natural a manner for Germany's women innkeepers as for its career army officers.

Then her face flashed into thoughtfulness and instantly into revelation. She'd just remembered something.

She looked to Jeremy. I looked with her.

He was sitting stiffly upright, playing the Foreign Office major.

"Did you find your telegram?" she asked.

He did a minute shift of his head sideways. A Cracker Jack flip book of a boxer's feint.

She went instantly on. "I knocked, but you didn't answer. I slipped it under your door."

"I did find it," Jeremy said. "Thank you."

He glanced at me, then back to her.

Jeremy and I ordered. She went away.

He turned to me, and I didn't have to ask.

He said, "The groups we must work with inside Germany—the *Republikaner* particularly—we've used their help for this, their resources, their bomb, and they feel invested in it. I'm obligated to stay in touch with them."

"Do they know of the special nature of the threat?"

That minuscule feint again. As if I'd just thrown a left-hand jab. But then immediately he said, "Not at all. We keep them informed. But only as much as we want them to know. To them, we're simply bursting balloons."

I figured I knew why he felt like dodging when the *Republikaner* came up. "You not real comfortable with those boys?"

He smiled at me. "You don't miss much," he said.

"It's their bomb but none of their business."

"Precisely."

"We okay for this?'"

"We're okay," he said. "And as to the pin for this particular balloon, everything is ready but the hour."

He still needed to set the clock on the time bomb he'd been assembling while I was at the air base.

"The bomb was one of the resources provided by the *Republikaner*," he said.

"Make it five minutes after five," I said. This was guesswork. How prompt would they be? Ziegler had stressed the importance of that hour to make it to the target on schedule. These were Germans. Their trains ran precisely. All this whistled through me quickly and I said, "No. Let's give ourselves a little more margin. The Zepps climb slowly anyway. Seven after five."

"Seven after," he said. "And you leave the inn at three?"

"If the weather's right."

"Then I have time to eat the sausages," he said.

I began to brief him on the events at the air base, and in the midst of it a man entered the inn and headed for the bar. The innkeeper, who was wiping down the zinc top, saw him come in and she instantly took up a stein, turned to the tap behind her, and filled the vessel. She moved to the newcomer and put the stein before him, even as he was still taking off his peaked field cap and laying it on the bar.

A large, late-morning beer was this man's routine.

Though perhaps only on flight days.

It was Major Dettmer.

He and the woman spoke together for a few moments, low, their heads angling toward each other.

I doubted he flew drunk. But he needed some fortification.

The innkeeper moved away.

I had no interest in speaking to him, seeing as I intended to kill him this afternoon.

Jeremy was watching me watching something over his shoulder.

When I brought my gaze back to him, he flipped his face very slightly to the side, keeping his eyes fixed on mine. *What is it?* he was asking.

In a low voice I finished telling him about Ziegler and then about Major Dettmer, ending with: "Dettmer came in while we've been speaking." I slightly angled my head in the major's direction.

I looked over Jeremy's shoulder.

The man was heading this way.

Beyond him the innkeeper was clearing his stein from the bar. He'd made quick work of it.

I pushed back a little from the table. Preferring to flee, but recognizing the need to make everything seem normal, I rose.

Dettmer arrived, saluted.

I returned the salute, and I formally introduced Jeremy to the major.

"I do not wish to intrude," the major said, "but may I ask to sit with you for a few minutes?"

I could have said no. I was Colonel Klaus von Wolfinger, after all. Turning Dettmer abruptly aside would have been consistent with the character I'd created.

But if the man I was to kill felt the need to talk with someone in a bar before a mission that was plenty dangerous on its own, then it might as well be with me.

I nodded without comment at an empty third chair that placed him between the two of us.

He sat.

He put his peaked cap in his lap.

"Commander Dettmer will fly the LZ 78 this evening," I said to Jeremy.

"God punish England," Jeremy said to him. *Gott strafe England.* "May we order something for you?"

"Another beer?" I said.

Dettmer looked at me.

"You're drinking this morning," I said.

"Only what I allow myself on these days," the major said.

Outwardly I offered nothing for him to read at this. No smile. No frown.

Then I realized I was deliberately trying to make him uncomfortable.

"Merely one long beer," he said.

I was too much in character. I owed him better than that.

"We admire what you do," I said, making my voice go as warm as I dared without drastically altering my necessary persona.

He nodded once, in thanks.

We waited for him to speak. I realized he had nothing particular in mind. He simply needed a little conversation on the day of a mission. There'd been the words with the innkeeper. The brief pose, their two heads angled toward each other, suggested a closeness between them. Perhaps even more, something only a woman could give. But there were things on his mind a woman couldn't speak to. And the men were locals. Drunks or bores. He'd seen two of his own sitting here, and so he'd come to them.

"How do you keep warm up there?" I asked.

He laughed softly. I understood what he was about to go through. At the Zepp's operating altitude two miles above England, it would be a Chicago-winter fifteen below even in August. And it would be a slashing cold, with the head wind beating into the command gondola.

He spoke happily for a time about their woolen underwear and their leather overalls and their fur overcoats and the sheep's wool lining in their leather gloves. And their scarves and their goggles and the ineffectualness of all that.

He was happy to speak as if these were the things that brought him to his morning ritual of a beer and conversation on the days he flew.

He moved from goggles to dreams, however. A seamless transition. "I often freeze in my dreams," he said. "I can wake in a midsummer sweat in my rooms in Spich and continue to shiver from the cold in my dreams. In my dreams I have forgotten my overcoat or my gloves and I pay dearly for that."

Dettmer paused. He turned his head toward the bar, as if thinking he should have another beer.

But he looked back to me.

He said, "Or the opposite. I am on fire. We all have these dreams, you know. The day is soon coming when their planes can climb fast enough to catch us. Or when they create an incendiary shell that can reach us, and the first one to touch our airship's skin will turn us into a fireball. We will have a brief time to decide then, each of us. We carry no parachutes, you understand. And so my men and I have each made a decision. Some of us will leap and some of us will stay. Some will die falling to earth and some will die consumed by fire in the heavens."

Dettmer stopped speaking. His eyes moved to mine and then to the Iron Cross pinned to my chest. He smiled a faint smile at me. He figured I understood. He figured men could talk like this to each other if they each understood.

I did understand.

I wished it were for the reasons he assumed.

I wished I were fighting this war in a way that earned this moment between us.

Instead, I was barely able to remain seated in the chair.

But I stayed.

The innkeeper's boy arrived. He put the plates of sausage and kraut before us.

"Perhaps some food?" Jeremy said to Dettmer.

"Thanks," he said. "I have to go now to prepare."

Having remained in Dettmer's presence, I'd come back to my own obedience, my own place in this war that wasn't quite yet an American war. But things were being done in the world that should not be done. And as an American I was dealing with that.

Dettmer, at least, had established preparations to make. A clear and specific path to the completion of his mission, however arduous or frightful that might be. I was still improvising.

So I said to him, "What *are* the preparations to fly your airship?"

He was glad to come back from his dreams and to focus on the routine.

"I will put my men to work," he said. "The chief engineer, the helmsmen, the radioman, the gunners, the bombing officer, the sailmaker. The engines are to be examined, the elevator and rudder controls tested, also the telegraph and the Maxims. The bombs must be loaded precisely. The gas cells must be checked for leaks."

"When do you board?" I asked. "When are all the checks completed and you go to your stations?"

"We board in the hangar," he said. "The final taking on of gas and ballast and ordnance is a delicate thing. The balance of lift and load. That is part of the preparation. Our very body weight must be accounted for. Only the watch officer remains outside to oversee the ground crew at the launching."

The timing seemed terribly off.

My physical presence on the airship during preparations, which I'd blithely assumed to be possible, would throw off the weight adjustments. I would have no access to the interior. But there was nowhere outside to effectively place the bomb. Nor the opportunity to do it, in plain sight.

I'd trusted too much on my ability to improvise.

"I must go now," Dettmer said.

He rose.

I rose too.

He started to salute.

Instead, I offered my hand to him.

We shook.

He held my hand for a moment, even after I'd stopped the shaking. "Thank you, sir," he said.

My mind thrashed.

Dettmer turned to walk away.

And then I thought of the ground crew and their supervision.

"Major," I said.

He turned back.

"Does the watch officer fly with you?"

"Yes, of course."

"How do you account for his weight in your preparation?"

"He is the last to come on board, once the ship is outside the hangar. Till then we have a man with us to take his place."

My mind settled.

"May I have the honor of sharing the last hour before your launch? Perhaps I could take the place of your watch officer's substitute."

Dettmer straightened instantly to attention. Of course.

But he had a practical matter first.

He broke from his uprightness to give me a once-over.

Apparently I was close enough in size. He stood at attention again and snapped me a salute. "It would be *our* honor, sir."

Perhaps it was the sudden impression I had of myself as a fraud that prompted the question that came then to my mind. A fraud especially to this man before me. Perhaps the question was prompted by the way I dealt with that, thinking I was no fraud at all, that I was no more a fraud than any actor in any role, that my role in this drama was crucial, that I had lives in London to save and I had no alternative. Perhaps this most important reality led me back into the character of Colonel Klaus von Wolfinger and it was he who prompted me to ask the question. Or maybe it was my true self—the newspaper reporter looking for the arresting personal detail in a story of life and death—maybe it was Christopher Cobb the reporter, who could be as hardened as any secret service officer when necessary, who prompted the question. Whatever or whoever it was, to my shame, I finished with Major Dettmer by asking, "If the day comes that you dream about, which are you? Earth or sky?"

He did not hesitate. "I am afraid of fire," he said. "I will jump."

53

Major Dettmer saluted me smartly. I saluted him. I did not watch him leave.

Jeremy ate. I did not. We neither of us said a thing.

Then he rose.

"May I borrow your case?" he said.

It was sitting on the floor at my feet. I retrieved it and handed it to him.

We nodded at each other and he went off to activate the bomb.

I touched the handle of my coffee cup and I let it go. I did not know my way forward. Not yet. Which was the nature of improvisation, after all, not to know the next thing to do until the present thing is done. For now, sit here. That was clear. Receive a phone call. Passive things, however. The other actors in our little drama were the ones presently at work. The plot went forward only if the weather was clear. Which it likely would be. So after the waiting, my own next move would be to make sure that Sir Albert Stockman—British parliamentarian, crypto-Hun, aspiring poisoner of London, and paramour of a world-famous actress—was prevented from arriving at the Zeppelin air base this afternoon.

Did we need to kill him?

Was he intrinsically dangerous?

If either Jeremy or I made it out of this alive, Stockman would never be able to return to his phony life in England. He would be known for what he was and Germany would be stuck with him. And if our plan to expose and discredit the poison gas air attack worked, his dangerous usefulness would mostly vanish.

There were, of course, other considerations on this question, personal to me, that would fit into either pan of the balance scale. But, in fact, I did not have to decide right now. We couldn't kill him this afternoon anyway. Not in the hotel room, certainly. Not in broad daylight in a German town. We couldn't effectively remove him from the hotel, either living or dead.

Then I thought: The body could stay in place. Isabel could play the role of terrified witness and grieved lover with ease. But the deed might get noisy in the doing. And word of his killing could make it to the air base before the mission and stymie things.

I picked up my cup of coffee and drank from it. Thick and bitter and no longer hot. It was clear to me that Jeremy had to sit with Albert till my part with the Zeppelin was done.

That decided, I ate my lunch.

And soon thereafter Jeremy returned.

He presented my bag to me with both hands.

I took it into my lap and opened the weather flap.

Wedged inside was a dark blue tin that once held *Stollwerck Chocolade*. It nearly filled the dispatch case.

Jeremy sat in the chair Dettmer had occupied, nearer to me, and he drew it nearer still.

He said, in almost a whisper, "You're free, of course, to admire my handiwork in private, but I'd strongly recommend you let it be. I've packed it all tightly in cotton wool."

In answer I closed the flap and set the case gently on the floor.

Perhaps it wasn't answer enough. He added, "The connection from the clock to the device is delicate."

"I understand," I said.

"I wish we didn't have to trust it," he said.

"We have no choice," I said.

We let that be for a moment.

He remained near; we could still talk low; the bar was empty. I said, "We need to speak of what's next."

"Stockman," he said.

"Stockman."

Jeremy said at once, "It would be difficult to kill him this afternoon."

"I entirely agree," I said.

"You have a thought?"

"I do. As soon as the bell rings on the London raid, we go to the hotel, take the room, and you hold Stockman at gunpoint till I return."

He'd been listening to all this with his ear turned my way, his eyes averted. Now he looked at me. There was a grim fixedness about him.

I figured I knew why. "The *Stollwerck Chocolade* part is a one-man job anyway," I said.

He nodded. The grimness loosened. Then he had a sudden thought. He said, "You're putting the actress in the center of things."

That was true.

I said, "Can you think of another way?"

He tried for a moment, though I was sure he'd already been working at the Stockman solution for a while. "I can't," he said. "But I'm not the one who has problems with her."

"She'll know enough just to sit and look terrified," I said. "She'll be fine at that. She can act."

Did I believe myself? I had no choice.

Jeremy rose. He said, "Bring your lock tools."

He was right, of course. But a very dark shadow passed through my head. I would have to slip unbidden and unwanted into a hotel room that held my mother and one of her men.

Jeremy went away to sleep, and I ordered a beer.

Merely one long beer.

Dettmer's limit.

When I lifted it, I paused as if to touch steins with the major.

54

Over the next few hours I looked at my watch a dozen times.

My twenty-one-jewel, railroad-grade Waltham.

I had time to admire the watch.

The minutes went slowly.

At last it was three o'clock but no call came and then five more minutes went by without a call and then at last, at ten minutes past three, I heard the ring of a telephone from the direction of the kitchen.

I stood up.

I waited.

The innkeeper appeared at the doorway.

As soon as we made eye contact, she turned and disappeared.

I put the strap of the dispatch case with the ticking bomb over my head and onto my shoulder and cupped my hand beneath the case and pressed it against my hip. And I followed.

She was standing in the doorway to a small office immediately before the entrance to the kitchen. She stepped aside.

I went in and took up the telephone and put the receiver to my ear. I said, "Wolfinger."

"Colonel." It was Ziegler. "We have good weather."

"Thank you," I said. "Allow me to deliver the news to the English gentleman."

"As you wish, sir."

We rang off.

And I stood before Jeremy's door and I knocked and the door opened only moments later.

He was putting on his peaked cap.

We went out of the Boar's Head and into the Torpedo and we drove to the Hotel Alten-Forst.

We parked the car and I left the bomb on the floor of the tonneau and we strode through the lobby of the hotel and into the elevator and we arrived at the second floor.

And things slowed down.

The flower-wrought-iron door clanged open. The elevator boy spoke some chirpy words that I did not hear. Jeremy and I stepped onto the long Turkish runner carpet. We turned toward Room 200.

We moved off. One long stride and another, and then together we knew to slow down, to walk softly, one short soft step and then another, and I would not let myself remember anything, creeping toward my mother's hotel door. Not remember, not anticipate. I focused on the details at hand. Had I told Jeremy along the way that I'd drive the Torpedo to the air base? Or had I only intended to tell him, running the words in my mind as I approached his room at the inn but forgetting to say them? No. I said them as we got into the Torpedo in the side yard of the Boar's Head. I'd said that I'd take the car.

My mind thrashed on to find some other preoccupation. But now we slowed even more in our walk to Room 200. We trod more quietly still. And the door before us loomed large, squeezing everything else out of my head.

And we stood before it.

Jeremy gently drew his Luger. I gently drew my lock-picking tools. We looked at each other. We were both ready.

One of us needed to listen at the door.

Not me.

I nodded for him to do it.

Jeremy turned his head and brought his ear near to the door. His face was angled toward me.

He listened.

Then he smiled a small, wry smile.

And so it took all the will I could muster to open my leather pouch of tools and work the pick and the torque wrench gently into the lock. I manipulated the pins one at a time, choosing silence over maximum speed, though I was plenty fast, happy to focus unthinkingly on this task of the fingertips.

But the distraction of professional concentration vanished with the click of the lock and my withdrawal of the tools and my reflexive step back from the door, my body ready to run away. Jeremy pushed in front of me and wrenched the knob and threw the door open and rushed in.

We dared not fail at this. I had no choice. I followed him, not pausing to put the lock tools away but dropping them on the floor, drawing my Luger. He'd turned sharply to the left and was lunging through the bedroom door and my mother screamed—in her authentic, unperformed voice—and though my legs were leaden and my chest was clamping shut I also pressed through the doorway as well, even as Jeremy, inside, cried *"Halt!"* and then again "Stop!"

I took my place beside him and let myself see.

The bed was strewn with rose petals.

Whose idea was that?

Stockman had halted. He was standing beside the bed and was squaring around, his hands rising, showing us his palms. Showing us more, perhaps, if I'd looked closely, which I did not, but at least he was not naked. He was wearing his union suit. His body did, however, register on me as athletic in the tight throat-to-ankle cling of his underwear.

And I had no choice now.

I turned my face to my mother.

I released a breath I had not known I was holding. Nothing utterly private was visible on her either, though barely so—she wore a peach silk and lace chemise and matching corset with black stockings gartered at its hem—did we interrupt them just before or just after?— and in spite of her scream, she was now arranged in an alertly sitting, arm-braced, chest-forward pose worthy of a cigarette card. Her eyes, however, were wide in *Shock and Terror*, wide enough to play to the back row of the Duke of York's.

Was this what I'd feared all those years?

This scene?

This pose?

It was no more than what I'd imagined whenever I tried to imagine it as mundane.

At some other specific moment in the half hour just past or in the half hour to have come, perhaps it would have been different for me. Worse for me. But this was how it finally had happened.

We stared at each other, my mother and I. She glanced away for the briefest moment—to check out Stockman—and then she looked back to me and let the *Shock and Terror* mask fall from her face.

And this face was naked.

This was perhaps the most utterly private part of her body, this face.

I wanted to turn away from it but it held me.

This face was weary.

This face was old.

This face was mortal.

This was the face of a woman who would hold very tightly to a man of skills and looks whose love she had lately won, having feared never to find such a man again.

Having sorted through a lifetime of such men.

And she held all the more tightly to this one because he was also a man of great means, a man of significant power, a strewer of roses.

He was, however, also an aspiring mass killer.

I was done looking at her.

I turned my attention back to Stockman, whose own eyes were wide as well. Legitimately so. His new pal Josef Jäger was holding one of two pistols that were presently pointed at him. And Jäger was in a new guise.

Everyone was very quiet for a few beats, all of us taking in the scene.

I said, speaking English, "You can put your hands down, Sir Albert, and join Madam Cobb on the bed. Chastely, however, at this opposite edge."

I flipped the Luger in the direction I wanted him to go and he obeyed without a word.

As he adjusted and arranged himself, I said, without taking my eyes from his face, "And you, Madam Cobb, can relinquish your fetching pose and relax at your end of the rose garden."

I could see her movement in my periphery.

She complied.

"Allow me to introduce myself," I said. "I am Colonel Klaus von Wolfinger of the *Auswärtiges Amt*." I hesitated for a moment, having used the German phrase, as if I were in the process of remembering there was a non-German speaker in the room. I did not look at her, however. Not a glance. I said, "That's the *Foreign Office*, Madam Cobb. I am willing to think you are an innocent outsider in all of this. Naturally so. You have some other function in Sir Albert's life. But for now I am sorry we must insist you be subject to certain restrictions along with him."

Through my little speech, Albert and I were focused on each other. His eyes were subtly dynamic, however, with tiny narrowings and widenings and brightenings and darkenings as he listened to me, as he absorbed my new manner, assessed my surprising appearance, reread all my words and actions since we'd met. He was having trouble with all this.

My mother said, "I'm sure there has been some terrible mistake. With regards to Sir Albert as well as me."

I turned my face to her.

And for a second time I found her to be blank. As blank as when I'd told her about Albert and the poison gas.

I said, "Forgive me, Madam Cobb. You are used to a starring role. But I'm afraid you have no lines in this scene."

Not even that could stir up a reaction in her eyes, or around her mouth, or with her nostrils, or upon her skin. Nothing flickered or twitched or flared or stretched.

So perhaps even the blankness was an act.

It made no difference.

I looked back to Stockman.

His eyes grew steady. He found his voice. He said, "If you are who you say you are, you must put your weapons away at once, you must accord Madam Cobb and me the dignity of our privacy, and you must instantly call your superiors. Ask them to contact Colonel Max Hermann Bauer of the General Staff. He will put you straight."

Though the words themselves were measured enough, he had mustered his full umbrage and toughness for these instructions. He paused now for them to have their effect.

I smiled faintly at him and made my own words sound sickly sweet in tone. "Surely, Sir Albert, you are not under the illusion that Colonel Bauer received higher authorization for your little escapade. Even as we speak, he is also being detained."

Stockman had no answer for this. Once again his mind began to grind behind restless eyes.

I said, "Did you really think you could poison the ancestral home of the Kaiser's English mother and grandmother and expect him to approve, even after the fact? It is a matter of blood, Sir Albert."

I gave that line a moment of silence to play in his head.

Then I invoked his own invented word from our first discussion of blood. "*Der Überglaube*," I said. The overarching belief.

And his restless eyes grew still.

Had he just capitulated?

It was his own argument. Albert knew the risk he'd taken. Like the manly university swordsman he admired and wished he'd been, he seemed to stand straight and lower his saber and accept the wound. That odd respect I'd occasionally felt for him nibbled at me for a moment.

Only for a moment.

"I will leave you now," I said. "Sir Albert, I think you know Major Ecker. He worked for you briefly."

Stockman finally took his eyes off me. He turned his face to Jeremy. He looked at him closely for the first time since we burst in. He recognized him. "You were the one," he said, the killing tone of his voice reminding me that Stockman had actually wept for his man Martin. He glared at Jeremy, though he seemed to address me: "So does the officer corps of our Foreign Office tolerate a common murderer?"

"That's quite enough, Albert," I said. "The Foreign Office is more concerned with *uncommon* murderers."

Stockman shifted his glare to me.

But he said nothing.

"Make yourself comfortable, Baronet," I said. "Major Ecker will sit with you, and he is authorized by the highest Foreign Office authorities to shoot you dead if he deems it necessary."

Stockman sniffed and turned his face away.

He understood.

I looked at my mother for the last time in this scene. "I do not mean to alarm you, Madam Cobb. And surely it will be unnecessary. But he has the same authorization regarding you."

She straightened a little in the torso and played a defiant heroine worthy of her Duchess of Malfi: "He may shoot me if he chooses, but I will follow Sir Albert to the end."

I had no idea what part act, what part truth was in this declaration. I doubted that even she knew.

I made no reply.

I turned my back on her.

Jeremy and I exchanged a nod and I passed into the sitting room. I gathered up my lock-picking tools and I put them in my pocket and then I was striding down the hall, wrenching my mind away from the fact that there was one more confrontation to come with Albert Stockman and his lover.

55

I leaned into the Torpedo and lifted the dispatch case from the floor of the tonneau. I stepped out, holding it close. I opened the passenger door and laid it gently on the seat.

Inside the case was the ticking of the clock, but I could not hear it. The ticking was muffled into silence by the cotton wool and the tin.

I looked at my Waltham.

It was five minutes to four.

The matter of Stockman and my mother had taken too much time.

I started the engine and drove away fast.

At the air base I was tempted, because of the time, to drive up to the place where the colonel's driver had parked this morning. But if something went wrong, if the bomb went off with the Zepp still on the ground—by a delayed takeoff perhaps—I wanted the car in a place away, a place I could run to and not have to throttle and spark and crank while phosgene rolled immediately over me.

So I stopped in a stand of birch trees near the entrance to the air base grounds, just off the road to Uckendorf. There was no security out here and the camouflaged Torpedo was inconspicuous among the trees.

I hung the bag over my shoulder and walked away from the Torpedo, taking my watch out to see the time and hearing it tick—the Waltham had a loud tick, muffled by my watch pocket but audible in the open air—and I thought of the ticking in the bag, and it was five minutes past four o'clock.

I hustled on, wanting to jog the half mile to the hangar area, but slowing myself to a brisk walk for the sake of the bomb under my arm, its delicate wired connections. I reached the administrative building in a little less than ten minutes.

Ziegler was in his outer office, on his feet, and he spun to me, strode to me at once. "Good," he said. "Come."

I followed him out of the administrative building and into the hangar through the same side door we'd used this morning.

LZ 78 loomed instantly above me. And *against* me, its gray vastness feeling like a palpable weight upon my eyes, my face, my chest. It staggered me, made me work hard to steady myself on my feet. It made the thing hanging from my shoulder feel dangerous only to myself.

"The commander is forward," Ziegler said.

I dragged my body away, moved my legs, followed Ziegler along the length of the ship, the upwind doors wide open now, the sky going pale white from a thin spew of clouds, a breeze funneling into the hangar and into my face.

The breeze made me think: The Torpedo was well away from here, but it was downwind. Gas released in the launching zone would roll my way. I would have to run fast, if it came to that. I would have to start the car fast.

But if the flight went off on time, I would surely have time to get away. Where exactly would LZ 78 be at seven minutes past five?

"Colonel," I said, "are we still on schedule for a five o'clock launch?"

"From what I gather," he said.

"Good," I said.

All along the airship's length there was the bustle of ground crew, in gray shirt sleeves and soft caps, unfurling the handling lines.

The lines were slack. The hangar ballast was still on board.

We reached the control cabin, a long, boat-shaped, enclosed gondola suspended a man's body-length beneath the great gas-packed hull. An exposed aluminum ladder went up from the gondola and into the keel walkway.

"Here we are," the colonel said.

He stopped at the foot of a rope ladder leading to the forward compartment of the gondola.

He motioned for me to go up. "I'll leave you here. They don't want extra weight. They're expecting you."

We snapped off a simultaneous salute to each other.

He said, "When you've finished, would you care to join me at my office to watch the launch?"

"Of course, Colonel," I said.

And I went up the ladder into the major's command area.

The place felt unfinished, with the web of aluminum braces visible overhead and along stretches of the lower walls. The focal working parts were prominent panels under the windows at the front and along the sides, holding gauges and instruments for heading and for incline, for altitude and for speed, for hydrogen pressure and for fuel level, and standing before the panels were wheels and levers for rudder and elevator and ballast.

The place bustled with half a dozen men in leather jackets and heavy scarves doing their pre-flight checks. In the midst of them was Dettmer with a clipboard in his hand, speaking intensely with one of his officers.

I waited.

I was prepared to insert myself into his awareness. But I felt the need to seem casual about all this, to plausibly portray a benign observer. I had a few minutes of margin. Ideally I'd plant the bomb somewhat nearer its detonation to minimize the possibility of its being discovered in time to disarm it.

Another officer approached the two men, and his arrival drew Dettmer's eyes up and over to me. Immediately he excused himself and stepped my way.

He saluted.

"No need for that, Major," I said. "This is your domain."

His chest lifted and he smiled, grateful for the sign of respect.

I wished I could order him to use the parachute they'd put on board for Stockman, if something were to happen.

But he was a dead man.

All these men around me—I'd roughly parsed them as executive officer and helmsman, navigation officer and chief engineer and telegraph operator—these were all dedicated professional soldiers in obedient service to their country, and all of them were dead men if I did my obedient service to my own country and to my country's ally. As was the watch officer a dead man, whom Dettmer now temporarily nodded off the ship to execute his duties with the ground crew. I was there to compensate for his weight.

"How long do I have on board?" I asked.

Dettmer looked at his clipboard. He looked at his own watch, which he drew from his tunic pocket on a dull gold chain. "Half an hour certainly. Perhaps more. We can wait till the weighing off to reboard the watch officer."

I said, "My official duty is to check on our special bomb. But I'd like to see some of the ship."

Dettmer nodded and went immediately thoughtful. I presumed he was trying to think of someone to spare as my guide.

"I know your men are busy," I said. "After being led to the bomb rack for inspection, I'd need only a little orientation from someone. You wouldn't mind my respectfully and carefully looking around on my own, would you?"

"No sir," he said. "Of course not."

He summoned one of the other officers nearby.

He introduced Lieutenant Schmidt, his telegraph operator, a lanky young man with hollowed cheeks and callused hands, the perfect image of a rube off a farm in southern Illinois, down where you couldn't tell the difference between Illinois and Kentucky.

"This way, sir," he said.

He stepped to the aluminum ladder in the middle of the floor and I followed.

We climbed through the gondola roof and into the open air for a few steps, the smell of hydrogen suddenly strong around us, and then into the hull.

We emerged on the wood slat floor of the keel walkway. It stretched the length of the airship within a tight A-frame of aluminum girders, but this end of the ship was in darkness at the moment, with only swatches of self-luminous paint defining the path. The lieutenant switched on a tungsten flashlight.

"We won't have light in here till we are under way," he said. "The generator."

"I'm fine," I said.

"You would be astonished," he said, "how carefully insulated all the electrical devices are."

He led on, heading aft. He shined his light here and there, identifying whatever his beam fell upon, trying to be a proper tour guide: the vast flanks of the gas cells, covered in goldbeater's skin to prevent leaks; the wiring and the cables, for rudder controls and engine telegraph and speaking tubes; the containers for ballast, full of water laced with alcohol to keep it from freezing at ten thousand feet. He even pointed out the tools and spare parts and the rigging ropes. He loved his airship, this apparent rube of a Lieutenant Schmidt, who was not such a rube after all. He had a mechanical turn of mind.

I tried to ignore him.

I had my own agenda.

I took most careful note for myself of the eighty-gallon aluminum fuel tanks clustered like cave-growing mushrooms along the walkway, their flammable contents piped down to the Maybach engines below, kept away from any engine spark.

Behind these tanks would be a fine place to deposit my dispatch bag and its bomb.

We were in a dark stretch. The lieutenant kept his light forward. I could hear a faint ticking.

It was my own watch.

But I was very aware of the ticking I could not hear.

And now there was some daylight ahead, coming from the floor.

We approached, and the defile of the walkway opened up, the planking vectoring around an open keel hatch.

In the upspill of light I took my watch from my pocket and checked the time. Twenty-five minutes after four.

"We take on supplies here," Lieutenant Schmidt said.

The hatch also had another function. This was clear to me. Directly over the opening was an array of iron hooks welded into a horizontal level of girders. The hooks were within easy reach, outward and upward, just above one's head. This was where a man could hang the break-cord tether of his Paulus parachute and then leap through the hatch. The tether was attached to the top of the silk canopy of his chute, which was folded with its lines into the rucksack on his back, the top of which was closed by another break cord. His plunging body-weight reached the end of the tether, which grabbed at his parachute, which broke through the top of the rucksack and billowed open and snapped the tether. And the leaper was free and floating. He escaped. He did his duty as best he could and then he lived.

And yet all the men on LZ 78 had refused parachutes.

I could understand why.

They were brave and they were dedicated and they were professional. They were soldiers. To make their way here and do this thing successfully, they would have to abandon their ship early in its distress. Which they refused to do.

I was killing men like this.

But Albert was not a man like this.

He'd insisted on being one of them to share their glory, but he'd also insisted on a way to escape them if they were to die.

At last I realized it would be easy for me to kill Albert at the end of this night.

A bullet in his head.

Simple.

At my hip, the bomb ticked on.

I'd stopped to ponder all this.

The lieutenant drew near.

I was staring at the array of hooks.

"You know what that's for?" he asked.

"I do," I said.

"This is where they are supposed to be kept," he said, and he flashed his light into a rack in the dimness beyond the hatch.

He snapped his head back.

He'd clearly expected the parachute storage rack to be empty, a testament to the crew's scorn for any plan to abandon their ship.

But a single, rucksack-shaped bundle lay on one of the shelves. Albert's.

And then Lieutenant Schmidt surprised me a little. He was a shrewdly practical man, as guys stupidly mistaken for rubes often were.

"Someday," he said. "They will make a parachute that needs no anchoring in the ship. It will be light and easily worn and you can simply jump. Even at the very last moment, when you have done all that you can do. You will jump from wherever you are and deploy your own canopy."

Briefly—not as Klaus von Wolfinger, not as America's secret service agent, not even as the Cobb who wrote news stories—but briefly, as one guy hearing another guy and knowing what he means, I thought to say to him, *May you still be flying when they start issuing those.*

But the words snagged on a goddamn irony in my head, and instead I said, "We should see the bomb rack. Time is growing short."

"Sorry, sir," Lieutenant Schmidt said, and he led me farther, to midship and another open hatch, a large one, with the walkway skirting it.

Over this opening, however, the cross girders supported a tenement-garden-size release mechanism. The bombs bloomed in neat rows, fins unfurled, awaiting their headlong harvest.

Beneath them, crouched low and leaning head and shoulders over the hatch opening, was an officer in the uniform common to the command gondola.

Below him was the watch officer I'd displaced.

I did not hear the words they exchanged but the watch officer saw me in the shadows and nodded the crouching officer's attention toward me. The man turned his head and leaped to his feet. He saluted.

I returned it.

"Sir," he said. "Lieutenant Kreyder, bombing officer of LZ 78, awaits your command, sir."

"At ease, Lieutenant," I said.

"Thank you, sir," he said, and he spread his legs a little and clasped his hands behind his back.

"That's not enough at ease, Lieutenant," I said. I was out of character now. Too soft. I was going a little out of my mind meeting and naming these men one by one.

"Sir," he said. "It's not often I have the honor of showing a colonel my little garden."

He was repressing a smile. He was seeking my permission to laugh a little with me.

I wanted to tell him that he and I had the same image of his bombs.

I wanted to have a little laugh with him.

This was no way to fight a war. For either of us.

This all had to stop, this saluting and naming and talking together.

I had to think about the people in London who were, at this very moment, dressing for the theater. Not soldiers at all.

I knew I had to make quick work of this phony rationale for standing inside the LZ 78.

I had to plant my bomb and walk away as quickly now as possible.

56

So this officer pointed out Albert's bomb, hanging with the others. It looked different from the rest only in subtle ways. The shape of its striking point, the angle of its fins, the sheen of its metal body.

I saw these things and I let them go.

The lieutenant spoke reassuringly on and on to this special colonel who was taking a special interest in this special bomb. "We will drop no others until that one has done its work," he said. "We have studied the target area carefully, the navigation officer and the commander and I. We have flown over this district before. It is relatively well lit even when it is farther down our route. But tonight we will go straight there."

I backed away. "That's enough, Lieutenant. I am satisfied. Thank you."

He was beginning to salute, but I turned away from him.

The rube was still near me.

I said to him, "I will examine the ship on my own for a while, as your commander mentioned."

"Yes sir," he said.

"You can return to your post now."

His hand came forward. He was offering his tungsten flashlight.

I had my own in my pocket. But I needed to continue acting like Wolfinger, who would have made no such preparation.

The lieutenant said, "I know this ship like the back of my hand."

The rube figured he'd read my thoughts in my brief moment of hesitation. Figured I'd give a damn about his finding his way in the dark.

I took his flashlight.

What matter did it make now if I dropped out of character to let this boy think Colonel Wolfinger would care about his welfare? So I said, "Thank you."

He straightened and lifted his hand into a salute and he held it there. I waved it off. "Go," I said.

"Sir," he said, and he vanished into the dark of the walkway.

I shifted the flashlight to my left hand and put my right hand beneath the dispatch case and cupped it and drew it against my hip.

I gave the lieutenant time to distance himself from me along the walkway.

I switched the flashlight on, and I headed forward. My destination was the mushroom garden of fuel tanks feeding the engine at the rear of the command gondola.

But moving through the dark I could not stop thinking about these good Germans all around me.

And I thought of my own good German. Jeremy Miller. No. Erich Müller. *Müller* was the German. I was lucky to have him on my side.

My side. But I was American. And I was killing the men on this airship in defense of England. For Jeremy. Who was not a German, in reality. Jeremy the Englishman, he said. Jeremy the Brit.

I heard his own words: *There are no pro-Brits in Germany*. The Germans in this country who were *his* allies, and therefore my allies, those Germans might wish to defeat the Kaiser and his generals and their way of governing; they might wish for a better Germany, a democratic Germany, a bona fide republic. But they were *not* pro-Brit.

And there was Jeremy's mother. His own mother. She loved her Kaiser, who took them to war against the Brits. The Kaiser who hailed the sinking of their great passenger ship in the North Atlantic. Who justified a thousand dead civilian Brits. She was certainly not pro-Brit. Not like her son.

And I saw that little echo of his boxer's move in my mind. The head feint.

What was the punch his old reflex made him dodge? A question from the innkeeper. *Did he find the telegram she'd slipped under his door.*

Sure, he said. And to me: *These were the groups we worked with inside Germany. The* Republikaner. *We were obligated to stay in touch with them.*

I remembered his back turning away with the *Republikan* at the garage where we fueled up the Torpedo. Their intense conversation. Backs turned.

We were *obligated* to them?

Having to provide a little easily censored information to a tractable collaborator would elicit a *shrug*. Not a feint. It was the question itself, spoken in my presence, that elicited the feint.

And he'd slipped one other punch.

Did they know the special nature of Albert's bomb? I'd asked.

And he did his little head feint to me. *Not at all*, he'd said.

I stopped now.

I switched off my flashlight.

I stood in the dark.

He'd gone out of his way to make sure I didn't open the bomb.

He gave me good reasons.

But he said it and he knew I understood those good reasons and yet he said it again by stressing its delicacy, and again, by regretting our need to trust the device at all.

The lady doth protest too much, methinks.

I knelt down on the walkway.

I would be careful. Just in case I was presently being a fool, I would handle my box of chocolates carefully and look carefully. But I would look.

I could not hold the light and do what I had to do, at least for the first part. I needed both hands.

I remained in the dark.

I pressed the lieutenant's flashlight into my tunic pocket next to my own.

I pulled the strap over my head and set the dispatch case easily, easily down before me. I opened the weather flap. I put my hands inside and pulled at the tin box. It did not yield.

I turned the case sideways and held it gently between my knees.

I squeezed the case just a little and pulled at the tin and it rose slightly and I squeezed a little harder and pulled and again and again, and doing this inch by inch I finally was holding the bomb invisibly in the dark before me.

I rotated it so that it was level.

I grasped it tightly with my right hand.

With my left hand I moved the dispatch case from between my knees and placed it to the side.

I dipped into my tunic pocket and withdrew one of the flashlights. My own, I thought.

I switched it on and held its beam on the tin box. *Stollwerck Chocolade.*

I used the light to guide the box to the planking of the walkway before me.

I could work with one hand now.

I put my thumb in the small lip at the center of the lid. I lifted. The lid rose. It was hinged on the opposite side and I opened it all the way back and let it go.

The white beam from the tungsten bulb showed a faint yellow tinge upon the white of the cotton wool.

He had indeed packed it tightly. I had to be very careful now. If he was, in fact, the Jeremy Miller I'd come to rely on, I had to take heed of his warning. I did not want to disturb the bomb.

I needed two hands again.

The hinges were holding the top of the tin box parallel with the floor. I laid my flashlight there, its beam shining back toward me.

I hesitated now.

And listened.

I could hear a clear ticking from within the box.

All right.

I leaned forward, turned my head to listen at the surface.

The ticking was coming from the left side.

I sat back up.

I looked at the dense surface of purified raw cotton. I tried to visualize the arrangement within. The stick of dynamite would be nearly as long as the longest dimension of the box. The clock was small. A travel clock. I figured the dynamite was laid in close to one of the long sides.

The safest way not to disturb the connection from explosive to clock was not to pull the packed fibers apart. I'd go in at the very edge and try to lift up the covering layer as a unit.

The stick of dynamite could be laid out at either edge. I chose the bottom edge, as it now sat before me.

I ran four fingers gently in, pressing against the side wall of the box. And then I touched the curve of the dynamite stick.

I backed my hand up a bit, found the lower edge of cotton wool, ran my fingers underneath. And I pulled.

The top layer of cotton wool began to rise up, mostly as a unit. I brought my other hand into play, gathering and recompressing and lifting back the clinging batches of wool fibers.

And then the business contents of the tin box were exposed.

Darkly, at the moment.

The lifted layer of cotton wool was blocking the beam of light.

I held up the cotton wool with one hand now, as if it were a second lid.

I took up the flashlight with my other hand and shined it into the tin box.

The clock was there. Ticking away. The stick of dynamite was there.

The wires from clock to dynamite were missing.

The two objects lay in the tin box utterly separate.

I flipped the flashlight beam toward the bottom edge of the layer of cotton wool, my mind lunging forward to figure out how to reattach the wires, how to make this work.

But there were no wires. No wires at all.

I flipped the beam back to the dynamite.

The blasting cap was also missing.

Jeremy's exact words about the bomb slithered through me: *I wish we didn't have to trust it.*

After the bomb I planted failed to explode and the Zeppelin flew on successfully to London, he wanted me to blame the device.

But it was him. Erich Müller.

57

I sat back on my heels.

I wanted to figure him out.

But I didn't have time.

I was down to my last fifteen minutes or so before I'd have to get off the Zepp.

I had no bomb.

I thought: *I'm sitting inside one.* I was surrounded by two million cubic feet of explosively flammable hydrogen.

But how could I both detonate it and escape it? Especially since the explosion would also instantly release a tempest of poison gas.

Was I ready to die for tonight's theater crowd in London?

A reflex voice in me cried *yes.* Faintly though, coming through a welter in my head. I knew the answer would be louder and clearer if it was Broadway. If it was my own country. Or if my mother was playing Hamlet at the Duke of York's.

But I had to believe that even tonight I'd be dying for more. I'd die for a chance at exposing and discrediting poison aerial attacks themselves.

Seemed like a good cause.

But no. I wasn't ready for that. Not the dying part. I had to work hard now to try to have it both ways.

Which made me think of Albert's plan.

His parachute.

I had a way to survive if I could figure out how to blow up the LZ 78 while it was in the air.

But the *how* had to include a long enough fuse.

First things first.

A few hours before takeoff, Dettmer had a man subtracted from his ship. For this, he'd be thinking to take things *on* board—compensating ballast—not off. Maybe that's why the parachute was still sitting there. But I couldn't depend on it remaining. I needed to secure the parachute.

I stood up and closed the lid on the tin box and picked it up with me. As if it were still useful. Without something to serve as a blasting cap, the dynamite wouldn't blow. Not till the airship did. Still, by reflex, I kept the box. I had few enough resources. It was all I had. Something might come to mind.

I opened the dispatch case and slid it back in.

I shined my light and strode forward.

At least for now I could get around the ship without anyone's close scrutiny. A Zeppelin had a crew of about twenty. At least half of them were mechanics. They were all with the engines. More than half the rest were presently in the command gondola. Everybody on board had a focused task. That would probably last till the ship was airborne.

A footlight shone ahead.

The hatch was still open.

I arrived.

No one was around.

I took the parachute from the shelf. It was heavy, a good thirty pounds. I put it under my arm.

I skirted the hatch on the walkway and walked forward, keenly aware of the distance I was covering, my distance from the parachute launching hooks and the hatch.

I was instinctively heading for the place I'd targeted when I still thought I had a time bomb: the run of tanks piping fuel forward and downward to the engine compartment of the command gondola.

That was still a volatile spot.

And it was only about a third-base-to-home sprint to the hatch.

I arrived at the fuel tanks and shined my light on them.

I lifted the light to the bloated clouds of hydrogen bags hovering overhead.

I looked back toward the hatch, a distant glow.

And back to the bags.

Gas.

A flame burning low and gas leaking in. The pace of the gas could provide its own fuse.

I had my Luger. For a quick, tight cluster of shots high up in one of the bags above me.

I had matches.

I needed something to burn slow and low.

I didn't know if my gasp made me clutch the tin box tight against me or if clutching it made me gasp. But I knew there was something inside. Sweetly, it was a thing Erich Müller never thought to render useless.

Cotton wool.

Cotton wool burned slow. Especially compacted tightly.

Of course, the first stroke of a match might ignite the fumes that already scented the air.

Or the contrary problem might assert itself. Cotton wool could burn itself out.

It was all timing. Timing. And I had no idea what the timing might be.

But the ticking in my watch pocket was the only time that counted now and it was reminding me that I needed to act.

I struck out forward along the walkway, moving as fast as I could into the dark with the beam of tungsten before me.

I had to get back to Dettmer and ask permission to stay aboard. He would surely let me fly with them tonight. After all, he'd been prepared for an Englishman to do so. Instead, he'd have a chance to impress the Foreign Office.

He'd want me to watch the takeoff of his airship with him. But I needed to get off his bridge and go to work as soon as possible afterward. For my larger aspiration in this mission, vivid, unmanageable word had to get out. The ball of fire should be seen at Spich, at least distantly. The Zepp and its phosgene had to fall on German soil.

I'd pull the trigger on the LZ 78 soon after takeoff. But long enough after to put jumpable distance between that hatch and the ground.

And then there was the scene from limbo being played out at the Hotel Alten-Forst.

I stopped abruptly, even though I needed to rush. This was a complication that only now reminded me of itself.

Who was Jeremy? What was his intention? He was sitting in Room 200 with a pistol on Stockman and my mother. Or at least he was when I left him. The two men could have been working together. Or they had lately begun to do so. They certainly had the same immediate objective: the gas bombing of London.

But I knew the truth wasn't simple.

And whatever it was made no difference to my actions in the next half hour or so.

I moved on.

Another hole of light in the floor was growing bright up ahead.

And then I was down the ladder and through the roof of the command gondola.

I landed and found Major Dettmer handing off his clipboard to his executive officer. The cast on the bridge was a little different now. The navigator and the telegraph lieutenant were off to their posts. The helmsman was at the rudder wheel and a junior officer was at the elevator control.

The executive officer crossed before me, caught a glimpse of me, and paused to salute.

"No saluting," I said. I would put them at their oblivious ease around me. "I am a fly on the wall."

But I realized I'd just translated an American idiom into German. It sounded odd in my mouth even as I spoke it. "As they say in America," I quickly added.

The executive officer laughed.

"The place is full of flies," I said.

He laughed again and Dettmer did too, having drawn near.

"They are all rubes in America, I think," Dettmer said. Not an exact equivalent of "rube" in German, but close enough.

The executive officer continued on his way and I turned to face Dettmer. "Major," I said, "may I ask a favor? Not only for myself personally, though it would certainly be that as well, but as a favor to the Foreign Office. We have removed the English amateur from your midst. Please allow me to take his place. Berlin has telegraphed me to ask for a firsthand report on the work the airships do. Particularly, of course, on the night when you deliver this important package."

As I expected, Dettmer snapped to. He would have saluted, but I lifted my own palm quickly to stop him. He stayed his hand and said, "Of course, sir. I'd be honored."

I offered him my own hand to shake, and he took it with warmth.

Behind me the executive officer shouted an order to someone below. "Prepare airship march."

I said, "I will freely explore the ship in flight, if I may have your permission. I want to experience everything. Your Lieutenant Schmidt gave me an excellent tour. And your Lieutenant Kreyder wishes to share more of his important procedures with me."

"As you wish, Colonel," Dettmer said. "As you wish. You'll forgive me if I am preoccupied for the next hour or so."

"Of course," I said.

Dettmer's eyes shifted over my left shoulder.

I looked.

His executive officer was crossing back our way.

"Captain," Dettmer said to him. "The colonel will fly with us tonight. At weigh off, release the extra ballast. And bring the extra cold gear. Only the takeoff necessities for now."

"Yes sir," the captain said, slipping away.

Dettmer looked back to me. "We'd brought these things for the other man. The overalls and the fur coat and the felt overshoes and so forth, the extreme cold weather things, these can wait until we are at a higher altitude. Your flying jacket will immediately make you one of us."

He laughed at this thought.

Courteous words from Wolfinger came to my mind. A comradely laugh even formed in my throat, ready to employ. I could make myself say or do none of it.

I was getting too close to these boys once again.

Dettmer paid no attention to my unresponsiveness.

He said, "The woolen underclothes you should take time now to put on. To sweat with the rest of us."

He laughed again, a softer one, this one while searching my face, suddenly afraid he was getting too familiar.

I could manage nothing but blankness for him.

He cut off his laugh.

This was Klaus von Wolfinger's likely response anyway. So be it.

The executive officer arrived with two contrasting articles of clothing folded one on top of the other, one rough-ribbed wool and one soft-cured leather.

Dettmer said, "You will need to put on the woolen underclothes at once, Colonel. There is privacy in the keel. In the crew space aft."

I was glad to have a chance to get away to myself.

I began to reach for the clothes.

Dettmer intervened. He said, "But first, please allow me." He took the leather flying jacket from the captain.

He held it up and spread it open for me.

He said, "You'll need to remove your pistol, Colonel."

I hesitated. As myself, and as Wolfinger.

Dettmer picked up on the hesitation. He said, quite respectfully, almost gently, "For the jacket. Of course you will retain your weapon. Though we ourselves carry none, for safety's sake."

"I promise not to discharge it, Major," I said.

He nodded to me.

I undid my pistol belt and laid it at my feet with the dispatch case.

"Thank you, sir," he said.

The air was cleared.

He lifted the coat a little.

This was a ritual I dreaded now. The bond of a uniform. The bond of personality, of camaraderie. I dared not bond with these men.

I had to focus.

These men were the enemy tonight.

They were the instruments of mass murder.

I made myself smile. I turned my back to him. I slipped the dispatch case off my shoulder and laid it on the floor at my feet.

Dettmer put the jacket on me.

I felt it like a second skin.

That was the danger.

And my mother slipped into my head. The mother she had always been, training her son the way she always had. In and around theaters. This was not a skin upon me. It was a costume. I was playing a role. I was an actor. I was a spy.

I shot my cuffs.

I began to button the jacket. With each button, a flourish of the hand.

I did not even need to turn to Dettmer for this. The gesture was for me. Working on my character.

My qualms were quickly dissipating.

I stopped buttoning about halfway.

Dettmer said, "There. You are now senior officer on the LZ 78."

I turned to him. I doled out one more faint smile. The smile of a superior officer pleased with his inferior for recognizing the appropriate protocol in an unusual circumstance.

He saluted. He held it.

I saluted him.

"You notice that the fit of your jacket is good," Dettmer said.

It was, indeed. Nearly perfect. "I do," I said.

"We'd heard that the Englishman was a larger man."

Albert was certainly larger than me. I had a flash of that first sight of him outside his castle, towering over my mother, leaning down to buss her on the cheek.

Even more dangerous than to think on these Germans at this moment was to think on my mother.

"We did not expect the jacket to fit *him* so well," Dettmer said. He let that settle in for a moment.

They'd arranged for him never to be one of them. His uniform would not fit.

And then Major Dettmer actually worked up the courage to give Colonel Klaus von Wolfinger a small, conspiratorial wink.

Wolfinger chose to overlook Dettmer's transgression. I said, with a large dose of duty and only a faint, condescending hint of faux camaraderie, "Things are as they should be."

58

I pitched my airship underwear behind a fuel tank.

I thought simply to stay here in the keel for the takeoff and on through my incendiary improvisation. But Dettmer expected me. He could conceivably do something officious if I didn't show up for the launch, could send someone to see if I'd found my way all right in the dark.

The walkway suddenly shifted a little beneath my feet. The airship trembled, and I felt a twinge of uplift in my chest.

I knew we'd thrown off our hangar ballast and had lifted from our bumper blocks and outside we were surrounded by two hundred ground crewmen holding hard at the handling lines, letting us hover but reining us in, keeping us centered in the hangar doorway.

I went forward and down the ladder and onto the bridge.

Dettmer was at the front window of the gondola, his back to me, framed alone against the sky beyond the hangar door. The sky was off white, as if it were packed with cotton wool.

He scanned outward and downward, from far left across to far right. And he commanded, "Airship march!"

The executive officer, leaning from a side window, cried, "Airship march!" and the order was taken up outside to port, to bow, to starboard.

At once, almost imperceptibly, we began to move.

Major Dettmer looked over his shoulder.

He saw me. I was where he'd hoped I'd be.

"Colonel," he said. "Please join me."

I stepped forward, stood beside him on his right.

Dettmer kept his eyes ahead.

Two wide-set guiding rails led from the hangar mouth out three hundred yards into the maneuvering field. Arrayed ahead were eight handling lines stretched forward by a hundred bent and straining *feldgrau* backs.

And the movement was clearly perceptible now.

We were floating into the daylight.

And from all around us—front and sides—a sound rose up. Men's voices—two hundred men's voices—rising as one. They sang. They sang of thunderbolts and clashing swords and crashing waves. They sang loud even though they strained hard to drag this vast machine of war into the oncoming night.

And when they began to sing the chorus, the men around me, Dettmer and the executive officer and all the others, joined in. *Lieb Vaterland, magst ruhig sein!* Dear Fatherland put your mind at rest. *Fest steht und treu die Wacht, die Wacht am Rhein!* Firm and true stands the watch, the watch on the Rhine.

Colonel Wolfinger sang as well. He sang louder than them all. Indeed, I have a pretty good tenor and so Wolfinger even drew an admiring turn of the head from the commandant of the LZ 78. Major Dettmer smiled at this powerful officer who had graced them with his presence. And I nodded my head to Dettmer, even as I lifted my voice with all these good Germans and entreated the dear Fatherland not to worry about a thing.

When the chorus was done, the men outside went on for another verse, though the officers on the bridge stopped singing and focused on their tasks.

Wolfinger was ready just to keep a stoic, watchful silence. He'd been warmer to Dettmer and his men than he'd been to anyone in perhaps his whole career. And his clamming up now suited Christopher Cobb just fine. Because I wanted simply to get through the next twenty minutes and on to my business.

Dettmer was going on and on to the colonel—to me—about guiding cars and a winch and wind headings and cloud cover and the moon and we were moving inexorably forward, and even as he spoke, I took my watch from my pocket to check the time.

It was a Waltham.

An American watch.

I put it away as quickly as I could without drawing attention to it, glancing at Dettmer, who was speaking to me at that moment but looking forward. I cursed myself for all the details I had not anticipated. This one I had failed to consider long before things got tough. Though why shouldn't a high-ranking officer in the Foreign Office have a fine American watch? It was a privilege that could readily accrue to his position. But I'd overlooked it. And that made me worry about what else I'd overlooked.

Perhaps Dettmer had seen me in his periphery as I read my watch. Perhaps he'd finally realized I was not responding to him. Maybe he'd finally said all that he could possibly think of to say to keep his Foreign Office observer informed and impressed. Whatever the reason, he did stop talking to me.

And then finally we were well free of the hangar.

And the airship was set against the wind.

And the water ballast was released and the watch officer returned and the engines began to pound and the lines were cast off and I stood through all this simply waiting, hearing the orders but not listening to them, feeling the bustle increase around me but not moving, holding even more still, waiting now to do what I had to do.

The floor was quaking beneath my feet.

The engines vibrated into my legs and into my jaw and into my brain.

Dettmer commanded engine revs and elevation angles and we were moving, we were rising, the distant tree line was beginning to sink below us, slowly. There was no necessary race forward as in an aeroplane. We crept upward.

"Major," I said. "I will leave you now."

Dettmer looked at me.

I tried to read his face.

I kept mine blank, inhabiting, in my actor's brain, my character's power, his independence, his arrogance.

Dettmer's face was blank as well. Rare for him, with me. But surely natural to him with others. He had his own power here. He was the commander of this ship. He was respectful of me, of the people I represented. Fearful even. Perhaps. But the self-possession and the exercise of power and independence that I was portraying to him were, in a real sense, conferred by him. Especially now that we were in the air. The captain of a ship on the sea was God. The commander of a ship in the air was no different.

I tried to see suspicion in Dettmer.

I could not.

But this look between us went on for a longer moment than was comfortable.

"With your permission," I said, and I lowered my head to him ever so slightly.

He said, "We each have our mission, Colonel."

I said, "My mission tonight is based on a surpassing respect for yours."

He smiled. Quickly, warmly.

How ardently this soldier, this commander, this master of a German warship craved personal reassurance. Craved approval.

How sad this all was.

"My ship is yours," he said.

I brought my right hand up sharply to my right temple. He straightened with a silent gasp. He was touched by my initiating this salute. He brought his own hand up and we held this for a moment, those few beats of amplified respect between two officers.

But through this whole exchange I could not look him in the eyes.

59

I turned to cross the gondola, and as if the cabin knew my haste it grabbed my chest and pushed at the backs of my knees and propelled me toward the ladder. The airship was climbing, of course, and I was rushing downhill.

Manageable still. The angle was maybe ten degrees. But I was very glad the ladder would let me face aft.

I put my hand to the ladder and the executive officer said, "Careful, sir."

I nodded without looking at him.

I climbed through the roof and out into the open air.

I let the angle press me tightly against the rungs, but almost at once I was dragged to my right. I grasped hard at the left side rail and held on tight. I stopped climbing. For now it was sufficient not to be slung into the air.

We were coming round a bit, perhaps adjusting to the head wind, perhaps taking a heading. But the outward pull eased now and I climbed hard and fast and I was inside the keel.

I had to get this done long before we were at our final cruising altitude. This angle would be a constant challenge.

The hull was still dark.

I held tight to the handrail along the walkway and shined my flashlight forward and I moved as quickly as I dared let myself, with this constant tugging in my chest threatening to fling me headlong into the darkness.

I passed over the gondola engine. Along this stretch of the walkway the sound of the forward Maybach, which was straining to help lift us, jackhammered in my head. It was a bit of a struggle to think in the midst of this but I knew at once I needed to do my work close to this place. The sound of my Luger plugging a gas cell would be masked here.

I pushed on aft for now. I needed to do two things before I could get to the matter of making fire.

There was no light up ahead. The forward hatch—my hatch—was, of course, closed. When I desperately needed for this to be open, I would not have time to open it. So I pressed on, pushing my center of balance downward, down into my legs, into my knees, pressing hard at each footstep, leaning my torso backward, holding tight to the handrail, my flashlight beam bouncing before me, lifting as far out on the path as I could throw it.

And then I saw in my beam the walkway turn up ahead, where it skirted the hatch.

I arrived.

I braced myself against the starboard turning of the railing and I flashed the beam to the closed hatch and then, beyond it, to its portside. I was looking for a lever or a handle or a wheel, some way to open this thing. It wasn't there. I scanned the beam and I found it, at the forward end of the hatch, a wheel with protruding handles set in the bulkhead.

I moved toward it.

The rail along the walkway ended and I angled my body hard to my right—the ship's upward incline seemed greater now by a few degrees—and my target, clear in my flashlight, was another rail along the bulkhead.

I lunged for it.

I had it.

I made my way along to the wheel, and with my left hand I grabbed one of its handles and then, needing the wheel to both open the hatch and hold myself steady, I grasped a second handle with my right hand.

The dispatch case lifted off me. My chest clamped in panic even as the shoulder strap grabbed at my neck.

It was okay. The strap held. The bag and the tin box were safe. The angle backward was a good fifteen degrees. Perhaps more. It felt like fifty. Two powerful hands pulled at my shoulders.

I strained at the wheel. It turned, bit by bit, bearing my clinging weight with each torque of the gears of the hatch. Light was dilating into the keel behind me.

And then the wheel would turn no more.

I looked. The hatch was fully open.

I let go of the wheel, one hand at a time, quickly grabbing downward and reattaching at the handrail. And now I had both hands secure there and I dragged myself along the bulkhead and approached the corner going forward.

I stopped.

I clung hard. The pull on me was strong, trying to fling me aft. I knew the danger. The light was all around. I sensed the hatch gaping behind me. The maw of a bright-faced beast. If I let go I would tumble directly out of the Zepp.

I turned my head. I looked.

We were running over rooftops and now over a paved road, and now a dense stand of trees was passing and passing. Had we circled back over Spich? A public relations move upon takeoff?

I looked away.

We were up a good three hundred, four hundred feet. I remembered newsreel clips of parachutes being tested off the London Bridge and the Eiffel Tower, so I figured I needed about six hundred feet minimum to jump.

I inched along. And I turned the corner into the walkway.

I climbed, the spill of the light of the hatch fading behind me. I switched on the flashlight, and up ahead I saw the silver flank of the nearest fuel tank. I approached and flashed the beam into the deepest shadows beyond.

The parachute was there. I would carry it forward with me. The ticking would really begin after the fire was lit. I'd need to have this thing attached to me when I struck the match.

I needed an extra hand. I extinguished the flashlight.

I bent to the parachute, drew it out. I wrapped my right arm around it and held the rail with my other hand. The next milepost was based on sound anyway.

I climbed onward.

The hammering approached, the piston roar of the Maybach. I moved into the very center of it.

The walkway was elevated a foot or so from the aluminum skin of the keel, and the fuel tanks were welded to the keel and set about the same distance off the walkway edge. I lifted the parachute over the railing and wedged it between two tanks for now, and I moved forward one fuel tank.

I turned and faced aft and sat down on the walkway, bracing myself with a foot against the near edge of the next tank.

The engines were hammering through me not just as sound but as a bone-deep vibration, from where I sat, from where the bottom of my foot pressed against the side of the fuel tank.

But I was thinking just fine. I was thinking clearly.

If the army played a few minutes to the locals before heading out to do its business—and the German imperial propaganda machine was already as well oiled and powerful as the Maybach engine I was sitting over—then perhaps we'd level off soon and give the people a good look at the new Zepp in flight and feed their war fervor. This was the newest model, after all. Lately delivered.

I had to make a tough choice. Sit and see if my guess about our location and heading was right and risk a more remote blast if I was wrong or work in this tilt-floored Coney Island Pavilion ride and risk fumbling the tin box and letting it tumble down the walkway.

I drew the box from my case.

I opened the lid but kept the box in my lap for now, my flexed legs holding it more or less level.

I found my matches and pulled them from my pocket. I laid them on the cotton wool.

Where would I set the box so that it wouldn't slide while the cotton burned?

And what about the parachute? Trying to put the harness on and carry the chute rucksack down this incline and hook it properly for a launch would be a terrible challenge at this angle.

I had to roll the dice.

I had to wait.

And I did.

I sat for a few moments and a few moments more and I thought that the angle was softening a little, but then perhaps not.

And then yes.

And we began to turn again.

Another portside turn.

If we'd passed over Spich, as I'd thought, and then over the Alten Forst, we'd now be turning north again, finding our bearing toward England, and in lovely, level flight we'd pass once more over the good citizens of Spich, who'd been alerted by our first passage and now were crowded into the streets to wave and cheer and throw their hats in the air. *Gott strafe England.*

I had no intention of blowing up the LZ 78 and its payload directly over Spich.

But it was a small town.

We'd cross it quickly.

And the upward angle was declining.

I felt I was right.

I waited.

We were leveling.

I waited.

And now we were level.

I rose up. I placed the tin box on the walkway and I stepped aft to the parachute and unwedged and withdrew it from its place against the fuel tank.

I turned back and flashed my beam to the box sitting open there on the walkway, matches on top of cotton wool. I approached it, the parachute cradled in my right arm.

And the lights came on.

60

It came from above and from below. The light was muted—the bulbs and their fixtures double-contained in glass—but the hull was illuminated clear enough. Plenty clear enough for me to look far ahead along the walkway and see a figure coming this way.

I glanced back aft to see if I'd soon be surrounded.

No one in that direction.

Back to this figure, advancing rapidly now.

Lieutenant Schmidt. My canny rube.

I dropped the parachute to my side.

He was smiling. He was preparing to salute.

And then he wasn't. He was looking at the parachute as he approached and he was recognizing it and then he was looking at the box in front of me.

He was maybe thirty feet away now.

He slowed.

It would have been impossible for him to figure out anything close to my plan. But he knew something odd was going on.

He was ten feet from me and he stopped.

I lifted up to full height to stand before him as a far superior officer.

He wavered.

I could have found these things here myself. However odd they were, if their presence in the middle of the walkway was sinister, then surely his first impulse would be that it had nothing to do with me. I was a very high ranking officer in the *Deutsches Heer*. I had found these suspicious things myself.

The Maybach pounded loudly on.

There was no need to speak to him anyway. I was righteous in my rank, in my place here on the LZ 78.

I motioned him closer.

I pointed at these things. The parachute. The box. The matches.

I cried above the engine roar, "See what I've found, Lieutenant. What do you make of it?"

He looked more closely at the box.

He began to bend toward it.

"Close enough!" I commanded.

He stopped himself. Stood upright.

My rank was prevailing.

He saluted. He waited.

I had no time for this.

The engines roared around us both.

There was nothing more to say anyway.

He could not be allowed to walk off now. He would, of course, speak of this to the executive officer or the commander. Even if he was not suspicious of Colonel Wolfinger, even if they were not either, even if, instead, they thought I'd shrewdly uncovered a plot, perhaps a further plot of the Englishman, they'd still send somebody up here to me.

I could not let that happen.

Lieutenant Schmidt would be dead in a few minutes anyway.

I drew my Luger.

I pointed it at him.

His face went blank. Of course he hadn't suspected me. And he could not even begin to imagine what was happening now or why.

We looked at each other.

When he and his fellow crew members imagined their death in the night sky, what had been his choice? To burn or to jump?

His face was a rube's face now. Not canny at all. Uncomprehending. No. Not a rube. Just an overgrown kid from some backwater Black Forest town who loved his telegraph and his airship.

I motioned him to move back a few steps.

The Luger was pointed at his chest.

He was starting to get it. He began to raise his hands.

I shook my head *no*.

He took a couple of steps back and I stopped him with a flip of a palm.

A quick ending for this boy now was surely better than an extended burning ten minutes from now. Or a leaping. That terrible, time-stretching fall to the earth.

I stepped over the box and drew near him.

His face showed no fear. It showed something far worse. Betrayal. A previously unimaginable betrayal.

Betrayed by a colonel in the German army.

Too bad he wouldn't be able to put this worthwhile lesson to good use.

I wanted nothing more to do with his face. I motioned for him to turn around.

He obeyed.

He stood straight and still before me. His ears were splayed. I hadn't noticed that before.

I lifted my pistol and pointed it at the back of his head.

The engines hammered on.

This wasn't necessary.

It would be sufficient for him to sleep.

"I'm sorry about this," I said. I said it aloud. But even I could not hear the words in the din of the Zeppelin's engines.

I drew my right hand wide and focused on the center of his parietal bone and I swung hard and caught him there with the flat bulk near the Luger's breech block and Lieutenant Schmidt fell sideways into the handrail and then collapsed onto the walkway, and he did not so much as twitch a finger.

Sleep on, young man. At least you've been spared a nasty choice.

Mine already having been made.

I holstered my Luger.

I turned and crouched before the tin box.

We'd be clear of Spich by now.

I took up the matches and laid them aside. I expected the cotton would burn slow and low. But I wanted the flame at that level for only a minute or two. I lifted the top layer and exposed the dynamite and the clock. I took the clock out and tossed it aside, leaving a hollow there. I spread the fibers, loosened them all around in the inner space. When the flame in the slower-burning, packed fibers reached this pocket of oxygen, the fire would flare up.

I laid the top layer back in place.

I rose and moved to the parachute and brought it back and knelt again before the tin box, on its aft side. I unfurled the external harness and placed it around my shoulders and cinched it at my waist. I laid the rucksack next to me.

I took up the matches.

The pound of the Maybach abruptly reshaped itself inside me. It became the sound of my heart. It became the coursing of my blood. It was music now. It was like the piano player whaling away in front of a motion picture screen where some terrible calamity was on its way.

I could smell fuel oil. I could smell hydrogen.

Why hadn't I noticed them this strongly before?

Maybe I'd die for London after all.

Maybe all it took was the strike of this match.

I held it low, as near to the cotton as I could.

And I struck it.

It flared up and I thought it would keep flaring until all the air around me was afire.

But it didn't.

I was still here.

The flame receded a little.

I lowered it to the cotton wool.

I touched the flame there.

And I flinched back and away.

The cotton flashed up instantly.

Too fast. No explosion but it was burning way too fast.

Then this flame receded as well. The fumes immediately around it were consumed.

The cotton was burning.

Very nicely.

Get the hell out.

I stood up. I lifted the rucksack. I turned. I strode off. Fast. But controlled. My knees were a little weak, a little reluctant to hold me up. But I moved. And I moved. And the light was before me.

And I stopped.

The goddamn gas bag.

I turned. I strode back to the box.

A faint wisp of a smell, like burning leaves.

The flame was spreading.

I looked up to the gas cells.

I drew my Luger and I looked forward. I felt a slight movement of air, from the hatch at the gondola ladder. I judged the flow of air and I looked up again. I made a guess at an angle to compensate and I chose a spot in the whale-gray flank of the gas cell above me. I lifted the Luger.

I readied myself once more to go up in flames with all these boys and their airship, and I fired once and again and again and the explosion waited inside there and I fired again and twice more and it was enough, a tight cluster of six shots into the gas cell, and I holstered the Luger and I turned and I ran, ran as fast as I could and still keep my footing on the planking beneath me and the deep hole of light was before me and growing larger and I ran and I reached the turn in the walkway and I took it and I went around to the long side of the hatch and I stepped over the railing and I looked down—though I dared not wait no matter how high I was—and an empty field was passing there, a good six hundred feet below, and I grabbed the loop at the top of the rucksack and I leaned and I hooked it and I leapt.

I fell and I fell and I fell with the air pounding at my eyes, I fell though a part of me was breathlessly inert, was not moving at all, was waiting for the saving clutch of the tether, waiting. And it came, a wrench at my shoulders and at my waist and a thumping compression of my chest. And the falling abruptly turned to floating.

I floated and I floated and I breathed and I looked down to the tops of my shoes and an empty field beyond, and I was hearing the piston drone of Zeppelin engines.

I lifted my face and lifted my hands to grasp the risers and I turned my head around and looked up.

All I could see was the shade-darkened inner canopy of white silk, my parachute billowing above me, and I could see the high, cloud-smeared sky beyond.

And almost at once the LZ 78 emerged from its silken eclipse. It was dark and vast and gliding away from me. Serene, I thought. Secure and serene and murderous, I thought. I've failed, I thought.

The sound of its engines Dopplered lower and began to fade as the Zeppelin sailed on, though it was still quite large against the late afternoon sky, the forward tapering of its colossal hull, the splay of its fins making it look like an aerial bomb of the gods, flung personally from Valhalla by Odin. I had, of course, been destined to fail.

And in the flank of the Zepp, at the very bottom, the sunlight flashed briefly.

No. I craned my head. Not the sun. It was a lollop of flame and now it was a rapid blooming, a golden rush from that spot and forward along the skin of the Zepp and then came a billow of flame breaking through the hull and swelling into the air and the front third of the Zeppelin reared up like a frightened horse, the ship cracking apart, and the flames soared gelatinous now, great thunder clouds of cumulus fire. And it was all strangely silent in this first surge of things, in the igniting of the hydrogen and the inward flash of the gas cells and even in the vast uplift of flame torching the sky, there was only silence. And I remembered I was falling.

I looked down and the ground was rushing at me and I thought to keep my legs loose, ready to flex and fall away, diverting the direct blow, like jumping from a porch, like a kid who's used to jumping, and my legs jolted and instantly I diverted the fall to my left, hitting at calf and thigh and hip and side and I was down and I was all right, I could tell that my legs were okay, my body was okay, and silk was falling softly against me, clinging to me.

And now from on high came a clap of Odin's thunder pounding into my head and rattling my bones and then a concatenation of thunderstrokes, smaller sounds but sharper, and then another larger boom that rolled over me, and I pulled the silk covers around me, a kid still, awakened in the night in a terrible storm, hiding in the covers, and I waited, and the sound rolled on and away, and then there was silence.

I sat up and pulled at the canopy, dragged at it, wrenched at its insistent hold, and finally it came free and I looked up.

The sky was filled with the black billowing of smoke and the blood-orange flare of falling fragments and the back quarter of the Zepp was buoyed still, briefly, though it was starting to burn, and then it plunged and disappeared behind a distant line of trees with an upswell of smoke.

I had seen enough.

I stood up.

I turned my back on all that.

The air smelled faintly of malt.

Nearby was a stack of barley straw bales.

Stockman's bomb was dead.

But that was all I knew for sure.

61

By reckoning from the verging sun, whose disk I glimpsed briefly through a scrim of clouds, I struck out to the southeast. At one point early on, I skirted a copse of pine but I diverted into the trees. I found a downed and rotted trunk and stuffed the parachute into a hollow beneath it.

It felt to be a long while because of the uncertainty of my path and the fading light, but in fact I made pretty good time to a stone wall at the eastern edge of a pasturage, beyond which I found a graveled road.

I followed it south, though it was angling me back to the southwest, and I ended up walking into the little town of Liebour, where a crowd had gathered around its central fountain in the town square.

They'd assembled half a dozen wagons and were calling out for volunteers to board them.

I knew what this was about.

The nearby calamity.

They were heading to the place of the crash.

I figured the active gas was dissipating, but they would find clear evidence of the phosgene.

I stayed back from the crowd, striding with purpose around the outer edge of the square. Those who noticed me started and stared or shrunk back or saluted.

I ignored them and pushed on, and I reached the road sign leading away from Liebour. I was very glad to recognize two choices. One to

Uckendorf, from which I could find the road east toward Spich that passed half a mile from the air base. The other choice, which angled farther east, led to Stockem. I'd studied Jeremy's portfolio of maps well enough in our long trip to remember this town lying on the same Uckendorf-Spich road but closer to Spich. A shortcut.

I struck off in that direction, walking fast, and thinking hard, now that I knew where I was going. I tried to figure out why Jeremy had arranged for Stockman's bomb to succeed. Which raised the question of why he did so with such an elaborate first two acts in his little play, their elaborateness difficult to explain.

I didn't have an answer for that. Not right away.

I knew only that something was rotten.

And it occurred to me: maybe the explanation was not quite so difficult if our Erich Müller—stage name Jeremy Miller—was working for the German secret service. Not so difficult if they approved the attack but wanted Stockman out of the picture. Albert had control of his bombshell design, and maybe part of his selling price was for him to be directly involved in the mission. All this drama could have been intended to deflect Stockman and still use his device to attack London. They could blame the American secret service, in cahoots with the Brits. And with Jeremy appearing to help in such an elaborate way—secretly setting up the failure of the British-American plan at the last minute, with the simple failure of the time bomb to be blamed—he would effectively preserve his own central secret, that this dynamic English secret service agent was, in fact, an agent for the German secret service. The rococo acts one and two were the solution.

Was I thinking clearly?

It all seemed very complex.

But what seemed simple was the logical end of Act Three of this play. The Germans wanted Stockman alive. Of course. He was a member of Parliament, after all. Inside eyes and ears. If they'd wanted him dead, this would have been a much simpler play. Jeremy had never intended to let me kill Stockman. He was going to have to prevent that now. And through Jeremy, the Germans knew that my mother was also an American spy. They knew it from the outset. So in the climax of Act Three—for a German audience very satisfying in its Aristotelian inevitability—we would have a poisoned London and two dead American agents.

I was afraid one of them was dead already.

62

I hit the macadam road from Spich to Uckendorf with the light beginning to dim. I turned east and pressed on and soon the land to the south of the road was denuded of crop and tree and animal. The air base's thousand acres. A wire fence took up, and then, ahead at last, was the stand of birch. I turned in at the road leading to the hangar and entered the trees.

With the light fading and the Torpedo's camouflage working, I was stopped cold at my first glance ahead. I thought the car was gone. But I stepped and stepped again, looking more closely, and there it was and I rushed to it.

I opened the driver's side door.

Upon the seat lay a Luger.

I pulled back.

Before I could even start to think rationally about this, Jeremy's voice said, "It's mine."

I spun around.

He was standing only a few paces away.

His hands were raised. As if I were holding a pistol on him.

I wasn't. I put my hand to my own Luger, but he was not moving and he even lifted his hands higher. I did not draw.

"I have no other weapon," he said.

I looked at him closely. He was still buttoned up tight as a German officer.

He nodded down to his tunic. "They don't make provisions for concealed weapons, do they."

I said nothing.

"You did it," he said.

"You sound surprised," I said.

"As you know."

"As I know," I said. I drew my own Luger now. Calmly, slowly. I pointed it at the center of his chest.

"I suppose I *shouldn't* be surprised," he said. "They all think highly of you in London and Washington, and I could see why all along."

"They think highly of you too," I said. "In London and Berlin."

"No," Jeremy said, instantly and ardently. "Not Berlin. Not the way you mean it."

In the silence now I pondered his tone. I understood performance. It was the gift of my upbringing. He sounded real.

"Our little bomb," I said.

"Our little bomb," he said. "We came to Spich. We took our rooms at the inn. We slept. We ate breakfast and I assembled the bomb. Nothing had changed. It was to go as we both had expected."

"Your telegram," I said.

"My telegram."

He paused.

Okay. True enough so far. But. I said, "It wasn't the Brits who ordered you to allow the poison gas attack on London."

Jeremy hesitated. He looked away. Not to prepare for a lie. Not an aversion of the eyes. He flipped his face a little to the side and his mind worked at something and he squared his gaze around to me again. As if I'd slapped him across the face and even though he was a man trained to counterpunch, he accepted it as just.

His hands were still up and he seemed utterly oblivious to the fact. They were natural there.

"Not the Brits," he said.

"You pulled a Stockman," I said. "You were the one dropping the gas bomb." I heard my vehemence. I'd once liked this guy.

He gave a single sharp nod, casting his eyes down.

And then he looked at me straight.

"I work for the English," he said, "but only when their goals are the same as the goals of my own country. I am German. But the Kaiser is not my country. Hindenburg and Moltke and Falkenhayn are not my country. None of the Kaisers. None of the generals. *My* Germany wishes to be like your country. A country governed by the people and protecting the people—all the people—from their government and from themselves. A republic."

I believed he was speaking the truth about himself.

I said, "And what of the people of London tonight?"

"It was not my decision to make," Jeremy said. "We have our own leaders. They know we will never remake Germany as long as the Kaiser rules and these generals are heroes. The march into Belgium. The poison gas at Ypres. The sinking of the *Lusitania*. These acts of cruelty and the government's rabid defense of them are already undermining its position. Not just in the world but here among the true Germans. The attack on London could have been decisive."

"But it would have been your attack as well," I said.

We looked at each other in silence for a long moment.

Jeremy said, "I'm glad you are good at what you do."

I could only shake my head at this.

He laid the poisoning of London upon his leaders and then did what they asked. He laid the salvation of London upon me and was passively glad it went that way. I doubted this was a viable frame of mind for an aspiring republic.

He misinterpreted my reaction. He said, "I'm here, am I not? I didn't have to come. I came with hope, even though it was scant. Hope you were alive. The explosion rattled the windows at the hotel. I was afraid you'd died in the deed. You are capable of that sacrifice. I knew that. I'm very glad you were good enough also to survive."

I still found no words.

He said, "I gave you my pistol freely. My hands are raised. For my betrayal of you, I am happy to offer this proof of my regret and of my regard for you."

He turned around.

He offered me his back.

He did not look over his shoulder.

He did not see that I was indeed still holding my Luger steadily upon him.

He said, "If it is your decision now to kill me, I am ready to accept that."

I lifted the Luger and pointed it at the back of his head.

He waited.

I waited. Not to make a decision. That was made. I waited to adequately clear my head of how dangerous this well-intentioned and obedient man was.

"Turn around," I said.

Jeremy did so, slowly.

The Luger was pointed now at the center of his forehead.

He waited.

"Put your hands down, Jeremy," I said.

He did.

I lowered my pistol.

He let out a held breath.

I slipped the Luger into my holster.

"May I shake your hand?" he said.

I thought about that. Briefly.

"Yes," I said.

And we grasped hands.

63

When our hands parted again, I said, "What have you done with Stockman and Madam Cobb?"

"You underestimate her," he said.

This didn't sound good.

"We had a useful chat," he said.

"When?"

"Not to worry," Jeremy said. "Stockman was out cold and tied up."

I was worried.

Jeremy had left Stockman with his lover. A woman so blind with love she still couldn't accept or reasonably assess what he was capable of doing. But this man before me was capable of at least one of Albert's most heinous intentions. And he'd been my friend. He was quickly becoming my friend again. Mother's feeling for Albert, her desperate *need* for her feeling for him: couldn't I understand that?

"We should go to them," I said.

"I'll crank," he said.

And he did. When he slid into the passenger seat, I handed him his Luger.

I drove out of the trees and turned east onto the Uckendorf road.

Jeremy said, "From what you must have thought of me, you need now to understand. I was never allied to Stockman. I am ready for us to kill him. I will do it myself if you wish. He will compromise us both."

I looked at him. It was only a glance, but just before I took my eyes from him, he glanced too.

He knew what I was thinking.

"I will not return to England," he said. "I'm asking you to keep no secrets about me."

"Good."

He said, "I will be a more serious enemy to Berlin by working here for the republic."

I advanced the throttle in this open, empty stretch of good road.

I said, "So did you leave her guarding him?"

"Not to his eye, if he wakes," he said. "She's got the right stuff, but I don't think she realizes we intend to kill him and I didn't say otherwise. She thought it prudent that she continue to seem his ally. We feigned her bonds. She can slough them off at will. But she wants him to think they were in it together."

This was all right.

Perhaps she was still taking her role as spy seriously.

I had something to do now. The thing she did not yet see coming.

It would be for the sake of Jeremy and his work. A democratic Germany could perhaps prevent another great war. It would be for the sake of my work, for the work of the American republic.

And it would be for me.

For her.

I sped into Spich.

Then I had to slow down drastically.

The town square was dense with people. As in Liebour, Spich had turned out to share this disaster and do what it could. I eased the car in among them, and when people felt others yielding, they turned and yielded too, all of them doing so willingly, readily, respectfully, many of them greeting us, officers in their army.

We crept through them and Jeremy and I found ourselves acknowledging these people's nods and waves and salutes. As if we were one with them in their loss. It went with the uniform.

And then we were free and soon we pulled into the parking field next to the Hotel Alten-Forst.

I switched off the engine.

I had been thinking this out as we drove.

I needed to do this alone. Twice today I'd put a gun to a man's head and twice I'd spared the life before me. Even if only temporarily. This would not happen a third time. Stockman would die directly by my hand. And my mother would instantly be cast in a great and complex role. I would tie her up properly. She would go on to play the devastated lover, having witnessed the death of the man she'd loved most in all her life.

"I have to do this alone," I said.

He looked at me. He did not understand.

"It's not a matter of trust," I said. "It is a thing between the actress and me."

"I'll be here if you need me," he said.

"Be ready to drive us to Berlin," I said.

I needed to visit the American embassy. It was nearly time, as Trask put it, to leave the country abruptly.

64

I shed the flight jacket into the back seat, swapped the clip in my Luger for the full clip from Jeremy's, restrapped my holster over Colonel Wolfinger's tunic, and with a final nod between us, I left Jeremy in the Torpedo.

I strode across the hotel courtyard and through the lobby, taking note of who might be here when I followed a gunshot out of the hotel. The lobby was singularly empty. An old man sleeping in a corner chair. One liveried man clerking behind the desk. Even the visitors to Spich were in the street on this night, being Germans together, awaiting word, sharing their righteous rage.

It was a good night for an assassination. The shot would be two floors up and at the back of a nearly empty hotel in a distracted town.

The elevator operator was also gone and I went up the staircase. I emerged on the second floor and entered the long corridor to Room 200. I slowed a little. I approached with measured, muffled footfalls on the Turkish rug.

Mother wanted to continue to play her role. So be it. I would not knock. If he was conscious, I would not invite her to reveal the phoniness of her bonds. I would use my tools to enter the room.

And Room 200 was drawing near.

I measured my breathing as well. Careful now. Professional now. I stood before the door.

I drew out my tools. Pick and torque. The lock yielded. I did not turn the knob at once. I put my tools into their loops in their leather wrap and I put the wrap into my inner pocket. I used the movements to calm myself.

This was all feeling too personal.

That could cloud my judgment.

In fact, it already had.

I put my hand to the knob and turned it and opened the door wide.

Mother was sitting directly before me, in the chair where she'd sat last night among the roses.

The flowers whose petals had not been plucked and strewn on their bed this afternoon sat meagerly in their vases.

She wore a kimono negligee. The peach-colored chemise, which was her costume for the afternoon cigarette card pose, showed at her chest.

I took a step into the room.

She was not bound. Even in a phony way.

She looked at me oddly. The expression must have been genuine, because I couldn't for the life of me read it.

I took another step.

This was way too personal. Only now did it fully strike me that she shouldn't be sitting here.

I moved my hand to my Luger even as the door slammed behind me.

But before I could draw, a pistol barrel touched me at the back of my head.

Stockman said, "Pull it out slowly and hold it to the side."

I had no choice.

I drew the Luger from its holster, grasping it as if I would use it, just in case, since he'd given no instruction about that.

I extended my arm to the right, straight out.

I had no possible move other than this.

He nudged my head with the muzzle of his pistol.

"Toss it away to the right," he said.

I flicked my wrist as little as I could and still seem to comply. My Luger fell heavily to the floor.

The steel vanished from the back of my head.

"Don't move," he said.

I didn't.

I heard the bolt slide into place at the door.

"Turn around," he said.

I did.

He looked clear-eyed but beat-up. A welt as fat as a three-hour cigar emerged from his hairline and fell across his right temple. His pistol hand was steady. He was holding a Webley break-top revolver. He and his German blood carried a very British weapon. I chose not to comment on this. That I even *thought* to comment was inappropriate under the circumstances. But he had the drop on me, and though I was toying with ironies on the jittery surface of my mind, I was thrashing around for serious options in the core of me as well. The ironies kept me a little detached. Calmed me. One of the ironies: in spite of the beating and the hog-tying, he still looked very much like my mother's chisel-faced leading man.

"Who are you really?" he said.

There were certainly some ironies surrounding that question.

"The man who blew up your poison gas bomb over German soil," I said. "Along with the LZ 78 and the rest of its payload."

The pistol wavered a little.

I said, "Weren't you conscious for the blast? It was a good three or four miles away but it rattled your windows."

I realized I was provoking him. But I had no choice.

I said, "It was unfortunate to poison some Westphalian cows and lose a Zeppelin, but I had to stop you from disgracing our Fatherland and embarrassing our Kaiser. The measure was extreme, but he had to learn about you and Bauer waging your own little war. You are traitors to the Kaiser and to the Fatherland."

Somewhat to my surprise, the pistol grew steady again.

Stockman said, "That's all irrelevant now. I don't give a bloody damn about the bomb or about the Kaiser. Not anymore. I know what's important here."

I had no idea where his mind had just leaped.

He said, "I know what's important after all these years. And you are the man who would blow it up."

I waited for more.

"Do you want to confess?" he said.

I said, "I have no idea what you're talking about."

"You think I haven't suspected from the start?" He glanced quickly over my shoulder. "I'm sorry, my darling," he said. From the angle and height of his glance, Mother had apparently risen from her chair and had moved off a little to her right.

"I'm sorry I haven't discussed this with you, my darling," he said. "But that's because I don't blame you. Not at all. It's this man. It's *his* fault. He would destroy us."

And now his eyes fixed on mine.

He said, "You are Isabel's lover. It makes sense of all the little things. You are her lover even still."

He seemed to want to say more, but words failed him. He pushed his pistol forward a little. It was holding steadily upon the center of my chest.

A heart shot.

Into a heart I heard thumping heavily in my ears.

The Webley was a double-action. I hadn't heard the cocking yet. But I knew it was coming.

Any second.

And my mother said, from behind me, "My darling Albert."

Stockman shifted his eyes.

The pistol stayed where it was.

His eyes went a little wide.

His brow furrowed.

And he began to move his shooting hand, the pistol shifting slightly to his left, in Mother's direction, moving even as his eyes had moved, even as they widened and his hand was moving faster now, the pistol was moving and I started to move as well, to my left, I thought to turn away from the line of fire and lunge and grab his arm and lift it, I visualized this even as I began to move and I was twisting away and his pistol hand was moving and we were both of us nowhere near to the place where we wanted to be and the room rang loud and the center of Albert's forehead blossomed instantly as red and as full-petaled as a rose and he flew back and his pistol jerked upward and he flew and he fell and the room rang and then it stopped. Then all was quiet.

I straightened.

Stockman lay dead on his back.

I turned.

My mother had my Mauser pocket automatic in her right hand, which was cradled in her left, the pistol still aimed, still wisping.

She looked at me.

Nothing showed in her face. Nothing.

She lowered the pistol. She squared around. She stepped to me and she reached out and took my right hand and lifted it between us. She laid the Mauser in my palm, and she looked me in the eyes.

"There," she said. "I hope you're happy."

65

On the way out of the Hotel Alten-Forst I put two bullets from my Mauser automatic pocket pistol into the mahogany front desk, scaring the hell out of the clerk, whose account would help convince any inquiring minds that a mysteriously untraceable German military officer was responsible for the killing in Room 200. The famous actress Isabel Cobb would be found tied up tightly on the bed, the love of her life dead in the next room. I received no reports, but I had no doubt that everyone who witnessed her performance on that terrible night was deeply moved.

In the following weeks Isabel Cobb went on to a great triumph performing as Hamlet in two languages in Berlin, though I had to learn this from the American newspapers. The London newspapers, in the summer of 1915, were disinclined to report on the night life of Berlin.

They did report, however, on the mysterious disappearance of Sir Albert Stockman, a distinguished member of Parliament, who was thought lost in the Strait of Dover on a night when U-boats were known to be in the area. He was rumored to have armed his personal yacht with a deck gun and used the vessel to lure the submarines to the surface and engage them in battle. The country mourned the presumed death of a true English hero.

A month later, a Zeppelin dropped a dozen bombs in the theater district. The second of them fell on Wellington Street in front of the

Lyceum Theatre, where a number of theatergoers were buying oranges and pastries and sweets from street vendors during intermission. Seventeen people were killed, twenty-one were badly injured. That bomb contained no poison gas. None of the bombs did, though several of them were perfectly placed for the purpose.

The first bomb had fallen before the Gaiety Theatre in The Strand, where an American musical comedy was playing by the name of *Tonight's the Night*.

Needless to say, as I tied my mother up, there were a few questions I thought to ask. Like what was in her head when she untied Albert. Was it blind love? Did she think the two of them could just run away from all this? Did she shoot him only when it was clear he was about to kill her son? Or did she let him go expressly to arrange our little climax? She would certainly see it as a far better scene for Isabel Cobb to play. But we spoke not a word. Even up to the moment of my closing the door of Room 200 behind me. Not a word. Sometimes, between a mother and a son, there were things you just didn't want to know.

AN EXTRACT FOLLOWS FROM
ROBERT OLEN BUTLER'S NOVEL
THE HOT COUNTRY,
THE FIRST 'KIT' MARLOWE COBB THRILLER

THE HOT COUNTRY

1

Bunky Millerman caught me from behind on the first day of Woody Wilson's little escapade in Vera Cruz. Bunky and his Kodak and I had gone down south of the border a couple of weeks earlier for the *Post-Express* and the whole syndicate. I'd been promised an interview with the tin-pot General Huerta who was running the country. He had his hands full with Zapata and Villa and Carranza, and by the time I got there, *el Presidente* was no longer in a mood to see the American press. I was ready to beat it back north, but then the Muse of Reporters shucked off her diaphanous gown for me and made the local commandant in Tampico, on the Gulf coast, go a little mad. He grabbed a squad of our Navy Bluejackets who were ashore for gasoline and showers and marched them through the street as Mexican prisoners. That first madness passed quick and our boys were let go right away, but old Woodrow had worked himself up. He demanded certain kinds of apologies and protocols, which the stiff-necked Huerta wouldn't give. Everybody started talking about war. Then I got wind of a German munitions ship heading for Vera Cruz, and while the other papers were still picking at bones in the capital, I hopped a train over the mountains and into the *tierra caliente*. I arrived in Vera Cruz, which was the hot country all right, a god-forsaken port town in a desolate sandy plain with a fierce, hot northern wind. But I figured I'd be Johnny-on-the-spot.

Anyways. That Bunky Millerman photo of me. I saw it for the second time some weeks later, after a bit of derring-do that gave me what I expected to be the scoop of a lifetime and a king beat on the other boys, who were all stuck in Vera Cruz sparring with the Army censors over an invasion that clearly wasn't moving out of town. Seemed there'd been something else going on all this time, right under our noses. When I'd finally gotten the real dope on that and figured out how to cable it to the home office uncensored, I got an immediate wire back from my editor in chief, Clyde Fetter. He called it a knockout of a story—and it was—the only problem being his wire ended with a "but" as big as Sophie Tucker's wagging away at me: Before he could go to press with this, he needed me back in Chicago in person, as soon as I could get there.

So I found myself in Clyde's Michigan Avenue office at the *Post-Express* on a hot afternoon in May. His eighth-floor windows were thrown open to the lake but it wasn't giving us *nada*, not enough breeze even to nudge the match flame he'd just struck up. What he didn't do was cross his feet up on the corner of his desk for what has become the traditional cigar-lighting at the start of one of our big-story sit-downs. I was still attuned to ominous signs after all I'd been through lately, so I didn't miss the significance of his feet being on the floor. He had more on his mind than figuring out the front-page layout and how to ragtime up our leads. Whatever he really had on his mind was awkward enough that he went cross-eyed focusing on the end of the cigar in his mouth, and he wasn't saying a word.

"So," I said. "Is our man going to file for the Senate race?" By which I meant Paul Maccabee Griswold, the Hearst of Hyde Park, Clyde's and my überboss. He had till June 1 to file for the primary and he was getting itchy for power of a different sort. I intended the remark simply as small talk to loosen Clyde up.

"Word is," he said, without so much as glancing from the end of his cigar.

And then I saw the postcard on the cork wall behind his desk. It was surrounded by clippings and Brownie shots and news copy, but it jumped off the wall at me. Clyde was still stalling, so I circled around him and looked close.

It was me all right. Bunky had snapped me from behind as I was walking along one of the streets just off the *zócalo*, which was the main square they call the *Plaza de Armas,* and there'd been a gun battle. Bunky had it printed up on a postcard-back for me, and I sent it off to Clyde. I'd inked an arrow pointing to a tiny, unrecognizable figure way up the street standing with a bunch of other locals. In the foreground I was striding past a leather goods shop. The pavement was wide and glaring from the sun. Even from behind I had the look of a war correspondent. There but not there. Unafraid of the battle and floating along just a little above it all. Not in the manner of Richard Harding Davis, who came down for another syndicate after the action got started and who wore evening clothes every night at his table in the *portales.* Not like Jack London either, who was in town looking as if he'd hopped a freight from the Klondike. I had a razor press in my dark trousers and my white shirt was fresh. We boys of the Fourth Estate love our image and our woodchopper's feel for words. It's an image you like your editors to have of you, and so I sent this card, even though by the time I did, I'd already begun to learn a thing or two I wouldn't put in a story for the *Post-Express* or anybody else. Did the lesson of those first few days help lead me to the big story? Maybe. I'd have to think that over.

But first I pulled the card off the wall and turned it over. I'd scrawled in pencil, "After the battle notice the pretty Señorita's in this photo. The one in white does my laundry." I drew my thumb over the words, compulsively noticing the dangle of the first phrase, which was meant like a headline. I should have put a full stop. "After the battle." And I've made "Señorita's" singular possessive, capitalizing it like a proper name. Maybe this was more than sloppiness in a hasty, self-serving scrawl on a postcard. It was, in fact, true that I had no interest in the other girls. Just in whatever it was that this particular señorita had inside her. Luisa Morales.

Clyde took a guess at where my mind was. "Good thing we've got a copy desk," he said, a puff of his relit cigar floating past me.

"If I were you I wouldn't trust a reporter who bothered to figure out apostrophes anyway," I said. But I wasn't looking at him. Now that I had him small-talking, I didn't care. Something more absorbing was going on.

I turned the card over once more and I looked at Luisa, dressed in white, far away. And I was falling into it again, the lesson I was about to learn in the photo seemingly lost on me. Because what I was *not* looking at in the picture or even while standing there in Clyde's office, really, were the two dead bodies I'd just walked past, still pretty much merely an arm's length away. A couple of snipers, also in white, dead on the pavement. That's what they paid us for, Davis and London and me and all the rest of the boys. To take that in and keep focused. I got the head count and I worked out the politics of it, and I could write the smear of their blood, their sprawled limbs, their peasant sandals without a second glance. I could fill cable blanks one after the other with that kind of stuff while parked in a wisp of sea breeze in the *portales* over a glass of *mezcal*. If I got stuck finding the right phrase for the folks on Lake Shore Drive or Division Street or Michigan Avenue, I just tapped a spoon on my saucer and along came a refill and inspiration, delivered by an *hombre* who might have ended up on the pavement the next morning showing the bottoms of his sandals.

"So what became of your señorita, do you suppose?" Clyde said.

I looked over my shoulder at him. He'd drawn his craggy moon of a face out of his collar and had it angled a little like he'd just sprung a horsewhip of a question on a dirty politician.

I ruffled around in my head trying to think if at some point I'd suggested any connection to him between the one in white and the one in black. It felt like a year ago I'd sent him that story, though it was only a few weeks. But I felt certain I hadn't. "Did I get drunk and send a telegram I don't remember?" I said.

"Nah," Clyde said. "Call it a newsman's intuition."

I shrugged and looked away from him again. But I wasn't talking. And that shrug was just for show. It was all still there inside me. The whole story.

2

She more or less came with the rooms I rented in a house just off the *zócalo*. I'd barely thrown my valise on the bed and wiped the sweat off my brow when she peeked her head in at the door, which I'd failed to close all the way. These two big dark eyes and a high forehead from her Spanish grandfather or whoever. "Señor?" she said.

"Come in. As long as you're not one of Huerta's assassins," I said in Spanish, which I'm pretty good at. I figured that accounted for the smile she gave me.

"No problem, señor," she said. She swung the door open wide now, and I saw a straw basket behind her, waiting. "I'll take your dirty things," she said.

"Well, there was this time with Roosevelt in San Juan . . ." I said, though it was under my breath, really, and I let it trail off, just an easy private joke when I was roughed up from travel and needing a drink.

But right off she said. "You keep that, señor. Some things I can't wash away." She did this matter-of-factly, shrugging her thin shoulders a little.

"Of course," I said. "It's probably a priest I need."

"The ones in Mexico won't do you much good," she said.

She kept surprising me, and this time I didn't have a response. I just looked at her, thinking what a swell girl, and I was probably showing it in my face.

Her face stayed blank as a tortilla, and after a moment, she said. "Your clothes."

My hand went of its own accord to the top button on my shirt.

"Please, señor," she said, her voice full of weary patience, and she pointed to my bag.

I gave her some things to wash.

"I'm Christopher Cobb," I said. "What's your name?"

"I'm just the local girl who does your laundry," she said, and I still couldn't read anything in her face, to see if she was flirting or really trying to put me off.

I said, "You've advised me to keep away from your priests even though I'm plenty dirty. You're already more than a laundry girl."

She laughed. "That was not for your sake. I just hate the priests."

"That's swell," I said. Swell enough that I'd said it in English, and I spoke some equivalent in Spanish for her.

She hesitated a moment more and finally said, "Luisa Morales," and then she went out without another word, not even an adios.

And I stood there staring at the door she'd left open at exactly the same angle she'd found it when she came in. And I'll be damned if I wasn't disappointed because I couldn't explain to her about my name. Christopher Cobb is how I sign my stories but Christopher Marlowe Cobb is my full name and my editors right along have all wanted me to use the whole moniker in my byline, but I find all those three-named news boys—the William Howard Russells and the Richard Harding Davises and the George Bronson Reas—and all the rest—and the host of magazine scribblers and the novelists with three names are just as bad—I think they all make themselves sound pompous and full of self-importance. And it's not as if I don't like the long version of me: My mother gave me the name, after all, when she first laid me newborn in a steamer trunk backstage at the Pelican Theatre in New Orleans and she went on to become one of the great and beautiful stars of the American stage—the eminent, the estimable, the inimitable Isabel Cobb—and Christopher Marlowe was her favorite, though he didn't understand women and probably didn't like them, because he never wrote anything like a true heroine in any of his plays, and maybe that tells you something about my mother's taste in men. She did love her Shakespeare as well, and she played his women, comic and tragic, to worldwide acclaim, but she named me Christopher Marlowe and she called me Kit like they called him, and Kit it is. I just keep the three names packed away in a steamer trunk, and if Luisa Morales had only stayed a moment longer, I would have told her to call me "Kit"— everyone close to me does—though no doubt that would have meant nothing whatsoever to her, and if I'd actually explained all that about my name the day I met her, she would have thought me a madman. Which is what I was thinking about myself. I was a madman to want to explain all this to a Mexican washer girl.

About Us

In addition to No Exit Press, Oldcastle Books has a number
of other imprints, including Kamera Books, Creative Essentials,
Pulp! The Classics, Pocket Essentials and High Stakes Publishing
> oldcastlebooks.co.uk

For more information about Crime Books go to > crimetime.co.uk

Check out the kamera film salon for independent, arthouse and world
cinema > kamera.co.uk

For more information, media enquiries and review copies please contact
Frances > frances@oldcastlebooks.com